12974

FX
PE ART, J

D0458185

GWEN BALLOCH
MEMORIAL LIBRARY
625 North Main Street
Spearfish SD 57783

WITHDRAWN

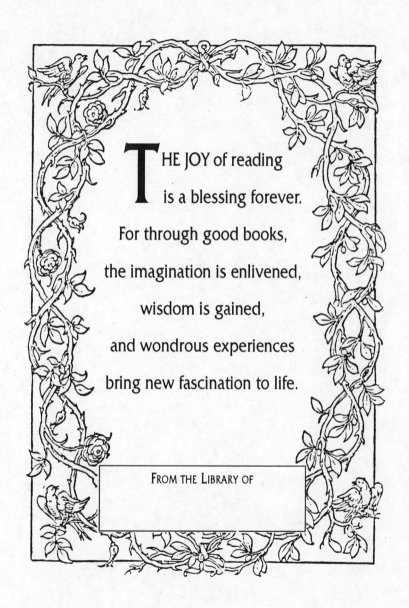

THE JOY of reading
is a blessing forever.
For through good books,
the imagination is enlivened,
wisdom is gained,
and wondrous experiences
bring new fascination to life.

FROM THE LIBRARY OF

EXCLUSIVE FAMILY BOOKSHELF 2-IN-1 EDITION

WESTWARD DREAMS

Where Tomorrow Waits

A Distant Dawn

JANE PEART

GRACE BALLOCH
MEMORIAL LIBRARY
625 North Fifth Street
Spearfish SD 57783-2311

COMPLETE AND UNABRIDGED

Family
BOOKSHELF
Since 1948, The Book Club You Can Trust

Where Tomorrow Waits
Copyright © 1995 by Jane Peart

Requests for information should be addressed to:

 ZondervanPublishingHouse
Grand Rapids, Michigan 49530

Library of Congress Cataloging-in-Publication Data
Peart, Jane.
    Where tomorrow waits / Jane Peart.
       p. cm. —(The westward dreams series : v. 3)
      ISBN 0-310-41291-9 (soft cover : alk. paper)
      I. Title. II. Series: Peart, Jane. Westward dreams series : bk. 3
PS3555.E238W48   1995
813'.54—dc20   95-16603
                                                                 CIP

All rights reserved. No part of this publication may be reproduced, stored in a
retrieval system, or transmitted in any form or by any means—electronic,
mechanical, photocopy, recording, or any other—except for brief quotations in
printed reviews, without the prior permission of the publisher.

Printed in the United States of America

---

95 96 97 98 99 00 / ❖ DH / 10 9 8 7 6 5 4 3 2 1

First Combined Hardcover Edition for Christian Herald Family Bookshelf: 1996

F
PEA

GRACE BALLOCH
MEMORIAL LIBRARY
625 North Street
Spearfish SD 89-2311

WITHDRAWN

12974

12974

THE

WESTWARD DREAMS

SERIES

Runaway Heart

Promise of the Valley

Where Tomorrow Waits

A Distant Dawn

WESTWARD DREAMS SERIES

Where Tomorrow Waits

WESTWARD DREAMS SERIES

Where Tomorrow Waits

JANE PEART

Book 3

ZondervanPublishingHouse
Grand Rapids, Michigan

A Division of HarperCollinsPublishers

Where Tomorrow Waits
Copyright © 1995 by Jane Peart

Requests for information should be addressed to:

 ZondervanPublishingHouse
Grand Rapids, Michigan 49530

Library of Congress Cataloging-in-Publication Data
Peart, Jane.
    Where tomorrow waits / Jane Peart.
       p. cm. —(The westward dreams series : v. 3)
    ISBN 0-310-41291-9 (soft cover : alk. paper)
    I. Title. II. Series: Peart, Jane. Westward dreams series : bk. 3
PS3555.E238W48   1995
813'.54—dc20   95-16603
                                                            CIP

All rights reserved. No part of this publication may be reproduced, stored in a retrieval system, or transmitted in any form or by any means—electronic, mechanical, photocopy, recording, or any other—except for brief quotations in printed reviews, without the prior permission of the publisher.

Printed in the United States of America

---

95 96 97 98 99 00 / ❖ DH / 10 9 8 7 6 5 4 3 2 1

PART 1

A BECKONING DREAM

Chapter 1

*H*ave you ever thought much about California, Penny?"

"California?" Penny Sayres glanced at her sister-in-law, who was picking berries beside her. "You mean about the gold rush?"

"No, not exactly that"—Thea shook her head—"about the place itself?"

"Only what I've read—in school mostly. About Balboa discovering the Pacific Ocean. But I've forgotten most of it."

"I mean about going."

"Going? To *California*? You mean on a wagon train?"

"Well, yes, what it might be like—"

"Not really. . . ." Penny paused for a minute and stared at the slim, dark-haired young woman. "Why do you ask?"

Thea shrugged. "Just curious, I guess."

They went on picking berries for a few minutes more until Penny exclaimed, "Whew! It's sure hot for this late in September!" She whipped off her broad-brimmed straw hat and fanned herself to cool off. "Don't you think we have enough? Look." She held out her nearly full basket.

"I guess so." Thea sounded uncertain.

"Oh, I'm sure it is." Penny declared. "Anyway, I'm quitting. Come on, let's go on home and get us something cool to drink. We've picked plenty to make a nice batch of jam. Grams will be pleased as punch."

"Well, if you say so," Thea said even as she added a few more to her almost overflowing basket before setting it down. Then she turned to her plump, fifteen-month-old baby girl sitting on the blanket on the grass behind them. "Come on, Belinda, honey. Let's go see your daddy's grandma," she said, lifting her up into her arms.

"Grams is at Mrs. Bristow's. Quilting bee this afternoon," Penny told her, then made a silly face at her adored niece to try to make the baby smile. "Want me to carry her?"

"She's getting to be quite a load," Thea admitted.

"Here, you take my basket, and I'll give her a piggyback ride." The exchange was made, and Belinda crowed with delight as her aunt swung her around, settled her securely, and started jogging across the meadow toward the white frame farmhouse nestled under tall oak trees. When they reached the porch, Thea set down the baskets and took Belinda.

"Are you and Grams planning to go to the church service this evening?" Thea asked.

"Oh, I don't think so," Penny replied. "Grams has had some trouble with her hip lately, and sitting too long on those hard benches gets to be a trial."

"It's not going to be just the ordinary Wednesday night prayer meeting. Tonight there's going to be a special speaker just come back from California. He's going to talk about the need for missionaries to the Indians in the western territories."

"So that's why you were asking me about California?" Penny smiled. "Frankly, I'm not much interested in that."

"Please, Penny, come with us!"

8

Penny, surprised at the urgency in her sister-in-law's voice, repeated, "Come with you?"

"Yes. I'd like you to hear what the man says too, because—Brad's all excited about it."

"Brad?" Penny said in surprise, knowing her brother had never been an overly zealous churchgoer. "Don't tell me *Brad's* interested in—" She halted, then asked in obvious disbelief, "You don't mean being *missionaries!*"

"Oh, my, *no!*" Thea shook her head. "It's the West he's interested in hearing about." Penny listened in amazement. Thea continued, "In fact, he's been reading all about it in all those pamphlets about how glorious everything is in the West."

"I've seen those posters in town, all about wanting emigrants to settle in the West. I've even read some of those frontier romances! But I don't believe any of it. Surely, Brad doesn't?"

"Oh, no! Not the romances!" Thea sounded shocked, then both of them laughed. "But he has read some of the written accounts about the real journey and about California. And he's interested in hearing the speaker tonight, because *he's* actually made the trip *twice.*"

They went inside. The house felt cool after the warmth of the afternoon and the exertion of rambling among the berry bushes.

"But what's that got to do with Brad wanting to go to *church* tonight?" Penny tossed her straw hat down and went over to the small mirror hung above the kitchen sink. She twisted her waist-length auburn braid into a knot on top of her head and secured it with a couple of hairpins she took from the pocket of her pinafore. "Brad's not exactly what you'd call a pillar of the church—" She halted suddenly then whirled around to face Thea "—that is, unless. . . ." She paused, then demanded, *"Unless—*he's

9

not—Brad's *not* seriously thinking about going west? *Is* he?"

Thea's large eyes widened as she nodded solemnly and answered, "Yes, I truly believe he is."

Penny frowned. Ever since the news of the discovery at Sutter's Fort had spread east and been written about in the newspapers, a lot of men had got "California fever." Even in the small rural community of Dunwoodie, Missouri, several men had left wives and families to go in search of gold. With a sinking heart Penny knew it was exactly the kind of thing that would spark her brother's impulsive nature. All those tall tales of instant riches would be just the thing to catch his imagination.

Warily Penny asked, "You don't mean Brad's thinking of *prospecting*, do you? Not *gold*, for heaven's sake?"

"No, not gold but land. You know if you homestead you can get acres and acres for practically nothing."

"But, Brad's doing so well.... You just got your house finished, and his carpentry business keeps him so busy...."

"Yes, I know, but—he's been restless lately. He keeps talking about all the opportunities there are out west for a man...." Thea shrugged. "*You* ought to know your brother, Penny."

Penny did indeed. From the time he was a little boy, Brad had a reckless streak and was easily bored. He was always looking for some new excitement. After their parents' deaths and they'd come to live with Grams, Penny often used to wonder out loud if he was going to live long enough for Grams to raise him. He was always doing something dangerous, reckless, taking chances.

Thea smoothed Belinda's cheek. "She looks sleepy. I think I'll put her down on Grams' bed for a little nap, if that's all right. Then we can talk," Thea said over her shoulder as she carried the little girl, whose blond curly head was drooping onto her mother's shoulder, into the bedroom right off the kitchen. While Thea was out of the room, Penny squeezed lemons, stirred sugar into the juice, then mixed it with water from the kitchen pump. Frowning, she got down two tumblers from the whitewashed oak cabinet and put them on the table along with the pitcher and a plate of molasses cookies.

Why had Brad gotten all stirred up about going west? Just when everything was going so nicely! When he had fallen in love with the gentle Althea Rawlings and married her, both Penny and Grams had breathed a sigh of relief, thinking that he would settle down. But evidently he hadn't. After not quite three years of tranquil domesticity, Brad was thinking about going west?

"Her eyes closed the minute I put her down," Thea announced as she came back into the kitchen. "Mmm, that looks lovely. I'm thirsty." She pulled out one of the ladder-back chairs and sat down at the table.

Thoughtfully Penny studied her brother's wife. Small, slender, delicate featured, Althea Rawlings hardly fit the picture of the stalwart pioneer woman taking over the reins of an ox-drawn covered wagon. Neither did she resemble one of those daredevil heroines of the dime novels Penny had sneaked upstairs to read under her covers as a girl. Actually they had been so preposterous she had ended up tossing them aside in disgust. She was sure the reality of the West was different from what either the novelists or the recruiters for wagon trains had written about it.

Thea took a long sip of lemonade. "The main reason Brad wants me to go tonight is to hear firsthand what it's like. Surely, a church speaker wouldn't make up something that wasn't true." Thea reached across the table and clutched Penny's hand. "That's why I want you and Grams to go and hear what this Brother Carmichael has to say. I'd like your opinion—you *and* Grams—your impressions. I trust Grams' judgment, and if she doesn't think it's a good idea . . . well, maybe she can persuade Brad."

Penny shook her head. "I don't know if Grams has that kind of influence on him anymore. After all, Thea, he's a grown man—" *And an impulsive one,* she added to herself. There was no use pointing *that* out to Thea, who adored her husband. His word was her command. If Brad wanted to go west. . . .

Thea's hand tightened on Penny's. "What I really want to know, Penny, *if* he *does* decide to go. . . ." She hesitated, then in a rush she asked, "Will *you* come with us?"

"Come with you to the *West*? On a *wagon train*?"

"Yes. That is, *if* Brad decides to go—"

"Oh, Thea, I don't think so. How could I leave Grams?" Penny withdrew her hand. "This is my home." She looked around at the rows of gleaming blue-and-white china on the oak hutch, the copper pans hung above the shiny black stove, the crisp, blue checkered curtains at the windows where the late afternoon sun streamed through the panes. "I've lived here all my life."

"I know, Penny, I feel that way about our little house too. It's the only real home I've ever had. But wherever Brad is, that's where my home should be. Doesn't even the Bible say that or something like it? 'Where your heart is, there also will be your treasure?' Brad is my heart—and Belinda. If he wants to go. . . ." Her voice trailed away tremulously; her beautiful eyes glistened with tears. "If that happens, Penny—" Thea bit her lower lip, then added earnestly, "—it would make all the difference in the world to me, Penny, if you'd say yes. Of course, I know you'd have to think about it, but there'd be plenty of time for that. Brad has to find out all about what he'd have to get to take and all. But if I thought you were going too, well. . . ."

Thea did not finish her sentence. She didn't need to. Penny understood. She and Thea had been inseparable since childhood, more like sisters than friends. Even now that they were grown up, hardly a day passed that they didn't spend at least part of it together.

For a minute they were both silent. The only sound was the ticking of the wall clock, which seemed suddenly loud. After a while, Thea got to her feet and took her empty glass over to the drain board. She paused and placed her hand on Penny's shoulder. "Please, Penny, at least think about it—I mean, about coming to church tonight."

Immediately Penny felt a reluctance to attend, as if by going she would be making some kind of commitment. So she put off giving Thea a definite answer by saying, "I can't promise. I'll have to wait and see if Grams feels up to it when she gets home from the quilting bee."

Thea's sigh was resigned, as she knew that was all she was going to get from Penny at the moment. "Well, I better wake Belinda up and be on my way. Brad wants an early supper so we can get to church and get seats near the front. It's bound to be crowded. Posters have been put all over town about Brother Carmichael's talk tonight."

A few minutes later Thea emerged from the downstairs bedroom carrying Belinda. Penny touched her niece's tousled curls, and Belinda removed her thumb from her mouth long enough to give a dimpled smile.

Penny walked with them to the door and out onto the porch.

Thea shifted Belinda to her other hip and went down the steps. At the bottom she turned back to Penny. "You *will* try to come tonight, won't you, Penny? And promise you'll think about what I said, won't you?"

Penny didn't like being pressured. Thea had always depended on her. How many times in their long friendship had Thea persuaded her to do something she didn't want to do, go someplace she hadn't planned to go? Penny didn't want to be placed in that position now. But it was hard to turn down Thea's pleading eyes. And this time there was an anxiety about her request that Penny was quick to hear. She knew her so well. Instinctively she responded to that anxiety and said, "Yes, I'll try."

Still standing there, leaning on the porch railing, Penny watched Thea go out the gate. Just beyond a grove of alders Thea turned, took Belinda's chubby little hand in hers, and waved. Penny waved back. Her heart gave a funny little twist. She loved them both so much. How would it feel if Thea's guess was right? If Brad really intended to go west? Instantly Penny felt the loneliness that would be hers. She took a long breath. "Drat that brother of mine! Why is he never content? Maybe this is just one of his passing phases—like so many others he's had over the years. Maybe."

Back in the house, Penny stirred up the fire in the stove. Grams would be home soon, and if, as she'd half promised Thea, they went to the church meeting tonight, she better get things started for an early supper.

While setting the table Penny thought over her conversation with her sister-in-law. Thea wasn't given to imagining things. If she thought Brad was serious about going out west, he probably *was*. Why hadn't he said anything to Grams or to her? Probably afraid one of them would dash cold water on the idea. California. She had to admit the name brought a tingle of excitement. She too had heard all the rumors, repeated by people who'd gone to the lecture last week. "Oranges big as melons growing on trees! Richest farmland you can imagine. Gold shimmering in creeks so you just have to scoop in your hand and bring out a fistful." The idea of it *did* send a tingle of excitement through her. Her brother wasn't the only one in the family who had an adventurous streak.

As a child Penny could run, jump, climb trees, and ride

14

horseback as well as Brad and some of his friends. She was always quick to issue a challenge or take a dare with the best of them. Grams had finally called a halt to her "hoydenish shenanigans" when Penny was thirteen, declaring it was "time she put down her hems, put up her hair, and start acting like a young lady."

As Penny got out the potatoes, peeled them, and put them on to boil, she thought of some of her wilder exploits—ones Grams had never got wind of. With a smile she was remembering them as the door opened and her grandmother came into the house. Penny gave a guilty start.

"Oh, Grams, it's you!"

Cordelia Sayres gave her granddaughter a curious glance. "Who else would it be?" she asked tartly.

Quickly dropping her paring knife and wiping her hands, Penny hurried over to help her grandmother off with her shawl, taking the basket of quilting patches from her. "Did you have a nice time? How were all the ladies?"

"Needles going as fast as tongues," chuckled Grams, handing Penny her bonnet to hang up. "And what have you been up to?"

"Thea came over and we went berry picking. We got lots for you. I started supper, because Thea wants us to go hear the special speaker at church this evening. Seems Brad's all het up 'bout California." Without saying just *how* interested Brad possibly was, Penny went on, "I told her I wasn't sure. I said you might be too tired to go. Are you?"

Grams pursed her lips thoughtfully. "Hmm, the ladies were talking about that this afternoon. Brother Carmichael's his name. Seems like everybody's plannin' to attend. So I suppose we shouldn't miss it."

"We don't *have* to go, that is, if you're too tired, Grams?"

"You're the one who don't seem too anxious, miss. Don't *you* want to go?"

15

Feeling disloyal to Thea, Penny quickly assured her, "Oh, I'll go. I just told Thea that I'd make sure *you* felt up to it— no, ma'am, I'll be glad to go."

"Then that's settled," Grams said, tying on her apron and moving over to the stove.

Penny knew it would have taken only a little more persuasion on her part to convince Grams not to go. But from what Thea had implied about Brad, maybe Grams *should* hear all that this Brother Carmichael had to say. Then she would be in a better position to judge what Brad had in mind. Even though he was a married man and had left home three years ago, Penny knew her brother still had great respect for their grandmother's judgment.

Grams had taken them in and reared them after their mother's death and their widowed father's fatal logging accident just one year later. To six-year-old Penny and her brother, who was then nine, Grams had given them more than a home. She had given them a sense of belonging, a feeling that they were special, the security of discipline, as well as concern and love. Somehow Penny felt it was important for Grams to advise Brad if he really was thinking of pulling up stakes and going west.

After supper Penny cleared the table, then said, "I'll go get ready," and went upstairs to her loft bedroom. Ever since she had first come to live with Grams this room had been her special place. Dormer windows looked out through the boughs of towering pine trees to the lake just beyond the end of the property. Its slanted roof gave her a cozy sense of privacy, her imaginative fancy play, like a princess in a tower.

She changed into a green merino dress, trimmed with darker green braid, and took her bonnet off its stand on the bureau. As she did, her glance fell on the framed daguerreotype of her parents taken on their wedding day. Her mother had been what Grams called an "Irish beauty":

dark, wavy hair; rose and cream complexion; and emerald green eyes. From the oval perfection of her mother's face, Penny critically surveyed her own face in the mirror. No resemblance. None at all. *She* had taken after her father's family. She was tall for a girl and boyishly slim; her eyes were slate blue; her nose too long and her mouth too wide. Thankfully her hair had darkened from vivid carrot color to auburn. But she had the kind of fair skin, sprinkled with freckles, that goes with red hair.

It was ironic that throughout her growing up years her best friend was the prettiest girl in Dunwoodie! Althea Rawlings. If Thea hadn't been such a dear, sweet-natured person, Penny might have been jealous. Their friendship bond had been forged early as they both were left motherless.

Thea's father had remarried less than a year after her mother had died. Her stepmother, Veda, was a stern, unloving woman. The only warmth, affection, and acceptance Thea received was here in Grams' house. Even now, as a grown woman, wife, and mother, Thea was still emotionally dependent. In fact, Penny had always found it hard to refuse Thea anything. Like going to church tonight!

With a sigh, Penny put on her bonnet. Tying the ribbons firmly under her square chin, she made a grimace at her image. Then she forced a saccharine smile that widened as she observed that at least her teeth were white and straight. People said she had a nice smile.

When Penny and Grams arrived they saw the small wooden church was unusually crowded for a midweek service. News of this speaker, recently arrived from the West, had spread quickly throughout the community. Interest in the westward movement was already high, which was probably why more men were present than ordinarily came for the Wednesday night prayer meeting.

As Penny and her grandmother approached the church,

a tall, young man detached himself from the group of men talking in the churchyard and came diffidently forward.

"Evenin', Mrs. Sayres." Todd Farnum touched the brim of his hat, then added shyly, "Evenin', Penny."

"Well, Todd, what a surprise to see *you* here on a Wednesday night." Penny's eyes twinkled mischievously. "You suddenly got religion or California fever?"

Grams gave her a sharp nudge with her elbow. "Penny! What a thing to say!"

Undaunted, Penny kept looking at Todd as if for an explanation. "*Well?*"

Obviously discomfited by Penny's words, Todd shifted from one foot to the other, stammering, "Can't rightly say. . . ."

Penny laughed, but her grandmother told him, "Don't pay a bit of mind to her, Todd. She's got a wicked tongue for teasin'. Whatever your reason for comin', it's nice to see you. How's your ma?"

"Doin' much better, ma'am, thank you kindly."

Penny's eyes still sparkled with merriment. Todd should be used to her having fun at his expense. They had been playmates as children, going all through school together. In age he was between her and Brad. Now that they'd grown up, Todd would have preferred their friendship to become a courtship. Even Penny was aware that most of Dunwoodie expected them to marry someday. But not *her.* Marriage was a long way off in Penny's future.

To Gram's annoyed and vocal despair, Penny—even at twenty, an age when many a Dunwoodie girl started worrying that she was moving perilously close to being an "old maid"—was in no hurry. Several young men had tried courting her, but none more persistently than Todd Farnum. So far none had been successful. Grams said it was because she was too independent and outspoken: "You'll never get a man to put up with that, young lady," she would caution. But Penny would retort, "Flirting is silly and being coy worse. If a man doesn't like me the way I am, I wouldn't be interested in spending the rest of my life with him anyway!"

To Penny, the idea of settling down to domesticity did not have the appeal it had to most of the girls she knew. There always seemed to be something beckoning from some distant horizon, just over the hill, like music only faintly heard. Oh, she knew she was a daydreamer; she'd been told that often enough. Maybe it was the Irish blood in her veins, inherited from her mother, that made her like that: Ireland, the faraway land of poets and saints. Well, not the saint part, but perhaps she had a bit of poetry in her soul—or as Grams might say acerbically, "A bit of blarney."

After a few more pleasantries they left Todd and went up the steps into the vestibule. As she entered the church, Penny saw Jeremiah Bradshaw out of the corner of her eye, and she felt a pang of dismay. She had to suppress a shudder. She hoped he hadn't seen them come in, for he would surely try to join them in the same pew. Taking a firm hold of Grams' arm, Penny steered her to the opposite side of the church, and as she did, she received an irritated glance from the independent little lady. Once they were seated, Grams remonstrated in a whisper, "For pity's sake, Penny, why did you push me like that—as though I can't manage on my own!"

Penny didn't want to explain, so she just whispered, "Sorry." Still, she had the feeling that Jeremiah *had* seen them, and she felt a tingling sensation along the back of her neck, an awareness that she was being observed. Why did she have such an aversion to him?

There was just something about him. Was it his fawning overeagerness, his almost uncanny ability to spot her at any gathering, to appear at her side instantly on countless occasions, making no effort to conceal his attraction? It was an attraction she certainly did not return. Was it this unwanted attention that made her so uncomfortable? Or was it something more? Something that made her skin crawl, made her want to draw away from any contact with him? Worse still, nothing seemed to discourage him. No matter how cool she was, he persisted in pursuing her.

To make matters worse, everyone else seemed to think Jeremiah Bradshaw a fine, upstanding young man and considered him an eligible bachelor. In the eyes of most of the town's matchmakers, he was a "good catch." He was well educated, by Dunwoodie standards, having gone off to college for two years, and was now a clerk in the County Recording Office. He was well mannered and good-looking. Tall with even features and dark, wavy hair and gray eyes with long lashes any girl might envy. No one, not even Grams, could understand why Penny would not be flattered by his interest.

But when he looked at her, Penny felt like shivering. How could she say what only she sensed? Something frightening behind the ingratiating manner, a cold shrewdness in those eyes? The feeling that he was manipulative and could not be trusted?

Even as she thought about this, Penny felt irresistibly drawn to glance his way. To her horror Jeremiah was staring at her. The minute their eyes met, Penny immediately averted her head, but not before he had smiled. A smile that sent an icy sliver of repulsion all through her. Why didn't he find some other girl who might welcome his attentions?

Gradually the hum of voices dimmed to a murmur. The rustle of people finding seats and settling into place began to quiet. A hush of anticipation fell as Reverend Thomas came into the pulpit to introduce the speaker.

"Brothers and sisters, tonight we are going to hear an amazing story, told by a person who has seen some of the glories of God's creation that none of us here have seen. He's come back with a vision to share with us. I feel sure you'll be astonished and inspired by what he is going to tell us tonight." He turned to the tall, lean man who had accompanied him to the front of the church. "Brother Willis Carmichael, will you come forth now?"

The craggy-faced man stood behind the lectern and began to speak in a dramatic voice. He talked of the splendor of mountains, the vast plains, the rivers brimming with an abundance of fish, the forests thick with game and wildlife of all kinds, rich land to be farmed.... Penny listened but only half believed what the man was saying. Was it truly possible that the place he was describing could be the modern version of the biblical "Promised Land," as he declared? It sounded almost too good to be true. Yet she could feel all around her the readiness to accept the picture he was painting—especially in the men. They were leaning in their seats toward Brother Carmichael, hanging on his every word.

The enthusiasm *was* contagious, however. Penny could feel the excitement stirring among the congregation. Brother Carmichael appealed to every man and woman in his audience who had ever felt the frustration, the drabness, the workaday ordinariness of their lives. He was offering them a chance to change their lives in a glorious way.

Then, Brother Carmichael leaned forward on the pulpit and his voice deepened dramatically. "But, my friends, in all this manifestation of God's creation, his providence, his bounty, there lies a profound need. A need that cries out to be filled. There are some of you here tonight who will hear and respond to that call. I beseech you to search your hearts and souls and discover if the Lord God is asking you to forsake all and go out west to minister to these poor souls...." Brother Carmichael's voice broke as he struggled to continue. "Oh, my brethren," he intoned, "if ever there

21

were fields white for the harvest, it is in the western territories, where Indians live under savage conditions, long deprived of the refreshing waters of baptism, the breath of the Spirit. The opportunities are enormous for those willing to sacrifice their comfortable lives in this part of our beloved country to track new pathways of salvation for those less fortunate ones who have never heard the reviving words of the gospel. For you few who respond generously, there are blessings awaiting you here on earth in a glorious new, unspoiled land out west, just as later on there will also be eternal rewards."

Having concluded, Brother Carmichael came down from the podium. Immediately he was surrounded by people anxious to ask questions and find out more information.

Grams had nodded off during some of the more repetitious parts of the talk, so when Penny whispered, "Let's go," she was ready to leave. Penny saw Brad among those clustered around the speaker. Thea was sitting in one of the front pews, holding a sleeping Belinda in her lap, patiently waiting. There was no real opportunity to talk to either of them. Knowing Thea would surely tell her their reactions later, Penny maneuvered Grams toward the back of the church and out the door, hoping also to escape Jeremiah.

Outside, on the church steps, however, Jeremiah was waiting. He courteously greeted her grandmother first. "Good evening, Mrs. Sayres. Good evening, Penny." Instinctively Penny stiffened, suppressing an involuntary shudder. He went on smoothly: "May I have the pleasure of escorting you home?"

Penny started to give Grams' arm a warning pinch, but it was too late. Jeremiah had already offered his arm to Grams, who had taken it. There was nothing Penny could do. Luckily it was only a short walk. As the three of them walked back along the moonlit streets, Jeremiah began expounding. "What a powerful message, wouldn't you say?

I was most impressed, weren't you?" Not pausing for her answer, he continued, "I certainly need time to ponder some of the things he spoke of, weigh them carefully. He has certainly given *all* of us something to think about."

Penny checked the urge to make some sarcastic remark. Jeremiah was *so* pretentious it set her teeth on edge. Was she the only one who saw through Jeremiah? Always trying to impress, as though he had deeper insight than anyone else? It was not too soon for Penny when they reached their front gate.

"Thank you for seeing us home, Mr. Bradshaw," Grams said politely. "Since it's rather late, I won't ask you in this evening."

"Of course, Mrs. Sayres, I understand," Jeremiah replied, then added insinuatingly, "But *another* time, perhaps?"

"Of course. We'd be most pleased." Grams nodded, and Jeremiah unlatched the gate for them both to pass through.

"I'll look forward to it with great pleasure," his voice followed them.

The minute they were inside and the front door closed, Penny gave an exasperated moan and demanded, "Oh, Grams, why ever did you invite him for? You know I cannot abide the man!"

Grams looked shocked. "Well, now, miss. It's still *my* house, I reckon, and I can invite whoever I like, I should think. What did you expect me to say when he practically invited himself?" Grams untied her bonnet strings and patted her gray coronet of braids, then hung up her shawl and started for the kitchen. Over her shoulder she said, "Your hoity-toity ways are not going to keep me from employing common courtesy, miss! And why do you have such an aversion to him? Mr. Bradshaw seems nice enough to me and if you weren't so persnickety you'd acknowledge that. Why, some girls would be mighty flattered that such a gentlemanly fellow was paying them some attention."

"Well, I'm *not*. So be sure to let me know when you issue him an invitation so that *I* can be *sure* not to be here!"

Grams threw Penny a disapproving glance but didn't say anything. She put the kettle on and got out an apple pie from the pie safe and proceeded to cut two slices.

Grams' silence always spoke volumes. Penny knew she had been rude. Contrite, she went behind her grandmother, put her arms around her plump waist and gave her a hug.

"I'm sorry, Grams. But, I can't help it. There's just something about Jeremiah Bradshaw—"

"Well, then, why were you so unkind to poor Todd Farnum?"

"*Unkind*? I wasn't unkind! Todd knows when I'm teasing. Why, I've known him forever—"

"He's not still a boy that you can tease and torment, miss. He's a grown man, and he's got a fine farm and a good head on his shoulders. And if you don't watch that tongue of yours, you'll be left on the shelf."

"Left on the shelf? What on earth does *that* mean?" Penny grinned, knowing very well what it meant. With an impudent flounce of her tiered skirt she sat down on one of the chairs at the round kitchen table and stared at her grandmother with widened eyes.

Grams sniffed. "It *means*, miss, for your information, all the eligible men in this town will be gone to girls smarter than you—at least smart enough to keep their mouths shut and not spout out the first silly thing that comes into their heads to say. *That's* what it means, Miss Know-It-All!" She emphasized her statement by setting the plate of pie down in front of Penny with a little click.

"Maybe I don't want to get married, Grams." Penny shrugged. "Maybe I'd be perfectly happy to be a spinster."

Grams poured the water from the hissing kettle into the teapot, which had been kept warm at the back of the stove.

24

Then she took a seat opposite Penny, regarding her over her spectacles for a long moment before replying, "I've heard ducks quack before."

Penny knew better than to continue this line of discussion. Instead she took a bite of her pie and asked, "So, what did you think of Brother Carmichael and his talk?"

Her grandmother stirred sugar into her teacup thoughtfully. "I feel he's going to stir up a great deal of unrest in the community. Firing up men with dreams of free land, all that sunshine and fruit growing so easy, to say nothing of gold just lying there waiting to be scooped up.... Didn't say much about how long that journey is, what hardships there would be for women and children along the way.... I don't know, Penny, but I'm a little wary of people who talk about pots of gold at the end of the rainbow and fancy it up with spiritual calling...."

"You saw Brad up there with the first of them, didn't you?"

"Yes, I did, and Brad's just the kind that would be taken in by it all."

"He's *already* interested, Grams. Even before tonight. Thea told me he's been talking a lot about it. He's read all the accounts in the paper. Says he's become more and more discontent with what he calls his 'dead-end life' here in Dunwoodie. Keeps saying out west things would be different. Thea says he's rarin' to go...." Penny paused with a forkful of pie halfway to her mouth. "But I don't think *she's* all that eager to go."

"And why *should* she be? She's got a nice house, a sweet little baby, family and friends nearby. Why would she want to pack up and go God knows where?"

"But if Brad wants to go—"

"If that's what her husband wants to do, Thea will go, I expect," Grams sighed. "She'll do what all women through the ages have done: follow her man."

25

Penny didn't comment. Her grandmother's declaration conveyed exactly why *she* wasn't in any hurry to marry and give up her independence.

Chapter 2

*P*enny woke up the next morning feeling out of sorts. The meeting the night before had been unsettling. She felt disturbed by Brother Carmichael's oratory and particularly the men's reaction to his talk—especially Brad's. She had the same worries Grams had about her brother. Brad was easily influenced and likely to be carried away by the extravagant claims made for the distant land of California. Coupled with Thea's suspicions, the eloquent descriptions of the night before might have been the proverbial last straw. Much as Penny loved her brother, over the years she had observed that his impulsiveness was often followed by a quick loss of interest. Still, she was wary that his restlessness might cause him to do something foolhardy. Penny recalled how Brad's eyes were shining with excitement last night. And Thea—well, she had looked anxious and unhappy.

Penny punched the pillows behind her head and frowned. Thea wasn't cut out for months of roughing it on a long wagon train journey. Penny knew Thea better than anyone. From the time they were both six years old and Penny had spotted the shy little girl standing on the edge of the schoolyard on the first day of school, she had kept a protective eye on Thea. Even after Thea had married Brad, Penny remained her confidante and closest friend. It was more than anxiety Penny had seen in Thea's eyes. That's what worried Penny most. Something else was troubling Thea, and Penny didn't know what.

Penny heard movement in the kitchen downstairs; the smell of coffee and bacon frying wafted up the stairwell. In spite of going to bed later than usual, Grams had probably been up since dawn. Penny knew she should be down there too, bringing in more wood for the stove and getting water from the well, although it sounded as if Grams had already done so. Although she seemed as spry and active as ever, Grams wasn't getting any younger.

"Penny!" Grams' voice called from the bottom of the steps. "Are you going to be a slugabed this morning? Breakfast's almost ready. I'm taking the biscuits out now."

"Coming, Grams!" Guiltily Penny threw the covers back and got up. As she washed and dressed, Penny kept thinking of the real possibility that Brad was planning to join the trek west. Brad was so enthusiastic, and optimistic to a fault. What really bothered Penny was that she knew he could talk Thea into going against her wishes and even against her better judgment. His own excitement was infectious. Grams said he could talk bugs off a potato vine.

Maybe she should stop fretting over Brad and Thea's plans. No matter *what she* thought, Brad would make the decision and Thea would go along with it. But why did Penny have the distinct impression Thea was terrified of the whole idea? Was there some secret reason she hadn't said?

Penny poured water from the pitcher into her washbowl, splashed her face several times. As she dried it she looked at herself in the round mirror above the pine washstand. Instead of her own, it seemed as though she saw Thea's delicate face, the violet blue eyes staring back pleadingly. What was she trying to say?

"Penny, food's getting cold. You comin'?" Grams' voice came again.

"Coming!" Penny tossed the face towel aside and ran down the steps. She had just seated herself at the table and begun eating her scrambled eggs when she heard footsteps on the porch. A minute later the front door opened and Brad walked in. If Penny felt *she* had been short-changed on looks, her brother had not. Brad Sayres was tall, well built. He had a wide, friendly smile and intensely blue eyes that shone with good humor from his handsome, sun-tanned face.

"Mornin', Grams! Sis!" he greeted them cheerfully.

He sauntered over to the stove as casually as if he still lived here. He lifted the lid on one of the pots and inhaled rapturously. "Ummm, smells mighty fine, Grams. Marmalade?"

"Yes, it is. Help yourself to some coffee, boy. Or would you want some bacon and eggs?"

"No thanks, Grams. Had breakfast. However, . . ." He straddled the bench on the other side of the table and reached into the basket, covered with a blue checked cloth. "I think I'll just have one of these biscuits . . . if I may?"

"What brings you out and over here so early?" Penny asked, a funny premonition stirring in her mind.

Brad took his time, slathering butter onto his biscuit and taking a bite before answering. "Well, now . . . I was kinda curious how you all reacted to Brother Carmichael last night. Didn't see you afterwards . . . left pretty quick, didn't you? Why? Not interested? Didn't like him?"

Grams exchanged a glance with Penny, then said, "Oh, he seemed sincere enough, I'm sure. But my goodness, Brad, could California be all that wonderful? He made it sound like the Garden of Eden before the fall."

"Well, he ought to know, Grams. He's been out there twice. Made the trip two times."

29

"If it's all that great, why don't he stay?"

"Yes, why not?" Penny joined in.

Brad's eyes, so much like Penny's, twinkled as his voice took on an oratorical tone. "He came to bring the message. Didn't you hear him say? 'Fields white for the harvest' and all that?"

"Don't tell me *you're* thinking about becoming a missionary?" Penny blinked with exaggerated disbelief.

Ignoring his sister's sarcasm, Brad grinned, "I believe I'd like a cup of coffee, Grams."

"I'll get it," Penny said and rose, giving her brother a dubious look.

"He *was* pretty eloquent, I must say," Grams commented dryly.

"Well, Grams, maybe you didn't know, but I was pretty interested in the West *before* Brother Carmichael came," Brad said as he accepted the steaming mug Penny handed him. "But I thought if Thea heard it preached about in church, she might be more willing to think about *us* going."

Grams set down her own fork and stared at her grandson. "You mean you're *really* thinking about it?"

"I'm doing more than thinking about it, Grams. I'm going. I'm putting the house up for sale. I'm goin' to start buildin' a wagon and be ready to join a wagon train leaving from Independence in the spring."

"And what does Thea say about all this?" gasped Penny.

"She's all for it," Brad answered blithely, then amended, "at least, she's all for it if that's what I want to do. But I want to do what's best for *us*. It's the greatest opportunity young people ever had since the first settlers came here. But here in Dunwoodie, opportunities are limited. You know that, Grams. I'd never get enough money together to buy a farm of any size—or land. In California you can get government land for a low down payment on a homestead.

Acres and acres of prime farm land for the taking . . . you just have to live on it for a full year and—"

"But it's such a long way. It's so far and. . . ." Grams' voice wavered a little.

"You could come with us, Grams."

"Not me, son, I'm too old, too set in my ways. I've lived in this house since I was seventeen when I came here as a bride. I had all my children here, including your father. I raised 'em here, lost 'em here. I plan to end my days here. . . . Besides, I couldn't leave your Uncle Billy."

Uncle Billy was Gram's younger brother who had been disabled by a hunting accident years before. He lived in a small cabin by himself nearby, and although fiercely independent, he took supper with them several times a week and was a part of the close-knit clan.

Brad glanced over at Penny. "What about *you*, sis? Doesn't the idea tickle *your* adventurous streak? Thea would be even more willing to go if you'd come along."

Penny didn't want to betray the fact Thea had already broached that subject. She needed more time to think about it. She still felt she didn't know the whole story; Thea was holding something back.

"*Me?*" she echoed as if she'd never heard the suggestion.

"Sure, why not? Might even find you a husband," he teased.

"Who says I want one?" she retorted.

"Well, old Todd's still moonin' away for you, come to that. I know Todd's seriously thinking about going too. We could make us up a party, two wagons—"

"Oh, hush! How many times do I have to tell everyone? Todd's a friend, not a beau!"

"Not to hear him tell it!" Brad retorted. "Then what about Jeremiah Bradshaw? Nobody could miss those calves' eyes he's castin' your way every time you're in sight."

31

Irritated, Penny balled up her napkin and aimed it at him. He ducked, laughing, caught it and threw it back.

"Now, stop it, you two. Looky here. You're not young-'uns anymore," Grams said with mock severity. But her eyes were merry behind her glasses, and her mouth tugged at the corners trying not to smile.

Brad glanced over at Penny. "I'm serious, sis. It would be great if you decided to come along."

"Could I bring Mariah?" she parried. Mariah was her saddle horse, given for her fourteenth birthday, a gentle dappled-gray mare.

"Sure thing," Brad nodded. "Think it over? A once-in-a-lifetime adventure?" he grinned. "Better'n just readin' all those romance novels."

That was all that was said about it then. Brad launched into some further details of what he had learned about the necessary preparations for the overland journey west. Grams and Penny listened without making further comments.

After Brad left, Grams poured them each a second cup of coffee, something she didn't usually do. Usually she was up and busy getting to her next chore. Bringing their cups back to the table, she sat down, folded her arms, and leaned forward on them. She asked Penny, "Well, what do you think, honey? Want to go along on the great adventure? Or are you waiting to see if Todd Farnum's going to join the Westward-Ho bunch?"

"Todd? Oh, Grams, that's just Brad's foolishness."

"Not altogether, missy, so don't play the innocent with me." She fastened her eyes on her granddaughter so that Penny couldn't look away. "What Brad said is just what everyone in Dunwoodie knows. Todd's been sweet on you since you were out of pinafores and pantaloons. Are you waiting to see if he's going to propose marriage or a wagon train trip to California?"

"I don't think Todd has any notion of going west."

Penny shook her head. "And he certainly hasn't asked me to marry him. And even if he did—either one of those things—well, his decision wouldn't have anything to do with *mine*."

Grams raised her eyebrows. "Oh, I've no doubt of that. You're not like Thea, who jumps when Brad snaps his fingers."

"You think that's wrong?"

"Not wrong. No, not at all. Not for Thea. But you're a different story. You've always had a mind of your own since you were knee-high to a grasshopper. And although Todd's a fine fellow, I'm not sure he's the right one for you."

"Why not?"

"Maybe because he'd be too easy for you to lead around, for one. But mostly because I think, in your own way, you're as adventurous as Brad. I think you've a hankering for new sights, new places, new challenges. And until that's out of your system, I can't see you settlin' down with some- one as placid as Todd." Grams finished her coffee, then got to her feet, and with a crumpled cloth napkin wiped up the damp ring it had made on the table. "Remember, you marry the life as well as the man. If you have any doubts about marrying anyone, it's better by far to wait. To do oth- erwise would bring misery on both of you."

"Why, Grams, just last night you were warning me about being 'left on the shelf.'"

"Well, maybe I changed my mind. I'm an open person, always ready to listen, to see things from another view . . . and that's what I've done." Then her tone turned sharp: "Come on, miss, we've got baking to do."

Chapter 3

*B*rother Carmichael was scheduled to give two more talks in Dunwoodie, one the following night at the Town Hall and another on Sunday at the church. Neither Penny nor Grams planned to attend, and Brad certainly did not need any more encouragement to take off for the West. Penny had heard all she wanted to about California. She had more than a few misgivings about the rich rewards awaiting across the prairies and mountains to the golden West. She was particularly troubled by Thea's silence about the venture on which Brad seemed set to embark. Besides Uncle Billy always took Sunday night supper with them, and the three of them looked forward to their usual good time together. Uncle Billy was a wonderful storyteller, and he and Grams swapped stories about their childhood, each trying to outdo the other.

It was a warm, wonderful evening of family fun. Grams didn't mention Brad's plans to Uncle Billy, and Penny's worries were temporarily put aside. But the next day she was unexpectedly forced to face the whole subject of California.

On Monday afternoon Grams sent Penny to take a basket containing jellies and two loaves of fresh baked bread to a sick friend's house. Mrs. Bristow, confined to her bed for an entire week, was eager to talk and hear all the latest news, so Penny had to stay for a cup of tea and a chat. By the time she started home it was beginning to get dark. Deciding to take a shortcut through the woods, she hurried along the path thick with pine needles. Suddenly she heard a voice call her name: "Penny! Wait, Penny!"

Surprised, she halted and turned to see who it was. A man was running along the trail behind her. *Oh, no!* She felt instant dread. It was Jeremiah Bradshaw! Not waiting for him to catch up, she started walking again briskly.

"Hold on, Penny," he called again.

"I'm in a hurry, Jeremiah," she said over her shoulder.

"But this is really important. I have something important to tell you." He reached her side out of breath. "Actually, it's *providential* that I saw you."

Penny quickened her pace. "I really don't have time to stop and chat, Jeremiah," she said, annoyed. "It's getting late, and Grams will be wondering where I am."

"Wait until you hear what I have to say, Penny," he said, matching his stride to hers. "It's something Brother Carmichael said about—"

"I've heard all I want to hear about California."

"Not *this* you haven't," Jeremiah said, not seeming at all disturbed by the irritated look she gave him. "I'm sorry you and your grandmother weren't there to hear for yourselves." There was a hint of reproach in his voice. "You missed a powerful message—"

"And I've heard all I care to hear of Brother Carmichael's messages as well!" she declared and added, "I have a strong feeling he exaggerates."

"You're wrong, Penny," Jeremiah pronounced solemnly. "Furthermore, there was a *personal* message last night *you* should have heard."

"What do you mean?"

Jeremiah took a few long strides ahead, then turned so that he was facing her so that she had to stop walking. "Listen, Penny. At the close of the meeting Sunday night Brother Carmichael asked each of us to search our hearts to see if God was trying to tell us something. He asked for silence so that we could all quietly examine our minds and souls . . . and—" Jeremiah paused dramatically "—I *did* and . . . Penny," here Jeremiah's voice deepened, "what I got very clearly was that *you* and I should go *together* out west . . . be missionaries."

Stunned, Penny looked at him aghast. "*What?* That's the most ridiculous thing I ever heard! Jeremiah, you must be mistaken."

Satisfied that he had caught her attention, Jeremiah's expression was smug. Penny protested, "I mean, you certainly *are* mistaken. I have no intention of going to California in the first place, much less as a *missionary!*"

Jeremiah shook his head, and his eyes speared into hers. "You can't fight the will of God, Penny. We are to start preparing to go out west and minister to the savages—"

"Jeremiah, I'm not even going to discuss this," Penny said indignantly. She started to walk away from him, but he reached out, caught her by the arm, and swung her around to face him. His eyes were burning, his pupils dilated. Penny's heart began thrumming as Jeremiah's fingers tightened on her arm.

"The Lord has shown me you *are* to be my wife. . . . If you refuse to listen, Penny, you'll pay the price."

Jeremiah was frightening. Penny felt an icy trickle of fear run down her spine. Determined not to show it, she lifted her chin defiantly, "That's impossible! Why would he show *you* this and not *me?*"

"Because you've closed your mind and your heart. You're running away from what you know deep down is his will—"

"I know nothing of the kind, Jeremiah," she said firmly, trying to pull away from him. But he held her fast. His fingers pressed so hard into her arm, even through her wool jacket, that it hurt. "Let me go!"

"You're afraid to admit that you know I'm right, aren't you?" His eyes glinted triumphantly; his mouth twisted in a grotesque smile. He gave a short, ugly laugh. "You're proud, Penny, and that's one of the deadly sins, the one the Devil uses to get people to disobey God. You'll have to come to repentance."

"You're mad, Jeremiah. You don't know what you're talking about. . . ." Combined fear and anger gave her strength, and she yanked hard at the arm he was holding. "Let me go, Jeremiah!"

"Go then!" He let go so suddenly that she was thrown off balance and stumbled backward. "But you won't forget what I told you. I can see that you know it's true, and you will eventually have to bend to God's will for us."

Realizing she was free, she turned and began to run. Jeremiah's voice followed her: "You can't run away from your predestined duty. You'll reap what you sow, Penny. Retribution—," Jeremiah's dire threats echoed hollowly in the woods.

She ran blindly, empty basket bumping against her until the pain in her side made her stop to lean on a tree, gasping for breath. Fearfully she glanced behind her to see if Jeremiah was pursuing her. The woods were darkening fast. Her heart was hammering against her ribs, and the pain was like a dagger, but she was afraid to remain longer. Jeremiah was crazy. She was convinced he had lost his reason.

Then she heard a branch crack, a twig snapping as if a foot had stepped on it. Panicking, Penny picked up her skirts and began running again. In sight of the house, she stopped. Panting, she leaned against the fence post, taking huge gulps of air into her hurting lungs. Her legs were shaking and her breath was coming in short gasps. The fact that she had escaped from the frenzied Jeremiah brought tears of relief. Spontaneous prayers of gratitude sprang up, inarticulate but heartfelt, scattered words from various psalms—"The Lord is my shield, my shelter, a high tower, thank you, Lord."

She felt ravaged by Jeremiah's venom, his scathing words. What right had he to say the things he had? Deep, shuddering tremors shook Penny. But what if—? She gave her head a little toss, straightened herself. No, she wouldn't even allow herself to think that way. Jeremiah was deranged. He must be if he thought. . . . Penny retied her bonnet strings, adjusted her cape, and went through the gate into the house.

Grams was in the kitchen when she came in the front door. "How was Mrs. Bristow, Penny?" she called.

Penny took a long breath, trying to regain some semblance of calm. She closed her eyes for a few minutes, debating whether or not to tell her grandmother about the experience. Quickly she decided not to upset her and managed to answer, "She's much better, Grams."

Not wanting her grandmother to notice the state she was in, nor ask more questions, Penny went to the stairway and said over her shoulder, "I'll be down in a few minutes." She hurried up the steps. Upon reaching her bedroom she flung herself down on her bed. Penny began to shake. Jeremiah Bradshaw *must* truly be out of his mind! But even if he wasn't, it still had been a terrifying encounter. Gradually her pulses slowed, her breath came more evenly. It was only then she saw that one of the buttons on her jacket sleeve was missing, the dangling thread from it hung reminding her of Jeremiah's viselike grasp, the fierce struggle she had been forced to make to free herself.

With tremendous effort Penny composed herself. She did not want to upset her grandmother. She needed time to think it through, to decide how she could manage to avoid Jeremiah in the future. She certainly did not want a repeat performance of this harrowing confrontation. Of course, he was deluded. Even so, the chilling predictions of what would happen if she didn't accept what he believed made her shudder. She must try to forget about it for now. She'd think of some way to deal with it and *him* later.

After supper, while she and Grams were doing the dishes, Penny asked casually, "Grams, do you believe the Lord gives other people messages intended for you personally?"

Grams went on wiping a plate for a few seconds before answering. "Honey, what I believe is if the Lord wants to tell me something, he does it straight out. He don't need nobody to do it for him. 'Course, you gotta be listening to hear what he has to say. But he don't play guessing games."

Penny breathed a sigh of relief. Coming from Grams, the best Christian she knew, that was reassuring. Most certainly Jeremiah Bradshaw was crazy. And vindictive too. He resented the fact that she had always discouraged his overtures, refused to allow him to become a 'serious suitor,' even snubbed him overtly when she could. Maybe she hadn't been kind. But how else do you deal with someone who won't take a polite no for an answer? And because he was rejected, he was trying to get to her with this kind of manipulative *religious* ploy.

How terrible to use the Lord for his own purposes. He just wanted to frighten her. She should just forget it, Penny told herself firmly, and put the whole horrible episode out of her mind.

Chapter 4

It was harder than Penny imagined to put the unnerving encounter with Jeremiah out of her mind. She woke up the next morning with a vaguely oppressive feeling. She tried to tell herself that his predictions of disaster were meaningless threats. Or was it remotely *possible*—Penny shuddered—that she really *was* thwarting God's will? No! Penny refused to believe that. Jeremiah was just trying to intimidate her. If he thought he could convince her of something so out of character for her as *that*, he was *very wrong*! Still, Penny could not entirely shake the feeling that something dark was hovering over her. Every once in a while, when she least anticipated it, the memory of that incident in the woods would come back to haunt her.

However, to her great relief she heard something that put the whole disturbing episode into better perspective. She heard Jeremiah had quit his job, left Dunwoodie to join Brother Carmichael on his travels, preaching and lecturing about California. At least she didn't have to be afraid of running into him, feel his reproachful glance upon her, or listen to anymore of his wild "visions." Maybe he would find someone else to fulfill his own dream of going west to "save the heathen Indians."

Besides, Penny had other things to think about. The holidays were coming, a season when there was much baking to be done in preparation for the annual family gathering always held at Grams'. Grams set great store in celebrating both Thanksgiving and Christmas. She did everything to make it special. They decorated the house with pine boughs and holly, got out the best tablecloth and napkins and Grams' best Blue Willow china. Aunts, uncles, cousins, and folks they just called "cousin" and "auntie" even if they were no real kin were invited, and most of them came. Hospitality was for Grams a virtue and a joy. Food was plentiful, talk was constant, music and singing filled the old farmhouse with melody. Uncle Billy played his fiddle for the young folks to dance.

There was also a load more dish washing and cleaning up to be done with all the meals cooked and served. It often turned out that it was Penny and Thea who ended up doing these chores together. They didn't mind, because it gave them a chance to talk.

One evening when they were doing the dishes, Penny commented, "I sure hear Brad holding forth on the wonders of going west. Talking about 'going to see the elephant,' isn't he? Is it just talk or is he truly serious?"

"Going to see the elephant" was the slang expression everyone used when talking about the great migration to the West. It meant that those who went on the journey would see sights they'd never dreamed of seeing before.

"Oh, he's serious, all right," Thea answered, and she wasn't smiling at Penny's teasing remark. "He's been making lists, drawing up plans to build one of those covered wagons they travel in, figuring out how much equipment and all would cost, how much he could get for our house and—"

Penny halted, drew her hands out of the soapy water,

dried them on her apron, placed them on her hips, and stared at Thea. "*Really?* He's *that* serious?"

Thea nodded. "Of course, it wouldn't be until spring that we'd go. That is, if he could sell the house and get everything ready—"

"And how do *you* feel about it?" Penny demanded.

"Well, of course, it's kinda scary to think about—going so far and all. But Brad says it would be wonderful—he's read all about it, and he says our life there would be so much better. There are so many more opportunities for an ambitious man like Brad—"

"Restless, I'd call it," Penny said dryly. "Of course, he talked to Grams and me about it. But that was right after Brother Carmichael was here and—I don't know, I guess I figured it was one of those things he'd got real excited about then forgot. . . ." She let her voice trail off. Evidently her brother hadn't forgotten about it. She looked at her sister-in-law, and suddenly Thea's eyes turned moist with tears.

"Oh, Penny, I hate the thought of leaving you! What will I do without *you*?"

In two seconds the girls were hugging each other. "Why don't you come with us?" Thea asked in a choked voice.

Penny stepped back. "Oh, I couldn't, Thea. Leave Grams?" She shook her head emphatically. "No, I couldn't do that."

Just then one of the uncles came in on his way to the spring house to get another jug of apple cider and stopped to tease and chat with them, so Penny and Thea did not have another chance that evening to pursue the subject.

It was weeks before the two friends had another chance for a private talk. In January Brad's plan to take the big step of traveling by wagon train to California was common knowledge. He wasn't the only Dunwoodie man who had "caught California fever," but he was the only one so far in the small community who was forging ahead with actual preparations to go. He had put their house up for sale and was buying lumber to start building the wagon to specifications for the long journey.

The thought of Thea, her best friend from childhood, as well as her brother and her darling little niece going so far saddened Penny. She tried not to show it around Grams, knowing it was probably equally hard for her. Maybe even more so. At Grams age, saying good-bye to Belinda meant knowing she might never see her again.

Penny's unnatural quietness around the house did not go unnoticed. One cold January morning at breakfast Grams gave Penny a speculative glance. "What on earth ails you lately, girl? You act like you're comin' down with something. Maybe you need a good dose of sulfur and molasses."

"Oh, no, Grams!" Penny put on a horror-stricken face and held up both hands. "The last time you managed to give me that was when I was twelve years old!"

"And I had to chase you halfway round the barn to do it, as I remember!" chuckled her grandmother. "Well, if it ain't that, what's come over you? You sure seem like something's bothering you."

"I guess it's the thought of Brad, Thea, and Belinda leaving come spring."

"Yes, I know, child, but that's life. Leastways, it is nowadays. Used to be, people stayed put. But not now! Got to go 'see the elephant,' I reckon."

Then, late in February, early one afternoon Thea came by, and Grams immediately took possession of Belinda. She took her into her bedroom, where she kept a small box of toys and playthings especially for when Belinda came to the house.

As soon as the two friends were left alone in the kitchen,

Thea pulled Penny close. She grabbed her arm and, squeezing it, whispered, "Penny, I've got to talk to you. I have something to tell you, but you've got to promise you won't tell a soul."

Penny stared at Thea. "Secrets?"

"Well, yes, at least for a while. But first I have something else to say. Brad and I have talked it over, and we both want you to come with us."

"To California? But I've already told you, Thea, I wouldn't think of leaving Grams."

"Don't say no until you hear all I've got to say, please, Penny. Just think what an adventure it would be, and besides, you'd be company for me and a great help with Belinda—Brad agrees with me. He really wants you to come, too. And Grams wouldn't be alone. She never is. Somebody's always visiting here. And there's Uncle Billy. I'm the one who'll be alone if you don't come. And Penny, I really need you—"

Thea's fingers were pressing into Penny's arm. She drew it away, rubbing it as she looked curiously at her sister-in-law. There was something more to all this, but she couldn't figure out just what.

"Is there something you're not telling me, Thea?"

Thea glanced over her shoulder as if afraid she might be overheard, then she drew Penny over to the kitchen table, and they both sat down. In a low, breathless voice Thea began. "First, you've got to promise not to say anything about what I'm going to tell you. Not to *anyone*. Not to Gram, and especially not to Brad."

Penny looked doubtful. "Oh, I don't know—"

"Please, Penny, *please!*" Thea begged. "We've always kept each other's secrets, and this is maybe the most important one I've ever had."

Penny wondered, *Why on earth does Thea seem so frantic?*

What could be so important? Then, seeing the desperation in Thea's eyes, she agreed, "Oh, well, all right. Go ahead."

Thea lowered her voice to a whisper. "Penny, I'm going to have another baby."

Relieved that it wasn't some dark, awful indiscretion she had promised to keep, Penny exclaimed. "Oh, Thea, that's wonderful! A little brother or sister for Belinda. Won't Brad be—," then she broke off and said accusingly, "You haven't told Brad, have you?"

"No. Not yet. And I don't intend to. Not until we're on our way. . . . I'm only a few weeks along, and if he knew. . . ."

"But this changes everything, . . ." began Penny.

"That's just it, it *does.*"

"But if he knew about the baby he wouldn't want—oh, Thea, I think you *should* tell Brad," Penny said firmly. "I'm sure it would change his mind . . . at least make him consider waiting until after the baby comes."

"I can't, Penny. Don't you understand? It would spoil everything for him. He's got so many plans. He's pretty sure he's got a buyer for the house, and he's drawing up plans to build our wagon. He's so excited, so optimistic. . . . I just can't do that to him."

Penny would have liked to argue more. But the determination in Thea's face stopped her. As gentle as Thea was, she could be stubborn, and where pleasing Brad was concerned, nothing could move her.

"And how about *you*, Thea? Do you really think this is a good idea? Do you really want to move out west?"

"If it's what Brad wants, I want it too. Brad and Belinda are my whole life, Penny. You of all people ought to know that. Just think what my life was like before Brad loved me."

For a minute both were silent. Images of Thea's stern, unsmiling stepmother came into their minds.

"Besides, going means getting away from Veda." Thea

45

said her stepmother's name with a rare trace of bitterness in her tone. "She's at me all the time, Penny, about Mama's things. She doesn't seem to believe Mama left them to *me* in a separate will. Says they rightfully belong to her because they were in the house when she married Papa."

Penny knew Thea's stepmother to be a stingy, humorless, house-proud woman. She knew how hateful she had been all these years to her friend. It had shown most obviously at the time of her wedding. Everyone was astonished—actually shocked—when the bride showed up at the church wearing *black*. Penny was the only one prepared for *that*. The week before the wedding Thea had come over in tears. Sobbing, she had told Penny that Veda was not willing to spend money for an appropriate bridal gown. "One good black dress is all anyone needs and, what's more, all you're going to get. Foolish expenditure for a fancy outfit you'll only wear once!" Thea quoted her stepmother as saying.

Even so, Thea had been a radiantly beautiful bride— thanks to Penny's grandmother. When she heard about the black wedding dress, she immediately trimmed a scuttle-shaped polished straw bonnet with tiny pink rosebuds and blue forget-me-nots and blue satin ribbons and took it over to Thea the day before the ceremony.

Thea's stepmother had been a grim, unsmiling presence at the wedding. To this day she seemed to try her best to cast a shadow over the young couple's life. The first Mrs. Rawling's possessions, the china, the linens, a rosewood clock, a cedar hope chest, a few pieces of jewelry, still remained a bone of contention between them. Periodically Veda would stir up trouble claiming them.

Thea covered Penny's hands with both her own small ones and pleaded, "I don't mind leaving everything else. In a way, it will be a chance for Brad and me to start a new life together. So you see why I can't let anything stand in

Brad's way of having his heart's desire." A tremulous smile lifted the corners of her pretty mouth. "'Goin' to see the elephant.' That's what they call it, you know. The chance of a lifetime to see something you've never seen before. That's why I can't tell him about the baby. You do understand, don't you, Penny?"

Penny was still hesitant. "I don't know. . . ."

"Just until we're on our way, Penny. Then, of course, I'll tell him. He'll be so happy. He wants a son." Thea's smile made her face radiant. "Just think, a son born in *California!*"

Penny had never seen Thea look happier. Maybe that's what life was *really* all about. Loving another person more than yourself, more than what you wanted. A small nagging question in Penny's own heart demanded, *Would I ever love someone that much? Would anyone love me like that?*

"The next part is the *really* important thing, Penny. Please, *please,* think about coming with us." Thea held up her hand as Penny started to protest. "Don't you see, Penny? With a new baby coming—I need you." Thea pressed Penny's hands tightly. "So will you? Think about it seriously?"

"But Thea, there's Grams. What about Grams? For both of us—*all of us*—Brad, me, you, and *Belinda*—you know she adores the baby! To just go off and leave her alone. . . ."

"She could come too! But of course, she wouldn't leave Uncle Billy, I guess. But he has Aunt Betsy and Aunt Dora too. And so many friends. It wouldn't be like he was completely by himself," Thea countered. "I think she'd want you to go, Penny. And it wouldn't be forever. If you don't like it after we get to California, you can always come back."

"Well, all right, I'll think about it!"

"Oh, wonderful! Thank you, Penny." Thea hugged her, then jumped up. "I better be going. I've a million things to do." She started toward the kitchen door to go out to the garden when she turned back and putting her forefinger to her lips, asked, "And you do promise not to tell?"

Reluctantly Penny nodded.

Chapter 5

$\mathcal{P}$enny's promise to Thea lay heavy on her heart. Whether she should have made it at all worried her. Especially troubling was keeping something so important from Grams. Even more burdensome was Penny's other secret; she still hadn't told her grandmother her decision to go west with Brad and Thea. After much inner struggle, she had decided to go. That Grams was nearing seventy made it harder. In the last two years Penny had taken on the heavier household chores: chopping firewood, bringing water in from the well, filling the copper tubs for the weekly washing, lugging out baskets loaded with wet laundry, hanging it out. Could Grams manage without her? Was Thea's need really greater? She realized in good conscience that she couldn't delay telling her much longer.

The morning she knew she couldn't put it off any longer, Penny puttered around the kitchen, making busy work. Grams sent a couple of curious glances her way but didn't say anything until Penny blurted out her news. Grams was standing at the stove, her back to her, and for a minute after the words were out, Grams seemed to stiffen. Then, a moment later, she turned and, to Penny's astonishment, she didn't seem too surprised. Still holding the pancake turner she nodded briskly and said, "So you've made up your mind at last, have you?"

"How did you . . . ?"

"Well, I figured something was brewing," Grams replied. "You've been mighty quiet lately, and *that's* not like you. I thought you must have something pretty serious on your mind." Then, spearing Penny with her "now tell the truth" look, she asked, "Was this your own idea?"

"Yes," Penny answered. "Of course, both Thea and Brad have asked me to go with them. . . ."

Grams again surprised her by saying, "Well, I think it's a good idea. You're young and strong. You'll be a good support to both of them. Besides there'll be enough work for the two of you keeping tabs on Belinda at her age." Grams seemed about to add something else, then must have thought better of it and just gave a firm nod of her head. "The more I think about it, the better idea it seems to me that you go along. You've got a good head on your shoulders, and Brad needs some balance; he's often apt to go off like a firecracker, and Thea'd rather perish than cross him." Penny knew Grams had hit the proverbial nail on the head. No matter how unhappy Brad's decision might make her, Thea would never refuse to go.

Later, when Penny told Thea she would definitely go with them, Thea was ecstatic. She grabbed and hugged her, and the two of them danced around Thea's kitchen a few times. "Oh, Penny, I think I would have died if you hadn't said yes. I couldn't bear the thought of leaving you behind. You're my best friend. I can't imagine my life without you. And it'll be such an adventure and you and I will have such fun and Belinda will be so happy her Auntie Penny is going too. Oh, Penny, I promise you, you won't regret it."

Thea's use of the word "regret" made Penny think of the ugly scene with Jeremiah. "Regret" was the same word Jeremiah Bradshaw had flung at her for not accepting that *he*

50

had received a word from the Lord that *they* should be married and go to the West as missionaries. In spite of Thea's assurance, Penny had an uneasy feeling that she *might* regret both agreeing to go *and* keeping Thea's secret. As a troubling afterthought, she wondered what Jeremiah Bradshaw would say when he learned she was going west after all.

Penny was relieved she had finally broken the news to Grams. But she still felt uncomfortable hiding the *real* reason she was going. Grams deserved the whole truth. Surely she had the right to know. Grams loved Thea like her own and would welcome the prospect of a new grandbaby.

Even though she was committed to going, at least once a day Penny voiced her concern about leaving her grandmother. She would say, tentatively, "You're sure you won't be too lonely, Grams? Maybe I shouldn't—"

Finally Grams became exasperated. "Don't be silly, child. I'm not in my dotage. Leastways, not yet. And Uncle Billy'll help out much as he can. And Sister Dora and Cousin Tom don't live so far that they can't come over and give me a hand if I need it. Not that I won't miss you. I certainly will . . . but it won't be forever, now, will it?"

"No, Grams, just until they're settled and then. . . ."

That was what Penny and Thea had agreed upon. Yet no real plans of how Penny would come back east were actually discussed.

Penny found herself repeating that same assurance to Todd Farnum one evening when he came by to check for himself on the rumor he'd heard. Penny was out by the stable, grooming her mare, Mariah, when Todd arrived. He stood awkwardly for a few minutes, making circles in the loose dirt with the toe of his boot before he asked, "Is it true? Are you going along with Brad and Thea to California?"

"Yes, I'm going, to help on the journey and to get them settled. With the baby and all. . . ." She went on brushing

Mariah's mane. Glancing at Todd, she was shocked at how stunned he looked.

"I don't know about that, Penny."

"About what?"

"That's a mighty long way to travel to turn around and come right back. Are you *sure* this is what you mean to do?"

"Yes, I'm sure, Todd," Penny said gently, then added, "It's not as if it's forever."

Todd shook his head.

"I don't know, Penny. I have a feeling it *is* forever. I don't think you'll come back."

For some reason Penny couldn't try to convince him that she would. The words wouldn't come. Todd looked at Penny with hopeless longing. Although his emotions ran deep, he didn't have the ability to express them. He'd known her so long, loved her ever since ... well, since he knew what that meant. They had been children together, climbed trees, ridden horseback, waded in the creek and gone fishing. Everyone in Dunwoodie—except Penny evidently—expected that they would likely marry someday. At this moment, any chance of that happening slipped away, and now that she was out of reach, she seemed even more desirable to Todd than ever.

"Well, I reckon, I'll be going." Todd's disappointment made his voice thick. He took a few steps, then turned back. "I just hope you won't regret it."

Penny watched him walk away. Regret? *Regret!* That word again! She started vigorously wielding the curry brush. She was tired of hearing it. Hadn't she read somewhere the quotation "Better remorse than regret"? Didn't remorse mean being sorry for not taking opportunities when they came? If she let Brad and Thea go without her, wouldn't she feel remorse for missing such an adventure? Surely *that* would be much worse.

52

Grams, sewing in the lamplight, looked up as Penny came in the door. Penny went over to the stove, lifted the blue spackle coffeepot, and shook it to see if it was still full. She took a mug down from the shelf, poured herself a cup, and brought it over to the table across from where Grams was seated in her rocking chair.

Stirring sugar into her cup and said quietly, "I told Todd I was going."

"And I suppose the boy took it hard."

"Yes, ma'am."

"I think he always planned that someday you and him. ..."

"Yes. I know. And I'm sorry if I've hurt him."

"Well, just so you don't regret it when it's too late."

Regret! That word kept cropping up! Why did everyone use it? Wasn't it possible that she would think back on her decision as the best one she had ever made?

However, Penny made no comment. She couldn't share with Grams the *real* reason she couldn't back out now. She was caught between two loyalties. The one that bound her to Thea was strong. Thea needed her in a way Grams never could. Grams was a giver, generously pouring out love, acceptance, support to everyone. Thea was an emotional pauper.

While Penny had received an abundance of love from Grams, Uncle Billy, and a wide assortment of relatives, Thea had grown up in a loveless home. She had once confided to Penny that she could never remember being hugged or told she was loved—until Brad.

When Grams knew about the baby, Penny was sure she would understand and approve of her decision to go west.

She soon kissed Grams good night and went upstairs to her loft. There she took down her Bible from its shelf above her bed and, holding it, knelt down. She wasn't sure what she should pray about, but she was sure God knew what she needed. Thumbing through the pages she found in

Exodus 33 the heartfelt plea that spoke to her own situation: "Lord, show me Thy way that I might find favor with Thee. If Thy presence does not go with me do not lead me from here."

Penny got into bed feeling assured that if it wasn't right for her to accompany Brad, Thea, and Belinda something would happen to prevent her going.

She bunched the pillow more comfortably and settled herself for sleep, but she lay awake for a long time. Now that she had told Grams her decision, Penny's imagination ran free. Ever since the whole idea of going west had taken hold, she had felt a stirring excitement. That's why the word "regret" fell on deaf ears. Instead she had the strongest feeling that what lay ahead was better than what she was leaving behind. Maybe the unknown promise beyond Dunwoodie, where all her tomorrows waited, was something splendid.

Chapter 6

𝒥n the weeks that followed, preparations for the westward journey got underway. The first order of business was the building of the wagon in which they would travel. Brad had secured plans for the commonest type of conveyance, strong and sturdy enough to withstand months of rough terrain. These vehicles were called "prairie schooners" because of their shape, and it took only a little imagination to concede they *did* resemble a sailing ship. Built of oak, the rectangular bed of the wagon was approximately four feet wide and about twelve feet long. A sturdy tool chest was built at one end. The wheels were iron-rimmed wood. The axle assemblies were built with special care and strength, because the probability of the "emigrants" reaching their destination, over plains, deserts, and mountains, depended on its durability and safety. After yards of sturdy canvas cotton were stretched over the bent hickory supports arched from one side to the other, they were then painted with several coats of linseed oil to make them waterproof. All along both interior sides extra pockets and slings were sewn to provide more storage space. It was easy to see that the interior of the wagon, which served as the travelers' living space, would be cramped.

Penny felt a little awkward when she found out Todd was helping Brad to build it, working nights and every weekend in Brad's barn. She told herself it was only natural that Brad ask for his help or for Todd to offer. After all, they had been friends since boyhood. Penny tried not to see the mournful glances he cast her way when she looked in on their progress, but since she could not avoid him, she did her best to act casual and friendly around him.

Penny knew her decision to go west had become the subject of gossip. Dunwoodie, like most small towns, had no secrets. Talk had come back to her that people wondered how she could go off to California and turn her back on a potential husband as nice as Todd.

But Penny was independent enough to feel she did not have to explain or apologize to anyone. Let them buzz all they wanted. On the whole, she herself never paid much attention to gossip. However, she was secretly glad to learn that Jeremiah had left town to travel with Brother Carmichael. By this she assumed that he was genuinely serious about his own "calling." Well, it didn't concern her and it certainly didn't *include* her. Penny pushed aside her disturbing thoughts about him. Gradually the frightening encounter in the woods and his bizarre proposal faded in the busy preparations for the long journey.

Once the wagon was built, the packing began in earnest. Loading, shifting, and rearranging began. Almost every day, more "necessities" were decided upon, and the whole process had to be gone through again. Bedding and tent supplies, blankets, feather bed, pillows, tent, poles, stakes, ropes, and cooking utensils, Dutch oven, kettle, skillet, coffee grinder and pot, knives, tableware, precious matches placed in a glass jar—all had to be accessible for each night's camp on the trail. Places had to be found for their food provisions—stores of flour, baking soda, coffee, cornmeal, dried meats, vegetables and fruit, molasses, vinegar, pepper, salt, sugar, rice, and tea—which would have to last either the whole two thousand miles or until they reached a settlement where they could be replenished. They had to be very selective in taking Grams' wonderful home-canned delicacies; the glass jars took up too much room and could be broken too easily.

Decisions about clothing were the hardest to make for Penny and Thea. What would life on the trail be like? What might they need when they arrived in California? Daily discussions were held on these weighty matters. Then Brad put his foot down, declaring they each could have only one trunk and Thea would have to share hers with both him and Belinda. That settled, both women packed judiciously, one wool dress apiece. Anticipating it would be the hottest part of summer when they were to cross the prairies, they packed lighter weight gingham dresses. Grams contributed two denim pinafores for each of them, saying, "There'll be lots of dust and dirt to deal with, housekeeping in a traveling wagon." Penny and Thea exchanged a knowing glance, and with a wink and a giggle, each of them packed a party dress—"just in case."

Grams had taken on the job of packing the medicinal supplies. "Young people never think they might get sick. But with a little one along it's best to be prepared," she said as she fitted a small wooden box with some of her own time-tested remedies for stomachache, along with laudanum and camphor for headache, quinine for malaria, hartshorn for snakebite, citric acid for scurvy.... "'Cause, for sure, after a while you'll run out of fresh fruit and vegetables." She gave a definitive nod, then slipped in a large bottle of castor oil and another of peppermint essence.

The three of them spent hours making mattresses to place in the back of the wagon where they'd sleep, and Grams busily finished up an extra quilt to add to the ones already packed. "There'll be plenty of cold nights, I'll be bound, even if you'll be travelin' in summer. I've heard tell even in the Sahara Desert, nights get freezing cold. You'll be glad to have these, more'n likely."

Only a few "luxuries" were permitted. Brad watched doubtfully as Thea lined up the things "she could not bear to part with" to be placed *somewhere* in the wagon. Her mother's set of china, silver teapot, a few books, a Seth Thomas clock with brass trim, and Belinda's cradle. At this, Brad balked.

"We don't need to take *that*, Thea. She's almost outgrown it; she can sleep on a pallet, like the rest of us."

Under Thea's pale skin appeared a blush turning her quite pink. Penny knew Thea was very tempted to tell Brad then that they would certainly *need* that in a few months. There was a moment's hesitation, then Thea said softly, "Please, Brad. My grandfather made it for my mother when she was a baby. I slept in it and Belinda, too—it's a family heirloom."

Penny saw her brother chew his lower lip in frustration; then resignedly he said, "All right, if you insist. But something else'll have to go."

Thea threw a look that said "help" to Penny, and together they scrambled back into the wagon and started shifting things around again. Thea's gaze landed on a box containing some embroidered linens and pillow slips. Thea pointed at it. Penny knew that Thea had carefully packed her wedding bonnet in among them so that it wouldn't be crushed. She knew how much sentimental value Thea attached to it. It was a symbol of so much—but she also realized the cradle meant more. It would be for the new baby, to be born in the new country for which they were heading, in the new life to which they were going.

By the first week in April everything was packed. The wagon was finished, loaded, and ready to go. The day of their departure for Independence was set.

During that last week before they were to leave, Penny awoke every morning with a funny little feeling in her stomach. Though she had been counting the days, marking them off on the Farmer's Almanac calendar, now that she was about to leave, each day brought a special awareness. Things she had taken for granted, hardly noticed—the first signs of spring, the first green leaves, the bulbs beginning to poke through the ground, the first robin—took on a new significance. Next spring she would be in *California* seeing all kinds of new things.

Though she felt a happy excitement, there was also a melancholy about these last days. Penny found she could not glance at Grams without tearing up. One morning Penny came downstairs, paused on the stairway, and, looking into the kitchen, saw her grandmother moving briskly about fixing breakfast. Penny marveled at the small, straight body, her quick, deft movements. At an age that is considered to be elderly, Grams was as spry as ever.

Penny felt a sharp clutching sensation in her heart. Grams seemed dearer than ever now that she was leaving her. They had both been so busy this past week, there hadn't been a spare minute or an idle hour to talk, to tell her all the things she wanted to say. Penny wondered if that hadn't been her grandmother's purpose, keeping so busy that she wouldn't think too much about them leaving. She knew it would be particularly hard for her to say good-bye to Belinda, who was Grams' special "pet."

There were so many things Penny wanted to tell Grams if only she had a chance: how much she loved her, how much she appreciated all the years of devoted care. Especially she wanted her to know what her unselfishly "freeing" her to go with Brad and Thea meant, not making her feel the least guilty about leaving. This evening, for sure, Penny would say all those things that until now had been in her heart.

When Penny returned from taking a few last-minute things to be placed in her space of the wagon, Grams was sitting in her rocker working on her patchwork. She looked up when Penny came in. "You know, I've been thinking that it'll be some time 'fore you can get to a post office and send a letter back to me. So I want you to keep a journal, Penny. Write something down every day about where you are, what's goin' on, and what it looks like out there." Here she turned her head, looking out the window so Penny couldn't see her suddenly bright eyes. "I reckon you'll see sights that'll be beyond description, but I want you to try to write it all down as best you can. Then when you get to California, you can send it back to me. That way when I read it, it'll be like I was with you all that way."

Impulsively Penny went over and hugged her. "Oh, Grams, I wish you were going with us. Won't you change your mind and come? There's room."

"Land sakes, child, no! Mercy! I can't leave Uncle Billy, and Sister Dora's been hinting she'd like to spend some time over here . . . now that Clem's married. . . . I don't think she likes her daughter-in-law much, and I told her once you all were on your way . . . I'd enjoy the company."

Penny only half believed her. She knew Grams was being brave, putting up a courageous front. It must be very hard to part with the two people she had raised as her own children, to say nothing of Thea and Belinda.

She studied her grandmother's face she knew so well. There were still traces of the young woman that the old daguerreotypes proved had once been Cordelia Sayres. Her silver hair had dark streaks that hinted of lustrous color. But more than past beauty were the lines that life had etched on her face. The happiness, sorrow, wisdom had all left their mark, and it was a lovely legacy.

One of the many things Penny's grandmother had taught her by example was the ability to accept any circumstance, that life itself had something to teach, that you did the task that lay immediately at hand, and trusted God for the rest. Penny had never heard Grams complain, no matter how difficult things seemed. It was an important lesson. Even though Penny admired that quality in her grandmother she had no idea how valuable it would become to her in the days, weeks, and months that lay ahead of her.

PART 2

THE ADVENTURE BEGINS

Chapter 7

*A*t last it came! The day they were to start for Independence. There they would join the other wagons setting out on the Oregon Trail. Brad had made arrangements with a Captain Harding, a veteran of many cross-country treks, to join a train of twenty-five wagons he was leading to the coast, scheduled to depart on the fifteenth of April.

That morning Penny and Grams breakfasted alone early. Later Brad would arrive, driving the wagon with a brace of four oxen, two saddle horses, and their cow, tied to the back end. Then there would be the final farewell. Penny was sure her face must show some of her tension and anxiety about leaving.

As if reading her thoughts, Grams said, "Now, no last-minute nonsense, young lady. You're doing the right thing, Penny. Even though she didn't say anything to me direct, I expect Thea's going to need a sight more than company on this trip."

Penny darted Grams a sharp glance. Had she guessed about the new baby? Although both girls had been careful not to let anything slip, nothing much escaped Grams. But she didn't let on, if she did.

"And you won't forget about keeping a letter-journal, will you?"

"No, ma'am." Penny could hardly speak over the lump rising in her throat, realizing that this was the last time she'd be sitting across the table from her grandmother for a long, long time.

When Brad showed up, Grams bustled about, directing the loading of Penny's belongings, with an extra basket of food she had filled for them. Then followed a great deal of confusion, as other relatives, neighbors, and friends began to gather to see them off. Belinda was handed around to be kissed and hugged by all, and Brad had to listen to Uncle Billy's instructions and Aunt Dora's warnings about trusting strangers. Grams drew Penny aside and whispered, "We'll say our good-bye in here, not in front of the others. Don't want to make a spectacle of myself." She sniffed, then said sternly, "Nor do I want you blubbering, missy!" She gave Penny a hard hug.

Held tight in the arms that had rocked, comforted, and consoled her all the years of her life, Penny held her tight, loath to let go or move out of the embrace.

It was Grams who pulled away first, at the sound of footsteps on the porch and Brad's voice calling out, "All set, Penny? We're ready to roll."

They hurried out and Penny climbed into the wagon from the back. Brad cracked his long-handled whip, and with a neck-jolting jerk, the wagon lurched forward amid the yells and shouts of good-byes.

Penny leaned out as far as she dared, waving frantically. Grams was on the porch waving something in her hand. It looked like a dishtowel. The last thing she saw was that white cloth flapping before they rounded the bend at the end of the road.

Thea was sitting up front on the driver's seat with Brad, holding Belinda on her lap. Since there was no one to see,

66

Penny let the tears come and roll down her cheeks unchecked. For a few awful minutes Penny had the nightmarish feeling that maybe it was an awful mistake to leave her childhood home, all those dear to her, even Todd Farnum, a good man who loved her. . . .

As they rolled through the town where she had grown up, passing all the places she had passed hundreds of times on her way to school or to the church or to the store all these years, mixed with the nostalgia, Penny felt a ripple of excitement. Soon she would be seeing another landscape, another part of the world.

She was, after all, on the brink of the greatest adventure of her life, where anything could happen, where anything was possible. She might even find love—stronger, richer, deeper than she had ever imagined—waiting for her beyond the prairies, over the mountains. They were going to travel into a strange new land. . . .

She took out a newly sharpened pencil and the notebook Grams had given her and balanced it on her lap. Opening it to the first page, she wrote, "The sun is shining, the air is April fresh, and we are on our way. California Ho!"

Then an old thought occurred to her that she had not dared share with anyone: Would she find a love, stronger, richer, deeper than any she had ever imagined or known? Maybe it was only a foolish, romantic dream, but where she was going, she just might find it.

Chapter 8

*I*ndependence was congested, its streets jammed with wagons, carts, and jostling crowds of men, mules, and horses. The noise was deafening: merchants hawking their wares to the westward-bound "emigrants"—what they declared were the "necessities" for the long journey. The ring of blacksmithing shops was constant. Long lines of people stood waiting their turn to get their horses and oxen shod. The banging, hammering, braying, and shouting was mixed with hundreds of discordant voices rising to make themselves heard over the constant din.

As Brad maneuvered their wagon and team through the crowded thoroughfare, Thea and Penny, holding Belinda, peeked out from the protection of the canvas curtains. They exchanged horrified glances as they took in the scene. Were all these people on their way to California too? Were they all trying to escape from wherever their homes to find a better life in the "promised land"? They exchanged expressions of thankfulness that they had stocked their wagon with supplies before arriving in Independence. At least they wouldn't have to stop to wait in endless queues to purchase them. Brad finally managed to get them out of the center of town and onto a less crowded road.

From there they would go to a place called Maple Grove, the rendezvous point. Here they would join other westward-bound wagons and meet the wagon master, Captain Harding. Once everyone who had signed up for this train was assembled, the men, the heads of each family, would gather for an organizational meeting. At that time guidelines for the journey would be explained: what routes the train members would take, the daily schedule they would travel by, the routine that they would follow, the rules they would obey. Brad admitted there were quite a few details he didn't fully know, and he admitted he had a good deal yet to learn about this venture and so he looked forward to meeting with the other journeyers.

They were all really eager now. Penny had come up to the front of the wagon, stepping over boxes, rolled up mattresses, quilts, and trunks to crouch behind the other three on the driver's seat. They couldn't stop talking. Here at last was the "jumping-off" place of their journey, the gateway to the exciting new life ahead. Suddenly Brad pulled on the reins to bring the wagon to a stop.

"This must be where we turn," he said, pointing to a crudely printed sign on a rough wooden board nailed to a tree, a painted arrow under the words Maple Grove.

Penny thrust her head between her brother and Thea to see. It didn't look much like a grove. There wasn't a maple tree in sight. It was just a large open space in the middle of an overgrown meadow. They made the turn and slowly went forward. Soon they saw three or four wagons scattered over a wide area. A few horses grazed on the scraggly grass that edged the rutted center. A small group of men huddled to one side and looked around indifferently as Brad drove the wagon into an empty space. For a full minute they all sat there, stunned. Where was the large gathering of wagons ready to go west? At length Brad said, "I'll go see what's goin' on."

Penny sensed that he was trying to sound matter-of-fact, but she guessed he was just as bewildered and disappointed as she and Thea were. The scene before them certainly didn't look like what they had pictured. Nor did the people seem like the band of enthusiastic fellow-adventurers they had anticipated meeting and socializing with and sharing the excitement of the journey with.

Neither Thea nor Penny voiced their apprehension. They remained quiet as they watched Brad, hands in his pockets, assuming a nonchalance they were sure he didn't feel. He ambled up to the small cluster of men, who regarded him curiously.

Belinda, who had fallen asleep with the rocking motion of the wagon, stirred and awakened. "I hungwy."

"In a minute, honey. Let's wait and see what Daddy finds out. Then we'll find a nice place and have supper." Thea soothed her, but her tone did not evidence much hope of finding the "nice place" she promised.

"Do you think one of those men is Captain Harding?" Penny asked.

"I don't know. I sure thought there'd be more people than this, didn't you?"

"Brad said there'd be at least twenty-five or thirty wagons all together. They won't start west with fewer than twenty . . . not safe because of Indians, I guess."

Thea gave a little shudder, and Penny wished she hadn't mentioned Indians. That was one of the hazards of the westward journey that the "emigrants" most feared. She remembered Brother Carmichael calling them "wild savages" that needed to be "tamed." She quickly tried to undo whatever mischief she'd caused by bringing up the subject.

"Of course they're mostly exaggerated—Indian attacks." She was quick to add, "It's those made-up Wild West stories. Actually, from what I've read most of the Indians are peaceable, just want to trade. That's why we brought all that extra stuff, the calico, combs, trinkets. Remember? That information was in some of the information Brad got when he wrote to Captain Harding. And certainly *he* ought to know. He's led eight wagon trains, it said."

Thea only nodded. Penny hoped that she had allayed her sister-in-law's worries. She wondered just *how* afraid Thea *was* about this whole venture. Thea hadn't talked much about it. The most emotion she'd shown was relief and gratitude once Penny had agreed to come along. She glanced at her sister-in-law with new respect. Hadn't she read somewhere that real courage was when you *were* afraid of something, but did the thing you feared anyway?

Penny felt Thea had hidden her fears because of Brad. Few people could resist Brad's persuasive ways. Penny remembered times when he was a little boy wheedling for an extra piece of pie or cake so that even Grams found him irresistible. And she'd never seen Thea disagree with him about anything. But if she really was afraid and didn't want to make this journey—maybe, it would have been better if *this* time Thea had dug in her heels and said no. Even let him go it alone. But of course, Thea would never have done *that*!

Before Penny's thoughts could go any further down this dangerous path, Brad returned. Penny suspected the grin on his face was planted to offset any misgivings the two women might have.

"It's all right," he told them with heartiness. "It'll be another day or so before Captain Harding gets here, as well as everyone else who's signed up. They're coming from all over—Maine, Mississippi, as well as Missouri. We're lucky we got here early and can have our pick of a spot to park our wagon, let the oxen and horses feed . . . pitch a tent." He glanced at Thea. "Now don't look that way, Thea. It's going to be fine. Everything's going to work out."

Penny hoped Brad was right. Anyway, she made up her

mind to help him bolster Thea's obvious flagging spirits. She was just tired. The day-long trip in the unaccustomed wagon had been tiring, and Belinda was fretful. She'd be all right once they had eaten.

Determined to be cheerful, Penny got busy helping Thea spread out a blanket on which to set Belinda down. She got out the picnic basket Grams had handed them before they took off and opened it. Just as she had hoped she would she found something to give the child to nibble on until they were able to fix a real supper. Inside were all manner of goodies: blueberry muffins, oatmeal cookies, apples, homemade bread, sliced ham, cold fried chicken, a mound of sweet butter wrapped in cheesecloth. Penny sent up a silent prayer of thanksgiving! What a blessed grandmother they had.

After two long, tedious days Captain Harding still hadn't shown up. Penny kept telling herself it would all come all right. Two or three more wagons pulled into camp, and their occupants would ask the same questions they had asked when they arrived. Nobody seemed to know for sure when the wagon master would come, when the organizing meeting would take place, and, most of all, when they could start west. Some of the men were getting restive. Some even talked of pulling out and joining up with another wagon train. But all it amounted to was talk.

Little by little, some of the women made friendly overtures to Thea. Belinda was such a pretty baby, she always drew people's comments and was clucked over. The women largely ignored Penny. But she was used to being ignored around Thea. All their growing-up years, especially when boys began to take an interest in the opposite sex, Penny had been mainly known for having a "beautiful friend." Boys who had been hers and Brad's playmates for years suddenly hung around, hoping for a chance to be noticed by

Thea. Of course Thea only had eyes for Brad, who had taken a long time noticing his little sister's best friend.

But this time, being ignored was different. Penny finally understood why she was being left out of conversations and not sought out. It dawned on her that it was because she was *unmarried*—the *only* unmarried woman in the group thus far. Maybe they regarded her as a threat? How silly! She certainly had no designs on *any* of their husbands. She decided she wasn't going to let it bother her, although it did make her feel a bit awkward.

Brad was getting irritable and restless with the delay. Then on the third day, as if by magic, a group of ten, then another fifteen wagons pulled into Maple Grove. The already assembled bunch greeted them with shouts and cheers. Now it began to look like a real wagon train, and spirits rose. Everyone grew more lively, optimistic, and cheerful.

As every few hours a new wagon filled with other eager "emigrants" pulled into the Maple Grove clearing, good feelings became contagious. Some particularly elated folks painted signs on their canvas tops, with sayings like "California, Here We Come!" Finally Captain Harding arrived, and the collective sigh of relief was almost audible. Now things would *really* get underway, and they would soon be heading out onto the Oregon Trail.

An organizational meeting was scheduled for that evening, and Brad said they'd have to have an early supper so he could attend. All afternoon the whole camp buzzed with supposition of who would be voted spokesman for the group, the one to whom people could go when they had a problem or a dispute to settle. The rumor was that the men would draw up and agree upon a code of general regulations for the order and mutual protection of the whole train. Each family was independent, providing for their own food and welfare, but every man was expected to do his share of general work: guard duty and livestock picket assignments.

It all sounded splendid to Penny. Penny secretly hoped Brad would be chosen as spokesman. She was proud that Brad already seemed to be well regarded by the other men. Not only was he personable, outgoing, and smart, but he was also generous in offering help to others. His carpentry skills were in particular demand. He readily lent a hand in helping to pitch tents, tend livestock, and drive oxen. There were a surprising number of men who seemed to be lacking in necessary tasks of camping and wagon train living: storekeepers, owners of small businesses, a schoolmaster, and a law clerk were among some of the most eager, enthusiastic would-be western travelers. Penny wondered how a wife felt knowing her husband's obvious inexperience and ineptness as they ventured out on the long journey over plains and mountains, with homesteading and farming as their end goal.

Well, that was one thing about being single. She had no one to worry about but herself. Already she was getting the hang of outdoor living and leading a "tinkers-style life," and she loved every minute of it.

All afternoon a festive air continued to circulate among the camped wagons. Their once flagging spirits were revived by the presence of Captain Harding and the promise of an imminent departure.

Just before they were to prepare Brad's early dinner, Penny and Thea were sitting on the back of the wagon, waiting for Brad to return from taking the oxen for water. They were greeted by a cheerful voice: "Howdy, young ladies."

They turned to see a large gray-haired woman approaching. Smiling, she held out a dish covered with a blue checkered napkin and said, "Just thought you all might enjoy one of my apple pies."

Thea was holding Belinda in her lap, so Penny hopped down and accepted the unexpected but welcome gift. "Why, thank you," Penny said, holding out her hands for the plate.

This was the first open gesture of friendship they'd experienced since they'd pulled into Maple Grove. Each wagon load of travelers seemed to keep to itself as if everyone were waiting for everyone else to make the first move. From Brad, who had been around talking to the other men, they heard that several of the wagons were made up of two or three related families all moving west together. These groups had plenty of company among themselves and were either too shy or too cliquish to extend the circle. But this woman seemed ready not only to be neighborly, but to tell them about herself and to get to know them.

"I'm Nelldean Hardison," the woman said, her weathered face wrinkling in a wide smile. "Me and my grandson Nate's making this trek together. You two sisters?"

"Sisters-in-law. I'm Penny Sayres, and this is my brother Brad's wife, Thea."

"And who's this little sweetie?" Nelldean asked, holding out a finger for Belinda to grasp. Belinda dimpled and held out a chubby hand.

"Belinda." Thea smiled proudly.

"My, ain't she a picture?" Nelldean beamed. "So you're ho for California? Nate and me'll be partin' ways at Fort Hall. We're set for Oregon. Goin' to homestead there. Folks think I'm pretty old to be settin' out for a new country, but I say it's never too late." She chuckled merrily and went on without being prompted. "He's all alone in the world now 'cept for me. My son and daughter-in-law, his ma and pa, went out to Oregon two years ago. Nate was supposed to go with them but got the typhoid, near lost him, but we pulled him through. He was too puny to go with his folks, so he stayed with me until they got settled. They sent us the money to get the equipment we needed to outfit our wagon, and we started planning this here trip. Well, that was over a year ago, and just as we wuz about to leave, we got word both his folks had got sick real sudden and—," Neldean snapped her fingers "—just like that they wuz both gone to glory." Nelldean sighed. "But we'd bought the wagon and had it fitted out, and Nate was rarin' to go, so anyway, well, I couldn't let him go by hisself now could I? He's got a homestead waitin' in Oregon, so that's where we're plannin' to settle. So how about you folks? Going to California to mine or to homestead?"

"Homestead," Penny replied. "At least Brad and Thea are; I'm just along for the ride. I'll be going back once they're settled."

Nelldean gave her a skeptical glance but didn't say anything. They chatted a few more minutes, then Brad came back tired and ready for a supper they hadn't yet started. Penny introduced him to Nelldean, who shook his hand and said, "Well, I'll be goin' and let you folks get your supper." When they thanked her again for the pie, she waved her hands dismissively. "Jest hope you all enjoy it. I believe in bein' neighborly. Even when we're all on the move. Never know when you might need a helpin' hand, and it's nice to know the folks you're travelin' with. I'll bring Nate by so's you can get acquainted with him too." She nodded to Brad. "Good for a boy to have an older man he can look up to and kinda ask for advice he might not want to ask his old gramma for!" She chuckled and went on back to the wagon parked up away from theirs.

Penny and Thea worked together to get their belongings ready. The fact that this meant they were really going to get started on their great adventure made for a lightheart-

GRACE BALLOCH
MEMORIAL LIBRARY
625 North Fifth Street
S__ ___ SD 57783-2311

edness in contrast to the worry of the last few days. The two women went about setting things out on the small makeshift table, joking and laughing. Watching them Belinda clapped her tiny hands and laughed along with them. This made them laugh all the more. The result of all this merriment was a meal more like a carefree picnic.

An hour or so before Brad was to attend the men's meeting, Penny and Thea got out the makeshift table of small, square boards nailed together, and they set out their supper. Thanks to Grams, they had another bounteous meal— sliced ham, homemade bread, quince jam—and they opened a jar of Bartlett pears. Belinda seemed happy as a little gypsy, sitting on the ground and eating with both dimpled hands. Every so often she crowed with delight. Thea and Penny alternated between excitement and silliness. The least little thing sent them into hilarious giggles.

Nelldean's pie was delicious—better than either of them could make, Brad teased them. "I encourage you two to keep up *that friendship.*" More than the treat of the pie, Penny appreciated Nelldean's obvious generous nature. It gave her a sense of security to know that there was an older woman who had raised a family of her own, suffered the ups and downs of life, and had a wealth of experience and knowledge that neither she nor Thea possessed. As the jovial woman had said, you never knew when you might need a neighbor. Certainly there were unknown hazards in this moving caravan of people on this uncharted journey west. It was good to know Nelldean Hardison was on their wagon train.

After supper Brad walked over to the organizational meeting with some of the other men, and Thea took Belinda inside the wagon to put her down for sleep. Left to herself, Penny leaned against the wagon and looked up at the sky. It was just beginning to get dark. A few tiny stars

12974

began to appear, and the pale line of a new moon etched itself against the gray-mauve background.

Just then she heard the creaking sound of yet another wagon turning into the campground, its humped outline rocking as it moved awkwardly forward over the rutted surface of the ground. The driver was obviously searching for a place to camp.

A man and woman sat on the high driver's seat. Slowly the wagon advanced, then pulled to a stop directly in front of where Penny stood. The man turned his head so that Penny saw his face clearly. For a moment all she could do was stare, horrified. Then she drew in her breath sharply. "Oh, no!" The man was none other than Jeremiah Bradshaw.

Chapter 9

$\mathscr{P}$enny's first horrified reaction was to duck out of sight. Not wanting him to see *her*, she crouched behind the wagon, her heart pounding. Jeremiah Bradshaw! Of all people she had never expected to see—never *wanted* to see! If she imagined the worst possible thing that could happen to her, it would be to have him on the same wagon train.

How had it happened? He had left Dunwoodie to travel with Brother Carmichael before she had decided to go with Brad and Thea. She had been so glad not to have to see or talk to him—to have him out of her life! Now, here he was back in it.

Gradually Penny collected her wits. His wagon passed theirs. Sure that he had not seen her, she crept from her hiding place, watching as his wagon went toward the center of the campground where the large campfire was burning. Most of the menfolk were gathered there at the organizational meeting, and Captain Harding would be there to greet the newcomers.

Who was the woman with Jeremiah? His *wife*? It *must be*. It certainly wasn't his mother, and he didn't have a sister. When had Jeremiah married? And *who* was she?

79

After Jeremiah's wagon passed by, Penny climbed into the wagon. As she did Thea looked up. She was just covering Belinda, and she put a finger to her lips, warning her to be quiet so as not to wake up Belinda. Something in Penny's expression alarmed Thea, and she crawled over to where Penny huddled at the edge of the wagon and whispered, "What ever's wrong?"

"You'll never guess." Penny shivered and told Thea what she had seen. In hushed tones she said, "How can I possibly avoid him if they're going to be traveling with us?"

"I don't know." Thea looked forlorn. "Poor Penny. I know you couldn't stand him. None of us could figure out exactly why—"

Involuntarily Penny shuddered, remembering the effect Jeremiah's unwanted attention had on her. "I can't explain it. He's just so—so—" She shook her head.

Thea patted her shoulder sympathetically. "Don't bother. I understand. I'll try to find out more about them tomorrow. I'll ask some of the women—without mentioning you, of course. I've been talking to some of them, the ones with small children. Mothers always talk to each other. About their little ones—how old are they, when did they start to talk or walk, that sort of thing."

Penny knew Thea was being tactful. *She* had been more or less ignored by the other women. Be that as it may, she'd let Thea do her detective work about the Bradshaws.

Actually it was Brad who brought back the information they had been curious about. He shared the news that he had been temporarily voted spokesman for their group of wagons, but it was his other bit of news that interested Penny personally. "Say, Penny, an old beau of yours just turned up to be part of our wagon train. Jeremiah Bradshaw. He's got a wife with him though, so I guess his heart wasn't broke too long," he told her teasingly.

"He was no beau of mine!" Penny declared indignantly. "What did he have to say?"

"He seemed mighty surprised to find out you'd come along with Thea and me."

Penny and Thea exchanged looks.

"What *exactly* did he say about me?" Penny asked.

"Oh, just something about you always were a will-o'-the-wisp." Brad shrugged. "We didn't talk much. He sat in on the meeting and made a few suggestions. Which weren't well taken, I must say, as he had just arrived on the scene and didn't know anyone. Seemed kinda pushy."

"You said his wife is with him. Is she from Dunwoodie too?" asked Thea.

"No, funny thing. Brother Carmichael—you remember him?—well, seems like he had been to this woman's town and convinced *her* that she too was to go west as a missionary, then introduced her to Jeremiah and married them."

Penny would have liked more details about this startling occurrence, but Brad yawned and said he was going to "hit the hay." "Coming, Thea?" He held out his hand to her, and she took it and, with an apologetic look back at Penny, went along with him into the wagon.

Penny stayed by the campfire a little longer, knowing that sleep would not come easily for her this night. What would having Jeremiah in such proximity for the next several months be like? She couldn't bear the thought. She knew one day soon the encounter she dreaded would have to happen—was bound to happen. She doubted if he would create a scene as long as she was under Brad's protection. Still, a cold shudder went through her. All the joy and excitement she had felt about the trip drained away. The menacing figure of Jeremiah loomed over her like a giant shadow.

Only a few nights later Penny came face-to-face with

Jeremiah. Thankfully, she was with Thea and Brad. The whole company had been called to a final meeting before getting under way the following day, to receive last minute instructions on the order in which each wagon would pull out and in what sequence. Their eyes had met for one terrible moment. The saying "If looks could kill . . ." flashed through Penny's mind. Quickly she averted her head as though listening intently to what the wagon master was saying. When the meeting was over, Jeremiah and his wife had disappeared. Still, Penny was glad she had not been alone this first time he had seen her.

PART 3

ON THE TRAIL

Chapter 10

There were thirty wagons in their train now and so much for each group to do every day that Penny assured herself there was little chance of her having to deal with Jeremiah. Even less when the wagons were lined up in the order of their arrival so that when they finally pulled out, the Sayres' was near the front, while the Bradshaws', among the last to join the train, was at the end. When the wagons circled at sunset, they were camped a long way from Jeremiah and his wife.

At the few glimpses she had of Emily Bradshaw, a slight, pale girl with light brown hair and large, frightened eyes, Penny's soft heart felt a nudge of sympathy. She looked sad, anxious, as though she were longing for a kind word, a show of friendship from some of the other women, but too shy to make any gestures herself. Most were too busy with their own chores and children. Even moved by pity, Penny knew *she,* of all the women, could not take any step toward friendship. Whatever she did would be wrongly construed.

For the most part, Penny tried to forget that Jeremiah was in the wagon train and live her own life. She had taken to this unusual way to travel, as Grams would say, "like a duck takes to water." As a child she had often fantasized about the gypsy life, having a little painted caravan, and going wherever the road led. Traveling in the huge canvas covered wagon was far different, but in those first few weeks of the journey Penny enjoyed it thoroughly.

She also tried to keep her promise to Grams of keeping a letter-journal of their days to post at the first mail house or military fort they came to along the trail. She tried to give her grandmother a picture of what life on the trail was like—a life that Penny knew would seem strange to a woman who had lived in the same town all her life and in the same house since she was seventeen!

Life on the trail was so much busier than she had imagined with so many chores to be done—and quickly. In the morning, at the wagon master's shout, they had to be ready to pull their wagon into line in its correct position.

They had been traveling for two weeks before Penny figured out the best time to write to her grandmother: usually the noon break. That was when the wagons pulled off to give the mules, horses, and oxen some rest and for the weary travelers to get a bite to eat. Penny would settle herself at the side of the wagon in the shade, prop her copybook on her knees, and begin to write.

Dearest Grams,

I've tried to jot down something every day that will keep a record of our journey, but I've done a poor job of it so far. But there has been so much to do, so much to see, well— that's my excuse—the days are so full and busy and by nightfall we're all too tired to do much but fix and eat supper, go to bed. I'm still trying to get the hang of this life on the trail. Let me just tell you how it goes.

Morning begins at daybreak. You'd laugh to see me jump when the guard-duty men's rifles go off with a shattering bang. That lets us know we were kept safe and sound through the night by these brave fellas. It's also the signal that we have just two hours to get breakfast, wash up, pack up, and get "ready to roll," as they say around here, before pulling out on the trail for the day's journey. We're supposed to make ten to twelve or more miles per day in order to get to the mountains and cross them before the first snows that sometimes come early in the Sierra.

There's not much chance of sleeping in because there's racket aplenty as folks rouse themselves and get their breakfast going. You never heard such clanging of skillets, banging kettles to say nothing of barking dogs. You'd be surprised how many folks brought their dogs along on this trip. I try to get up first to give Thea time to get the baby up and dressed. I'm getting fairly good at starting a fire. Brad, who was never a morning person, as you may remember, hauls himself out of the wagon, groaning as he gets the team, who aren't that eager either, yoked up. I can sympathize with the poor beasts being hitched for another hard day on the road. We do everything to lighten the load for them. Often Thea and I walk alongside, as do the other women and children. We take turns carrying Belinda who's getting mighty heavy. We've become good friends with a very nice older lady, Nelldean Hardison, who walks with us most days.

Penny paused. She thought of the conversation she'd had with Nelldean the other afternoon when Thea had taken Belinda to the wagon for a nap. Penny always enjoyed Nelldean's company. She was always cheerful and talkative and never complained or whined like some of the women.

Noting that Penny was bareheaded, Nelldean told her, "You've got a fine head of hair, my girl, but what you need is a good sunbonnet, elseways you're going to ruin your complexion and might get sunstroke to boot. I made me a couple 'fore we started out, with broad brims stiffened with narrow wood stays. They'll keep the sun out of your eyes, protect your skin, and keep you from gettin' your brains fried." She chuckled. "I'll make you and your sister ones too. She looks right delicate. Don't see her out walkin'. Is she ailing?"

Penny shook her head, wondering if it might not be a good idea to tell Nelldean Thea was expecting, in case—in case, what? That question stopped her. After all, it was Thea's news to tell, and since Brad didn't know yet, Penny felt she better not. Penny simply said, "She's fine; it's easier for her to nap when Belinda does."

Nelldean didn't make any further comment. But it made Penny wonder if she ought to tell Grams. It wouldn't make any difference now for her to know. Still, she hesitated.

Nelldean spoke again. "Women need a lot of strength for this journey. And more when they get where they're going. Homesteading takes all a body's got and more." Penny felt Nelldean's quick, inquisitive glance. "Did you mean what you said the night I met you? That you're just 'along for the ride?' Why, I'd think a young woman like you'd be up for adventure yourself. I seen you riding your horse the other day, and I said to myself, 'That young lady's going to make a fine homesteader.'"

"Well, you see, I live with my grandmother. She reared Brad and me, and I'll be going back home after I help Thea get settled—well, that's just the way I planned. I only promised Thea I'd stay until—," Penny caught herself before she blurted out Thea's secret.

"I see." Nelldean nodded.

Penny had a feeling the woman guessed what she had not said and in some way it comforted her to know somebody else knew.

Penny went back to her letter-journal. Her pencil skimmed over the pages as she gave her grandmother as vivid a picture as possible of what her far-away family was experiencing. She tried to give her an idea of what a "normal" day on the trail was like for them. She knew it was impossible to describe it to her as it really was, but she tried.

Two hours after sunrise the wagons are ready to roll. At noon the wagons turn off. The teams are not unyoked but are loosed from the wagons to graze nearby. Sometimes while people eat an "in hand" meal of bread or cheese, the men hold meetings to take care of any business that may need to be discussed or any arguments to be settled. You'll be glad to know Brad is very well regarded among the other men. He's matured a lot and become much steadier and more responsible.

Brad has been voted one of the seven duty captains, whose responsibilities are to assign jobs and oversee some of the wagon repair and other chores on the wagon train. My particular charge is taking care of our two saddle horses, Brad's and mine; Mariah is doing real well. I often put Belinda up in the saddle in front of me and ride. She loves it.

She stopped writing for a minute, pausing to think what to say next. Penny did not know how much to tell of some of the unexpected things that went on: the petty arguments, the problems no one was prepared for, the hardships, and the physical stress of this journey. Much of these were offset by the camaraderie of the other travelers and the congenial companionship the three of them shared. The main thing she didn't tell her grandmother was the arrival of Jeremiah Bradshaw and his wife. It took her only seconds to decide not to say anything. At least not yet. So far, she had managed to keep her distance from both the Bradshaws. She hoped she could maintain that distance all the way to California.

Instead Penny told Grams about the funny things that happened: their new style of cooking over an open fire, the words Belinda was beginning to say, and some of the mishaps of wagon train living.

Penny scribbled busily until she heard the familiar "Wagons! Pull out!" The noon break was over, and they had to start moving again. She quickly put away her notebook and pencil. Once the call was given, everyone hastened to be ready to move out. Over and over they had heard repeated how important it was to make those ten or more miles every day and keep up with the other trains. "A day lost is lost forever." It was necessary to keep the teams of animals in good shape so that there would be no delays. More than once Penny heard Brad repeat what he'd heard the scout and wagon master say: Worst thing you can do is fritter one day on the trail.

All that was necessary to keep the worst laggard moving was to mention the dread words "the Donner Party." Every emigrant knew the tragic story of the members of an earlier wagon who had been caught in a blizzard and were trapped for a horrible winter. There were stories of starvation—or worse.

Tucking her book into one of the pockets of the canvas marked for her belongings, Penny grabbed her new sunbonnet, tied the strings under her chin, and started walking alongside the wagon. "Coming, Thea?" she asked her sister-in-law.

Thea looked up from the pallet on which she was resting beside the sleeping Belinda. "I think I'll stay in for a while. I have a little headache," she said wanly.

Penny started to say something but thought better of it. Just the other evening she had begged Thea to tell Brad. But Thea shook her head, "Not yet, Penny. Just till we get further on our way. I don't want to give him any reason to turn back. I had some of the same queasiness with Belinda; it will pass. I'll just be careful. Please, Penny. Brad is so happy. He's in his element, can't you see that? We can't spoil it for him."

The pleading in Thea's beautiful eyes was impossible to refuse. Penny jumped off the back of the wagon, and as Brad cracked his whip and the wagon made a jolting start, she fell into step alongside.

Lately Thea had been staying in the wagon more than

walking, and Penny was worried. Two other women in their company were also expecting, sooner than Thea, however, from what Penny could tell. She would have to be more aware of Thea's condition and take over some of the heavier chores, like lifting and carrying Belinda or placing her in front of her on her saddle when Penny rode Mariah.

Penny did not mind walking. It gave her time to think. She still wondered what it would be like when they reached California, still miles and months away, and how long she would stay. At least until Thea had the baby. Then she would return home. Would that be as hard to do as it had been to come? She could not help wondering if it would be the golden land of promise it had been portrayed as being.

Preoccupied with her own thoughts, time passed quickly for Penny, and soon the signal was given for the wagons to pull out at the end of the day. Penny followed along as Brad guided the oxen into their place in the circle that the wagons always formed for the night for protection from any possible attack by hostile Indians. Thank God, so far there had been none.

At the end of the long day everyone felt relief. This journey was far harder than anyone had anticipated, for both humans and animals. While the men unhitched the teams, the women greeted each other and stood chatting for a few minutes, and the freed children ran around playing tag with friends from some of the other wagons.

Penny and Thea got busy preparing the evening meal. At supper there generally wasn't too much talking; they were all too tired. Gradually things quieted, voices got lower, the night guards left to take their places, beds were unrolled, and children were hushed and readied for sleep. Brad soon left them to crawl wearily into the wagon to sleep. Belinda usually fell asleep in Thea's arms and she took her inside. Penny always insisted on cleaning up and dousing the fire before climbing into her blanket roll. Brad

91

had helped her pitch her small tent at the back of the wagon, not too far from where both horses were tethered for the night. She liked hearing their soft whinnying, the movement of their hooves on the grass, and she liked being able to look out through the flap at the sky. As they reached the prairies the sky seemed bigger than ever. Tonight it was pinpricked with brilliant stars.

Penny, even though tired, didn't usually go right to sleep; her mind always seemed too busy. There was so much to see and learn as they traveled westward. She lay there listening as the night deepened, and a restful silence hovered, then gradually settled over the campground. On nights like this she was glad she'd been persuaded to come along on this journey. Finally her eyelids grew heavy, and Penny drifted slowly off, thinking, *I wouldn't have missed this for the world.*

Chapter 11

$\mathcal{F}$or the most part, Penny's daily entries into her let-ter-journal to Grams were full of the funny incidents and the things she noticed about people, events, happenings that would interest her grandmother as she read it.

You probably recall when we went to hear Brother Carmichael, he went on and on so about what coming west would be like—"Friends, you are traveling to the Garden of Eden, a land flowing with milk and honey"— I'm sure there were some who believed every word. I've begun to think it would have been well for some to take all that with your often counseled "grain of salt." I don't know what California will be like exactly, but I doubt "the clover in Oregon grows high as your chin." However, the wildflowers on the prairies we've passed through are the prettiest and most colorful I've ever seen.

We are becoming fast friends with the Hardisons. Hardly a day goes by that there isn't some sort of exchange between our wagons. Nelldean reminds me something of you, Grams, wise and witty and as cheerful as the day is long. Nothing seems to daunt her. She's a treasure trove of information, which is very helpful to us as we make do with the housekeeping chores while being constantly on the go. You see, Nelldean has already made this cross-country trip once.

She and her husband came shortly after the discovery of gold, so she knows more what's ahead of us than anyone else. Nelldean's grandson, Nate, a gangly, freckled sixteen-year-old, is shy but just as generous and open-hearted as his grandmother. Belinda adores him, and he's real sweet with her. Of course, it is Belinda who is the center of attention in our small party. I wish you could see her, Grams. She is growing prettier every day, blonde ringlets now curling around her neck, her skin rosy and healthy from being out-doors so much. And with the sweetest, cunningest ways.

Jotting down the simple details of everyday life on the trail, Penny deliberately left out telling her grandmother about Jeremiah Bradshaw's harassing presence.

The fact that in the few weeks since the Bradshaws had joined the wagon train she had managed to avoid any direct contact with Jeremiah gave Penny a certain compla-cency. A false sense of security, as it turned out.

One afternoon when Penny was coming back from draw-ing a bucket of water from the barrel at the rear of the wagon, a tall figure suddenly loomed in front of her. Jere-miah. Instinctively Penny stepped back, heart thundering. Without any greeting, he planted himself in her path. His mouth twisted sardonically. "Well, Miss Sayres, I thought you didn't want to go west," he snarled.

Penny tried to keep her voice even and remain calm. "I hadn't planned to—"

"Don't lie to me. Don't you know falsehood will not go unpunished? And he who speaks lies will not escape but *perish*?"

"I'm not lying," she said coldly.

"What about your grandmother?" he sneered. "You told me you couldn't leave your grandmother. Or was that another lie?"

"Of course not. I wasn't lying. I came because Thea needed me and—"

"So it was just with *me* you didn't want to come?"

Jeremiah's eyes were dilated, his nostrils quivered, a muscle in his cheek twitched. Penny's mouth went dry with fear. She remembered that awful encounter with him in the woods back home, and she shrank from a repetition. Any minute he could lose complete control. There was no use trying to deal with Jeremiah. He only saw things the way he wanted to see them. Just like he had insisted he had a divine word that *they* were to go together as missionaries. She felt the old revulsion of him rise up within her, but she knew better than to enrage him further. All his fury at her rejection of him was more physical than spiritual. He was using her failure to go along with *his* vision as a cover for his crushed pride. Penny prayed frantically for help.

"That was it, wasn't it?" he demanded. "You risked disobeying God because you didn't want me? You think you're too good for me, don't you?"

"I don't owe you any explanation, Jeremiah," Penny said, trying to control her inner trembling. "Now, let me pass—"

"Not yet. Not until I get an answer."

"You had your answer, Jeremiah, back in Dunwoodie."

He shook his head, eyes blazing, his fists clenched. "You're so proud, aren't you, Penny?" He flung the words at her sarcastically. "Well, you know what pride is? One of the deadly sins! And *you'll* see—pride goeth before a fall, Penny. There's retribution for people like *you*—"

He's crazy, stark raving mad! Penny thought frantically. *I have to get away from him.* She tried to pass by him, but he grabbed her wrists.

"Let me go!" Angrily, she tried to pull away, but his grip was too strong. Desperately her eyes darted to the left and right, hoping someone would break this up just by walking by! But there was no one. She was wedged between the two wagons, hidden by their height and bulk, shadowed by the fast-falling dusk, and caught here alone with Jeremiah.

His fingers gripped harder, his voice thickened. "You like tormenting me, don't you, Penny?"

"Of course not, Jeremiah. Why should I?"

"Because you know how much I wanted you to be with me, how it grieved me that you wouldn't listen to what I know was meant to be—"

He pulled her to him, one hand roughly forcing her chin up, his mouth coming down bruisingly on hers. Penny dropped the bucket and felt the cold water splash onto her skirt hem and shoes as it fell to the ground. Then she put both hands against Jeremiah's chest, pushing with all her strength. Taken off guard, he staggered back, stumbling. She drew back her hand and slapped his face as hard as she could.

Jeremiah's palm went to the side of his cheek, already turning red from the stinging blow. His expression went from stunned surprise to total blankness. For a second he neither spoke nor moved. Only his burning eyes betrayed his anger.

"You'll regret you did that, Penny."

"And what about *you*, Jeremiah? You're a married man," she retorted in a low, furious voice. Something buried deep in her memory came into her mind. She decided to flog him with his own weapon: Scripture. "Matthew five, twenty-eight! Think about it—"

The brief glimpse Penny had of Jeremiah's face before he swung on his heel and marched away gave her the satisfaction of knowing that her words had hit their mark. As he disappeared from her sight, she shook her hand, her fingers still tingling from the slap. A feeling of weakness swept over her, and she had to lean against the nearest wagon wheel to steady herself. For a wild moment, the urge to laugh almost overcame her. She knew she must be on the edge of hysteria. Slowly a sense of thankfulness followed. A psalm she had memorized as a child came to her in all its beauty and truth. It was Psalm 18:48: "You have delivered me from a violent man, therefore I will give thanks to you—and sing praises to your name." "Thank you, Lord," she whispered. With a grateful heart she blessed Grams for insisting she memorize Bible verses every week.

That night as she lay sleepless in the dark of the little tent Penny had no doubt whatsoever that she had a Father in heaven who was watching over and protecting her.

Shuddering at the memory of that encounter, resolutely Penny determined to push the nasty incident with Jeremiah out of her mind. How dare he use Scripture to twist and distort? How had she caused him to be so vengeful? She hadn't meant to and she was sorry if she had.

Penny pulled the covers up around her chin, trying to banish the hate-filled scene from her mind. But in spite of her resolve, Jeremiah's voice still echoed hauntingly: "Pride goeth before destruction and a haughty spirit before a fall."

Dearest Grams,

Remember the saying that journeying west was "going to see the elephant"—meaning, I guess, that we were bound to see sights we never had before or could imagine? Well, I have yet to see an elephant, but I've just seen my first buffalo! One day a herd came thundering toward us; it looked like a great dark cloud, a moving mountain coming on with terrible speed. I have no idea how many there were—it seemed a monstrous group, making awful noises, hoof beats clattering, wild snorting, heads down, tails flying. It was an awesome sight to behold. When stampeding, they do not swerve to the left or right but go straight ahead, not stopping for anything. Our scout, waving his arms and shouting, rode down the line telling us to move out of the way of this bunch of animals moving ever closer like a marauding army. But some wagons could not pull out soon enough, and two were overturned as the buffalo rushed by. Two buffalo were shot and their carcasses stripped, butchered, and divided among the wagon train. A huge fire was built, and the meat barbecued. At first I was not eager to try it, but persuaded to taste it, I found it richer and gamier than beef steak. Some said the rest would be made into jerky. Not particularly appetizing to me, but perhaps as we go further and food rations get scarcer, anything will taste good.

Sometimes our evenings are quite lively. As a company of fellow travelers we seem to have come together as a constantly moving band of neighbors. After supper, when the evening chores are done, a group of us often gathers around a campfire. One man is a talented guitar player, another accompanies him on his harmonica, playing familiar melodies that we can all join in singing: "Old Kentucky Home," "The Girl I Left Behind Me," "Maryland, My Maryland." But when they swing into "Home Sweet Home," it touches many a pensive heart, and soon there is a chorus begging them to play something more cheerful. Obligingly they go into "O Susannah" or "Turkey in the Straw." But all in all it is as pleasant a time as can be imagined after the long, wearying days.

I have found there are several other unmarried women in our wagon train, all younger than me! At the ripe old age of twenty-one I'm considered a "spinster," I suppose, and so out of the running for the three bachelors among us. One is a law student and can be seen with a thick tome of jurisprudence open, studying it as he walks alongside his team. The other two are taking "absence without leave" from their college education, but one of these is our harmonica player so we are all happy he did so to make our campfires so enjoyable.

So the social life here at the end of the day is remarkably active! Thea has provided me with an interesting—but I must say "creative"—history. She tells people the story of a "broken engagement" that she says I am bravely recovering from—wouldn't Todd be surprised to know he supposedly jilted *me*? Anyway, it seems to have earned the sympathy of some of the women who had been "snubbing" me for being single, and everyone is quite friendly now.

In her letters to her grandmother, however, Penny still left out many of the things she thought might worry her, things that were burned deeply into her own memory. Penny knew she would never forget them. She might even write about them—someday.

They had been a little more than two months on the trail now, and many disasters had struck their wagon train. Some of the livestock had died, some from overwork, some from a mysterious prairie-induced illness. A few wagons had not been well-built and broke down, beyond repair. Those families had to unload, leaving some of their belongings strewn beside the trail, and join with relatives in their already overcrowded wagons. As wagons broke down, more women and children were forced to walk during the day and bed down in camp on blankets on the ground at night because the interiors of the remaining wagons were too full for any kind of comfort or sleep.

There were disputes and conflicts, even fistfights, as tempers grew raw and nerves taut. There was illness. Once a fever or disease hit one group, it seemed to sweep through the entire wagon train. There were hastily dug graves to join the ones they had seen earlier, then averted their eyes from as they moved along. A few of the water barrels, staves swollen from the desert heat, sprung cracks, leaking precious water and causing a rationing of water for both humans and animals. This commodity could not be wasted. They had to hold out until they reached Fort Laramie, where some of the supplies could be replenished. Nelldean told Penny that these things were all things expected to happen on such a long journey and that the wagon train had been fairly lucky thus far with no epidemics like cholera and no Indian attacks. Her comment didn't make things any more bearable, but it reinforced Penny's decision not to pass all this along in her letters to Grams.

The children on the wagon train were the only ones who

seemed carefree. Never had they been allowed so much freedom as they had on the trail. However, there had been some accidents. Tragedies. A couple of children had been run over by wagon wheels; another, running along behind, had tried to jump onto the end of the wagon but slipped and was crushed under the oxen-pulled wagon just behind. There had been illness too, sudden unexplained fevers that took one child, who had been running and playing the day before. The child was quickly buried, and the grieving family had to move on.

Jeremiah Bradshaw remained the "fly in the ointment" for Penny. She hated the feeling of looking over her shoulder, so to speak, always dreading another nightmare encounter. She couldn't entirely avoid him. Every so often she'd see him at a distance, and if he was able to catch her eye, there was always a dark, glowering stare. She didn't think he would seek her out again. But there was always that possibility, and that bothered her.

Nelldean and Penny's friendship strengthened with each passing day. Penny realized she was transferring some of her affection for Grams to this woman, on whom she found herself relying more and more for advice and counsel.

Nelldean's late husband had been in his thirties when gold was discovered in California. "We were both young and full of beans," she reminisced. "No hardship seemed too much for us. We was goin' to make our fortune, you see," she chuckled. "But it didn't turn out that way. Johnny didn't strike it rich. He was a farm boy who got carried away with all the tales of how easy it was going to be. We come back and took over his father's farm. We had to stand all those "I told you so's." Nelldean laughed heartily. "But Johnny proved himself a good farmer, and we raised our family. Four boys. Lost two early on, now the other two both gone. That's why coming with Nate was so important for me. And then that boy's got a good head on his shoulders. We're going to homestead, and it'll work. The good Lord willin' *this* time it's all going to turn out just fine."

Nelldean's optimism and faith were inspiring. They gave new strength to Penny's own hope of how it was all going to be once her brother and Thea got to California.

Dearest Grams,

I think yesterday was one of the happiest days we have had on the trail. There's such a feeling of optimism among us all. We're right on schedule, and it looks as though if we keep up the daily mileage our captain has set for the wagon train, we'll reach the mountains in early September, long before any chance of winter snows, which is considered the most dangerous part of the entire trip.

At Soda Springs we camped by the river for a few days, and we had a chance to catch up on our laundry, pick berries, and generally enjoy a welcome respite from the daily grind of endless travel. This is a beautiful spot. Rocky rims glow all around, golden in the sunlight, grassy slopes dotted with cedar trees stretched out in front of them. You've never seen such wildflowers. They seem brighter and more vividly colored than any back home.

But best of all I want to tell you about our "escapade." When Thea and I had finished our washing, we felt pretty proud of what we'd accomplished. Then, I guess, that mischief in me, which you've always known was there, nudged me. The river was shimmering in the sun so invitingly, I simply couldn't resist. I whispered to Thea, "Let's go downstream a little, round that bend, where no one can see us, and go swimming!" Thea looked a little shocked at my suggestion. But not too much so! We gathered up Belinda, took off our shoes and stockings, waded past to where there was a private spot, and we divested ourselves of skirts and petticoats and in our camisoles and pantaloons went into the cool water. After all the days of dusty travel I can't tell you how delicious it felt against our skin. We held Belinda between us, and she had such a time kicking her feet and splashing as we dipped and bobbed, paddling her chubby little feet in the water. We passed Belinda back and forth, taking turns, and we were soon having the time of our life, just like the children we used to be.

By mid-June a change took place that no one had counted on; some thought it was positive, some negative. A wagon train, made up of Iowans, had left Independence less than a week behind theirs and had now caught up with them. They wanted to join the Missourians, which would add about twenty wagons to the train. It seems they'd heard from folks coming back along the trail that there might be Indian trouble ahead. The men whom the Iowans had sent to a joint meeting felt it would be safer to have a bigger train, more men, more guns. If the Missourians agreed, they would need to vote on a new leader for both caravans. Captain Harding called a meeting of the men to hear the Iowans' proposal and vote on whether or not to join the two wagon trains. Right after supper Brad departed to join the circle of other heads of families who were gathering for discussion.

Penny was left alone by the campfire while Thea went into the wagon to put Belinda down for the night. Penny wished the women had some say-so about the matter. She had her own reservations about joining up with the Iowa wagon train. From the little she had observed while they had all been camped by the river, the Iowa emigrants had little in common with the Missourians. In fact, the two camps, waiting to start on the trail, couldn't have been more different. The Iowans deemed it all right to work on Sunday if they were to be ready to leave the first of the week, but the Missourians strictly observed the Sabbath and did nothing, which made them have to scramble to get all the chores done, everything in readiness for the dawn departure.

Penny just had an uneasiness about joining forces. If an Iowan was voted leader, for instance, would the Missourians get a fair hearing if any disputes arose? She had felt far safer with the slow-speaking Alvin Wright, whom they had voted to be their trail leader before leaving Independence.

She didn't share her misgivings with her sister-in-law when Thea rejoined her at the campfire. But she was eager to know the outcome when Brad returned from the meeting. He seemed in a thoughtful mood.

"So what was decided?" she asked.

"We decided to think it over and then come together again tomorrow night and vote on it."

"Do you think it's a good idea?" Penny persisted.

"I'm not sure. Of course, they've got a point—I mean, *if* there *are* hostile Indians ahead, the more, the better...."

Thea moved closer to Brad, who put a protective arm around her shoulders.

In her tent that night, Penny hoped her doubts about the wisdom of joining the two wagon trains were unfounded. After all they had almost two thousand more miles to travel before reaching California, and what lay ahead no one could be sure. Maybe Brad was right, the more men and guns, the less danger.

But the next evening when Penny went to fetch their water, she overheard something that did nothing to reassure her. Moving between two parked wagons, with two heavy water buckets, Penny stopped to catch her breath for a minute before shifting them from one hand to the other. That's how she happened to overhear two men talking. She hadn't meant to eavesdrop, but they made no effort to lower their voices. They were discussing the proposed meeting of both wagon trains for the evening clearly. Even before their voices dropped, she overheard part of their conversation: "Most of them Missourians aren't dry behind the ears yet. A bunch of farmers, don't know nuthin' about what's in store on the trail."

103

"Takin' a full day off on Sundays—lot of nonsense, if you ask me."

"Once I'm in charge there ain't goin' be no pampering, let me tell you. We gotta git through those mountains before winter. If they can't keep up, we'll just leave them greenhorns."

"Well, let's be sure we got a majority. Even if it takes some arm twistin'."

There was a rumble of laughter, then the other voice said, "And majority goes."

The tone of their voices and what she'd overheard didn't bode well for the Missourians. Should she warn Brad, tell him what she'd overheard? But there wasn't a chance. When she got back to the wagon two other men were waiting for her brother while he ate a plate of beans and biscuits, then they all hurried off to the meeting. She just had to hope it would all work out for the best.

It was late when Brad returned. Penny and Thea had waited up, anxious to know what had been decided. He told them Iowan Thomas Meecham had been elected leader.

"By a majority," Brad told them adding cynically. "Seems like he spent most of the day drumming up support for himself. So it took only one vote all around."

Instinctively Penny had the feeling Meecham might have been one of the men she had overheard. But there wasn't any point in repeating what she'd heard. It was too late. Meecham was in charge now.

Meecham, a tall unsmiling man with an arrogant stride and a harsh voice, went around the wagons after they were in their places for the night, barking orders and corrections to anything he could find to object to. Brad, like most of the Missourian men, would usually grumble in his wake. Although Brad didn't seem too happy about the selection either, he told Penny, "It's the same as on a ship at sea: the captain's word is law on the trail. You gotta hand it to him.

104

He's keeping to the strict schedule of ten or fifteen miles a day. He's gettin' us to the mountains 'fore it snows."

Penny felt it best to keep her own comments to herself. Brad was right; maybe what they needed was a forceful, "no-nonsense" leader to get them to their destination safely. Penny was keeping a lot of things to herself these days. Lately she had experienced an unexpected nostalgia for Dunwoodie. It would hit her at odd moments, mostly in the evenings at the end of a long day. Maybe it was the smell of wood fires or the plink of a guitar being picked hesitantly, its player trying for the right chord, or the sweet, sad twang of a harmonica, that would bring on a kind of homesickness. As a feeling of sadness came over her she would get busy at some chore, distracting herself. This homesickness didn't happen often. Most of the time, Penny realized she was having a "once-in-a-lifetime" experience and relished it.

The week of July Fourth, she wrote in Grams' letter-journal:

> We reached Independence Rock, which seems a fitting place to celebrate the nation's birthday. We spent two days here, camping, doing our wash, and catching up on chores you can't get to when traveling. Some of the more adventurous among the younger men climbed up onto the rock to carve their names thereon—"for posterity," I suppose. Throughout our whole wagon train there's a certain feeling of pride that we've come this far. Many of us are as surprised as pleased that we've proved ourselves to be so hearty and have become seasoned campers, learning new skills. Of course, some of our fellow travelers have suffered greatly due to losses of children or spouses through illness or accident. But as you would say, Grams, it's all part of God's plan, and we'll know why someday.

Penny stopped here, wondering if she should mention

that though they had been warned of the possible Indian raids, so far there had been no sign of any hostile Indians. A few mildly annoying ones followed them as they drew nearer to Fort Laramie, begging and wanting to barter, but they soon disappeared. Better pickin's farther from the fort, everyone guessed. Deciding not to mention the Indians, Penny went back to writing.

The celebration started early in the day by the most verbal and visible "patriots." There was speechifying, pounding on tin pots and pans, rifles and pistol shots into the air, yells and wild whooping, hollering and shouts. The men gathered in small groups to talk politics loudly. Sometimes these "discussions" became shouting, while tempers and patriotism ran high and got mixed-up. A few even ended in fisticuffs. Although there is a rule about no whiskey or other spirits on the train, somebody had smuggled in something that was at the root of most of the disturbances.

Late in the afternoon all we ladies put on our "best bib and tucker," as Nelldean calls it, and everyone joined in for a barbecue and some high jinks for the children. In the evening guitar and banjo, with accompaniment of several mouth organs, provided music for some square dancing. The children were allowed to run wild while the grown-ups enjoyed the release from the deadening drudgery of trail life. The party went far into the night, and everyone declared it a high mark of the long journey.

Neither Jeremiah nor Emily put in an appearance at the Fourth of July celebration. It was the kind of gathering that Jeremiah probably considered "unseemly"—well, maybe it was for someone as inflexible as Jeremiah. But it was certainly the kind of harmless relaxation that most of the weary travelers needed. Penny's sympathy for Jeremiah's unfortunate wife mounted.

Chapter 12

Fort Laramie

The night before they reached the military post at Fort Laramie, the guides, as usual, rode back down the line of wagons telling each driver where they would camp overnight. Penny, who was riding Mariah alongside the wagon, heard the scout shout up to Brad, "Twenty miles today—good day's trek. We're pulling out about a mile from the fort and camping there."

Fort Laramie would be the first chance in all the long weeks of travel to replenish supplies and stock up on some things like salt and sugar, which were running low.

The very next morning the fort's commander, with two aides, rode out to welcome the wagon train. He was an impressive-looking man, with a narrow, handsome face and a full mustache, the epitome of a West Point graduate, all "spit and polish." The wagon master and the Iowan captain, Thomas Meecham, met him. Through them the colonel issued an invitation to the emigrants to attend the dress parade of his soldiers that afternoon.

Eagerly Penny and Thea looked forward to this rare diversion from the monotony of life on the trail. They put on their sunbonnets and, carrying Belinda, found a shady spot from which to watch the cavalry officers go through their paces. The uniformed men, erect in their saddles, the sun gleaming on their swords belted to their gilt sashes, presented a splendid sight. At the different bugle calls, their mounts were instantly alert, their ears twitching, the arched necks taut. Then on signal the beautiful animals, in perfect alignment, wheeled and marched in formation, with never a misstep nor a wrong turn. It was thrilling, and Penny felt a sense of pride simply watching the riders in well-trained troops go through their paces. They could not have done better if they were being reviewed by the president as commander-in-chief of the army himself.

To their further excitement and surprise, later that afternoon officers from the fort arrived at the camp to invite all the ladies to a dance to be held that evening at the headquarters.

"Oh, of course, you must go, Penny," Thea said. "It will be good for you to get dressed up for a change, do some dancing and a little flirting!"

"I don't want to go by myself!" protested Penny. "They invited *all* the ladies, you know. *You* can go too."

Thea's cheeks flushed, a glint of possibility showing in her eyes. She ventured hesitantly, "Do you think Brad would? . . ."

"Let's ask him," suggested Penny, adding with a teasing smile, "He can't object if we take Belinda along for a chaperone!"

They laughed merrily at the thought and went together to look for Brad. They found him talking to Mr. Walker, who looked amused when the two girls posed the question. Brad hesitated only a minute, glancing over at the older man, who gave an imperceptible nod. Then Brad smiled. "Don't see why not. You two deserve a little fun. Just so long as you keep your wedding ring and Belinda in plain sight, Thea," he cautioned with mock severity.

Back at the wagon Thea opened her small humpbacked

trunk and began digging into its depths. "Here, Penny," she said, holding out her lace shawl. "You must wear this and carry my fan."

The rest of the afternoon the girls pondered what to wear, primped, and practiced new hairstyles in a frenzy that reminded them of old times. They giggled until they were quite giddy.

"Here, try this." Thea tossed Penny her lace shawl to add an elegant touch to the simply made, periwinkle-blue dress. Thea's early pregnancy had just given her tiny figure a pleasant roundness. They hid the fact that the last hooks on her bodice didn't meet by cleverly adding a wide sash to her full-skirted, peppermint pink-striped dress. At last they were ready. They got Belinda up from her nap, dressed her in her prettiest dress and ruffled bonnet, then went to show Brad before leaving.

"Never saw three prettier young ladies," he told them.

"Sure you don't want to come along?" Thea asked.

"And spoil the soldiers' evening?" he teased. "Nah! You all go along and have a good time."

They left him at the wagon and went to join the contingent of other wagon train ladies waiting for the promised transportation over to the fort.

There was a flurry of exchanged compliments as the women eyed each other's hurriedly assembled finery. A good number of ladies had shown up for the night's festivities, even some of the older ones, like Nelldean. They had no intention of dancing, but just were hungry for some music, some gaiety, and some lighthearted fun. Penny noted that Emily Bradshaw was not in the group. Probably Jeremiah had not allowed her to come. Poor soul! If anyone needed a little change, it was someone confined to the company of the dour Jeremiah all these weeks.

Soon the wagon sent by the fort's commander arrived. With much laughter and joking the ladies were helped up into it by courteous soldiers. As they set off toward the fort they had an escort of four cavalry men in spotless blue uniforms, brass buttons blazing, boots shining. They were mounted on gleaming horses and rode alongside.

As they mounted the wooden steps into a mess hall, which had been transformed for the occasion, Penny could hear music. All at once, all her worries and doubts of the last few weeks that had been so hard to shake fell away like magic.

Later Penny described the evening to Grams:

The minute we stepped inside we were surrounded—ambushed might be the "military" way to say it—by officers, all of whom were handsome, charming, and gracious—and clamoring for a dance. Believe it or not, I was whirled away at once by a blonde, mustachioed man (a lieutenant, no less!), leaving a number of other disappointed young men looking soulful. (A totally *new* experience for me, especially attending a dancing party with *Thea!)*

But, as I'm told, at Fort Laramie, as in all army posts, especially one as isolated as this, the men always outnumber the available ladies. Only the senior officers are allowed to have their wives with them at this fort. The result of this rule is that for months many of these gentlemen have not set eyes on a woman, other than the wives of their superior officers or the Indian squaws who come in to trade. With so many bachelor officers doing their first duty after graduating from West Point, these were especially anxious to make the most of this rare social occasion. Having never known such popularity in Dunwoodie, I can tell you I was pretty nigh overcome. But Grams, I do have enough common sense to know that I couldn't possibly be as pretty, as witty, or as good a dancer as I was told over and over during the evening. I am also human enough to thoroughly enjoy such attention.

Not that Thea was left on the sidelines, by any manner of means. As usual, her picture-perfect beauty, her sweet smile, and her manners had her at the center of male admiration.

The few times I had a chance to glance her way, she was always at the center of an admiring coterie of officers. Sometimes engaged in conversation with one or more officers while Belinda was held alternately by one or the other. That young lady—probably a foretaste of things to come, when *she* will certainly be the "belle of the ball"—was having the time of her young life, clapping her tiny hands happily to the tunes of the regiment's band who were providing the dance music. Nelldean took over the lap-sitting several times during the evening so 'Thea could dance. I saw her gracefully waltzing with one or the other of her attentive officer admirers. It was so good to see her happy and not anxious as she has sometimes been on this journey.

A buffet supper was served at midnight—food such as our sore eyes have not beheld in many a long day! Platters of sliced ham, turkey, salads, spiced peaches, bowls of nuts, relishes, and a raspberry "bombe." Such an astonishing array was set forth that I was hard put not to "make a spectacle of myself," as you would say, Grams. After weeks of the monotonous trail diet I had to exert great control not to try everything and seconds at that!

After that there was more dancing. Finally, to accumulated groans of protest from the gentlemen , the band struck up the traditional "Good Night, Ladies," and the unusual evening came to an end.

We ladies were reluctantly led back to the wagon in which we'd arrived and again escorted back to the wagon camp, this time accompanied by more than a dozen officers who had saddled up to escort us home in style.

When Penny finished this description of the party at Fort Laramie, she tore it out of the notebook and folded it in with the other journal-letters she'd written, planning to mail them at the post exchange when they went there the following day to replenish their supplies.

The next day, Penny and Thea wanted to take advantage of the chance to stock up. While Brad worked on the wagon, oiling the axle, checking wheels, renailing the sideboards that had loosened on the miles of jolting travel, Nelldean accompanied Penny and Thea, carrying Belinda, to buy provisions at the fort's store.

It was good to see all that was stocked there. Although only a few wives of army officers were posted so far west with their husbands, the store had many things that would catch the feminine eye: bolts of brightly colored materials, ribbons and bonnet trims, buttons, and yards of lace and eyelet ruffles. Even though they could not afford much, Thea and Penny enjoyed looking at all the luxuries, almost forgetting the list they had compiled. Penny was particularly tempted by a patterned paisley when she felt Thea pinch her arm and whisper, "Look over there."

"What?" Penny glanced questioningly at her sister-in-law. Thea shifted her eyes slightly to the right. Penny looked in the direction Thea indicated. All she saw was a tall, slender, dark-haired young woman standing nearby. Penny gave a shrug and glanced back, puzzled, at Thea. Just then the woman turned her head toward Penny, and she realized why Thea wanted her to see the young woman. Though otherwise attractive, the young woman's face was oddly disfigured with black markings. Her clear, gray eyes met Penny's stare coldly; then deliberately she turned her attention back to the length of red calico she had been examining. Embarrassed, Penny quickly began to discuss with Thea the idea of making new sunbonnets for the three of them.

A few minutes later the strangely marked young woman made her purchase, then left the store. Penny hoped that she hadn't made her feel self-conscious. She almost felt like going after her to apologize. But that would only make matters worse. Surely she must be used to people's curious glances.

"What do you suppose happened to *her*?" Thea asked.

Nelldean came up alongside them. "You're curious about the girl who was just in here?"

"We didn't mean to be rude."

"No, of course you didn't. I saw her the other day and asked one of the soldier's wives about her. It's a sad story actually. Her name is Celina Preston. She's the foster daughter of some people here at the fort. But when she was not much older than Belinda, her whole family was attacked by some marauding Apaches. All the rest of the family were killed except her and her sister. They were both taken captive. No one knows for sure what happened to the sister, but about four years later Celina was found. She'd been traded to the Mojave Indians by the Apaches, and that is their custom. They cut into the flesh, then rub charcoal or dye into the wounds." Nelldean shook her head. "She was brought to the fort and adopted by some people who had known her real family. They've tried to erase those tattoo marks but—it's not easy, no easier than erasing the memories of her years with the savages."

Thea, visibly moved by the story, shuddered and clutched Belinda closer.

"Does that happen often?" she asked. "Indians taking children?"

"Not often, although it does happen—" Then, sensing Thea's unspoken fear, Nelldean spoke reassuringly, "But the Indians around here and from this point on are mostly friendly. I haven't heard of a wagon train being attacked for a long time."

All Penny's recollections of Fort Laramie would have been pleasant ones if it had not been for one horrifying incident just before the wagon train pulled out to continue its westward journey.

One morning she, Thea, and Nelldean went to do some last-minute shopping at the fort's commissary. They were just leaving the store to walk back to their wagon when the sound of screaming reached their startled ears. It was so frighteningly high-pitched, like a wounded animal or some tortured creature, that they stopped dead in their tracks, clutching each other in fear. As they stood on the commissary porch, an army ambulance came rattling around the corner of the building. The two horses pulling it scrambled to keep their footing as the vehicle careened almost on two wheels. At the front of the infirmary on the quadrangle of the officers' quarters, the driver shouted a loud "Whoa!" and pulled the horses to a skittering halt.

As Penny and Thea stared, the soldier beside the driver jumped down from the seat and ran back to the ambulance's double doors. A minute later, two uniformed men emerged from the infirmary dragging a woman between them. Her hair was wild and streaming behind her, she was tightly held by both arms but struggling, kicking and yelling for them to let her go. Following them out onto the porch were two uniformed men. One, his head bowed, obviously distraught, was supported by a fellow officer as he walked unsteadily from the door of the building. He was openly weeping as the men holding the still-screaming woman finally lifted her into the ambulance and climbed in after her. The doors were slammed shut and bolted, and they all drove off. In silent horror, Penny and Thea watched, their eyes widened in shock.

Nelldean, who had followed them out of the store came alongside, saying in a sad tone of voice, "Poor woman! The storekeeper told me she's one of the officer's wives. They're taking her back east. Hopefully, once she's back in familiar surroundings, and with her family if she's got one, she'll recover." Nelldean shook her head. "Some people can't take it. It's especially hard on women, left alone much of the time when their soldier husbands are gone for weeks or

114

even months on patrol. Go mad with the isolation, the loneliness. Tragic for her husband as well. . . ."

Some movement behind her caught Penny's attention. She half turned just in time to see Emily Bradshaw standing a short distance away in the entrance to the fort commissary. Penny had not noticed her in the store, but she too must have witnessed the dreadfully distressing scene. As Penny turned, Emily dropped her shopping basket and swayed, then clung to the wooden frame, her face ashen. She looked as if she might faint.

Spontaneously Penny went over to her. "Are you all right?" she asked. "Maybe you should sit down. I'll see if I can get you some water."

Just then a man's voice spoke harshly, "We don't need your help."

Penny recognized that voice and whirled around to see Jeremiah striding toward them. He brushed rudely by her. "I can take care of my wife. We can manage."

Immediately Penny stepped back. Jeremiah took his wife's arm, keeping her from sagging to the ground. "Come, Emily." She leaned against him as if all her strength had left her. He roughly grabbed her basket, then, still holding her by her arm, half dragged her down the steps and across the compound in the direction of the wagon train.

Biting her lip in helpless indignation, Penny's hands clenched. How insensitive Jeremiah was! Couldn't he have shown his wife some compassion, some gentleness?

Nelldean echoed her thoughts. "I'm afraid that poor, poor woman is one of those I meant. I doubt if she'll make it, one way or another." Thea looked pale and shocked. Linking arms, they walked back to their wagons. Both scenes had brought sharply into focus the dangers, the risks, the terrible possibilities of what they had never realized at the outset of the journey west.

In the days that followed these two heartrending scenes

flashed vividly into Penny's mind. She kept seeing the girl with the tattooed face and the mad woman. Although they never discussed it, Penny was sure Thea was haunted by them too. Penny wondered at Nelldean's seeming acceptance of the horrors that sometimes happened in the western territories. But then she must have seen it often: the hopelessness of women broken by their husband's choices and expressing it in various ways—some by accepting it and saying, "nothing to do but stay"; others by plunging into madness.

One day when she and Nelldean were walking together, Penny confided, "I can't get that officer's wife out of my head. It makes me wonder about myself, if I would crack like that given her circumstances."

Nelldean shook her head emphatically. "Not you, Penny. *You've* got the stuff. I spotted that in you right away. And I've watched you. You ain't afraid to take on somethin' you've never tried before," she chuckled. "You've got what they call the 'pioneer spirit' and a bit of stubbornness too, I reckon. No siree, Penny, I'd count on *you* makin' it no matter what."

Nelldean's appraisal comforted Penny a little. Still she hoped she would never be put to the test.

Chapter 13

*P*enny was concerned about Thea. Brad was too busy with all his responsibilities to notice, but as the days went on, Penny was very conscious of Thea's waning strength. The ceaseless rattling of the wagon gave her headaches, and sometimes she seemed so lethargic, sometimes so dazed with fatigue, that she did not seem to notice what was going on. More and more, Penny took over the care of Belinda who, at two and a half, was becoming quite a handful. She was so active now and into everything. She had to be watched every waking minute to keep her out of mischief and away from disaster. They had to be careful not to set thoughtlessly aside a knife or a boiling pot unattended. Her curiosity was unlimited. One day she nearly fell head first into a bucket of drinking water. Another time she picked up a greasy discarded rag Penny had used to scour a skillet and stuffed it happily into her mouth. It was all Penny could do to keep up with her. As for Thea, all her efforts seemed to be in garnering her energy to put on an animation and cheerfulness she could not really feel when Brad was around.

Penny would place Belinda in front of her in the saddle when she rode Mariah so that Thea could rest in the back of the wagon. Penny's thoughts were often troubled. Thea should probably have never have come. In a way, Penny blamed herself. Maybe *she* had been wrong not to tell Grams about Thea's condition and seek her advice as to whether Thea should attempt the journey. A word from Grams would have been enough to cause Brad to postpone their leaving at least until after the baby arrived. But it was too late now. She would just have to pray that they would reach California in good health and everything would be all right.

After leaving Fort Laramie, thinking they had said good-bye to "civilization" until they reached California, Penny and Thea mentally prepared themselves for the miles of wilderness stretching before them. To their amazement, the wagon train encountered eastbound visitors almost daily—travelers, some of whom had already made the western trek several times. The wagon train people surrounded them, eager to hear the confirmation of their hopes and dreams. Although the more skeptical among them doubted some of the "tall tales," for most it served to spur some of their original enthusiasm to see the country to which they themselves were headed.

The plains seemed to go on endlessly, broken here and there by jutting boulders or a mammoth rock structure. Heat shimmered relentlessly from the sun, turning the endless prairie into a tawny ochre. Before them they could see razor-edged buttes rising sharply and thrusting into the cloud-studded sky.

As they got closer to those jutting rocks what still lay ahead of the weary travelers began to dawn on them. The ever-present urgency to get through the Sierra before the chance of an early snow was always lurking in their minds. Now the morning and late-evening air had an autumn chill to it. All the livestock began to act strange, restless, spooky. Penny noticed it and mentioned it to Brad, who told her someone said it was the altitude that sometimes made them a little crazy.

That night, a men's meeting was called, and afterward, when Brad returned and joined Thea and Penny at the campfire where they sat waiting for him, his expression had a firm set.

"We've got to ditch some of our stuff. There's no other way. Everybody's going to have to do it. The wagons are overloaded, the oxen and mules' strength dangerously strained ... now, you both look over your things ... from now on we only take necessities. Everything else's got to go ... no exceptions."

Knowing her softhearted, easygoing brother, Penny realized he was putting on as stern a face as possible. From her own experience she knew Brad could be wheedled. Certainly Thea, in her gentle way, could most often win any argument. But this was different. Word had gone out from the captain that if they wanted to avoid disaster and make California before a blizzard trapped them in one of the mountain passes, the teams' loads had to be lightened.

They all retired in a somber mood. Brad's last words were, "Tomorrow morning we got to pile all the things we're not taking on the side of the road. So be thinking about it tonight. And by the way, ladies, I have the last word."

Penny might have smiled at her brother's warning. He was girding himself beforehand from any pleading, forlorn sighs, or wistful tears on their part.

Penny slept in the tent that night beside Belinda, leaving the wagon for Brad and Thea by themselves, thinking they might need some privacy to discuss the matter. When she woke up at daylight the next morning, she heard the low murmur of their voices and from the tone, she realized things had not been settled.

"No, Thea, I told you not to bring it in the first place. It's got to go along with the barrel of china and the clock ...

119

I'm sorry, but they're just too heavy. I can't make it any clearer—we've got orders."

Penny had never heard her brother speak so abruptly to his wife.

"Now, don't argue, Thea. And don't you dare cry! That's all there is to it."

Penny peeked out the flap of her tent and saw Brad jump down from the back of the wagon and stride off. Thea flung a shawl over her shoulders and ran to catch up with him.

Penny felt sure it was the cradle they were arguing about. Now Thea would *have* to tell him about the baby. And high time too! It's a wonder he hadn't noticed something. Thea's slender figure had daily rounded. But Brad was too distracted, too occupied with the demands of the relentless onward push during the day. At night he was so exhausted he nodded over his supper and soon flung himself into the wagon to sleep until dawn.

Penny left Belinda still curled up in her quilt, thumb in mouth, soundly asleep, and crept outside. She got the fire started, sliced some strips of bacon, and got out the last of the eggs to fry.

Within fifteen minutes she saw them walking slowly back to the campsite, Brad's arm around Thea's waist, her head resting on his shoulder. Brad looked dazed; Thea was smiling complacently.

When they stacked the extra trunk filled with embroidered linens, the bird's-eye maple chest of drawers, the china barrel, the Seth Thomas clock alongside some of the other emigrants' belongings and family heirlooms, the spool cherry cradle was not among them.

Penny was relieved that Brad had been told about the expected baby. It took some of the responsibility off her shoulders. She had disliked being a party to deception. She gave Brad credit that he never admonished her about it, never made a single reproving remark about her being a conspirator. He was simply a little more serious, showing Thea a little more consideration than usual. Penny knew he must be pleased at the possibility of having a son in the new land to where they were going.

In her letter-journal letter to Grams, Penny didn't have the heart to tell about all the things they had to leave behind on the road. It was hard enough to see how heartbroken Thea was. She had put on a brave face for Brad, but when they were alone she had not been able to keep back the tears.

"Maybe it's because I never felt I had a real home when I was growing up. I so much wanted Belinda to have the few things from *my* mother when we built our new home in California," she sobbed. "You don't know how much those things meant to me."

"Yes, I do understand." Penny tried to comfort her. "But Belinda will have other things, Thea. New kinds of things. In California everything will be different. She won't even miss those things, because she won't know anything about them."

As they traveled further, Penny and Thea saw that the members of their wagon train group weren't the only ones who'd had to discard belongings to make the burden on the mules and oxen lighter. Strewn all along the rutted trail were quilts, chests, trunks, rocking chairs, clocks, and sets of dishes. All sad reminders of cherished items some woman had shed tears over leaving behind. But even among themselves the women did not complain. They had come this far and were beginning to realize how far they had yet to go. The men's weary eyes told the story more clearly than anything they could say.

Chapter 14

A few days after the "great ditching," as Penny and Thea called the wistful discarding of special belongings, when the wagon train stopped at noon to feed and rest the animals, they decided to rearrange the interior of the wagon. With the addition of the new supplies purchased at Fort Laramie, even after the elimination of items Brad deemed "unnecessary," the inside of the wagon still seemed crowded. Working hard and fast, they soon became hot and tired. The canvas interior was cramped and stuffy. Finally Thea brushed back her hair from her damp forehead with the back of her arm, saying, "Whew, I've got to stop for a few minutes."

One glance at Thea's flushed face reminded Penny sharply of her sister-in-law's delicate condition, and she quickly agreed, "It's near noon anyway. Let's quit. Go outside and cool off. I'll go get us some water, and we'll make some lemonade." She held up the bottle of citrus oil they'd bought at the post store on Nelldean's suggestion that it was a passable substitute for the fruit to make lemonade. Thea seemed relieved and leaned wearily against the back of the wagon while Penny grabbed one of the pails and headed for the water barrel.

Brad was checking the wooden wheels, testing for cracks, tightening ropes, and generally looking over everything. Belinda played on the ground in the shade thrown by the arched top of the wagon.

It was hot. The sun beat down mercilessly as Penny came back lugging the heavy pail of water. They had a time discussing how much oil to pour into their cups before adding water, and then they sampled and tasted until the right mixture was achieved.

They offered a cup to Brad, who welcomed it, and Thea held one to Belinda's mouth for her to drink some, spilling most. Thea had pleated paper into fans, and they sat sipping their makeshift lemonade, chatting idly while enjoying the respite.

Suddenly a terrifying cry split the air and went ricocheting up and down the line of parked wagons: "Indians!"

At the screams of terror echoing from one wagon to the other both women looked at each other wide-eyed with fear. Thea seemed paralyzed with fright, while Penny was galvanized into action. She scrambled to her feet and snatched up Belinda. Reaching for Thea's hand, she jerked her to her feet then pointed to the wagon. "Under the wagon. Hurry!"

Brad was running toward them, waving both hands and shouting for them to hurry and take shelter under the wagon as Penny had said. Then he grabbed his shotgun. Penny shoved Thea first, then, clutching Belinda, Penny crawled after Thea. They lay there trembling with Belinda between them.

Dust whirled like great windmills from the thundering hooves of what seemed like hundreds of horses galloping past. The air was splintered with the sound of frenzied whoops and screeching yells. The sun glinted on the red-bronze skin of bare-chested men with garishly painted faces as they thundered by the wagon where the women were

123

hidden. Colorful headbands, bright feathers, long black braids, streamed behind as the Indians circled the wagons, brandishing spears and bows. Arrows whistled and popped with a sizzling sound as the riders turned their ponies sharply, causing them to skid as they swirled in a kind of wild dance. The pong and swish of bow strings and arrows mingled with the snapping crack of rifles as the wagon train men tried to scare the Indians off.

Terrified, shuddering at each shot, Penny and Thea squeezed each other's hands in a painful grip. Was this the kind of attack others had related in detail? Would the horrors of scalping, capture, torture, and worse follow? Eyes widened with shock, they stared at each other, speechless but questioning. Penny squinted into the sun's glare, trying to see what was happening. But dust clouds obscured her view. Then Thea began sobbing and Belinda started to cry. Penny put her arm over Thea's shaking shoulders and huddled closer, her own heart hammering out of control. Then just as suddenly as they had appeared, the Indians whirled around and, still yelling at the top of their lungs, galloped back up over the hill from where they had come. An eerie silence hung over the wagon train for at least a minute or two. Then suddenly, it was broken by great cries of relief rising up throughout the camp.

It wasn't until later that they discovered that, while part of the band had distracted the men of the wagon train by circling, shooting arrows, and yelling, other Indians had ridden over to where the horses were grazing and made off with some. To Penny's horror, Mariah had been taken.

Counting the losses, the men stood shaking their heads, trying to figure out how to divide the remaining ones and how to shift the weights in some of the wagons.

Sorrowfully Penny went back to their wagon. She wept unrestrained tears. The theft of her beloved mare, who had gallantly come this far with her, was a bitter loss.

The whole wagon train was sobered by the Indian raid. Although they were thankful no lives had been lost, the episode left everyone badly shaken.

There was no more grousing from the men about taking guard duty. Nerves were on edge. Trigger-sharp tempers flared over trivial things. Children got slapped by anxious mothers, who tried to keep them close by telling them dread tales of Indians taking little ones as hostage. Even the animals, sensing the humans' nervousness, were restless and spooked at the slightest sound.

In the evenings when people gathered around campfires, voices were low and tense. That was why everyone jumped one night when a woman's screams rent the air. Men reached for their rifles, and general confusion erupted. The screams soon dwindled to heartrending sobs. Startled people asked one another: Where were they coming from? Who was it? The silence that followed was almost eerie. Then the rumor ran through the wagon train like a prairie bush fire. The screams had come from the Bradshaw wagon. Emily Bradshaw was in hysterics. Nelldean and one of the other older women hurried over to see if they could help. The quiet that descended on the whole train was ominous. One by one each family went into their wagons, pulled the canvas curtains and kept whatever they were thinking to themselves.

Penny, however, waited outside her own small tent until she saw Nelldean making her way back to her wagon and stopped her.

"We gave her a dose of laudanum; that should calm her down and help her sleep. Her husband was beside himself." Nelldean shook her head. "More angry than worried, I'd say. A strange man...."

"He is, very strange indeed," Penny said, then in a burst of confidence she poured out her own experience with Jeremiah.

The older woman looked concerned. "I've seen his kind afore. So sure of themselves that it don't matter about other folks. He's right and you're wrong. Sad to say, a lot of the Lord's business is spoiled by the likes of him. . . ." She patted Penny's arm. "Just be thankful you didn't listen to him, and you're not in that poor girl's place."

With that Nelldean went on to her own wagon, leaving Penny to her troubled thoughts. She wished she could do something to help Emily Bradshaw. But she knew it would only be rejected and probably misinterpreted. It was a long time before she could fall asleep.

Penny was now regularly getting up and starting the breakfast, giving Thea the chance to rest in the wagon until Belinda woke up. One morning, two days after Emily Bradshaw's outburst, Penny went to get the water before the rest of the family awakened. Suddenly, as she was drawing water, she heard a man's voice behind her. "Penny, I have to talk to you."

Knowing at once who it was, she stiffened. She dreaded another ugly scene but did not know how to avoid it. For a long moment all was silent, except for the trickle of the water from the barrel into the pail. Still holding her pail under the spigot, she slowly turned to face Jeremiah.

His face was set in grim lines. There were circles under his heavy-lidded, bloodshot eyes, evidence of sleeplessness. His voice was strangely lifeless as he said, "I just wanted you to know we're turning back."

"You're turning back?" she repeated in surprise, then turned off the spigot.

"Yes. Emily isn't well . . . not well at all. I've talked to Captain Harding. He tells me that there should be an army patrol coming by here soon on their way back to the fort. We could travel with them as an escort in case—," he halted as if it were difficult to continue, "—of Indians

126

again. You see, it's the fear—she can't take anymore . . . her nerves, her physical strength. . . . I'll have to take her home. Some others are also leaving the wagon train. There'll be enough to be safe. . . ."

The note of defeat in his voice was strong. In spite of all that had passed between them, Penny could not help feeling sorry for him. Going west and being a missionary was what had driven him with such intensity. Wrongheaded as he might have been about *her*, this was still something he had deeply wanted for himself and for the woman he had married. To give up now seemed tragic. One look at his stricken expression revealed what a crushing blow this decision had been for him. How was she to express her sympathy without sounding false?

"I'm sorry, Jeremiah . . . I know how much coming west meant to you. . . . This must be a terrible disappointment. But of course, you must do what you need to do for Emily's sake—"

Jeremiah harshly cut her short. "It's *your* fault, you know."

"*My* fault?" The accusation stunned her. "How could it be *my* fault?"

His voice roughened angrily, "If *you* had not been rebellious and done what you were supposed to have done . . . this wouldn't have happened. If you had *listened* and *obeyed as you were supposed to do!* It would have been you and I, together. *You're* strong, Penny. *Physically* strong but weak morally." His mouth twisted in a sneer. "If *you* had only obeyed—"

Penny held up a warning hand, "Stop, Jeremiah! I don't want to hear this, and I won't listen—"

He reached out and gripped her upper arm. "But you will hear it, and you will listen. *Now* you *will* listen. Before you refused to, but see what your willfulness has brought about? *Your* pride has brought about destruction, just as I

127

knew it would." His voice became louder, ragged with emotion. "It was the Lord's will for *us* . . . *you* and me, not Emily—"

"No, Jeremiah! Don't say another word. It's wrong—" She lowered her voice, but she stared at him steadily. "Have you ever thought you might have mistaken the message? It's *you* who could be wrong, Jeremiah."

He shook his head, his voice cracked as he gripped her arm. "Penny, I loved you—*we* could have made it."

"No, Jeremiah . . . no." Determinedly she pried his fingers from her arm. "Don't say anything more you'll be sorry for. We shouldn't be having this conversation. Please go. Emily is your wife. She needs you. This must be difficult for her knowing she is disappointing you and yet—she cannot go on. You should be with her . . . just go."

The muscle in his cheek quivered as he struggled to regain his composure. His eyes were like burning coals. His mouth worked as if he still wanted to say something more. Gradually he loosened his hold and dropped her arm. Then just as suddenly as he had come, he turned and walked slowly away, his shoulders hunched, a broken man, his dream of glory shattered.

Had Emily's breakdown been brought on by witnessing the woman who had to be trussed and dragged into the ambulance a short time before? Had Emily been afraid of what might be awaiting her in some isolated mission post? Or was she having nightmares of what still might lie ahead along the endless trail before them, before they even got to California? Had the mere idea of it weakened her resolve and broken her spirit?

In the camps there were rumors, especially among the women, who spoke in low voices, afraid of being overheard. They told tales of relatives or friends of theirs who had been broken by the experience of the trail. The often-heard phrase "Nothing to do but stay" came to Penny's mind. They were at the halfway mark. A few days more and they would reach the "No Return Trail"—after which there would be no turning back.

Early one morning a few days later, Penny heard the sounds of horses' hooves and wagon wheels. She looked out through the flap of her tent to see Jeremiah's wagon and two others departing, escorted by a patrol of blue-uniformed troopers. Two other families had also decided it was too risky to go on. Watching them go, Penny was conscious of a funny sensation in the pit of her stomach. She knew one of the women who was leaving was expecting a child about the same time as Thea, and much as she tried not to let it, that worried Penny.

Penny shivered involuntarily. Had *they* made a terrible mistake to come? After the halfway point, it would be longer and more dangerous for anyone to turn around, one wagon alone along all those dreary, desolated miles. Penny pushed away all those daunting thoughts. Of course Brad would never turn back. Besides, things were going to work out beautifully for *them*. They would find a wonderful homestead, their crops would flourish just like people said, Belinda would be healthy and happy, and Thea would have the new baby, born in California, a son for Brad.

Ahead lay the Snake River and the last leg of the long journey. There was an urgency now to get on the other side of the river, as far away as they could get from hostile Indian territory. Who knew for sure if the savages might not again swoop down from behind the hillsides any moment?

"It could have been worse," Brad said grimly, his eyes traveling to his wife and child. Penny knew the fears that must be lurking in his mind. She tried to echo his comment, although her heart was still sore from the loss of Mariah. She now walked, carrying Belinda most of the time—to ease the burden of their oxen. Now that Brad knew about the coming baby, Penny felt some of the weight of guilt lifted. She didn't like keeping secrets. Also, Thea now did not try to hide her discomfort, her general ill health. Pathetic in her apologies, she more and more let Penny take the responsibility for Belinda.

Brad too relied more and more on Penny's help. He didn't want to ask anything of Thea that might be beyond her strength. So he started teaching Penny how to drive the wagon. He'd get her to take the reins once or twice a day. At first she found it totally different from riding a saddle horse or driving a light buggy with one horse. Her shoulder muscles ached with the strain, and her hands became a mass of blisters. But she had always had a stubborn, competitive spirit and now wanted to prove to her brother that she was equal to the challenge.

Chapter 15

The Snake River

*A*s they camped the night before they were to cross the Snake River a circuit of unspoken apprehension vibrated throughout the wagon train. There was a sense that danger lay ahead. The uncertainty of the undertaking made the worried men tense and apt to argue. Once more, tempers flared and brief arguments erupted into fights. That evening it clouded up ominously. Rain the next day would make visibility worse and make a safe crossing doubly difficult. A chill wind blew, which set the horses whinnying, the mules braying, and the heavy oxen moving uneasily.

During the night it rained lightly. Penny heard the patter on the canvas overhead. She heard Brad moving restlessly on the other side of the wagon and knew he was sleepless with worry about the next day's ordeal.

At Penny's first sight of the river, she realized why Brad had been so vigilant in training her to handle the wagon, adamant that she become competent. It was a scary prospect. Brad busied himself checking the ropes on the canvas, nailing any loose boards on the body of the wagon. Tersely he ordered Thea to take Belinda into the wagon, to secure themselves in a nest of quilts wedged in between the storage chests, and not to move until they got to the other side of the river.

As each wagon moved up to the bank in turn, Penny grew more nervous. She was sitting on the driver's seat beside Brad. Every so often she glanced over and saw his jaw was clenched, his eyes straight ahead, almost holding his breath as he watched wagon after wagon being pulled into the rushing river by the frightened animals. The wagon train had crossed other rivers on their way west, but none as wide as this one. There was only one wagon ahead of them now. It started down the bank, while its driver held tightly onto his mules' harness and shouted. The wagon swayed heavily as it reached the water. Penny caught her breath, sure that it was going to tip over. Her attention was brought sharply to their own problem.

"Here, take these." Brad thrust the reins at her and she grabbed them. "I'm going to lead the oxen down. No matter what happens, hold on. We gotta get across."

Penny doubled the leather reins around her wrists and held them tightly. She fastened her gaze on the opposite bank, not daring to look down, though out of the corner of her eyes she could see the floating debris of other wagons. Packs of possessions that had not been securely fastened had burst loose and were sailing downstream among the rocks and broken tree branches. It was frightening. Among all the sights and sounds around her, she was suddenly aware of the crack of Brad's whip as he urged the reluctant oxen into the water's rushing current. Penny tightened her grip on the reins. She could hear the hair-raising shrieks of the animals and the curses and shouts of the men. The turmoil was enough to chill the blood of even the bravest.

Then the wagon lurched and pitched as it hit the water. From inside she heard Thea's stifled screams and knew she must be terrified at the rocking motion of the wagon as they slid down the bank, then were caught up in the cur-

132

rent. Behind her she felt the canvas flap like sails as the wind ripped through it. Her heart felt as though it were in her throat. Every prayer she had ever learned flew to her mind until all she could do was gasp between her chattering teeth, "Mercy! Mercy! *Help!*"

Then just as suddenly, Penny knew they had made it when she heard Brad's voice ring out heartily, "Good girl, Penny! Good for you!"

He pulled the still-frightened animals into place on the opposite bank; then he ran to the back of the wagon to check on Thea and Belinda. Too weak to congratulate herself, Penny drew a long, shaky breath. She was slowly pulling herself together when Brad came alongside and said, "Take care of Thea and the baby. I'm going to see if I can help some of the others."

Penny climbed down from the driver's seat. As she started to walk she realized her legs were wobbling. She had to hold on to the side of the wagon for a minute or two to steady herself before she could go around to check on Thea and Belinda. Thea was pale as cheese and looked as though she might be sick. She handed Belinda over to Penny and started to say something when they heard a piercing scream from the river. They both stiffened.

"Something's happened!" Thea gasped.

"I'll go see." Penny slung Belinda on her hip and ran down to where a group was clustered on the bank. A woman was sobbing hysterically and some others were trying to comfort her. "It's my boy! He's going to drown!" she was crying over and over. A man's voice rose above the rest: "Come on, fellas, we gotta help pull them out. Get a rope, someone!"

Penny moved in closer. "What's going on?" she asked a couple standing at the edge of the crowd.

"A child fell out when a wagon tipped over. He was

caught in the current, swept downstream. A man dove in to save him, but the current shifted and now *he*'s in trouble."

A deep shiver shuddered through Penny. *Brad!* Instinctively his name sprang into her mind. Brad was an excellent swimmer. Summer days had always found him in the deep pond behind Grams' house. It would be natural for him to leap in to save a child. With Belinda in her arms, Penny pushed through the crush of people to stand at the edge of the churning river so she could see better. The onlookers, who at first seemed mesmerized by the drama taking place in front of them, had turned into a cheering section for the would-be rescuers.

Penny's premonition had been correct. It *was* Brad floundering in the whirlpool of the river. As he spun and turned she could see a child's arms flailing. Over and over, Brad's head went under the water. Then he came up holding the boy's head above water, both gulping desperately. She felt as though a steel vise were gripping her throat. She wanted to scream but could make no sound. She tried to pray but no words came. Her arms tightened around Belinda, who squirmed and twisted, saying, "Too tight, Auntie!" Distractedly Penny loosened her hold on the little girl.

A rope had been slung around the trunk of a tree and knotted at the base. The other end was thrown like a lasso out into the water. People were yelling frantically now. The rope—their one hope of rescuing the pair—had sunk out of sight.

The current was too strong, too swift. Man and boy, captured in its grip, were caught in its fast-moving flow, too fast for anyone to help. Someone whipped out a machete, whacked at a low-hanging branch, and tried to throw it to Brad. As everyone watched, horrified, Brad's arm rose out of the churning water, his hand making a futile grab for the branch. But before he could reach it, he was swept into the whirling vortex. They had one last glimpse of him as he struggled frantically in the spray; then his head went down, one hand lifted desperately above the water, then that disappeared as well.

The voices of those on the riverbank rose in unified moan, then died away in gasps and sobs as everyone realized it was too late. Brad Sayres and the boy he had fought so gallantly to save were beyond help, beyond hope.

Stunned, an unbelieving Penny stood rooted to the spot. There was a stirring in the crowd behind her. Intuitively Penny turned to see Thea, with wide frightened eyes in a white face, coming through the parted crowd. "What is it, Penny? What's happened?"

Penny's lips trembled as she stammered out the words, "It's Brad, Thea. He's—he tried to save a little boy from drowning and he. . . ." She let Belinda slip out of her arms onto the muddy grass at her feet and held out her arms to her sister-in-law. "Oh, Thea, I'm so sorry. . . ."

Devastated, the hushed crowd fell back, casting furtive glances upon the two women locked in each other's arms. Thea's head sank limply on Penny's shoulder, her fragile body like a dead weight against her. A grief too profound for tears bound both women. Belinda, sitting at their feet, tugged at Penny's skirt. And for the first time in her short life she was not immediately lifted into her aunt's comforting embrace.

Nelldean arrived while Penny and Thea were still standing paralyzed with shock on the riverbank. Gently she led them back to the wagon and helped Penny urge Thea to lie down, suggested a soothing dose of laudanum for the grief-stricken woman. Then she took Belinda, fed her, rocked and sang to her. Finally mother and daughter were both asleep, and an exhausted Penny joined Nelldean at the back of the wagon. "What now, Nelldean?" she asked brokenly. "What in the world do we do now?"

The older woman reached for Penny's hand, held it quietly, and said, "Anything Nate and I can do, honey, you know you can count on us."

"I know, Nelldean." Penny nodded. "But I don't know what we're going to do. Without Brad. I just don't know. It's too late to turn back, and Thea's condition . . . I just don't know how we can go on."

"First things first, Penny. One day at a time. That's how all of us get through the hard times in life. You're young and strong, and you'll make it."

"I wish I felt sure of that."

"Remember, Penny, the Lord gives us strength just for the day. That's all he promised. Lean on him. As the Scripture says, 'When I am weak, he is strong' and 'He will not fail thee, nor forsake thee.' That's been proven to me over and over in my life, Penny."

Penny nodded and squeezed Nelldean's hand, wishing somehow she could borrow her faith at this desolate moment when her own was lacking.

"And Nate and I will help in any way we can."

"Thank you, Nelldean, I'm grateful." Penny knew Nelldean meant what she said, but after all, she and Nate were going to Oregon, while Brad's homestead was in California. That's where *they* were headed. Or were they?

The next day, some of the men searching along the riverbank found the bodies of both Brad and the little boy he'd tried so hard to save. The urgency of "moving on" was the deciding factor; they had to ready them immediately for burial the following day. The wagon train was delaying its departure so that this could be done with some respect and decency.

That morning, Penny rose before dawn. Dazed with shock, she dressed Belinda and fed her breakfast. Penny was wrapped in a kind of wordless grief, like being swathed in cotton wool, beyond tears, beyond feeling.

Thea, due to the dosage of laudanum Nelldean suggested, remained traumatized, unaccepting of the reality of Brad's death.

Together the two women walked to the place of the improvised burial service. The parents of the little boy were in even worse emotional shape, the mother near collapse. Penny kept her arm around Thea's waist, supporting her lest she faint. There was no minister with the wagon train, and a man she hardly knew read a passage from someone's Bible before lowering Brad's body into the shallow grave.

It still seemed so unreal that Brad, with all his boundless enthusiasm and optimism, was gone, that they would never see his teasing glance nor hear his laughter. He had been the spur for them all. Over and over he had told them they stood to gain everything by this journey. It never occurred to him that they would lose everything—his very life.

When the brief service was over they returned to the wagon where Nelldean had been keeping Belinda amused. With a meaningful glance at Penny she indicated another spoonful of laudanum might be in order for Thea.

"It will get her over this first part, at least. In a day or two there will be time enough for her to come to terms with it."

With some misgivings Penny did as Nelldean suggested. What good would a few hours of oblivion do when there was so much to decide? Was it all going to be up to *her*?

Nelldean took Belinda with her so Penny would have some time to herself and so the little girl could watch some of the older children run and play.

Left alone, Penny faced the questions that had to be confronted—even amidst the horror of the tragedy that had overtaken them. What would she and Thea and Belinda do now? They couldn't turn back, they'd come too far; and without an escort—two lone women and a child in a wagon alone? It was out of the question. But with no man to drive the wagon, mile after mile over the mountains they had yet to travel, and with all the dangers and hardships they might be facing—that too seemed out of the question.

She was no closer to a solution to their problem when late in the afternoon Nelldean brought Belinda back. Thea roused briefly to sip some tea, then closed her eyes wearily and went back to sleep. As soon as it got dark, worn out with sorrow and emotional strain, Penny lay down beside Belinda. It was a miserable night, getting increasingly cold. Penny cuddled Belinda close, and huddled, shivering and sleepless, half the night. Every so often she would awake with a start when she heard the horses spooking and snorting on the picket ropes.

The little girl's soft, gentle breathing soon assured Penny she had gone to sleep. It was then that all her own misery returned. The scene of Brad's drowning came back in all its horror. Her grief was compounded by bitterness. She felt a quick, hot anger at the betrayal—against the people who had enticed them on this fool's journey, so full of untold hardships, misery, unseen dangers—and with probably worse to come.

First things first, Nelldean had wisely counseled. There was no time to grieve, no time to waste. The rule of the wagon train was "A day lost is never regained." Out of respect for Brad and the little boy he had tried to rescue, the wagons remained at the river a full day. But tomorrow morning they would pull out. Penny knew the first thing she had to do was go to the wagon master and ask him if somehow they could go on to California without a "head of household." Perhaps some of the other men could take turns spelling her, driving their wagon. Brad had certainly helped others out many times.

138

Penny had never had much contact with the wagon master. Brad had made all their arrangements, and, of course, only the men met with him regularly when anything had to be decided or voted on. She knew she was taking a big chance going to him and asking this favor, but she had to try! What alternative did she have?

Early the next morning, leaving Belinda with Nelldean, Penny walked down the line of wagons to where she saw Captain Harding sitting on a stump. Straightening her spine, bracing her shoulders, even while her heart raced, she approached him. He was holding a tin of canned peaches, spearing one slice at a time out with the tip of his knife, then bringing it dripping to his mouth.

Penny cleared her throat. "Good morning, sir. I've come to discuss with you the possibility of our moving on with the wagon train. Now that my brother's ... gone, my sister-in-law has claim to his homestead in California, and I see no other way than for us to continue on—"

The words faltered on her lips as Harding slowly turned his head toward her, his eyes narrowed. He wiped his mouth with the back of his hand before speaking.

"I'm sorrier than I can say about your brother, miss, but there's no way I can let two women and a baby—cain't take that kind of responsibility. In my train all the men pitch in to help out the others, take picket duty, help fix broken axles or wheels, take care of the livestock. A wagon with no man to share the work of the whole wagon train is a burden. I don't need anymore problems, miss. The combined Missouri and Iowa parties give me 'nuf worries as it is," he drawled, shaking his head. "No, ma'am, we're still in Indian territory. Sure as God made little green apples there might be more trouble than we can handle. Best thing I can do is let you go with us far as Fort Hall, then you can wait there for an escort goin' back east."

He gave her a sour glance. He didn't add "where you

belong," but he might as well have. Penny's indignation rose in spite of her despair. There seemed to be nothing more to say.

Fighting tears, Penny walked back to her wagon. Maybe if she had used these tears before—a woman's ploy—perhaps the wagon master would have softened. Maybe not. In a way, she could understand his point. Allowing them to continue might endanger all the people in the wagon train. He couldn't make an exception. Now it was up to her to figure out what the three of them were to do. To wait at Fort Hall for an escort back east seemed preposterous. They were more than halfway to California. To travel back through what they had already endured? And for what? To go back to Dunwoodie? And with Thea getting nearer and nearer to the birth of the baby? No, she had to think of something else. What, she had no idea.

Nelldean was waiting to hear the result of Penny's mission.

"He said no—out of the question." Penny lifted Belinda out of Nelldean's lap and cuddled her close. "He says we can go as far as Fort Hall, then stay there until we can get an escort back home. But Nelldean, how can I do that?"

"Well, honey, we'll just take it to the Lord. He'll show us what to do. Let's sleep on it, see what tomorrow brings."

Chapter 16

*N*elldean left and Penny tried to settle for sleep. These last few nights, sleep had been hard to come by, not only because of worry but also the weather. It had been hot, almost windless. Afraid her tossing and turning might disturb Thea, who needed her rest, she decided to make a lean-to at the end of the wagon and sleep outside. She had taken a length of canvas and propped it up with staves. Hoping to soon fall asleep, Penny stretched out on her blanket roll and closed her eyes.

But sleep proved impossible. Too many unanswerable questions kept her from relaxing. Soon she was wider awake than ever. She tried to pray. Bits and pieces of Scripture came and went in and out of her mind. As a child on Saturday nights she would lie in bed going over and over the Bible verse that she was supposed to have memorized and would be required to recite the next day at Sunday school. Tonight she couldn't seem to recall even one verse completely.

He must *hear me*, she thought plaintively. Nelldean believed *all* prayers were heard. But were they answered? Fragments floated just on the edge of her memory. But when she tried to capture them to repeat them for comfort, they faded away.

"Your word I have hidden in my heart." Hidden, all right, she thought ironically. *Why can't I remember something comforting, encouraging, strengthening? "If you abide in me and my words abide in you. . ."* then what? *"Thy Word,"* what is it, Lord? *"A lamp unto my feet, a light unto my path—"* That's what I need: a word of guidance. *What shall I do, Lord? If I hide your Word in my heart, what then, Lord? "Then you will walk on your way safely, and your foot will not stumble. When you lie down, you will not be afraid. Yes, you will lie down, and your sleep will be sweet—"*

She felt herself slowly drifting off.

Then suddenly hands were shaking her, a desperate voice in her ear. "Penny, Penny, wake up!"

Startled, heart pounding, Penny woke up. Her eyes flew open. She pushed back her hair, rubbing her eyes. Thea was bending over her.

"What is it? What's the matter, Thea? What's wrong?"

"It's the baby."

"Belinda?" Penny struggled up into a sitting position. "Is she sick?"

"No, it isn't Belinda, it's *me,* Penny."

"You? But—" Her words were cut short even before she had formed her question. Thea's face suddenly contorted. She closed her eyes, drawing a long, agonizing breath. Her fingers dug into Penny's arm where she clutched it.

The stunning truth hit Penny. The *baby*! It was the *new* baby Thea was talking about. All this flashed through Penny's brain, which was now fully awake and aware. *This couldn't be happening. Not now! It is too soon. Weeks too soon! Thea isn't supposed to have the baby until we reach California!*

Penny reached out, eased Thea down onto her mat, and held her until the spasm passed. Slowly Thea let out a long breath. "I'm sorry, Penny," she whispered. "I thought it was just ... I didn't wake you because I thought maybe ... I hoped ... but then, remembering how it was when Belinda was born ... I'm pretty sure—"

Penny scrambled to her feet, grabbed her skirt, threw it over her head, twisted it around her waist and buttoned it, then reached for her blouse.

"I'll go get Nelldean," she gasped. "*She'll* know what to do."

"I hate being such a burden—," Thea said weakly.

"Don't talk nonsense. But if the baby's really coming, we'll need help," Penny said sharply, too afraid herself to be too sympathetic. "Here, I'll help you back into the wagon, then I'll run over to their wagon."

Penny put her arm around Thea, helped her get to her feet, then supported her as they made their halting way back to the wagon. Just as she was about to step up inside, another pain gripped Thea, and she grabbed Penny, moaning. Penny felt Thea shudder, and she tightened her hold. All the prayers she couldn't remember a few hours before came flooding back to her now.

"Oh, God, an ever present help in trouble. . . . Therefore we will not fear." She had never felt so afraid in her life. Penny gritted her teeth. Thea seemed to slump against her.

"Over?" Penny asked her.

"For now—but they're coming closer."

"Easy, easy," Penny cautioned as she helped Thea gently up into the wagon. She pushed a pillow under Thea's head, put another one at her back. Thea was shivering uncontrollably, and Penny put an extra quilt on top of her. "Now, don't worry. I'll be right back."

"Wait, Penny." Thea put out her hand, tugged her skirt.

"Why? What is it?" Penny asked, impatient at the delay. She was fighting panic. From the little she knew about childbirth, she knew there was a need for haste. At least *she*

143

would feel better when someone older and more experienced was with her.

"You better take Belinda. Put her in your blanket roll—"

"Good idea," replied Penny, her breath coming fast. Quickly she lifted the peacefully sleeping child, who did not waken as she carried her out to the lean-to and gently put her down. Then she stuck her head back in the wagon. "You'll be all right until I get back with Nelldean?"

In the dim light from the cloud-shrouded moon, Thea's face was a pale mask; her eyes were closed, but she managed a slow nod and a murmur. Penny took it for a yes.

"I'll hurry, Thea, just hang on," she said breathlessly, and then she picked up her skirt and started running along the line of parked wagons to where Nate had parked the Hardisons'. Reaching it, Penny rushed along the side, bumping into Nelldean's tin dishpan hung there and sending it clattering. A dog barked at the noise, and Penny stumbled, then caught herself by grabbing the side of the wagon. A splinter from the rough wood jabbed sharply into her palm. Tears sprang into her eyes and she winked them back.

"Nelldean! Nelldean! Nate!" she called, shaking the canvas flap on the back of their wagon. "Please, it's Penny!"

It seemed an eternity until she saw Nelldean's sleep-wrinkled face under a ruffled nightcab stick itself out through the slit, demanding, "Land sakes, what is it, girl?"

"It's Thea! The baby. She's having it—*now!*"

"Be there in a jiff," Nelldean replied, then disappeared.

Breathing hard, Penny leaned against the wagon, weak with relief. "Thank God for Nelldean." Penny's confidence began to come back. An excitement began to surge through her. Maybe this would bring Thea back to life. With a new baby to care for, the future to think about, maybe things would work out. With God's help and Nelldean's faith and her own stubborn determination, they'd get through this somehow.

On their way back to the Sayres' wagon together, Nelldean assured Penny she had been a helper at a dozen or so birthings. "Thea's probably stronger than she looks. And she's young and has had one young'un already. Yes, I know it's sooner than expected, but maybe she miscalculated. That happens many a time. It'll be fine, God willin'."

The next few hours were a blur of following Nelldean's instructions, bathing Thea's face with cool cloths, holding the hand she gripped so hard, whispering words of encour- agement to her throughout the long night. Many times Penny was to repeat her grateful prayer for Nelldean's friendship, her calm presence beside her.

Penny wasn't sure when she became conscious of a change in Nelldean's manner. Alarmed, she turned to look at Nelldean, and she read something in the woman's face that turned her cold. "What is it? Is it taking too long?" Then she glanced back at Thea, who lay back against the pillows exhausted, her face chalky, with dark smudges of shadow underneath the closed eyes.

"I'm afraid the baby's dead," Nelldean said sadly. "Not moving, not at all."

A rush of anger, fear choked Penny. She looked down at Thea, her face a pale oval, the dark masses of hair tangled about it. There was a clamminess to her skin when Penny touched it with the dampened towel. *Oh, no, Lord, the baby might have saved Thea, might have—*

Dawn inched fingers of light through the gaping canvas flaps. Nelldean touched Penny's shoulder and whispered, "Maybe you better take Belinda over to our wagon, give her some breakfast. There's nothin' much more to do here but wait—"

"Let me stay, Nelldean. Belinda will go with you. She

loves Nate. You're right. It might be better for her to not be here if—" Penny could not bring herself to say anymore, for the lump rising in her throat felt as big and hard as a stone.

Nelldean nodded and stiffly moved to the end of the wagon and hefted the little girl down. Nelldean's leaving must have aroused Thea, for she opened her huge, shadowed eyes and at first seemed dazed. Then her gaze focused on Penny. She wet her parched and swollen lips with her tongue and in a raspy voice said, "Penny. Bend down. I can't talk any louder." Her thin fingers touched her throat. "Sore."

"Don't try to talk if it hurts."

"Have to. Something I must—"

Penny bent closer.

"Penny," Thea said again. "Promise me?"

"Yes, of course, whatever."

"Promise . . . ?"

"What do you want me to promise, Thea?"

With obvious effort, Thea swallowed and tried again. "Take care . . . Belinda?"

"Yes, of course, I will. We *both* will."

Thea made a motion as if to shake her head. She looked infinitely weary. Just then a wave of pain swept over her.

Fear gripped Penny. Where was Nelldean? Why didn't she come back? She didn't know what to do except hold Thea's hand, feeling the bite of her fingers and nails press deeply into the skin of her wrist.

"Please, Penny." Thea's eyes looked desperate. "There isn't time. If I don't . . . *you must*—"

"Don't say that, Thea. Don't even think it." Penny's voice choked.

Thea's eyes closed and Penny knew the end was near. Her friend could no longer hear her—would never hear her again.

Penny didn't remember how much later she had stumbled to the end of the wagon and hoarsely called Nelldean's name, knowing it was too late.

Other wagons were already astir with people at their morning duties, cooking fires were sending swirls up into the misty morning, and there was the usual clatter of kettles and frying pans. Penny was aware of voices, children's laughter. Everyone was going about their regular chores as if nothing terrible was happening. When the worst possible thing was happening. Thea's young life was ebbing out slowly, inevitably, irrevocably, just as her lifeblood was draining away and with her the little baby, who had never had a chance to live.

When it was all over, Penny knew Nelldean had done everything she could. Yet it had all been for nothing. Thea and the baby were gone.

Maybe there was no hope even from the beginning. Thea was too depleted in strength and will to live, the baby too small. There was nothing more to say. Nothing more to do. But to go on. Alone. Somehow.

Chapter 17

*P*enny huddled under her blanket. She couldn't stop shivering. Every once in a while a deep shudder shook the length of her body. It couldn't be true. It couldn't have happened. But it *was,* and it *had*! Thea was dead and the baby with her!

Nelldean had held Penny, who was wracked with sobs and clung to her. The older woman wisely let her cry until there seemed to be no tears left, then she said gently, "Maybe it's best this way, honey. I don't think the poor little thing wanted to live. Not after your brother died. The will just seemed to go right out of her. And the baby was just too tiny and too weak. . . ."

Was Nelldean right? Had Thea just given up? For the last few weeks, ever since Brad's drowning, there had been a kind of lostness about her. She had had to be reminded to eat, to respond. At the mention of Brad's name, her haunted eyes were always misty with tears ready to fall. She seemed enveloped in a web of grief from which she could not disentangle herself. She hardly noticed Belinda nor anything around her. It was as if her own spirit had departed with Brad.

Penny had never seen two people more in love than

Thea and her brother. Only recently, at one of several impromptu weddings held among the wagon train folks—some on very short acquaintance and with little notice—Penny had made the comparison. At Thea and Brad's wedding, even in the inappropriate black dress mandated by her stepmother, Thea had been radiant. Her face, under the bonnet Grams had trimmed at the last minute with flowers and ribbons, was shining with happiness. Brad had been unable to take his eyes off his bride. As they repeated their vows, they had seemed oblivious to everyone else. Saying the words as they looked into each other's eyes brought tears to everyone else's. At that moment, Penny had determined she herself would never settle for anything less than that kind of love.

Brad and Thea had so much to look forward to together, with Belinda and a new baby. Now they were all gone! It was too cruel that all that love could end so tragically. The three of them had grown up together. Brad and Thea were part of everything Penny remembered about her childhood; she didn't have one memory that didn't include them in some way. She couldn't imagine what life would be like without them. Penny felt like a part of herself had been ripped away.

Thea had been her playmate, her companion, her confidante, her dearest friend. They had laughed together, cried together, prayed together, kept each others' secrets, shared the good, the bad, everything. How empty her world would be without Thea.

Penny stuffed an edge of her quilt into her mouth to stifle her sobs so as not to disturb Nelldean, who had stayed over with her and Belinda that night.

The next day as they buried Thea and the baby she had not lived long enough to name the air seemed filled with dust. The wind blew, constantly covering everything with a gritty mask, stinging the eyes, crawling down the backs of necks. Penny, standing motionless with Belinda in her arms, felt as though her heart would break. The wind tugged at her skirt and blew her hair into her eyes, which were already blinded with tears. Heartsick, she watched as the men shoveled the clumps of sandy earth over the shallow grave, then began covering it with rocks. Penny knew the reason for the rocks. Many times they had passed graves along the trail that had been dug out either by marauding Indians looking for clothes or jewelry or, worse still, by wild animals. The possibility of such a fate for Thea and her baby filled Penny with horror. The pain of leaving her dear ones in untended graves was intense.

The weight of Belinda's little body in her arms reminded her that she was not completely alone. She had a new and sacred responsibility. She was all the child had now. Belinda was an orphan: no mother, no father, no little brother or sister. Now what? *What shall I do?* echoed Penny's mind hollowly. Above all, she was determined not to give way to fear.

In the end, it was Nelldean who offered the answer to Penny's agonizing question. Fort Hall was the turn-off point; there the emigrants going to California would part with those heading for Oregon. To wait at Fort Hall for an escort back to Missouri seemed useless.

"Why not come to Oregon with us?" Nelldean urged. "We can join forces. You know how to drive a team; we can share provisions and supplies. Nate can help you with the animals, and I'll do the cookin' and help take care of Belinda. When we get to Oregon, you can sell your outfit, then decide what to do next."

It seemed the only sensible thing to do. The decision was made. They went through the Sayres' wagon, taking what supplies were left, giving some things away to others who had less, moving a few possessions, and setting more along the wayside. Penny acted in a nearly automaton manner, motivated only by necessity. She still had not had time to fully grieve or to weigh all her new and enormous responsibilities.

In the days following Thea's burial, Penny's sorrow was too deep for tears then. Only later, sitting on the driver's seat, holding the reins as the weary team plowed on the increasingly difficult trail, did she let tears come. It had all turned out so differently from the high hopes and dreams the three of them had had starting out.

On those long, dusty days, she remembered all the glowing reports in the brochure articles, urging people to join the mighty emigrant movement west . . . they would be fulfilling the country's "manifest destiny." Had drowning been Brad's destiny? And a prairie grave for his widow and stillborn baby? Life seemed too cruel. Penny had never thought it would be like this. The great adventure was like ashes to her. Bitterly she asked herself, *What more could happen?*

What did happen was another stunning blow. Belinda stopped talking. In the midst of all her own indecision, her own uncertainty, preoccupied, distracted with everything that must be taken care of and decided, Penny did not notice it right away. Rather than the active little child who had been toddling about, chattering constantly, making up her own words for things in an attempt in real vocal communication, Belinda was suddenly mute. Penny could not be sure exactly when it had happened, but when she realized it, it came as a dreadful shock.

Panicked into action, Penny worked frantically to get her to talk again. She fashioned hand puppets from old stockings, making them dance and ask questions; she told stories by the hour, trying to get Belinda to guess the ending or say the names of the characters; she sang to her, hoping the little girl would join in as she used to love to do; but nothing worked. All her efforts, all the games she played

151

trying to trick Belinda into some verbal reaction, were in vain. The child refused to speak. Whatever world into which she had retreated she could not explain, share, or talk about.

"I wish I knew what to do, Nelldean. That lost, longing look in her eyes is enough to break your heart."

"Well, all my life I've heard people say 'struck dumb,'" Nelldean replied. "I think that's what happened to Belinda. She was so frightened she was struck dumb. I believe, in time, she'll talk again. It's certainly not that she don't understand what's being said around her. You've seen the way her eyes follow you and how she turns her head from one or the other of us when we're talking?" Nelldean nodded her head sagely. "You'll see it'll happen one of these days. You've just got to be patient."

But Penny was impatient. She longed to have someone else take over the responsibility for Belinda, to tell her what to do. It was all almost too much to bear. Penny felt her energy drain away. What had happened to her? What had become of her original enthusiasm for the journey, her optimism at the start of each new day? As they neared Fort Hall, where the ones bound for California would leave the wagon train, Penny was wracked with memories of how Brad used to say that once they got to California, everything would be worth it. To him it was the fabled rainbow's end. Thea had been a reluctant traveler, and Belinda had not been asked if she wanted to come. Penny remembered how she herself had looked at it as a chance for adventure, an escape from a humdrum existence. She had loved the journey at first. She had felt free of all the restrictions, expectations, and the proscribed future her Dunwoodie girlfriends looked forward to—having a husband and children, becoming a wife, keeping house, cooking, sewing, canning. She hadn't been ready for that . . . not yet. Not for a long time. The idea of independence had excited her imagination.

The irony was that instead of gaining freedom, she had gotten more responsibility than she had ever bargained for, with no one to help her carry the burden or share it with her.

Sometimes she felt like one of the Israelites wandering for forty years in the desert—except for *her* there was no pillar of cloud by day or moon by night, no manna, just day after grinding day, dust, heat, dryness, miles of parched grass stretching endlessly—a stark, cruel, yet somehow beautiful land.

Only by not trying to look ahead could Penny function at all. She tried to meet each day as it came, concentrating only on the task at hand. By not allowing herself to worry about the risks that still lay ahead, she could at least pretend they did not exist.

Caught up in each day's demands, her anxiety about Belinda hovered over her constantly. Would the little girl ever regain her speech? On the surface the child seemed much the same, though not smiling so readily. But there were no tantrums, no crying spells. She just didn't speak. If she missed her parents, there was no outward indication. She did not ask about them. For the last few weeks of her mother's life, she had become used to Penny and Nelldean taking care of her. Nate was wonderful with her, taking her for rides on his shoulders and playing his harmonica for her.

In gratitude to both Nelldean and her grandson, Penny did more than her share of the work as the wagon train moved into the valley that would eventually lead them into the Oregon Territory. Work helped Penny suppress her gnawing worries. The days became a blur. At night she was too tired to do anything more than crawl into her bed at the back of the wagon and, with Belinda snuggled beside her, pray for the oblivion of sleep, the absence of nightmares. Then to wake and wearily and sadly begin another day.

Finally Nelldean took her to task. "Penny, you can't go on like this, girl. This is not the end of the road for you. Count your blessings. You're alive, number one. You're strong. You've come through a mighty hard time, but you did and you're stronger for it whether you realize it or not. And Belinda needs you. You're all she's got."

At Fort Hall Nate helped Penny unload more of the contents of Brad's wagon, and some of Thea's treasured furnishings had to be left there. If she was to do the driving for the rest of the way to Oregon, the weight for her already weary oxen had to be lightened. Penny kept only a few things that later Belinda might want of her mother's belongings. She added one more sad postscript to the letter she had written Grams to be sent from there:

> I know it was Brad's dream to go to California. But there was no way I could persuade the wagon master to let me come with the part of the train headed there. I believe it was best for me to accept Nelldean and Nate's urging to join them. At least I will have the support of good friends until I know what I should do from there. Nelldean's faith had sustained me. As soon as we reach Oregon City, I will write again.

PART 4

JOURNEY'S END

Chapter 18

From Fort Hall Penny had sent the letter to Grams containing the tragic news of the deaths of Brad, Thea, and the baby. She knew what a bitter blow this would be to her grandmother, who had loved them all so dearly. But she also knew that Grams was brave and courageous, that she had known tragedy and loss before and survived. She would again. However, Penny was not as certain about her own ability to go on.

"Dearest Grams," Penny began her first letter from Oregon City,

Many times along the trail I wondered if our journey would ever end. Of course, I thought it would end in California, but here we are in Oregon. Main Street is an amazing mixture, with a variety of stores, saloons, boarding houses, more saloons, dance halls, a barber shop, a newspaper office, a general store, a doctor's office, a pharmacist, a dentist, a bank, a freight office, and who knows what else. Some of the buildings look flimsy, some well built. I'm told that on some of the backstreets can be found some very nice frame houses with gardens—the residences of those who came here twenty years ago and established a town like the ones they left back east. Further out are ranches, cattle and horse farms, and miles and miles of orchards. Fruit grows plentifully here, especially a luscious kind of pear.

We are staying in the home of Bess Fulton, a friend of Nelldean's son and daughter-in-law. She has kindly offered us her hospitality, as she has three empty rooms. Her grown sons have gone to the California gold fields, and she says she is glad for the company.

I got a good price for our wagon, the two oxen, and the equipment. I kept Brad's horse, although he is worn from the long journey. Still, he is better than what I've seen for sale at the local livery stable. With some good feed and care, he should recover from any bad effects of the trip.

Now she paused in her letter. The hard part came next: to explain what had happened to Belinda in the aftermath of her parents' deaths, then ask if she should bring the little girl back to Dunwoodie as soon as she could arrange it. Unsure herself about what was the best thing to do, Penny needed Grams' good judgment. She finished the letter by assuring Grams that other than that, both she and Belinda were in good health, Oregon was beautiful, and she would await her answer. Penny took the letter to the post office and mailed it.

Grams' reply was a long time coming. Even though Nelldean told her it sometimes took months for letters to be received and answered, Penny became impatient. With every day that went by bringing no word from Grams, she grew more anxious. Was Grams ill? Was something wrong back home? Why hadn't she heard from her?

"I'm worried. Why hasn't she written?" Penny fretted to Nelldean after another futile trip to the post office. "I've got to do something, Nelldean. I can't expect Bess to put us up forever. I've got to make some money to travel on when I take Belinda back to Dunwoodie."

"Are you sure that's what you want to do, Penny? You and Belinda could stay here, make Oregon your home,"

Nelldean suggested mildly. "You know, you could file for a homestead yourself. Women out here have done that— many of them."

"A homestead? Me?" Penny looked surprised, then slowly shook her head. "I don't think so, Nelldean. I think when I hear from Grams, she'll tell me to bring Belinda back to Dunwoodie—*home*." But even as she said the word, Penny felt a strange detachment. Home? Somewhere along the trail, she had lost the sense of home.

In the meantime Penny tried to find some kind of work in case she needed to earn passage back east. However, there were dismayingly few opportunities for employment for young women. Some took in boarders, did laundry, or baked bread to make a living. But none of these was a possibility for her. Penny was discouraged, and her hope centered on a letter from Grams with some money for her to bring Belinda back to Dunwoodie.

A month, six weeks, went by and still no letter. Coming back from yet another disappointing trip to the post office one day, she met Nelldean's questioning glance with a shake of her head.

"Nothing! No letter, no job! I'm so depressed, Nelldean. I can't help it!"

"Somethin's bound to turn up, girl. Just you wait and see."

"You mean a miracle; that's what I need," Penny sighed.

"Then you'll get one," Nelldean said with conviction. "You've just got to be patient, learn to wait for the Lord to act."

Nelldean sounded just like Grams, Penny thought nostalgically.

In the meantime at the beginning of November, the Oregon winter set in, with daily downpours. To Penny it seemed ironic that on the long, dusty trail they had thirsted for just one drop of water and here it seemed to do nothing but rain. On one such night, as the rain pounded like a drumbeat on the tin roof, Penny got out her Bible, searching for some encouraging passages to boost her flagging spirit. She remembered the desperate prayers she had prayed those nights, lying sleepless in the wagon. How she had dredged up fragments of Scripture from memory—"If you abide in me and my words abide in you, you shall ask what you will—" Had they been mindless, meaningless? Or was what the Bible promised true? Penny closed her eyes, clenched her fists. *Yes, I do believe. God will show me the way—the right way.*

Somehow she got through Christmas. Nelldean and Bess made a great occasion of it, and Belinda was the beneficiary of their love and talents. Knitted caps, scarves, and mittens. A rag doll with yellow yarn hair and a wardrobe of dresses and bonnets. Nate had built a small wooden cradle for it as well. They all attended church service in the morning (there were as many churches in Oregon City as saloons). Afterward they had a festive dinner with duck—Nate's contribution—creamed onions, vegetables, mashed potatoes, and three kinds of pie: mince, apple, pumpkin. Beneath all the gaiety, the laughter and fun, Penny felt a tinge of loneliness. Nelldean and Bess had done their best, but Oregon City wasn't home. Who would ever have thought she would be homesick for Dunwoodie?

Nelldean had been right. In January came the long-delayed letter from Grams, along with a much battered box containing Christmas gifts for them all. Penny tore open the envelope addressed to her at general delivery in Grams' familiar handwriting. Her eyes raced down the closely written page. But the letter did not contain what Penny had hoped nor what she had expected. She read it with a growing feeling of dismay.

Somewhere in the second paragraph, she read the news that Todd had married. It was like a jolt. She was surprised to realize that somewhere hovering in the back of her mind had been the thought that when she *did* return to Dunwoodie with Belinda, Todd would be there, still in love with her, still wanting to marry, and that together they might make a home for Belinda. She hadn't thought this out in any great detail; it had just been there. Just as Todd had always been there in her life, patient, caring, kind— waiting. Well, that wasn't the case now. It surprised her that she felt so let down, as unfair of her as that was. She had never given him any reason to hope. In fact, she had done everything to discourage him. Why should she feel betrayed?

Maybe this was all part of *really* growing up—to realize that nothing stays the same. Everything changes. *Her* circumstances, *her* life had. *She* certainly had. She was no longer the girl who had left Dunwoodie. Nor was she still the girl Todd had loved and wanted to marry.

Penny found other surprises in the letter. It seemed that Cousin Sara and Tom and their little Jenny had moved into the house to live with Grams. Her grandmother wrote,

> It's such a comfort to have them here. I wouldn't have told you for the world, but I was right lonely after the four of you left. Even Uncle Billy was lonesome for young folks—especially a baby. But Sara and Tom are as lively as can be, and we all have a great time together. They're expecting another baby in the spring, so we shall have a full house, but the more the merrier, I always say.

Except there's no room anymore for me, Penny thought. Her tears blurred her eyes as she read Grams' final paragraph:

> You have Belinda to raise now. Why this should be, why this has come about, we will find out someday. God works in mysterious ways, as we all know. It would be foolhardy for you to attempt the long trip back here to bring Belinda back. To what? You have friends who love you, a new life ahead of you, Penny. I'm sure all the things I tried to teach

161

you and Brad will stand you in good stead. You will always be in my loving prayers, and I know God will guide and protect you in all you do.

Penny reread the letter. In little less than a year since she'd been gone, Todd had found someone else, and Grams had taken on a new family to nurture and love. Her first reaction was hurt. Her throat felt sore with the effort not to cry.

Quickly she blinked back the telling tears. She was just being selfish, self-indulgent. She *should* be happy for Grams, happy for Todd. And she *was*.

That night as Penny got Belinda ready for bed she took the little girl onto her lap and hugged her. "It's going to be all right, honey. Things are going to be fine—just fine," she whispered, wishing she fully believed that herself.

Now that there was no going home, she knew it was up to her to find some kind of work and to make a home for Belinda. How that would be done, she had no idea. That miracle Nelldean had promised she'd get seemed far away.

At the end of February and in the first week of March signs of spring could definitely be seen and felt. With the arrival of the new season, Penny resolved to accept what had happened, make the best of it, build a life for herself and Belinda here in Oregon. First she had to find some way to support them both. Nelldean had told her she'd get her "miracle." And one day she did.

Oregon City was growing constantly. Main Street was being extended, with new buildings going up every day. New businesses were opening up: a millinery, a dress shop, a hardware store. Maybe she could get a job as a clerk in one of them. She wrote a neat hand, was good at sums. She walked along the wooden boardwalk, glancing from one side of the street to the other. Just then, passing Miller's

General Mercantile, she saw a sign in the window: BOOK AGENTS WANTED.

She halted. What did that mean? What was a book agent? A sales person? There was only one way to find out: go in and ask. Penny straightened her shoulders, took a deep breath, opened the door, and walked inside.

"Mr. Miller?" she tentatively addressed the man behind the counter, who stood near an impressive silver cash register.

"The same. Speaking," he said, regarding her with both curiosity and admiration. Not often did such an attractive young woman, neatly dressed in bonnet and gloves, come into the store.

"My name is Penny Sayres, and I've newly arrived in Oregon City. I came in with the wagon train," she added, to let him know she was strong, hardy, and able to work hard. "I'm staying with Mrs. Fulton, and I'm looking for work. I wondered—the sign in the window says book agents wanted—do you ever hire women as agents?"

Mr. Miller gave her a long, astonished look. But he'd always liked a woman with spunk and determination. He nodded his head as he spoke: "I don't know why not. Books is books. Readin' is readin'. The only question is can you sell? Agents get paid a sum for every book order they take, plus a percentage of the cover cost of the book. Don't matter who sells 'em. Do you have transportation? A small buggy or wagon? You may have to go quite a distance to peddle 'em. There's lots of women in ranches in the outlying districts who could use this here fine book." He picked up a large volume displayed on the counter and held it up so Penny could read the title. "It's called *Handbook for Housewives: A Complete Guide to the Art of Creating a Harmonious Home, a Happy Husband, and Healthy Children.*"

Penny felt something click inside. Of course she could do it. "A woman selling to women might be even better," she said almost breathlessly.

Mr. Miller's eyes twinkled, he nodded in approval. "Fine and dandy. You're hired." He then proceeded to pack a box of books and handed her a ledger to write up her sales. "There you go, Miss Sayres."

Lugging an armful of books and a sales ledger, Penny hurried home.

"Nelldean, I've got a job!" she called as she entered the house. Nelldean and Bess were in the kitchen where they were feeding Belinda. All three looked expectantly at Penny as she came through the door.

In a rush she told them what had come about. Nelldean looked pleased, even a bit smug. "You got your miracle then, didn't you?" she asked Penny.

Penny laughed.

Bess chimed in, "Well, it's sure better than doing laundry or housework and probably pays more."

"The man at the store said I can make as much as I'm willing to work at it. I'll have to rent a small buggy to make my rounds. Mr. Miller says most of my customers will probably be ranch wives on places that are located quite a distance from town. Will that cost much, do you think?" she asked Bess, who had lived in town a long time.

"Try Hiram's Livery and tell them Bess Fulton sent you. They knew my husband Jake real well. I think they'll give you a fair price."

At Nelldean's suggestion, Penny sold some of the equipment from Brad's wagon that they had stored in Bess's barn after Nate took what he needed for his homestead. She rented a small rig and a horse with that sum, which, the livery owner agreed, could be applied to their purchase if she wanted to later.

Penny was excited at the prospect of her new career. Her old enthusiasm for adventure returned, and she was determined to make a success of it. She knew enough about horses to select an older one, but he was healthy, mild natured, and in good shape. The small buggy was just right for one driver and a box of books on the seat beside her.

She had moderate success selling the book in town, although at first some women looked askance at her, with suspicion or condescension. The book, however, sold itself on most occasions. It was the kind of book that had wide appeal for women, especially women far from homes back east who were struggling to build a home in the new country, in the desolate mining communities, on isolated ranches and farms, as well as in town. Many of the women had no family or friends.

Although she obviously preferred to be with Penny, Belinda stayed with Nelldean when Penny left each morning. Both Bess and Nelldean doted on the little girl, and Penny was grateful for this and for her job. Soon she would be able not only to contribute to the household expenses and pay a small board and room to Bess, but eventually have enough money to take Belinda back to Dunwoodie.

Penny always had stories to recount when she returned home in the evenings after a day of selling. Nelldean and Bess took great interest in her adventures as a book saleslady. It also gave them many a laugh, for Penny was a good mimic, regaling them with tales of her experiences, some intimidating, some funny, some exasperating. After a few ludicrous trial attempts, Penny got better at her sales "spiel" and much more confident in her new role.

Penny's life was busy with her responsibilities and with the important decisions she was mulling over. She was seriously weighing Nelldean's advice and praying hard for some direct answers. She recalled Grams saying, "God don't play guessing games. If you want to know something, ask him." Maybe that was easy for Grams, who had had a long, close relationship with the Lord. But Penny was afraid her own had been sporadic, her entreaties being more the quick, desperate kind.

With new resolution, she did begin to seek his direction, reading her Bible every night before going to bed. As she searched the pages for wisdom and understanding she was sure Nelldean had given her wise counsel but that it was up to her to understand, to really know if this was what she should do. Would it really be best for her and Belinda to stay here and build a life for themselves thousands of miles from their nearest family? After all, Thea's stepmother was still alive and Penny's grandmother and her cousins and Uncle Billy too. Would it be better to go back, where they would be surrounded by old friends and where maybe a doctor could help Belinda regain her speech? Torn by indecision, Penny would look over at Belinda, sleeping curled up, one rosy cheek cradled in a chubby hand sleeping dreamlessly. The road ahead seemed shadowed, winding into the distance she could not see. Night after night she sought and prayed for an answer.

After counting up her receipts one evening she announced proudly to Nelldean, "Well, if this keeps up, I'll soon have enough money to take Belinda home."

She and Nelldean were sitting at the kitchen table having a cup of coffee together after supper. Bess had gone to her Wednesday night prayer meeting, and the two of them were alone.

"Are you still sure that's what you want to do, Penny?"

"I don't know what else to do, Nelldean. I keep thinking Belinda needs to have a family. Grams adores her and there's Uncle Billy and. . . ." Her voice trailed off uncertainly. "Shouldn't she be brought up near her family?"

"But you said Thea had no blood relatives, didn't you? Only a stepmother that she was never close to? You and your brother were orphans and your grandmother's over sixty? What would you be taking her back to?"

Nelldean's words struck a deep chord of truth—a truth

166

Penny had not really considered too closely—maybe because she didn't want to.

"When it comes right down to it, Penny, you're all Belinda *really has*," Nelldean reminded her gently.

"Except *you*." Penny reached across the table and patted Nelldean's hand. "She couldn't have anyone more loving than you to take care of her."

"Yes, I do love her like she was my own," Nelldean agreed. "But I'm past fifty and can't go on forever. You need to be thinking about the future, yours and Belinda's. Of course, someday I hope you'll marry. Find a man who will be a good provider, a loving companion—a good father. But until then—the best thing a woman can do is to act like she may not find someone to her liking. To make her own way, provide for herself."

"I'm trying my best, Nelldean. It's hard work and slow, trying to earn enough to support us both."

"I know, honey, and that's why I'm going to suggest what I've been thinkin'. There's opportunities out here in the West for a woman alone—even a woman with a child. Land, for one. Maybe you ought to consider adopting Belinda legally. That way you could file a claim for a homestead as head of a household. It would be a security for the two of you for the future."

"Homestead by myself?" Penny's voice expressed her uncertainty. "But what would *I* do with all that acreage, Nelldean?"

"There's different size parcels, I think. And you could always sell off some, if it came to that. All it takes to meet the requirements is putting up some kind of a shelter or shack. I'd help and Nate would too. Little by little you could build on it, plant a garden, grow vegetables, live on it at least part of the year. And you could do that while building. You've had experience roughin' it on the trail. You're a capable gal! I seed that with my own eyes."

"I don't know, Nelldean," Penny said doubtfully.

"Well, think about it. If you decide to give up goin' back east, that is. But don't take too long, Penny. More and more emigrants are coming every day. Pretty soon land is goin' to get scarce and expensive as more people pour into the territory. Now's the time."

In the days that followed, Penny thought a great deal about Nelldean's suggestion. She respected her wisdom and knew Nelldean was giving her this good advice with the best intentions and for what she thought was Penny's own good. But it seemed such a big step to take, an irrevocable one. . . . File for a homestead? It sounded frightening.

Chapter 19

*A*fter a few months of selling, Penny gained more confidence and self-assurance and felt she was doing reasonably well. Of course, there were bad days, when most of the answers had been noes mixed with a few curt rebuffs. On one such day, Penny was tempted to return home for the rest of the afternoon. The day was warm and she was tired and thirsty, but because she was determined not to end the day with no sales, she decided to try a new route, hoping she would have better luck. Taking a rutted country road from town, she soon found herself out in the rolling countryside.

When she saw a house on a hilltop at the end of a long, curving lane, she slowed her horse to a walk and read the sign on the rail fence: L. C. BOUDREY. Perhaps here she would find a lonely ranch wife who was eager for some company and who could easily be persuaded to buy one of her books. She might even be offered a glass of cool water or lemonade, she thought.

The gate stood open, so Penny turned in and rode up to the house, a rustic, well-built log-and-stone building. At one side was a corral with four sleek horses, on the other side was a nice vegetable garden with some flowers at the edge. *Uh-huh,* Penny said to herself, *a very good prospect indeed! Prosperous rancher, a wife who takes pride in her home. What could be better?*

Penny got out of her buggy, hitched the horse under a shade tree away from the corral so that he wouldn't spook the other horses. Then she picked up her satchel of books and her order pad and walked toward the house. Before she reached it, the front door opened, and a man stepped out onto the porch.

Penny halted, momentarily taken aback. She hadn't expected a man. Her second thought was that he didn't look like a rancher—at least, he wasn't dressed like one. He had on a striped shirt, the sleeves rolled up to the elbows, a brown vest, dark pants, and riding boots. As she tried to regain her poise, she wracked her brain: what kind of man would be home in the middle of the day? A teacher, a preacher? Someone who worked nights? A *gambler* in one of the saloons that lined Main Street? She fervently hoped not.

When he took a few steps to the edge of the porch, she got a better look at him. He was above average height and leanly built. He had a thin face with high cheekbones, a strong nose, and deep set eyes. Although somewhat flustered by his appearance, Penny quickly composed herself. Smiling pleasantly, she began her pitch, with a slightly altered opening: "Good afternoon, sir."

"Good afternoon," he replied, folding his arms he leaned against one of the porch posts regarding her quizzically.

"Mr. Boudrey, I presume? L. C. Boudrey?"

"The same," he said with a slight smile.

"May I introduce myself?" Penny continued. "I am a representative of the Addington Publishing Company. May I speak to the lady of the house?"

He shook his head. "No, ma'am, I'm sorry, but you may not."

170

His response startled her, but she attempted not to show it as she wondered, *Good heavens, why ever not? Was his wife ill? Does he not allow her to speak to strangers? Or something more bizarre? Has he kept her prisoner?*

Redirecting her random thoughts back to her purpose of making a sale, Penny determined not to be so easily defeated. After all, she had ridden out of her way to get here—she was not about to give up without making an effort. All the sales manuals advised making at least three tries to close a sale. Penny took a deep breath and another tack.

"Then may I make an appointment for another time? I believe I have something that will be of great interest to her and also bring happiness to *you* as well."

"Oh?" the man lifted an eyebrow. "How do you mean?"

Just then an errant wind arose, lifting Penny's bonnet so that it fell back from her head. As it dangled for a moment by its ribbons, he caught a glimpse of her coppery hair gleaming in the sunlight. Before she righted it, L. C. Boudrey saw the face that had at first been half hidden by the shadow of the brim. He saw there was a drift of golden freckles across a charmingly tilted nose, and her eyes were slate blue and her candid expression was earnest.

Penny made a quick grab for her bonnet, setting it straight again, and without missing a beat went right on talking. "I have a volume that is indispensable to every household. Indeed, sir, I can guarantee there are at least thirty suggestions that will provide this home with a new atmosphere of comfort, cleanliness, convenience, congeniality, competence, composure as well as new health, heartiness, habits to ensure energy, effectiveness, and enlightenment."

Encouraged that he seemed to be listening intently, Penny increased her momentum. "This book, which I am offering homemakers for a ridiculously low down payment,

171

payable in three easy monthly installments, will enrich the life of this entire household. It contains sound, practical advice on nutrition, innovative ideas to insure a happy, healthy environment. It includes many Scriptural quotations, beautifully printed at the beginning of each section applicable to the subject. These are under the headings of menus, medicinal remedies, food preparation, sewing tips, decoration for each room of the house, care of babies, domestic pets, and how to remove every kind of spot or spill. This is the complete household-management tool. It is an indispensable resource for every homemaker. . . ." She paused before making her best closing plea: "Could I not be allowed to present to your wife this wonderful compendium of reference for every possible circumstance or condition a housewife might encounter in the course of her daily life?"

"No ma'am. Regretfully, I'm afraid not."

Again Penny was astonished. She had thought she was making all her points and that he was receptive. To be turned down not only disappointed her, but she could not guess why. Hadn't she perfected her "sales pitch," achieved a persuasive approach, practicing it endlessly for a patient Nelldean? She *knew* she had done an excellent job. Why was this man refusing even to allow her to show and explain it to his wife?

Bewilderment made her bold, and Penny asked, "May I ask *why* you want to withhold this treasure of information from the lady of the house?"

That trace of amusement in his eyes moved to his mouth and he smiled almost apologetically. "Because, simply stated, there *is* no lady of the house. I am—alas—not married."

Caught completely off guard by this statement, Penny took a step back, embarrassed. Then suspecting he had led her on intentionally, she drew herself up in dignified indig-

172

nation and retorted, "Well then! Since you're a *bachelor*, living alone, *you* could probably make good use of the contents of this book *yourself!*"

At this the man threw back his head and laughed heartily. In spite of herself, Penny began to laugh too. Then he said, "I'm sorry. Do forgive me. I didn't mean to purposely mislead you. But you must admit—there was no stopping you once you got started!" He took a clean white linen handkerchief from his vest pocket, wiped his eyes, and smiled broadly as he reached for his wallet. "And *of course*, I want to buy one of those marvelous books! You've convinced me. I'm sure it *is* something *no* household should be without," he mimicked her description. "How much?"

The transaction was made. The book changed hands as Penny assured him that it would live up to its promises. Reasserting her professional posture, she walked briskly back to her buggy and climbed in. Without looking back at the man on the porch, who was still watching her, she turned horse and buggy around and headed out the gate and back up the road.

All the way back into town, Penny considered the incident. Used to the rough, rugged, unschooled frontier types that populated the town, coming upon someone like L. C. Boudrey was a pleasant shock. Everything about him was different: his manners, his speech—even though he was dressed casually, his clothes were good quality. His attitude was self-confident yet courteous. And obviously he had a keen sense of humor! Ruefully she recalled how he seemed to enjoy teasing her.

That evening after supper Penny sat at the kitchen table, going over her order book. On Saturdays she took in her receipts and collected her payment from Mr. Miller for the week's sales. Overall, she had done fairly well this past week; the last sale of the day, to L. C. Boudrey, had brought her total to the highest in any week so far.

Studying his signature on her copy of the sales slip, Penny knew it to be the fine penmanship of an educated man. What was such a man doing living alone on an isolated ranch? He was hardly a typical rancher, but she had yet to see a better homestead. She had caught a glimpse of a young orchard behind the house. The man certainly knew how to farm; still, she was curious about him. But then, she had found that all sorts of people had come out west for all sorts of reasons, none the same.

Like *herself*, for instance. She sighed. Someone else's decision had brought *her* here. Now it was up to her to make a go of it. Nelldean's repeated suggestion that she apply for a homestead kept coming back to her. Maybe she really *could*. Make a real home for herself and Belinda. She'd come this far—with God's help—so why not?

The only troubling part was that even though Nelldean constantly reassured her that someday it would just happen, Belinda still refused to talk. Maybe a homestead would be the answer. If they were settled on their own, maybe then Belinda would feel secure enough and become again the normal child she had been. Penny prayed earnestly that she would be shown clearly if this is what she should do.

Only a week or so later it seemed she got her answer, in the form of a means of additional income. When Penny went into Miller's Mercantile to get a new supply of books, Mr. Miller greeted her with the question, "What would you think of adding some new items to your line?"

"It depends on what they are," she answered cautiously. She wasn't yet so sure of her sales technique that she was ready to try to close one sale with the offer of something else.

Mr. Miller held up two engravings, one of Ulysses S. Grant and one of Robert E. Lee, suitable for framing.

"Take your pick," he said with a twinkle in his eyes. "American heroes both." He grinned. "Dependin' which side of the fence you're on."

Penny studied the two portraits for a moment, then said, "I'll take three of each. Let the customers decide which one they want."

Sales of the engravings were brisk. Westerners, Penny discovered, were patriotic and, whichever man they preferred, easily swayed by political persuasion and past regional loyalty. The engravings became a popular item. Some customers even purchased *both*! By the middle of the week, she had already made more than any previous week.

Chapter 20

*P*enny's spirits were high. The books were selling well, and with the added commodity of the engravings, her nest egg was building up beyond the modest hopes she'd had when she started.

"I knew you could do it," Nelldean told her. "Now, what's keeping you from going ahead and getting you a homestead?"

"You know, Nelldean, I think you're right. Maybe I'll just do it."

It was a Saturday morning bright with sunshine, not a cloud in the sky, and Penny was preparing to go downtown to pick up her week's wages from Mr. Miller. She was taking Belinda with her as a special treat.

"Good girl!" Nelldean said approvingly as she tied Belinda's bonnet strings and gave the little girl a kiss. "Have a nice time, you two," she called after them as hand in hand they went out the door.

As Penny came down Main Street she saw a tall man striding down the opposite sidewalk. She thought there was something familiar about him, and then she recognized him. It was the rancher to whom she'd sold a book a few weeks before. She watched him as he stopped, unlocked

GRACE BALLOCH
MEMORIAL LIBRARY
625 North Fifth Street
Spearfish SD 57783-2311

the door, and went into one of the buildings across the street. It was then that she noticed the small sign: ATTORNEY AT LAW. He was a lawyer! No wonder he didn't look like a rancher.

Penny went on into the mercantile. Mr. Miller was leaning on the counter perusing a mail-order catalog when she came inside. He glanced up and, seeing Belinda was with her, greeted them both warmly.

"Well, good morning, ladies! And how's that pretty little miss today? Looks like you might need somethin' sweet. Maybe a licorice stick? Is that all right with Auntie?" He looked at Penny for permission. "Shall we let her choose for herself?"

Penny smiled and nodded and let Belinda toddle over to the candy case. Putting two chubby hands on the glass, she stared in for a few seconds, then shyly pointed to a twisted pink-and-white peppermint stick.

Over her head he whispered the words, "Not talking yet, eh?"

Since they had become good friends Penny had confided her concerns about Belinda. She shook her head and said, "We're hoping it will happen soon."

He got out the candy and handed it to the little girl, then went over to the cash register and opened up the cash drawer. Penny followed him over to the counter.

"You know, her parents are both dead, and I'm thinking of adopting Belinda. I might be needing some legal assistance. Could you suggest someone trustworthy?"

"Boudrey," he said. "Couldn't find no finer fella than L. C. Boudrey. Smart as they come, but nice and as friendly as kin, what with all his ed'cation. To see him now you'd never have knowed how he looked when he first come here. Thin as a rail, he was. Pale as a ghost. He was in right poor health. Sent out here by his doctor for his health is what I heard. Mebbe to die? But before long he was fit as a

12974

fiddle. All this pure air, and workin' his ranch, goin' fishin' and ridin' his horses is just what he needed," Mr. Miller chuckled. "Jest what the doctor ordered, as they say. Anyways, after a while he opened his law office. 'Fore that nobody knowed he was a lawyer and all. No siree." Mr. Miller began counting out her money. "Well, now, here you are, Miss Sayres. You know, I'm thinking, come spring, we might add some other items to your wares. You've done mighty good selling, so there's no limit to what we could offer your customers. Might have to get you a bigger buggy—"

"That sounds interesting, Mr. Miller." Penny tucked the little roll of bills into her purse. "Thank you and thanks for the recommendation of the lawyer—Mister . . . ah, Mister . . . ?"

"Boudrey, L. C."

"Thanks," Penny said again. "Come, Belinda." She took the little girl's hand and left the store, feeling just a bit guilty for having rather deviously satisfied her own curiosity about the puzzling man she had met on her sales circuit.

From his office, L. C. Boudrey saw Penny coming out of Miller's Mercantile. He got up from his desk and went to the window. Ever since that day she had appeared at his ranch so unexpectedly, he had thought about her, wondered about her, hoped to see her again. He had not wanted to start tongues wagging in this small town by making direct inquiries about her, and so she remained a mystery. Usually he did not come into town on weekends; there was so many chores, work to do on his place. But today he had come in to go over some papers dealing with a land sale. This seemed like too lucky a coincidence to pass up.

He reached for his hat and was out the door within a minute. She was standing directly across the street when L. C. noticed the little girl with her and the striking resemblance between them. His heart sank. She must be married. And that was her child? Why was she working so hard as a book agent? So eager to make a sale? Could she be a widow? Or was her husband away at the gold fields? Many a gold-hungry man left wife and children behind. Like a good lawyer, he looked for evidence before coming to a conclusion. And as a lawyer, he had learned to be discreet. Still, he was determined to find out her status or stop thinking about her. He crossed the street.

"Hello, there," he greeted her, feeling foolish that he could not address her by her name, married or single. He blamed himself for feeling awkward. He should have looked at the sales slip for the book that was still in his waistcoat pocket. He had been so taken by her winsomeness, the very novelty of her occupation, so preoccupied by her selling ability that somehow her name had not even seemed important. More fool he!

Penny looked at him for a long moment before answering. It seemed uncanny that she had just found out all about him from Mr. Miller, and then suddenly there he was.

Mistaking her disconcerted expression for one of nonrecognition, Boudrey's self-confidence was jolted. She seemed to be trying to place him. With dismay he thought she did not even remember *him,* while *she* had made such an unforgettable impression on him.

Anxious to jog her memory and make a connection, he blurted out, "The book is most helpful. It certainly is everything you said it was ... I'm very pleased I bought it—" Surreptitiously he glanced at her left hand to check for a wedding ring. But the little girl was holding it, and he could not see. "Yes, indeed, most pleased, Mrs. . . . . ? Miss . . . ?"

"Sayres," Penny supplied the last name but not the title, so he was as much in the dark as ever. He tried again.

"And who is this pretty little lady?"

"This is Belinda," Penny answered, not thinking to identify the girl as her niece.

Frustrated, Boudrey shifted from one foot to the other and twisted the hat he had removed upon greeting her.

"I'm glad the book is proving helpful, Mr. Boudrey," Penny said and moved aside as if to go on.

Frantic to elicit more information, L. C. did not step aside. Instead he attempted to prolong the encounter. "Lovely day, isn't it? A good one to be out and about canvassing, I expect. I am sure there is a ready market for your estimable product." For once, his lawyer's fluency with words failed him and he came to a floundering stop.

Penny hesitated. Should she remind him this was Saturday, tell him she did not work on the weekends? Perhaps she should mention the engravings? He might buy one or both for his office. No, that would be too pushy. Suddenly Penny felt awkward. Was she getting a sales person's mentality?

Boudrey misinterpreted her silence as he made another futile attempt to discover her real situation. "It was very pleasant to see you. I hope we will meet again." *And often,* he added mentally.

Penny merely smiled and murmured, "That's probably possible," and she walked past him, adding, "Good day, Mr. Boudrey."

Watching her slim figure move gracefully down the wooden sidewalk, L. C. inwardly questioned his failure. Why had he not somehow persisted in discovering if she were married? Perhaps he might have asked after her husband's health in some subtle manner? If she had none, then he could possibly have asked if he might call on her? L. C. derided his own ineptness. At least he knew her name was Sayres and the little girl's name was Belinda. Nothing more.

Dejectedly, L. C. returned to his office. Seeing her for the second time increased the interest she had evoked at the first one. Her cheeks were a becoming pink from the wind, her blue eyes bright, strands of coppery hair had escaped from the rim of her bonnet and curled fetchingly about her face. But there was more than physical attractiveness about her. There was intelligence and sensitivity in her expression, forthrightness in her manner, candor in the beautiful clear eyes. Instinctively he knew there was much more to this lady than met the eye. But how could he get to know her better without being unseemly? Social protocol was not as rigidly adhered to out here as back east. Still, it was clear to see that Miss (Mrs.?) Sayres had a natural refinement, a reticence that precluded any action on his part that might appear crude or indicate that he had taken too much for granted on such slight acquaintance.

Chapter 21

*A*fter that Saturday, Penny and L. C. Boudrey encountered each other often enough for it to be more than coincidence. At least on his part. Since the windows of his office fronted Main Street and were directly opposite Miller's Mercantile, the occasions Penny went there for her books or engravings also seemed the same time Boudrey had the urgent need to purchase something at the general store.

They always exchanged greetings and a few pleasantries, but since Penny was usually in a hurry to start her day of making sales calls, these meetings were brief.

However, the day Penny finally filed for a homestead at the city hall, she met L. C. just as she was coming down the courthouse steps, the papers in her hand.

In a burst of spontaneous excitement she told him what she had just done. He seemed genuinely enthusiastic about her decision.

"Well, it's a big step, I know," she said impulsively, "and one I wouldn't have undertaken without a lot of urging from Nelldean and Bess, to say nothing of beseeching the Lord to be a 'light onto my path'!" Then she stopped suddenly, feeling self-conscious. Maybe L. C.

wasn't a religious man and wouldn't understand her frame of reference.

To her surprise he responded, "Nothing of importance should be undertaken *without* all those things: good advice of friends and people you trust, and prayer. I've seen too many people rush into big decisions without due consideration and deliberation, to say nothing of seeking providential guidance," he said, adding, "marriage being one of the main ones. Even Shakespeare cautioned against that in his most romantic of plays, *Romeo and Juliet*—what he said is applicable even today. People take on the responsibilities of marriage many times 'unadvisedly, suddenly, too like summer lightening.'" He paused, looking a bit embarrassed. "I apologize, Miss Sayres, I am too loquacious. A trait of lawyers, I'm afraid. Forgive me."

"There's nothing to forgive, Mr. Boudrey. I'm impressed by your familiarity with Shakespeare and how it applies to life. I've witnessed just such occasions of which you speak. On the journey west in our wagon train, there were several of those sudden marriages. An itinerant preacher would happen along, going back east mostly, and couples who hadn't said much more than 'howdy' to each other before decided that while he was there they might as well get married. I know Nelldean used to shake her head over them, saying she hoped that once those couples settled down, their marriages would prove to have been 'made in heaven,' not on the Oregon Trail!"

They both laughed and L. C. remarked, "Mrs. Hardison is both wise and witty."

"Yes. I rely on her advice and good sense," Penny said. Remembering Nelldean's most recent advice about adopting Belinda, Penny started to broach the subject, thinking L. C. could probably tell her what had to be done legally.

But before she could, he surprised her by asking, "Where

is your sweet little daughter today? It is certainly inspiring to see such devotion between mother and child."

"You mean Belinda?" Penny asked. "But I'm not her mother. She's my niece, Mr. Boudrey. You see, my brother and sister-in-law, Belinda's parents, both perished on the way here. Our original destination was California. But after their deaths—well, it wasn't possible for me to go on alone. Nelldean kindly invited us to join her and Nate in their wagon. That's how we happened to come to Oregon."

L. C.'s spirits soared. Although he felt a natural sympathy for the tragic circumstances Penny had just explained, he could not deny the truth. At last, to know that Penny was neither a married woman nor a widow but a single lady caring for an orphaned niece was good news indeed. His admiration for her fortitude and generosity skyrocketed. Recovered from his relief, L. C. intended to ask another question, but Penny said, "It was nice to see you again, Mr. Boudrey."

He quickly rejoined, "And a pleasure to see you again, *Miss* Sayres. Do give my kindest regards to Mrs. Hardison, won't you? "

"Mrs. Hardison? You've met Nelldean?"

"Yes, we were introduced by the Reverend Mr. McCall, with whom I happened to be conversing the other day when she happened along. She was kind enough to invite me to call. I hope that meets with your approval?"

Penny concealed her amusement but thought, *That sly boots, Nelldean! Always "Johnny on the spot," wasn't she? And never a word about the invitation!* Of course, L. C. Boudrey was not only a prosperous lawyer and rancher—handsome and personable—but he was also the perfect candidate, in Nelldean's opinion, of the *"someday"* husband and father for Belinda she was always assuring Penny would come along.

Suppressing a smile, Penny replied demurely, "Why, of

course, Mr. Boudrey." They parted at the post office, and Penny went on her way, planning to gently chide Nelldean about her matchmaking.

Dearest Grams,

I don't know whether or not you will be surprised at the action I have just taken. I have embarked on a great adventure! "Another one?" I can see you now saying, shaking your head as you read this letter. I think you will agree it is a wise decision, considering Belinda and I are now out here, I have a well-paying job, good, faithful friends who care for us both and support my action. As of yesterday, I am a homesteader. It is what Brad wanted to do, and in a way I am doing it for him and for his daughter. It will one day belong to Belinda.

It is getting to be spring now and Oregon is very beautiful. The land I've filed for is next to Nelldean's grandson Nate's. He stayed on his land all winter even when it snowed and he now has a nice building, a barn and plans to raise a dairy herd. On the other side of my claim is land owned by a local lawyer.

Here Penny paused and thought about L. C. Boudrey. Since Nelldean's none-too-subtle invitation, he had become a frequent visitor. The first time he had arrived at the house, he came, as Nate put it, "loaded for bear." He carried two bouquets, one for Nelldean, the other for Bess, both of which he presented with a flourish, as well as a box of chocolates for Penny and a shiny red top for Belinda.

Mindful of their conversation about his familiarity with Shakespeare, Penny had to bite her tongue not to tease him by quoting, "Beware of the Greeks when they come bearing gifts." She didn't want to make him feel uncomfortable when he was obviously trying to make a good impression.

Penny had to admit he was an excellent conversationalist. It was wonderful to have someone who had such a wealth of knowledge without being pompous or the least

185

arrogant. He could also laugh and talk on plenty of mundane subjects. He discussed ranching with Nate and even got down on the floor to spin the top for Belinda.

Although Nelldean and Bess always tactfully disappeared at intervals during Mr. Boudrey's visits, Belinda was their constant chaperone. Because Penny's work kept her away most days, when she was at home, Belinda hardly let Penny out of her sight.

Penny knew Nelldean was hoping the friendship would turn into courtship, but Penny wasn't at all sure how she felt about L. C. Boudrey's attentions. She had so much on her mind these days: Belinda, first and foremost, and all that lay ahead of her on their homestead. Putting all these random thoughts aside, Penny went back to her letter to Grams.

> When it gets to be summer, we will spend more time out there. Nate has promised to help me with the building that has to be erected on the property, and we'll probably spend the nights there while the weather is still fine. It will be a grand place for Belinda to play. I know you may feel some caution about what I've done, Grams—a woman alone with a small child. But really, things are different out here. Women have a great deal more independence. So many women are widows, having survived the long journey west but having lost their husbands on the way. There was much sickness—both cholera and smallpox—in our wagon train, taking a toll on those who had not been vaccinated. I see all around me women who have taken bold steps to support themselves and their children, opening boarding houses, restaurants, businesses of all kinds. There is a spirit here I cannot exactly explain; it's as if the ones who made it all the way out here are going to stay—not only "make the best of it" but to make the *most* of it.
>
> Nelldean has been a wonderful support. She could not be more generous, caring, helpful if we were her own blood kin. So has Bess. I feel they have become a second family to

Belinda and me. So I hope you won't worry too much about us. I have faith that everything will work out for us out here. I remind myself often of your favorite quote: "Everything works together for good for those who love the Lord and are called according to His purpose." I believe that everything that has happened so far has been for "His purpose," although I don't understand it all. Keep well, dear Grams, and God bless.

Always,
Your devoted Penny

Chapter 22

*T*hat summer was the busiest and happiest Penny
could ever recall, different from any other summer of
her life. She had never worked so hard nor enjoyed it so
much. Her days were filled, and her heart sang with praise
to the Creator who had given her a newfound joy in living.
Sometimes while on the trail she had felt a hundred years
old. Especially after Brad and Thea's deaths, she had been
weighted down with a thousand sorrows and uncertainties
about the future. Now she could see a new life forming,
one she had never dreamed would be hers, one that each
day brought more and more into reality.

Owning her own land deepened Penny's appreciation of
nature. When she would stop work at noon to eat the picnic lunch Nelldean had packed for her, Penny would sit in
quiet contemplation of the rolling hills that surrounded
her, listening to the whisper of the gentle wind through
her stands of pine and cedar. *Mine,* she would think bliss-
fully—*mine to marvel at and give thanks for; mine to cut for
wood to build a house with and to burn in the stove.*

Nate often joined them for their midday meal. From
the skinny boy he'd been on the trail, he had grown tall,
filled out with the build of a man. All his newly acquired

knowledge and skills, after nearly a year of homesteading, he shared liberally with Penny as little by little she developed her land. In spite of his new maturity, Nate still had a boyish grin and a endearing openness. He had a wonderful way with Belinda and had become like a brother to Penny.

And of course, Nelldean had grown even dearer. The bond forged between the older woman and Penny on the trail had become stronger than ever. More and more Penny turned to her for advice and just for the comfort of sharing her innermost thoughts and feelings—particularly about Belinda. What would she do if Belinda was still not speaking when she became old enough to go to school?

Over and over Nelldean would say, "You just have to trust God to work this out, Penny."

Penny knew she was right, but it did not always banish the shadow of fear that Belinda would always be handicapped by the tragedy that had blighted her young life. Sometimes Penny felt it was unfair to burden Nelldean with her own problems, but there was no one else. It wasn't as though she had a husband or Belinda had a father to help shoulder these concerns. She was, after all, alone in the world—and all Belinda had.

Penny tried not to dwell on this. She tried to follow Nelldean's admonition—to live and enjoy each day. For the most part that summer, that's what Penny did.

Another frequent visitor to the homestead that summer was L. C. Boudrey, whose own land was adjacent to Penny's. Once he had found out that Penny was single, his original attraction to her developed rapidly. Because of his uncertain health before then, he had postponed serious courtships. The doctors' dire prediction had been that he had, at best, only a few years to live, and that those would probably be spent in invalidism. Now, with new health and new land, everything seemed possible.

With a freedom he had never felt before, he sensed an optimism about the future and believed he had met the woman who would be his wife: Penny Sayres. Unlike most of the women he knew, she was not married to some miner, for whom she was waiting to return from the gold fields, nor to a soldier at some remote outpost where she and the child could not follow. Neither was she a widow mourning a warrior hero fallen in battle. Every time he saw her his feelings for her grew stronger. He was, however, unsure if she could reciprocate his feelings.

Although she seemed always friendly and glad to see him, grateful for his offers to help with the building and land, their relationship remained merely that of neighbors and friends. L. C. felt it hopeless to expect more. In the first place, he hardly ever had a chance to truly be alone with her. Nelldean, Bess, and Nate were never far away. And of course, there was always Belinda. Although he had not had much experience with children, he found the little girl very appealing and longed to do something to alleviate some of Penny's concern about her. There just never seemed to be an opportunity to discuss it with Penny. By the end of summer L. C. began to wonder if he were on a futile quest.

August merged into the early weeks of September, the most beautiful time of the Oregon year. As the days grew shorter and time out at the homestead grew even more precious, Penny was still making her rounds, selling her line of books, calendars, and almanacs every weekday and spending most of the weekends working on her shelter.

One Saturday in early September, L. C. rode out, hoping to have a little time with her. As he dismounted, he saw Penny just descending a ladder from the roof of the small shed she was building. He saw her but she had not yet seen him arrive. He tethered his horse under the shade of a giant fir tree and stood watching her as she caught Belinda up in her arms and swung her around. Then putting her cheek against the little girl's round, rosy one, she hugged her. Watching this scene, he caught his breath. He felt his heart move within him. Like a sudden shaft of light passing through his mind, he saw as clearly as if it were projected on a "magic lantern" screen his long-held dream come to life. During the long months of his illness, he had rarely allowed himself the luxury to dream. Life had seemed precariously uncertain. But now, seeing Penny and Belinda, the dream seemed a reality. The hope of happiness, of a wife and a child of his own ... Suddenly he *knew* Penny was that woman with whom he would want to spend his life, to be his heart's companion, the mother of his children. He had never visualized exactly what she would look like, but seeing Penny holding Belinda, their two heads touching, one golden-red, the other auburn, gleaming in the sunshine, L. C. knew.

He felt a terrible longing to make it all come true. But how could he tell her? Penny had always kept him at arm's length. Whenever the conversation had become the least bit personal, she had turned it by making some amusing remark or by finding something she had to attend to immediately. Always she remained somehow beyond his reach. Was it only coincidence or was it by intent? Did she sense his attraction and wish to discourage it? Yet she always seemed glad to see him when he came. L. C. sighed.

There was so much more to Penny Sayres—resourceful, courageous, strong. What a woman she was! But on the other side of the coin of his admiration was the question, Was she too independent to need a man—even a man who would love her for those very qualities and respect that very independence?

His thoughts came to an abrupt end when she suddenly looked over Belinda's head and saw him. After setting the little girl back on the ground, she waved.

"Come see how much we've done. Nelldean says we

should have a roof-raising celebration when we've nailed the last shingle."

L. C. walked over to where she stood. He looked up at the small building, now nearly completed, and admired it with her.

"Won't you stay and have some lemonade and gingerbread with us?" Penny invited. "Bess brought some out earlier, then stole away my helper," she laughed gaily. "She captured Nelldean to help her at the church this afternoon. They're having a blackberry festival this weekend. Like blackberry pie? There'll be a whole mountain of them at the social."

Penny went down to the stream that ran close by and brought back the tin container of lemonade they had placed securely between rocks in the water to chill. She poured them each a tumbler full, then opened the basket in which a loaf of gingerbread was wrapped in a blue and white checkered napkin, and cut slices for the three of them.

After they ate, Belinda took the rag doll Nelldean had made her on the trail, the one she was rarely without, over to a shady spot at a little distance from where Penny and L. C. sat. She placed the doll against the trunk of the tree and began making a playhouse from twigs and leaves.

A quiet peace settled over the little valley. L. C. glanced at Penny. She had never looked prettier. Golden freckles sprinkled across the bridge of her nose and on her lightly tanned skin. The afternoon sun sent small sparkles of light through her hair, which was twisted up carelessly into a knot on top of her head. He found himself longing to touch the stray curls that spiraled onto her neck. Would this be a good time to tell her that he had fallen in love with her?

Even as he asked himself this he saw the expression on Penny's face change. She was watching Belinda picking wildflowers and fashioning them into little bouquets. The tenderness on Penny's face as she gazed at the little girl brought a sharp question to L. C.'s mind. Uncertainty took the place of decision. Was there room in Penny's heart for anyone else? As he was asking himself this, she sighed and when she turned to him her eyes were moist.

"I wish I knew what to do. If only I could help her some way—to find her voice again."

L. C. recognized this as a rare opportunity. He did not want to ruin this moment of intimacy, nor did he want to overstep the bounds of the confidence she was tentatively extending.

She proceeded to tell him about their journey west, what they had been through, and how Belinda had stopped speaking after Thea's death. "That's why the decision to stay here was so hard for me to make, even though I really had nothing to go back to. . . ." Her voice trailed off. "I've wondered if I shouldn't have made the effort to go back for *her* sake. Maybe there's a doctor back east who could do something—"

"But from what you told me it's not medical—," L. C. ventured. "I mean, there's no physical cause for her not to talk. She talked before, didn't she—"

"Oh, yes. Well, not always understandable, except for a few words like Mama, Dada, Penny, milk cow—that sort of thing. But she babbled constantly as though she knew what she was saying. And she certainly isn't . . . well, there's nothing wrong with her mind. She's smart as she can be. Nelldean says in time she'll talk."

"Nelldean's right, you know. I know men who were in the war who went dumb from shock. Maybe that's what's happened to Belinda. From all that happened to your wagon train . . . I mean, how can a small child understand all those terrible things? Maybe the only way she could

193

handle it was to retreat back into babyhood—into not having to put it all into words."

The little frown that had puckered Penny's brows together over her troubled eyes cleared. "Yes. You're probably right. And Nelldean is too. I just need to have more faith. She keeps reminding me of Mark 7:37: 'He makes both the deaf to hear and the mute to speak.' I just hope Belinda's healing isn't dependent on my believing it will happen."

Penny looked so sad that L. C. longed to reach out, take her in his arms, and comfort her. Much as he longed to, he knew it was not the time. All uncertainty about his own feelings vanished. Everything within him yearned to comfort and assure her that she need not worry or go through this *alone*. He was sure now that he wanted to take care of her *and* Belinda, to make things secure and safe for her whatever happened. But he realized it was too soon. He had to make her trust him first. . . .

Just then Nate Hardison came thundering down the hill on his horse and the moment of intimacy ended. Nate was one of Belinda's favorite people, and as he jumped off his horse, she ran toward him. He lifted her up into his saddle, where she smiled happily.

"How's it goin'?" Nate asked Penny, cheerfully leading the horse and little rider over to where she and L. C. were sitting.

The conversation became general then, of tree felling, timber, boards, caulking, fence posts, and rafters.

Then Nate grinned and said, "Trout are plentiful in the pond upstream. How about goin' fishin'? Catch us a few browns we can have for supper? Gramma and Bess can fry us up a batch and some good ol' cornpone with it!"

From the look on Belinda's face, there was no doubt she understood what Nate had proposed. She began to clap her chubby hands together. Nate got her down from the horse, saying, "Come on, Belinda, let's cut us some birch poles for rods. I'll get one for you, Penny," he called over his shoulder as, hand in hand, he and Belinda headed for the edge of the stream.

L. C. got to his feet and said good-bye. As he mounted his horse, he saw Penny hurrying off in the direction Nate and Belinda had gone. He rode back to town wishing he'd been invited to go fishing too.

Chapter 23

One September evening not long after L.C.'s visit, Penny was on her way home from a long day of selling, and her thoughts turned to Belinda. Would she ever speak again? She seemed happy enough: no tantrums, no moping, no visible signs that might be attributed to the tragic happenings of her young life other than her refusal to speak. Every characteristic was that of a normal three-year-old child. Penny knew there was nothing wrong with her mind. Belinda reacted to everything about her, her eyes held intelligence and responsiveness. When Penny played word games or acted out stories with Belinda's dolls or played tricks that might make her react verbally, Belinda enjoyed it all immensely, laughing out loud, clapping her hands, playing the games. But still she didn't talk.

Penny sighed. She couldn't be with the little girl every minute. When Penny was out working on her route, Belinda seemed quite content to stay with Nelldean and Bess, who adored the little girl. Penny knew she was lucky to have them taking care of Belinda while she earned money to support them. But maybe—suddenly, a thought struck her. Just *maybe*—that was *it*! With the two grandmas catering to Belinda's every whim, anticipating her needs so that she never even needed to ask for anything, there was no necessity for the child to talk!

Penny put the buggy in the lean-to, unharnessed Jebo, slipped a feed bag over his nose, and went into the house, still deep in thought. She found Nelldean in the kitchen, sewing one of her sunbonnets. Since coming to Oregon City, Nelldean had got a thriving little business going making sunbonnets. Mr. Miller carried all she could supply and paid her a nice sum for each one.

She greeted Penny cheerfully. "Have a good day? Belinda's already in bed. She fell asleep whilst I was rockin' her. I kept your supper hot on the back of the stove. Sit yourself down and I'll serve you."

Penny pulled out one of the chairs and sat down gratefully.

"You're too good to me, Nelldean, you spoil me. Spoil us both. Me and Belinda!"

"Nuthin' of the kind!" Nelldean retorted. "I like doin' for folks. And you and Belinda's like my own. People what's been through what we've been together get like this—," she held up crossed fingers and quoted, "Ecclesiastes 4:9— 'a threefold cord is not easily broken.' That's us: you, me, and Belinda."

"What about Nate? Doesn't he fit in with us too?" Penny teased.

Nelldean put Penny's plate of steaming pot roast, potatoes, and cabbage in front of her, then sat down again across from her at the table.

"Well, I've got some news to tell you," Nelldean said picking up her sewing again and frowning at the ruffle she was slipstitching around the brim. "Nate was by here earlier; got me to sew on a button or two—all slicked up he was." She paused significantly. "Goin' courtin'." She glanced at Penny for her reaction.

"Courting? Nate?" Penny's fork halted halfway to her mouth.

"Yessiree. Zeire McCall, no less. Reverend McCall's daughter. Seems he met her at the blackberry social and, well—"

"Do you think—I mean is it serious?"

Nelldean chuckled, "Seems so. Leastways, he said he cain't wait till spring to frame up his house. Suddenly, sleeping in the barn he put up don't seem to suit."

"Nate thinking about getting married!" Penny shook her head.

"Well, maybe not right away, but—," she paused for a few seconds before going on. "It's the best thing that could have happened. I'm happy about it. She's a real sweet girl."

"But what about you, Nelldean? You came out here to be with Nate, to live with him on the homestead."

"Oh, honey, I didn't 'spect Nate to stay a bachelor forever. Nor do I 'spect to live forever. Nate's got a good head on his shoulders, smart and responsible for his age. He's got a nice homestead started, planted an orchard. It could've gone another way entirely—what with all the temptations out here for a single man. And you know what Scripture says: 'It's not good for man to be alone.'"

Nelldean stopped and looked over her spectacles at Penny for a long moment, as if expecting her to say something.

Penny suppressed a smile. Nelldean was always hinting that L. C.'s intentions toward her were serious, but Penny dismissed them. She had already taken on as much as she could handle. Marriage certainly wasn't in her plans. Not now, not yet. Maybe not ever. Her first responsibility was toward Belinda. Until Belinda was completely recovered, nothing else was important. But now she was concerned about Nelldean. With Nate making plans of his own, what about his grandmother?

Impulsively Penny reached across the table and squeezed Nelldean's arm.

"Well, you'll always have a home with us, Nelldean. Next spring my house will be going up, and we'll all live there as snug as can be."

Nelldean's eyes misted, and she had to remove her glasses and wipe them before replying. "Don't forget about yourself, Penny. You've got a life of your own too."

"I won't, and I know I do, Nelldean. But right now Belinda is more important. I've been thinking a lot about how to get her talking. I think I need to spend more time alone with her. And this is what I'm thinking. The weather is still nice; the mornings are cool, but the days are mostly sunny and warm." As she spoke a plan began to form in Penny's mind. "I want to take Belinda on a little camping trip this next weekend. She'd love it. Remember how I used to put her on the saddle with me on the trail? We'll take blanket rolls, gear, and enough food for a couple of days. We'll fish and hike, and maybe I can get her talking. If we're out there alone together, maybe she'll have to start asking for things—speaking!"

Nelldean looked thoughtful. "Yes, that just might do it. At least you can give it a try. She's a good little camper. It just might work, Penny."

With Nelldean's encouragement Penny went ahead with her plans. Although Bess was more constrained in her support of the idea.

"I don't know, Penny," she said doubtfully. "You folks ain't been out here long enough to know, but Oregon weather, especially this time of year, is mighty changeable. It might turn real quick."

Bess tended to be a worrywart, and Penny blandly dismissed her warning. "We'll take plenty of blankets and warm clothes," Penny assured her and went on packing.

When told about their adventure, Belinda seemed delighted and began to help getting ready, bringing her doll and a favorite raggedy blanket to be included in the packing. Penny filled the saddle bags with enough supplies for a couple of days. Then she placed Belinda astride the saddle, then mounted herself. With admonitions from Nelldean and Bess to be careful, they set out.

The morning was glorious. The sun touched the leaves on the trees, turning them to brilliant yellow and russet all along the roadway out of town.

"We're going to have such a wonderful time, honey," Penny told her. "We'll go out to the homestead first, then we can climb up into the hills, find a stream to fish in, explore the other side of their property, pick wildflowers—" She felt the child's arms tighten around her waist. "You'll like that, won't you, honey? They're so many fun things we can do. Then we can make a camp, build a fire to cook our meals. Nothing more delicious than fresh-caught fish fried along with potatoes sliced with wild onions found along banks of the creek, is there, Belinda? And tonight we'll sleep under the stars in our blanket rolls like a couple of cowboys!" She heard Belinda's lilting little laugh and knew the child was understanding and enjoying the prospect. *Please God*, Penny prayed. *Maybe, just maybe, when we're alone, Belinda might talk again.*

That first day was wonderful. The fresh air revived Penny, who had worked especially hard all week so as not to feel guilty by missing two good working days. The further they went, the more reassured Penny felt that she had not made a mistake deciding to stay in Oregon. They would be happy on their homestead; she would create a real home for Belinda and herself. As they rode along she could picture herself planting fruit trees on the sloping hills, putting in a large vegetable garden, perhaps, and having some milk cows and goats. More and more she could envision the life they could have here. If only Belinda would recover her speech. . . .

When the shadows on the hills began to shroud the sun,

Penny decided to camp for the night. There was a rippling stream and large trees with low sweeping branches under which they could be safely sheltered and spread their blanket rolls. She set Belinda busily gathering small twigs and branches to get a fire started while she got out a frying pan and the slices of bacon Nelldean had wrapped in cheesecloth in their food pack. She got a can full of water from the stream and made a pot of the best coffee she had ever tasted from the sweet clear water. They ate hungrily after the day out in the open, and afterward Belinda looked drowsy. As the moon began to rise over the tips of the pines, Penny gathered Belinda close in her arms and sang her to sleep with an old hymn she had learned in childhood: "How gracious you have been to me, O Lord, how bountiful in thy gifts." Her voice rose sweetly upward into the night air.

They awakened at first light. They rolled up their blankets and washed their faces in the stream. Penny stirred up the fire, made coffee, then they ate the potatoes they had buried in the embers the night before to roast.

It was a splendid cloudless blue day. Invigorated, Penny decided to climb higher up into the hills. The sun was gilding everything, the light frost melting away in glistening diamonds, the aspen trees along the path quivered in the crisp breeze. As they wound up through the wooded hillside they could look down into the valley and see the colorful patches of red maples, the golden willows, and the silver ribbon of the stream bending through. The way became steeper and every so often Penny turned the horse aside to let her rest and nibble at the grasses. It was a different kind of day than their first one but just as enjoyable, and the scenery at this level was even more spectacular. Penny was filled with awe at the wonder of God's creation.

At this elevation, however, the day seemed to darken sooner and she began looking for a place to camp for the night. They reached a clearing surrounded by magnificent cedars. The fallen needles had made a soft mattress on which they could lay their bedrolls to sleep in comfort from the wind that was growing quite chilly. Penny made a fire and they cooked the trout they had caught the day before. With a dessert of dried apples and shortbread brought from home they had a fine supper. By the time they finished it was already dark, so they tucked in for the night on a mattress of pine needles under a lean-to of sweeping cedar boughs. Belinda went straight to sleep, but Penny, though pleasantly tired from the exertion of the day, lay awake listening to the wind sigh through the branches, and she prided herself on her accomplishments. Who, knowing her back in Dunwoodie, would ever have thought that she could take a child and set out alone on a three day camping trip? It even amazed *her.* As she finally drifted off to sleep, she felt proud of her newly developed independence and capability.

But the minute she opened her eyes, the proverbial prediction popped into her mind: "Pride goeth before a fall." After waking, she lay there for a moment listening. She heard nothing but silence. Not a whisper of wind, nor the stirring of a tree limb. Slowly it came to her. It had snowed during the night and a white blanket of heavy snow covered everything for as far as she could see. Moving carefully she slid out from under her bedroll. As she did her head hit a low branch of the tree under which they were sleeping, and a shower of snow landed on her! After brushing the snow out of her eyes, Penny marveled at the beauty of it all.

Then slowly she realized their predicament. This must be one of those "freak" snowstorms Penny had heard about. After her first awe at its beauty, Penny decided they had better try to get back to town in case there was more snow in the offing. However, this proved more difficult than she anticipated. The snow was soft and deep, and the trail they had taken coming up was completely obliterated.

The sky, heavy with gray clouds, looked as if there might be more snow on the way. Penny debated whether to try to make it back to the homestead or to remain where she was. Riding a horse with a child clinging to your waist down a steep grade in a snowstorm would be no easy task. But there seemed nothing else to do but try. After a hasty breakfast, Penny packed their bedrolls and saddle bags onto the patient Jebo; then she lifted Belinda up and mounted herself. Slowly, they started back down the hill they had climbed so confidently the day before. Jebo valiantly did his best, but he kept stumbling. Penny held her breath, afraid that she would be pitched off with Belinda and tossed down over the unseen cliffs. Holding tight to the reins, they inched down the hazardous mountainside.

Every so often a tree limb, heavy with snow, would suddenly shift in the wind and dump its load down their backs. At last they managed to get down the mountain and reach a clearing. Penny got off and walked over to the edge where she could see down into the valley. There, very faintly, she made out the outline of the slanted roof of her homestead shelter.

"Oh, thank God!" she breathed a sigh. "It's all right, Belinda, we're almost home!" she called gaily to the child, who was so bundled up that only her little cherry nose peeked out from the scarf and cap.

Torturously they made the last hazardous few miles down. But afternoon shadows were lengthening rapidly and there was definitely a scent of snow in the cold air. Penny led Jebo into the lean-to beside their shack and unloaded him. She took off the saddle and bags, threw a blanket over him, then carried Belinda into the small cabin.

Keeping up cheerful chatter, Penny was grateful that Nate had installed a small stove in addition to her bunk and a couple of chairs. All this was done mainly to fulfill the homestead requirements of building a livable shelter on the property within a year of the claim. At least they had a few supplies here and enough firewood to keep them warm for a day or two.

Contrite at having put themselves in this risky situation, Penny blamed herself. She had been foolhardy and over-confident to take a small child on a camping expedition without making provisions for an emergency. She also knew that by now Nelldean and Bess would be concerned about them, and she felt bad to have caused them any worry.

If the snow continued—if it became one of those blizzards she'd heard about—they could be marooned for days. At the worst, they could freeze to death, if their wood burned out, or if their food gave out, they could starve before anyone could come to rescue them. Before her fears got out of control, Penny recalled Grams' often-used comment: "Don't borrow trouble" or better still "Sufficient for the day. . . ."

Give us this day our daily bread. She *had* that, Penny reminded herself as she unwrapped half a loaf, some cheese. *Manna.* She smiled to herself. God had provided for the complaining Israelites even if they had got themselves as lost in the desert as she had been in the foothills. "Trust in the Lord, and he will provide *all* your needs." *Why do we have to be brought to our knees before we really rely on his gracious providence? "O ye of little faith!"—I'm full of Scripture quotations today,* Penny chided herself in amusement. Nevertheless, she found them comforting.

She got a fire going in the little stove and put some bacon in a skillet. Scooping some snow from outside the door into two buckets, she set one aside to melt so that she could take it out for Jebo to drink. The other bucket she set in front of the stove so that she could later pour it into a kettle to boil for coffee. On the shelf she found a jug of molasses, some canned milk, and a tin of beans. "Enough for a fine supper!" Penny exclaimed triumphantly to Belinda. Their meal turned out to be delicious and satisfying along with fried bacon and what was left of the loaf of bread. Afterward, when Belinda's eyes began to droop sleepily, Penny wrapped her up snugly on the low bunk bed, and Belinda was asleep in a minute.

Sipping a second cup of coffee, Penny went to the window. All she could see was an endless carpet of snow. Involuntarily she shivered. Tomorrow she might have to turn Jebo loose to find the trail back to town. That way someone would surely come looking for them.

"And I'll be ready to eat some humble pie," Penny said to herself as she unrolled her blanket and crawled in beside Belinda. She lay there watching the fire until she too fell asleep.

To her amazement she slept dreamlessly. When she first awakened she could not remember right away where she was. She raised her head and looked around the small cabin. Gradually things came back to mind. Then she saw Belinda standing on a stool looking out the cabin window. "Morning, honey," Penny called to her as she got out of the bunk. Belinda turned to look at her, then pointed her chubby little finger and said over and over, "Snow, pitty snow!"

They were the very words Penny had repeated to her over and over the day before trying to keep her from being afraid as they made their precarious way down the mountainside!

The shock of hearing Belinda's voice momentarily immobilized Penny. Belinda had *spoken.* Actually spoken *out loud*! She *could* speak! She *was* speaking! O dear God, thank you! Penny almost choked on her own rush of thanksgiving. She jumped up and ran over to the little girl. Laughing and crying for joy, Penny hugged Belinda.

"Yes, darling, I see it, I *see* it! Pretty snow." Holding her, Penny looked out to where the new snow was falling, drifting like big goose feathers out of a milky gray sky.

All that long day Penny talked to Belinda and Belinda chattered back. She repeated whatever Penny said. Penny would point to articles of clothing, every item in the cabin, to her eyes, to her nose, to her mouth, her ears, her hair and teeth. The little girl would say it again and again. In between Penny could not resist hugging and kissing her, praising her, which made the little girl laugh merrily.

They invented games, and Penny began to tell her stories. "Once upon a time—," Penny would start, and Belinda would reply, "Once pont da time."

In her joy over Belinda's recovery, Penny alternated between laughter and tears, almost forgetting their predicament. Early in the afternoon she noticed that the pale sun was trying to penetrate the clouds and the listless snow had ceased to fall.

Later still, when she again went to the window to check the weather, Penny saw a figure on horseback coming through the drifts toward the cabin. Pressing her face against the glass, she peered out trying to see better. Had Nelldean sent Nate? But the rider looked taller, broader of shoulder than Nelldean's grandson. His sheepskin collar was turned high, his broad-brimmed slouch hat low so that his face was obscured. But there was something vaguely familiar about him. Penny rushed to the door, flung it open just as the rider dismounted. To her total astonishment she saw it was L. C. Boudrey.

"Oh, I'm *so* glad to see you," she called to him in a voice warm with gratitude. "How did you find us?"

He explained that he had seen them start out on their camping trip from his office window that Friday. Later, he had run into Nell on the street and, after judicious questioning, learned where they were going. Then with the snowstorm, he became worried about them. Since the homestead claim wasn't far from his ranch, he set out to find them—to rescue them, if need be.

"Come in, come in," Penny invited him, taking hold of his arm and bringing him inside.

"You're all right then?" he asked, brushing the snow from the shoulder of his jacket before stepping over the threshold. "And the little one, too?"

"Better than all right. Something wonderful has happened. It's Belinda." Penny ran over to the little girl.

"She's talking?" L. C. asked.

"*Talking?* She hasn't stopped since she first saw the snow early this morning." She picked her up in her arms and coached, "Say hello, darling."

"Heddo dawding!" the child repeated. Penny and L. C. looked at each other, then burst out laughing. Belinda, pleased that she had said something to make the grown-ups laugh, repeated it over and over—"Heddo, dawding, heddo dawding . . ."—interspersed with giggles, until they were all in a hilarious mood.

"It's Mr. Boudrey, Belinda. Boudrey," Penny prompted.

"Bouey! Bouey!" Belinda repeated, laughing.

Penny gave her a squeeze. "Oh, you're a little minx, aren't you! Now say hello properly to Mr. Boudrey."

Belinda stuck her chubby finger in her mouth, then in a very loud voice said, "Bouey! Bouey!" to another round of laughter.

"I can't tell you how happy I am. It's an answer to prayer. A great many prayers. I feel everything's going to be all right now." Penny smiled and poured L. C. a cup of coffee.

"Well, we better start back soon. More snow's predicted, and I'd feel better if we were safely on our way before that

207

happens. Mrs. Hardison and Mrs. Fulton were mighty worried. And, of course, so was I."

"It was so good of you to come all this way out here to find us."

Within the hour, L. C. had packed up, and then Penny and Belinda, bundled up again, mounted. They followed the trail made by L. C. earlier. It would be a slow trip but a safe one.

As they headed out, Penny said, "I can't thank you enough for coming. I'm not sure how long my firewood and food would have lasted."

"No thanks necessary. It gave me a chance I always dreamed about when I was a little boy."

"What was that?"

"Being a knight on horseback coming to rescue a damsel in distress. In this case, *two* damsels," he laughed, nodding toward Belinda.

"Well, it's nice to know dreams sometimes come true," Penny replied.

"Not all do, but we can keep hoping." L. C.'s eyes held amusement and something else Penny could not quite discern. "I must say, though, it was a pretty *capable* damsel I found. You could have done quite nicely on your own for another few days, I'm sure."

Chapter 24

*D*uring Penny's second spring in Oregon, two things happened that brought her to a decision. One was the celebration of Belinda's third birthday, and the other was the announcement of Nate Hardison's intention to wed the preacher's daughter, Zeire McCall. Ever since Belinda had recovered her ability to speak, she had filled the house with childish chatter, endless questions, and merry laughter. Nelldean and Bess were overjoyed at Belinda's recovery, and the child was even more the center of attention.

Penny now had enough money saved to hire a carpenter to build on to the original shed and construct a small house on the homestead where she and Belinda could live and where, when Nate got married, Nelldean would join them.

The night of the engagement party, Penny was late going to bed. She had insisted that Nelldean and Bess, both exhausted by all the preparations, go to bed and let her clean up the kitchen. After all was finished, she pulled a rocking chair up to the window and sat for a long time looking out at a beautiful moonlit night. A night for romance and lovers. She smiled, thinking of the looks exchanged between Nate and Zeire as they had accepted the congratulations and well wishes of friends. Sipping a cup of tea, Penny let her mind wander back to some of her own romantic dreams. Dreams that seemed to have been those of a girl she now hardly knew.

What had happened to her? All sorts of things had made her grow up and become a realist, a person who did not allow herself the luxury of dreams.

Enough! she told herself and quickly got up, put away her cup, banked the fire in the stove, and tiptoed into the small bedroom she shared with Belinda. Looking down at the sleeping child, Penny decided it was time to adopt her legally, time that they became a *real* family. She would need legal advice about how to go about the adoption. L. C. was the logical person to consult.

One day soon afterward she ran into him on Main Street as she was coming from the post office. As always, L. C. seemed happy to see her. Although after "rescuing" them he had been a frequent visitor to the Fulton house, lately he hadn't come quite as often. Penny wondered why. Nelldean had been more to the point when Penny remarked on it one day.

"Why not, indeed?" Nelldean said in a slightly indignant tone of voice. "The man's not a fool. Why should he keep minin' where there's no gold? He don't get much encouragement," she said with a sniff.

"Why, what do you mean? We're always glad to see him. Belinda always rushes to greet him. And I always enjoy his visits."

"Humph. Not so anyone could notice," retorted Nelldean with a little toss of her head.

"Why, Nelldean, how can you say that! I'll always be grateful to him for coming to dig us out that day and being so kind to Belinda."

"I don't think it's *gratitude* he's lookin' for." She gave Penny another look, seemed about to say something, then

210

pressed her lips together. She gave the cake batter she was beating a few hard licks, tapping the wooden spoon on the edge of the stoneware bowl, then said, "Mebbe he's findin' a warmer welcome elsewhere in town. A fine lookin' gentleman like him's bound to catch many a lady's eye and be ushered happily into any parlor in this town."

The conversation might have gone further, but Bess came in. Penny was just as glad. She had other things on her mind at the moment.

She was, however, recalling that exchange with Nelldean as she saw L. C. approaching.

"Good day, Miss Sayres." He tipped his hat and stopped. "How nice to see you."

"And what a coincidence seeing *you*, Mr. Boudrey."

"How's that?"

"Well, I was just thinking about you and—"

"You *were*?"

His eyes lighted up so eagerly she was almost embarrassed to tell him why she had been thinking of him.

"Yes, sometime soon, I want to consult you on a legal matter. I shall come to your office and discuss it, if I may?"

The light seemed to fade from his eyes, but he inclined his head and his voice took on the professionally correct tone.

"Any way I may be of help, I would be most happy to do so."

"I shall make an appointment then in a few days."

"Any time, Miss Sayres, it would be my pleasure." He paused slightly, then asked, "And how is Belinda?"

"Oh, fine! Chattering like a magpie all the time now." Penny was about to say something like, "Why don't you come see for yourself?" but checked herself. Remembering what Nelldean had suggested might be his reason for staying away, Penny felt reluctant to indicate that he had been missed or to issue a particular invitation for him to call.

211

They stood there for a moment, neither making a move to leave. Then L. C. tipped his hat again, bowed, and continued on down the street.

Penny looked after him, puzzled, then with a slight shrug walked home. Among the mail was a letter from Grams. She was anxious to read it since it had been at least three months since she'd heard from her grandmother.

The letter contained much heartfelt relief, happiness, and "Praise the Lords" over the news of Belinda's newfound speech. Grams also enclosed a clipping from the Dunwoodie newspaper, to which she attached an explanatory note: "I thought you'd be especially interested in seeing this item that ran in our *Independent* last week."

"Experienced Guide to Lead Group to California" was the headline. Penny's eyes widened as she read the article:

> Jeremiah Bradshaw, lay evangelist and seasoned traveler, successful traveler of the famous Oregon Trail, will speak tonight at the Town Hall and recruit emigrants to make the trip under his guidance to the rich western territory of California. Mr. Bradshaw's lecture will include pictures of the fruitful orchards, orange groves, and gold fields—

Penny finished reading the rest of the piece with growing disbelief. How could Jeremiah pass himself off as an "experienced guide" when he hadn't even completed the trip? And where was poor Emily in all this? Were they still together? Was she still alive even?

Penny tore up the clipping in disgust. She pitied the poor people who took him at his word and invested in expensive equipment to undertake the journey under his command. She could hardly suppress a shudder remembering her last encounter with Jeremiah. Well, thankfully, that was all in the past. At least *she* would never have to see him or have any contact with him ever again.

The following Friday afternoon, after completing her sales for the week, Penny went to L. C.'s law office. From his window he had seen her coming down the boardwalk. With admiration he watched her cross the street. How attractive she was! The proud lift of her head, the erect, purposeful walk. He went to the door and stood there, waiting for her knock.

"Come in, Miss Sayres."

"You act as though you were expecting me, Mr. Boudrey."

"You did mention that you might be needing some legal assistance, so I am not completely surprised. Won't you have a seat? Now, what can I do for you?"

"I want to fill out papers or whatever is necessary to adopt Belinda," Penny said as she settled herself in the chair L. C. drew up for her to the side of his roll-top desk.

"Since she has no other living relatives and you are her blood kin, that should be easily arranged."

"I want her to be co-owner of the homestead property or at least the beneficiary of my estate—I mean, whatever I accumulate in my lifetime—at my death."

"We can draw up that kind of agreement as well. They would be two separate documents, of course."

"I know nothing of legal matters. Will you take care of this for me then, Mr. Boudrey?"

"Of course, but may I ask a favor of you, Miss Sayres?"

"Certainly."

"Since we have known each other over a period of time now, could you bring yourself to call me by my first name?"

Penny looked surprised and rather amused. He was so serious.

"Why, yes. That is, except—"

"Except?"

"There's something I've wanted to ask you for a long time," she said.

"Ask away."

213

"Well, it's a rather personal question, and I've often been told I am too blunt—"

"Not for me. I like frankness. I encourage it in my clients." He smiled.

"You're sure?"

"Indeed. What would you like to know?"

"I'm curious, how can I call you by your first name when all I know is the initials L. C.?"

Something curious flickered in his eyes regarding her.

"My friends call me Lot," he answered,

"*Lot?* You mean like in the Bible?" Penny exclaimed. Then, thinking her amusement might seem like ridicule, she rushed on: "*Really?* It seems a rather strange name to give a child. Lot was *not* the most heroic of characters in the Bible. One would think that if parents were going to choose a biblical name, another selection, like Abraham or David, might—," she halted, her hand went to her mouth in embarrassment. "Not that I mean to criticize your parents for choosing it, but—" Again she stopped. "It *is* a little unusual, isn't it?"

He laughed. "I wasn't there at the time I was named, so I really had no say in the choice. By the way, is *Penny* your real name?"

"I asked you first," she parried.

"All right. But I warn you, I've only let a few people in on this deep, dark secret. Actually my name is Lancelot. My mother was a devotee of Tennyson and was reading *The Idylls of the King* when she was expecting me. She was entranced by the whole round table legend and named her only son after the shining knight." He smiled. "Unhappily, the famous knight turned out not be quite so chivalrous as she had supposed. I was born and named before she got to the end of the story. And then it was too late. As I was growing up, my family and friends all called me Lance. But when I came out west and hung up my shingle as a lawyer,

214

I just used my initials. Actually, no one else has ever asked me about it before now." He paused. Penny looked as if she were having trouble keeping a straight face. "I know it's pretty unlikely," he added. "I warned you."

"Well, it's not only funny. It's a kind of coincidence—"

"How so? You mean both our mothers gave us 'storybook names'? That is, if I'm assuming correctly that *your real* name, of course, is Penelope. Right? After the noble, patient, faithful wife of Ulysses?"

Penny shook her head. "No. Penny is a nickname from when I was little—and people used to tease me about the color of my hair." She drew out a strand from under her bonnet brim, "Coppery like a penny. Somehow it stuck. Probably because they were all disappointed."

"*Disappointed?*"

"You see, I was named for a distant relative, an elderly cousin, who everyone hoped would be flattered and leave me a fortune when she died. I think she must have been very wealthy, or why else would a family give a child such a name, unless they had hopes of a great inheritance?" Penny laughed. "As it turned out, she wasn't all that rich and in her will left most of her money to a number of cats she adored. Would you believe this particular relative was considered a little eccentric by the rest of the family—*bookish*—*" Mischief danced in her eyes. "That she was considered very suspect . . . a person who read a lot . . . poetry especially."

"But you still haven't told me what your name really is. What is the coincidence you mentioned?"

"Well, if you want to know the truth, my real name is . . . Guinevere!"

"*What? Guinevere? Truly?*"

"Yes, really and truly!"

He threw his head back, roaring with laughter. When

he finally got control of himself, he demanded, "You mean . . . ?"

"*Yes*—her favorite poetic characters were—," and they both finished together, "King Arthur and the knights of the round table!"

"So now we've found out all sorts of things about each other. Anymore hidden secrets, any other family skeletons in your closet you want to confess?" he asked teasingly.

"No, I don't think so. But there is one request I'd like to make."

"Granted," he said promptly. "You don't need to ask. Whatever you want, it's yours."

"That's an unwise statement. Especially for a lawyer," she admonished playfully.

"Go ahead. Ask away. If it's in my power to give it, I will."

"Oh, it is," Penny told him. "You said most of your friends call you Lot?"

He nodded.

"But I'm sure your mother didn't. What did she call you?"

His eyes softened and he answered, "Lance."

"Yes, that's much better. I like that. You asked me to call you by your given name. She must have loved that name. May I call you Lance too?"

"I'd be very pleased if you did—Penny." He said her name almost tenderly.

"Good. Then it's settled." Penny rose. "I must go." She went to the door and stood there for a moment putting on her gloves. "If you don't have other plans, Nelldean told me to be sure to ask if you'd come to supper this evening?"

On his feet, Lance smiled. "Delighted. Do thank her for the gracious invitation."

"I shall." Penny's cheeks dimpled. "See you about six then?"

"With pleasure." He walked with her to the door. There

216

she hesitated a second, then looked up at him with mischief in her eyes. "So what does the C stand for?"

"The C?" He frowned. "Oh, the C! Calhoun! My mother was a southern sympathizer," he laughed.

"Another family skeleton!" She joined in his laughter. "Well, good-bye for now."

His eyes followed her as she went down the steps and over to her small buggy. What a magnificent woman. How lucky any man would be. . . .

As Penny picked up the reins and flicked them lightly across Jebo's back, she glanced back to where L. C. Boudrey—Lance—was still standing in his office door. She waved and he waved back. As she drove off, she realized she was looking forward to the evening more than she had anything for a very long time.

A week later Lance stopped by the house. Nelldean answered the door, then went to call Penny, who was reading to Belinda. Diplomatically, Nelldean coaxed Belinda, with a bribe of cookies, to stay with her while Penny went into the tiny parlor where Mr. Boudrey was waiting.

"I hope I'm not calling at an inconvenient time, but there were a few questions I wanted to ask before I file your adoption request papers. I also wanted to make some suggestions that might facilitate a speedy resolution."

"Yes, of course. You don't foresee any serious problems, do you?"

"No, not really. There's one thing that, as your lawyer, I may want to advise you to change on the application."

"Oh? Well, of course, I should consider very carefully any advice you have. I want this done as speedily as possible. What would you have me change?"

He took a sheaf of papers from his thin leather briefcase and held the top one out for Penny. "See right here, where it says Guinevere Sayres: spinster—I'd like that changed."

"Changed? You mean you'd rather I use Penny, so it won't sound so—so fanciful—to some judge who will be making the decision?"

"No, Guinevere is fine as it is. It's the *spinster* I'd like to see changed."

Penny turned wide puzzled eyes on him.

"Penny, I want that changed to *married*. . . . I want—I am asking you to marry me. . . . You look so surprised. You never guessed?"

She shook her head.

"Didn't you realize I'm in love with you?"

"Perhaps you *think* you are."

"I'm not exactly a boy to confuse attraction or infatuation with love, Miss Sayres."

"And I, Mr. Boudrey, am no longer a girl—full of foolish dreams of romance and knights riding to the rescue on white chargers."

"Ah, but then. . . ." He smiled, rubbed his chin with one hand, his eyes filling with amusement. "You can never tell. And love means different things to different people—"

"Mostly different to men than to women."

"Maybe. But let me at least say this. That very first day we met, I *knew*—though I didn't know *how* I knew. And I didn't know exactly how it would all turn out, knowing life is not always a poem or a story with a happy ending. Still, I knew that somehow we were meant to be together. And I still do," Lance said softly. "Lancelot and Guinevere! Imagine! That is no ordinary coincidence. The more I think about it, the more convinced I am that our meeting was destined. It *had* to be . . . it was so ridiculous, so preordained . . . I'm *never* home at that time of day . . . usually . . . and then you came and—"

"You're too imaginative. Much too imaginative for a *lawyer*!" Penny chided him, trying to be severe. "Lawyers are supposed to be all facts, every *t* crossed, every *i* dotted. Not irrational or fanciful like the rest of us."

"Lawyers are human too, Penny. Lawyers *in love* are maybe even more capable of poetry and romance, because it's unusual for them. I *know* I love you, and I want you to marry me. It's not an impulse. I've been thinking of it for a long time. In fact, lately I've thought of nothing else. Will you, Penny? Will you marry me, change that word *spinster* and become my wife?"

Penny was quiet for what seemed a very long time. But he waited. As a lawyer, he knew about timing: he knew how to wait for a jury to absorb testimony and how to watch for a person to reveal something under cross-examination. He knew how to make a summary statement and assess its impact on a courtroom, how to debate the options and deliberate the verdict. So he waited, all the while longing to gently brush back the coppery hair, touch the smooth curve of her cheek, kiss the sweet, vulnerable mouth. He waited. . . .

The silence lengthened between them, then Penny spoke slowly, "I've been so busy, so preoccupied, I haven't allowed myself to dream of love. I do respect you, and I'm touched and honored that you have asked me to marry you. I think I need time—"

"I understand that. I don't mean to rush or pressure. As for this—," Lance gently withdrew the papers he had handed her "—you can go ahead with this as it is. I used it as a device to propose." He gave a rueful smile. "Lawyer's trick. Forgive me."

Penny studied him for a long minute. From the very first day, she had been impressed by him. As she got to know him she realized he had the all the qualities she had always admired in a man but had never found in one man before. He had overcome his own challenges well, regained his health, and established a law practice and reputation in a

219

new community. He was outstanding in every way: of obvious strength of character, with an optimistic faith, intelligent, honest, and with an expressed desire for a home and lasting love. Nelldean, a trusted judge of character, had extolled his virtues for weeks. Choosing her words carefully, Penny said, "If *we*—you and I—are to be together . . . Belinda and Nelldean come in the package."

"Of course. Just what I've always wanted . . . a family," he said, and reaching out, he took her hand. "Whenever you're ready, if the answer is yes—we can resubmit these papers with both our names on it." He raised her hand to his lips and kissed it.

Penny felt the sadness lift, the loneliness that had been her companion for all these months. Maybe it was possible to love deeply, to discover a life companion with whom to share the years that lay ahead of her, to create a real home for Belinda. A warm sweetness filled her as her eyes met the ones regarding her so lovingly.

They talked quietly of immediate action and future plans. When at length he rose to leave, she walked with him into the hall. At the door he turned, and she allowed him to draw her into his arms. He cupped her chin in one hand, raised it. Looking down into her upturned face, a powerful emotion swept over him as he realized his long-held dream was coming true. He bent and kissed her softly. Her response was all he had ever imagined.

When he had somewhat regained his composure, he whispered earnestly, "I want so much for us to be together to make a home for us and Belinda. A real home is what I've always wanted, and now I know who I want to share it with me."

"How can we miss?" Penny could not resist demanding. "That is, *if* we follow all the tenets expounded in *Handbook for Housewives: A Complete Guide to the Art of Creating a Harmonious Home, a Happy Husband, and Healthy Children*."

She could hear him still chuckling as he walked down the path and out the gate. Standing at the door, she was filled with optimism. "Lancelot and Guinevere! Maybe there *is* a Camelot, after all—and we've found it."

WESTWARD DREAMS SERIES

A Distant Dawn

WESTWARD DREAMS SERIES

A Distant
Dawn

JANE PEART

Book 4

ZondervanPublishingHouse
Grand Rapids, Michigan

A Division of HarperCollinsPublishers

A Distant Dawn
Copyright © 1995 by Jane Peart

Requests for information should be addressed to:

ZondervanPublishingHouse
Grand Rapids, Michigan 49530

Library of Congress Cataloging-in-Publication Data

Peart. Jane.
    A distant dawn / Jane Peart.
        p. cm. — (Westward dream series ; bk. 4)
    ISBN: 0-310-41301-X (softcover)
    1. Frontier and pioneer life—West (U.S.)—Fiction. 2. Women pioneers—
West (U.S.)—Fiction. I. title. II. Series: Peart, Jane. Westward dreams
series ; bk. 4.
PS3566.E238D57 1995
813'.54—dc20   95-35737
                                                      CIP

All rights reserved. No part of this publication may be reproduced, stored in a
retrieval system, or transmitted in any form or by any means—electronic,
mechanical, photocopy, recording, or any other—except for brief quotations in
printed reviews, without the prior permission of the publisher.

Edited by Bob Hudson and Robin Schmitt

Printed in the United States of America

95 96 97 98 99 00 01 02 / ❖ DH / 10 9 8 7 6 5 4 3 2 1

WESTWARD DREAMS SERIES

A Distant Dawn

Chapter 1

"*Look* at *that*, Sunny!" the boy exclaimed.

Sunniva Lyndall turned and read the sign to which her sixteen-year-old brother pointed:

WANTED: Young, skinny, wiry fellows, not over eighteen. Must be expert riders, willing to risk life daily. Orphans preferred. Interested persons should apply at the local Pony Express company.

"Well?" she shrugged. Then as she realized why he wanted her to see it she demanded, "Are you out of your mind, Tracy?"

The eagerness on Tracy's freckled face faded.

"Don't even *think* about it!" She held up a warning hand to ward off any further reckless enthusiasm.

"Ah, Sunny—," he protested.

"No! Don't say a word! I won't listen!" His sister's hazel eyes flashed. "You want to get killed before we even get to California?"

She moved away but he grabbed her arm. "Wait just a durn minute, Sunny! We're flat broke, remember? You got a better idea?"

Feeling sick dismay sweep over her at his reminder of their predicament, Sunny spoke more sharply than she intended. "No, I don't have a better idea at the moment, but I'll think of something." As an afterthought, she added, "And you watch your language, young man, you hear?" She walked on. Then, realizing he wasn't following, she stopped and looked back. Her brother was still standing there, hands thrust into his pockets, making a circle in the dusty street with the toe of his boot.

"Come on, Tracy," she called impatiently. For a long moment, Tracy remained staring at the poster. "Come on!" she repeated with increasing irritability.

Reluctantly and slowly her brother moved, mumbling under his breath. Sunny bit her lower lip in irritation. Weren't things bad enough without her having to deal with his childishness? To make matters worse, *she* was to blame for their plight! Blatantly swindled, out of money, stranded in a Missouri border town. Temporarily, at least. Surely when she found the sheriff of this town, explained what had happened . . .

How stupid she had been to trust that blackguard Colin Faraday. The whole sorry scene that had taken place on the train on their way here came back to Sunny in vivid detail.

It had seemed such a good plan, a great adventure, when they had set out from their small Ohio Valley community. Filled with excitement and high hopes, they boarded the train to Independence, Missouri. Even the name was significant to them. It was the "jumping-off place" to the West. There they would join one of the many wagon trains heading to California, where they would homestead and make their fortune.

Sunny remembered how optimistic they were but how hopelessly inexperienced in the ways of the world.

On the train, they encountered an affable fellow traveler. Seated across the aisle from them, he introduced himself as Colin Faraday and soon engaged them in conversation. He seemed so interested in them, asking them many questions

8

about where they were from, where they were going. His pleasant personality, his jolly laugh, and his self-assured manner soon won their confidence. They found themselves telling him their plans, their hopes for the future.

"Well now, if that ain't the best kind of luck. A sure enough example of being in the right place at the right time—and being the right man!" he said with a broad wink. "I don't know how many times I been on this same train and met up with folks like you going west. I have great admiration for people with that kind of dreams"—he leaned closer—"and I'm in the business of making them come true. Leastways, *helpin'* make them come true." He lowered his voice. "But you gotta be careful about gettin' your wagon, your mules or oxen, your supplies. ... The merchants and storekeepers at these towns where the wagon trains set out from are like foxes, ready to devour unsuspecting emigrants like yourselves. Not that you ain't got a good head on your shoulders, no siree bob. I seen that right away. You, young lady, and this here young man, I could tell you know where it's at, but ..." He shook his head. "Heard some sad tales of folks bein'—" a worried look crossed his face—"well, unless you know what you're doin'..."

At his words, Sunny suddenly felt the full weight of what they had done. Buoyed with enthusiasm, she had ignored all the warnings, relatives' dire predictions of the hazards of the undertaking. It was *she* who had read the glowing *Emigrants Handbook* from cover to cover, committing to memory just what they would need to purchase to become part of one of the wagon trains going west. Her hands clutched her small purse, in which was most of the cash they had received from the sale of the house, the furniture, the cow, their three horses. This was the first time since they had left home that she felt she might have taken on more than she could handle. Now the fear that she might not be able to choose wisely, make good assessment of value on buying a wagon, trust the merchants to deal fairly, made her weak with apprehension.

"Isn't there someone we could talk to, someone to consult?" Sunny had asked Faraday in a faltering voice.

"Yes, ma'am, there sure is!" Mr. Faraday laughed heartily. He jabbed his thumb into his chest. "You're looking right at him."

Faraday proceeded to tell them that he was willing to do for them what he'd done for countless others starting out to the new part of the country.

"More than willin'," he assured them. Then he explained how he could procure their "outfit"—wagon, mules, and other necessary equipment—for them and save them from being cheated by unscrupulous suppliers who fed off the ignorant.

"That is very kind of you, Mr. Faraday. But I don't know whether we should impose on your goodwill. Won't that take a great deal of trouble and time for you? From your own business in Fairfax City?" Sunny was torn by her natural reluctance to rely on a stranger. However, the relief of turning over the responsibility to someone more knowledgeable than she to outfit them for the journey west was greater.

"Well, ma'am, I took to you and this young fellow the minute I set eyes on you both. I sez to myself, sez I, now there's a pair of fine, upstanding, ambitious young people ready to face the future and expand this great country of ours. It would be a pleasure—no, let's say a downright honor—to assist such a couple."

He then told them the best way to handle the transaction. He drew a stubby pencil out of his vest pocket, searched in the pocket of his jacket and brought out a crumpled envelope, turned it over and started writing down a list of items to be bought, jotting the possible price in an opposite column. His lips moved as he counted—

audibly but under his breath and therefore unintelligible to them. At last, with pursed mouth and a frown, he gave a sigh and rattled off a sum.

"That's only a by guess and by golly based on the prices the last time I did this for friends. But I'm sure I can do better than this, given a little time." His eyes squinted as he beamed at them both. "And it *might* take time, searching around, comparing prices, gettin' the best deal. So what I suggest is this: When we get to the train stop right before Independence, a place called Cottonwood, you two get off and go to the hotel there, get a room. I'll ride on into town and do my bargain huntin' and finaglin'. Then when I've got your outfit hitched and packed, I'll bring it over so that you can take it on out to the Oakmont; that's where all the wagons assemble for a few days before leaving. They call it the *rondaysvoos* yard."

He handed the envelope over to Sunny.

She drew a sharp breath. The total was more than half of all the money she had. But they wouldn't need much money on the trail, except perhaps at the two army forts, where there were trading posts to replenish their provisions. Naturally, their initial outlay would seem exorbitant. If they had purchased a wagon and supplies at home before they left, it might have been better—but it was too late to worry about that now. She should feel glad they'd met this kind stranger who had so generously offered to help them. She knew she would have been helpless dealing with sharp merchants herself. So with only a few misgivings Sunny counted out the cash into Mr. Faraday's pudgy, outstretched palm.

"I've written to Mr. Lucas Flynt, the wagon master, reserved us a place in his wagon train leaving on the fifteenth of April," Sunny told Faraday.

"Flynt? Yep, know him well. He's top grade. You couldn't put your fate in better hands. Led dozens of wagon trains

11

safely 'crosst country. Heard tell he's had powwows with them Plains Indians."

"*Indians?*" Tracy's eyes lit up.

"Oh, yessir, boy. Some of the trains has run into Indian trouble. 'Cept Flynt's. None 't all." Mr. Faraday folded up the bills, tucked them into the inside pocket of his gaudy plaid coat.

"So then, Mr. Faraday, we'll wait at the hotel for you? And you will bring our wagon, mules or oxen—whichever you decide is the better animal for the long journey—along with our provisions there?"

"That's the ticket, little lady."

"When should we expect you to come?"

"Can't say for sure. These things take time, as I said. But if you don't want to. . ." Faraday made a gesture as if to retrieve the wad of bills and return them to her. But Sunny quickly halted him with a wave of one hand.

"No, no! Mr. Faraday, I just wanted to get some idea of how long we'll be staying at the hotel. I assure you, I appreciate very much what you're doing for us."

As Sunny recalled her words she shuddered. How could she have been so gullible? They had been proverbial lambs led to slaughter.

But he had seemed so nice, so truly concerned about their welfare, so anxious to help. How could she have guessed? She should have been warned by the flamboyant plaid suit, the two-toned shoes, the yellow silk handkerchief, the bowler hat. Now that she thought of it, all of it shouted *beware!* If she had only been smart enough.

At the hotel Sunny was given the only single room available, while Tracy shared a room with four other men on the top floor. Sunny spend a restless night. Noise from the streets of a town that never seemed to sleep, the sound of voices, high-pitched laughter from the saloon downstairs, the rattle of wagon wheels from a stream of seemingly endless traffic outside, made sleep difficult. The second night, worry added to the other things kept her awake. When two days passed with no word from Faraday, the awful possibility that he might not show up at all dawned upon Sunny.

At first Sunny did not confess her growing uneasiness to her brother. On the third morning of their stay, after some cautious questioning, Sunny discovered that no one had ever heard of Mr. Faraday nor of anyone offering that kind of service. Horrified, she came to the conclusion that they had been duped by a professional "con" man. The man had never intended to arrange anything for them; he had simply taken their money and disappeared.

Well, he wasn't going to get away with it. Not if she could help it. She would find some way to bring him to justice and recoup their "nest egg."

When she finally told Tracy, he simply stared at her speechlessly.

"You mean we can't go to California after all?"

"Didn't you understand? That—that *criminal* has stolen our money!"

"You mean like a bank robber?"

"Exactly," she replied grimly.

"What are we going to do?"

"The first thing I'm going to do is try to find Lucas Flynt. We'll go out to Oakmont, the rendezvous yard, and tell him just what's happened. He can probably get the man arrested or—something! I don't know. We've got to do something, Tracy. We're almost out of money."

The hotel desk clerk gave them directions to the livery stable, where they might be able to hire a horse and small wagon or buggy. That's where they were headed when Tracy spotted the sign advertising for Pony Express riders.

Sunny glanced over her shoulder at her brother, who still looked nettled. Her quick rejection of his idea had got his dander up. Realizing that it was only his way of trying to

13

help, Sunny felt contrite. Of course such a job would appeal to him. He rode like someone born on a saddle. They were both excellent horseback riders. Their father had put them both on ponies by the time they were three, taught them to ride. But a job like *that* was out of the question. Even the ad didn't hide the fact that it was dangerous. Said right out, "Must be willing to risk life daily. *Orphans preferred.*" Imagine! Well, they weren't desperate enough to allow Tracy to do *that*! At least, not yet.

Chapter 2

*S*unny marched determinedly ahead; her brother lagged in her wake at a slower pace. That's the way it had always been. Eight years older than he, Sunny had always been the leader. That's why she felt so horribly responsible now that it was *she* who had landed them in this mess. She was twenty-three and should have known better.

Going to California had been *her* dream. There to find the happiness and independence she longed for, away from her stepmother's nagging relatives. She read all the brochures, all the enthusiastic accounts of how it was a land of opportunity, of untold rewards for those who had the will and vision to work hard. It hadn't taken much to get her brother to become just as eager.

Tracy had been her special charge almost from the time he was born and certainly after their mother died when he was just two years old. Sunny pressed her lips together firmly. Yes, she might have got them into this, but she would get them out!

Even walking through town to get to the livery stable was chancy. Traffic was heavy, the street jammed with the heavy canvas-topped wagons drawn by oxen or mules on their way to Independence some fifteen miles away. Sunny felt a wrenching, indignant sensation as they stood on the wooden sidewalk and waited to cross, watching the wagons pass. *They* would be in one of those—*should* have been—if only she hadn't listened to that smooth-talking crook!

This town seemed to be bursting at its seams, growing, thriving, the gateway to Independence, which was the *real* starting place to the West. There were stores of all kinds—hardware, saddlery—and plenty of saloons! Sunny had noticed that when they walked from the railroad station that first night. The farther they walked, the more congested it got. In the distance, on the outskirts of town, they saw a number of tents. These, they learned, were the camps set up by some of the emigrants waiting for their wagons to be built so they could join up with a wagon train going west. Maybe that's where she and Tracy would have had to stay if they hadn't met up with Faraday, Sunny thought grimly. Maybe that was where they'd end up if—Sunny didn't even finish the thought. As soon as she talked to Lucas Flynt, everything would be straightened out.

At the livery stable all that was for hire was a rickety buckboard and a swaybacked nag who had seen better days and should have been put out to pasture long ago. But convinced that nothing better was available, Sunny paid what she considered to be an unreasonable rental and, after receiving indifferent directions, set out for the rendezvous yard, where Lucas Flynt's wagon train was assembling.

There were a few tense moments as they maneuvered their unreliable vehicle through the crowded thoroughfare until they were out on a rutted country road. Sunny drove while Tracy looked out for the sign with the word *Oakmont,* a name that sounded like a park for a camp meeting or a picnic. They had gone a good distance before Tracy spotted a wooden sign nailed to a fence post and shouted, "There it is, Sis!" He spelled out the crudely printed word. An arrow was painted below it. It was just another bend in the road, an empty spread of stunted pine trees and scrub oaks. Less than ten huge wagons with arched canvas tops were parked at wide intervals. They really did look like sailing ships. No wonder they were called "prairie schooners."

Sunny reigned the spindly horse, who seemed more than willing to stop and nibble at some scraggly grass at the side of the road. So this was the rendezvous yard? The place where their fellow band of adventurers would set off for the great migration across hills, valleys, prairie, and mountains to the golden country of California? Viewing it, Sunny felt a sinking sensation in the pit of her stomach. Somehow she had expected activity, energetic movement, eager prepara- tions being made, talk, laughter, children running about. Instead the only people she saw were a small group of men gathered in front of one of the covered wagons. It wasn't the picture she had held in her imagination all these weeks. Aware of Tracy's anxious eyes upon her, Sunny tried not to show any disappointment, even though it didn't look very promising. She wasn't going to let anything destroy their dream. Inwardly outraged at what had happened and deter- mined to seek justice, Sunny wound the reins over the wooden brake and got down. As she approached them the men turned curious gazes upon her. Sunny took a deep breath, then spoke. "Excuse me, gentlemen, I'm looking for the wagon train leader, a Mr. Lucas Flynt."

In unison three of the men swung their heads to the fourth one, who regarded Sunny with undisguised inter- est. He tipped the brim of a slouched felt hat back from his forehead with his thumb and took a step forward.

Sunny took his measure. He was slightly under six feet tall, lean—to the point of being lanky—but muscular. His skin, tanned almost as dark as an Indian's, had the look of polished saddle leather, making his eyes startlingly blue. He looked awfully young to be a wagon master. But since he was obviously the one she had to talk to, she said, "Mr. Flynt, we have suffered an outrageous wrong, and—"

Before she could continue, he held up one hand, halting her. "Sorry, ma'am, I'm not Mr. Flynt. I'm Webb Chandler, his scout."

Momentarily taken aback, Sunny said, "Oh, well then, it's Mr. Flynt I must speak to. We were to be a part of your wagon train leaving next week. But a terrible crime has been committed. On the train coming here a man presented himself to be an agent you have used on several occasions to procure proper equipment for the journey"—and here Sunny had to stop to catch her breath and swallow before going on—"and has evidently absconded with our money without purchasing our wagon, our supplies, our . . ." Under his puzzled frown, she came to a stop.

"So? Just what do you want me to do about it, ma'am?" he asked.

"Why—why, help me find him, or go with me to the sheriff and have him arrested if he can be found. He was supposed to meet us here hours ago and then take us to the rendezvous place so that we could join with your caravan . . ." Sunny's voice trailed off as she saw the expression on the man's face.

"Well, ma'am, I'm right sorry for your dilemma—I surely am. But that's not an uncommon occurrence." At her look of dismay his tone softened. "Unless you got somethin' to go on. You know his name?"

"Yes, I certainly do. It's Colin Faraday."

Chandler let out a long, slow whistle, shook his head. "Faraday, eh? Faraday's notorious for spotting—if you'll excuse the term—greenhorns."

Sunny looked shocked. "You mean to say you're not going to do anything to apprehend this thief—who, I

18

might add, used your boss's name quite freely in gaining our confidence?"

A pained expression crossed his lean face. "As I say, I'm sorry as I can be," he drawled, "but don't see as how I can do anything to help. That rascal's probably clear out of the county by now. 'Spect as he left on the next train out."

"With *our* money! And you say there's nothing can be done about it? Where is the law to protect people?"

"People foolish enough to trust strangers? Nowhere, I'm afraid."

Sunny felt a wave of hopelessness mixed with resentment at the condescension in the man's voice. The fact that what he said was the truth only made her feel worse. She didn't need anyone telling her she'd been a fool. She *knew* that. Her throat felt tight, and she felt the stinging sensation of tears at the back of her eyes. She willed them back. Evidently there was no help coming from *this* man. What were they to do? Desperately she groped for some way to rescue herself and Tracy from their dire situation.

"Is there any way we could join up with another wagon? I've still a little money left. Could we possibly pay our way by working? My brother's a champion with horses, and I could take care of children, help the other women in lots of ways."

Chandler looked beyond her as if searching for someone or something to say. Then he looked directly at her. "Ma'am, don't you think this whole matter could be better handled by your husband? Seems to me this is a man's problem."

It may have been spoken with an effort to seem patient, but to Sunny it sounded disdainful. She felt her face burn. Sorry she had revealed her desperation by appealing to his sympathy, she drew herself up and replied coldly, "I have no husband. And I am perfectly capable of handling this myself if you would be kind enough to direct me to the local law enforcement."

A smile tugged at Chandler's mouth, but he replied

solemnly, "The sheriff's office is right next to the Palace Hotel, ma'am. And if you don't get any satisfaction there, might I suggest you try Mr. Flynt himself. Although I doubt he'd tell you much different than I did. As I said, it happens all the time—"

"I don't want to hear about anyone else, thank you!" Sunny snapped. "It's *us* I'm interested in, and seeing justice done." With that she whirled around and started back toward the wagon, almost colliding into Tracy, who had come up and stood behind her during this exchange with the scout. Sunny brushed past him and he had to hurry to keep up with her. She was in the wagon, reins in hand, when he sprang up beside her. He was barely seated before she gave the horse a smart slap with the reins, turned around, and headed back toward town.

Darting a quick glance at his sister, he recognized that set of her jaw, the small, square chin lifted. He knew that look and he knew Sunny. He could almost read her thoughts. After all they'd been through to get here, she wasn't about to give up. She'd think of some way, do something. Tracy didn't know just what.

As the buckboard on its wobbly wheels pulled out onto the road, Webb Chandler looked after the young woman driving it. That lady had spunk and sass, all right. Spirited as they come, she might just be someone to stand up even to Flynt, he reckoned. Of course, she was obviously upset. Her face all flushed, frowning, her eyes sparking fire. Under other circumstances she might be attractive. Dressed too plain though, almost like those women in a painting he'd once seen of the Pilgrims landing on Plymouth Rock. Her high-collared dress was brown—a color Webb couldn't abide—and not a ribbon or bow or flower on her hat, either. While she had been talking she'd impatiently pushed back the untidy wisps of honey-colored hair straggling out from under the shelf of her stiff bonnet. Still, she was one of the prettiest women he had seen in many a day.

Chapter 3

$\mathcal{T}$hey returned the horse and wagon to the livery stable, then walked back to the hotel. In the lobby, Sunny went directly up to the counter. The man behind it, bent over a ledger, did not look up at her approach. Sunny drummed her fingers impatiently on the countertop, waiting for him to acknowledge her. Clearing her throat, she said, "Excuse me, sir." The desk clerk still did not move. Was he purposely ignoring her? She tapped the service bell twice. This finally got his attention. He turned, frowning. "Yes, ma'am?" The tone was annoyed but he came forward. Leaning on one elbow, he peered at her with narrowed eyes.

Meeting them, Sunny asked coolly, "I was told I could find a Mr. Lucas Flynt, the wagon master, here. Could you tell me if he is?"

The man jerked his thumb and inclined his head toward the other side of the lobby. "Most likely you'll find him there."

Sunny looked in the direction of his thumb to the far end of the room. Out from louvered doors swirled clouds of smoke, loud voices, laughter against a background of tinny piano music. Obviously the hotel saloon. Could she bring herself to go into a place like that—a "den of iniquity," as her stepmother would judge it? She saw the man behind the counter smirk, and something within her stiffened. Flynt's wagon train was due to pull out in three days. She had to try to convince the wagon master of some way she and Tracy could be on it. Straightening her shoulders, Sunny started toward the swinging doors of the saloon. Tracy caught her arm and said in a low, nervous voice, "Sunny, you don't want to go in there. It's no place for a lady!"

"The kid's right," the desk clerk echoed with a malicious smile.

His comment was like a red flag waving. Sunny's determination hardened. She'd had enough male condescension for one day. Their very future was at stake. Nothing was going to stop her now. Certainly nothing as trivial as something not being *ladylike*. Her fingers pried at Tracy's grip. Between gritted teeth she whispered, "Let go, Tracy. I've got to talk to Mr. Flynt myself. It's our only chance!"

Tracy knew his sister well enough to realize that once her mind was made up, there was no use arguing. Gradually his hold loosened. His expression was one of helpless resignation. "Well, all right, but I'm coming with you."

"It'll be all right. You'll see," Sunny said, wishing she was as confident as she tried to sound. Resolutely she crossed the lobby toward the saloon, Tracy her reluctant escort.

With only a second's hesitation she pushed through the swinging doors. The smoke-filled, stuffy air was sour with the smell of whiskey, and her nostrils quivered with distaste. The noise was almost deafening; loud bursts of raucous laughter mingled with the drone of voices, the din of the piano badly in need of tuning. Standing on the threshold, she took in the scene: men were huddled around tables, others lined up two deep at the long oak bar. She was only dimly aware of a few gaudily dressed women scattered throughout the crowd. Instead her gaze moved slowly around the murky room, eyes searching for Lucas Flynt.

How had the scout described him? Broad as a beam, a mustache red as a fire engine? Tracy's uneasiness mounted. Her own resolve was ebbing when she spotted him. Seated at a round table with a bottle in its center was a hulk of a man with a drooping, rust-colored handlebar mustache, playing cards. A wide-brimmed hat pushed up from his forehead, his shoulders hunched, he studied the cards in his large hands.

She was sure that was the man she wanted to see, to talk to, to persuade.

"There he is," she murmured to Tracy. "Come on."

"Uh, Sunny, I don't think this is a good idea...," was Tracy's hesitant response.

Disregarding his last-ditch attempt to stop her, Sunny threaded her way through the room to the table where Lucas Flynt sat. Reaching it, she dragged up her courage. "Mr. Flynt?"

One of the others at the table glanced up, nudged the man next to him, and drawled, "There's a lady wants your attention, Luke."

Still holding his cards, Lucas Flynt slowly lifted his head and pierced her with a look that sent her heart racing, knotted her stomach. The cheroot he held in the corner of his mouth tipped. "I'm Lucas Flynt," he growled. "What do you want with me?"

"I urgently need to speak to you."

The buzz of conversation at nearby tables subsided. Heads turned, chairs scraped back so their occupants could get a better look. This might prove interesting. The primly attired young woman, and the skinny boy standing behind, approaching "Big Luke" was no ordinary occurrence. And while he was playing cards! The possibility of something exciting happening sharpened the curiosity of the saloon patrons.

Flynt moved the cheroot to the other side of his mouth,

24

pulled a card out, tapped it on his chin, then laid it on the table. "You shure it's *me* you want?"

"Yes," Sunny replied firmly. She drew another long breath. "It's business I must discuss..Business of a very serious nature."

He frowned, bushy eyebrows meeting over the big, crooked nose that must have been broken sometime. He raised his steely gray eyes from his cards and gave her a glowering stare that would have intimidated someone less determined.

"This ain't exactly the place, lady."

She was about to stress the importance of her request when a man's voice spoke. "Excuse me, ma'am, but we don't serve ladies in here. You'll have to leave." She turned her head and saw a large, bald man in a striped shirt, with an apron tied over dark trousers—it was the bartender. "And no kids either." He indicated a mortified Tracy, whose face had turned beet red.

"I'm not here to be served. Neither is my brother," Sunny quickly explained. "I've come to talk to Mr. Flynt on business." She turned back to Flynt. "It will only take a few minutes. I implore you—"

"Can't you see I'm in the middle of a game?"

"I'm truly sorry, but if this weren't so very urgent, I—"

"Go ahead, Flynt. Talk to the little lady," one of the other cardplayers urged with a sly cackle.

"Some of your past catchin' up with you, Flynt?" another crony asked with an insinuating wink at Sunny.

Flynt shifted in his chair, breasting his cards, then glared at Sunny. "You'll have to wait till I play this hand. Then I'll meet you out in the lobby."

"Thank you very much," she said tightly. She'd accomplished her object, but now her knees felt weak. Her face aflame, Sunny turned away from the rudely gawking men. Acutely aware of the eyes upon her, the ripple of laughter, the remarks being exchanged among the saloon patrons, Sunny held her head high as she went back out to the lobby, Tracy hot on her heels.

Once outside the saloon, he turned on her furiously. "Doggone it, Sunny. You sure done it. Makin' a rare spectacle of yourself in there, and *me* too!" he accused her. "They were all laughin' at us."

She spun around and faced him. "Do you think I care what a bunch of uncouth, beer-guzzling *poker players* think?" she flung back. "This is about *our* money. I'm trying to find some way we can get to California! I'm trying to rescue us, boy! Don't you understand we're stranded here, almost destitute? Instead of being mad at me, you ought to be grateful. I'm doing the best I can."

Tracy got even redder. He lowered his eyes. Sunny's anger melted to understanding. She realized she had embarrassed him. But it hadn't been a Sunday school picnic for her either to go into that awful place. But she'd *had* to. *Somebody* had to. Tracy had just turned sixteen and was hardly more than a child. It *had* to be her, no matter *how* humiliating it was.

"Sorry," he mumbled. She put out her hand and touched his arm.

"It's all right. It's going to work out. It has to," she said. "Let's sit over there in that alcove and wait for Mr. Flynt."

She saw the desk clerk look up as they passed, a snide smile on his smug, pasty face. She would have liked to smack that face, she thought furiously. What if it was *his* mother or sister in the same predicament *she* was in? He wouldn't be grinning like an idiot then. He'd be proud of her. At least, he *should* be.

Glancing at Tracy, Sunny wasn't so sure *he* was. She went over, intending to say a few words to comfort him, reassure him. But when she put her hand on his arm, he shook it off and took a few steps away. His back to her, he stood looking out the hotel window.

26

His head was down, his chin nearly to his chest, his hands plunged into his jacket pockets. With a shock, she saw his bony wrists protruding. He was growing so fast, that jacket was almost too small for him already! The frightening facts of the situation assaulted her again. Alone in a strange town, money nearly gone. No one willing to help them. *Dear God, please!* was the only prayer Sunny could think of.

Sunny took a seat on one of the stiff, horsehair chairs and glued her eyes on the saloon doors hopefully. She watched every time it opened and men went out, but there was no sign of Lucas Flynt.

Just when Sunny decided Flynt wasn't coming, the slatted doors to the saloon swung open and Lucas Flynt stood there looking annoyed, his gaze sweeping the lobby. Sunny jumped to her feet, and then he strode toward her.

As politely as she could manage, Sunny told him her well-rehearsed story, explaining what had happened and finishing by asking if somehow she and Tracy could work their way to California, hitch up with some other family's wagon.

"We're both strong, both good with horses, and I can do all sorts of things to help the women—" Her voice failed along with her hopes as Flynt shook his head, pursing his lips under the shaggy mustache.

"No way, ma'am. No can do."

"But we signed on. We wrote to your outfitting company. We sent our deposit ... ," she protested.

"I'm sorry as can be, ma'am, but there ain't nothing I can do. It's written in the guidelines set up. Each emigrant has to have their own wagon, team, and supplies."

Shock and disbelief mingled in Sunny's expression. Then her face flushed with indignation. "But I told you. That man—that scoundrel—assured us he would buy everything we needed. He was to meet us here yesterday with—"

"That's a durn shame, ma'am. I cain't tell you how many

times I've heard the same sorry tale, but as it says in the Good Book, you gotta be wise as a fox—especially here, as well as in Independence. There's all kinds of scalawags and sharpies out to do in greenhorns."

Sunny bristled at the same term the insufferable scout had used about them.

Flynt shook his head again. "All I can suggest, lady, is you and the kid go back home."

"But we can't—" Sunny began, feeling betraying tears rush into her eyes. She blinked them back, bit her lower lip, which had begun to tremble. She wasn't about to tell this hard-hearted man that they didn't even have enough money for train fare back home. Plus, how could she ever face the "I told you sos" from all the relatives if they did go back?

"You mean there's no way—no possible way—"

"No, ma'am, no way I can see—none at all."

Flynt seemed to be about to say something else, then changed his mind. He was obviously uncomfortable in this situation. He gave the edge of his brim a little tug, then with another doleful shake of his head turned and walked back into the saloon.

Her knees suddenly weak, Sunny sat down. Tracy stood over her, watching her mutely. She felt like crying or screaming—or both. But it was still important to put a good face on disaster. For Tracy's sake. Sunny pressed her lips together. "Well, so much for that. There must be another way."

"Well, there is, but you won't listen," Tracy said, jumping on this moment of indecision.

"If you mean what I think you mean, forget it."

"Doggone it, Sunny, you're so durn stubborn—"

"Keep your voice down, Tracy," she said between clenched teeth. "Don't make a scene. Everybody's staring at us as it is."

Looking around, Tracy saw that her statement was true.

28

The few people in the lobby evidently witnessed their meeting with Lucas Flynt, perhaps even heard some of the exchange with him. A few had lowered their newspapers unabashedly while it was going on. Tracy shifted from one foot to the other.

Embarrassed, Sunny rose and said in a tense voice, "Let's go up to my room, where we can discuss this *in private*."

"No, I'm going out for a while to cool off," Tracy muttered, and he turned abruptly, stalking across the lobby and out the hotel door, leaving Sunny stunned, standing alone.

Chapter 4

*C*onscious of the desk clerk's curious eyes, Sunny gathered her shattered dignity like a ragged cloak and turned back to the counter. "My key, please," she said icily. He handed her the key attached to a paper disk on which was printed the number twelve. Ignoring his knowing sneer, she murmured, "Thank you." Then, holding herself very stiff and straight, she went up the stairs. Reaching the top, she went down the dingy corridor to the room she had rented. She opened the door, shut it behind her firmly, then leaned back against it with both hands behind her and closed her eyes for a long moment. What now? What on earth were they to do *now*?

She must pull herself together. She must not give Tracy the slightest cause to suspect that she didn't know exactly what they should do next, what steps to take. First she had to find out just how much money they had. She emptied out her purse, counting the cash out to the last penny. The result was that Sunny felt as if she were staring into an abyss. A dark, bottomless hole without a glimmer of light. She drew a shaky breath, feeling very lonely and very, very frightened.

There had been plenty of times in her life when Sunny had been told she was "unteachable." Her stepmother had often accused her of thinking she "knew everything." Well, this time she didn't. She had refused to listen when everyone tried to talk sense into her. Her stepmother's relatives had been appalled to learn that she had put the house and the valuable farmland up for sale. And when they found out what she intended to do with the money, they had descended on her, cautioning, remonstrating, chastising, even offering to buy the property themselves "to keep it in the family," in trust for Tracy when he came of age. Stubbornly she had rejected all the unsolicited but well-intentioned advice. They had left, shaking their heads. What would they think now if they knew that all their dire predictions had come true?

How could she go home to that kind of reproach? *Home?* There *was* no home to go to, not now, because of her reckless irresponsibility! Reckless. Irresponsible. The very labels *they* had given her.

But how could she have foreseen the possibility of being tricked and robbed?

Sunny put her head in her hands. A picture of Tracy came into her mind, his round, guileless eyes, his freckles, his little-boy grin. He had trusted her. And she had failed him. Swept away by those stories of the glorious opportunities for land and riches in the west she had believed. She had brought all this upon them. It was all *her* fault.

She had always felt hemmed in by the small town where she had grown up; she had always longed for new horizons, to travel and find what was at the end of that mythical rainbow. Going to California had seemed like the ultimate chance to discover it all. Her stepmother had often reprimanded her for daydreaming. California had been her daydream. Now those dreams seemed to have crumbled about her.

Sunny finally raised her head. Enough of this self-pity. She'd have to think of something. Her father had always

31

told them not to complain but to count their blessings. They were both young, healthy, and strong. Surely they could find some kind of work. Both had the skills they had planned to use in homesteading. Tracy knew all about horses. He could probably get a job at a livery stable or maybe a ranch. Sunny could do housework. Although that prospect filled her with despair, she tried to be optimistic. It only meant putting aside their dreams of going to California for a while. She *had* to believe that.

Her stepmother had told her often enough that her tongue was too sharp, her temper too short, and her comments too opinionated, that her attitude in general was unbecoming for a woman. In the future she'd have to be more tactful in dealing with Tracy. She was so used to taking the lead that her manner was sometimes authoritative, and he resented it. Almost always he had gone along with whatever she suggested or decided. Today was the first time he had openly argued with her over a decision. This hint of rebellion in her younger brother had shaken her. Sunny decided she owed Tracy an apology. When he came back, she would lay out her ideas, discuss them with him.

What no one ever gave her credit for was imagination, independence, and courage. If she and her brother were going to survive this major setback, these qualities would have to be employed. She wasn't yet defeated. She'd find a way out of this present dilemma. She *had* to.

Suddenly Sunny felt exhausted, bone-tired, worn out with all the stress of their ordeal. She unbuttoned her shoes, kicked them off, loosened her stays, and stretched out on the lumpy bed. Her eyelids felt heavy, and she shut her eyes. As naturally as breathing she went into prayer. *Dear Lord, don't let this be one of my awful mistakes. I know I'm impulsive, hardheaded, and stubborn, but please, Lord, don't punish Tracy because of me. I got us into this; now please give me the wisdom I need to get us out.*

Outside the hotel Tracy stood looking about glumly. He was furious with his sister and wanted to be away from her worried eyes, her sharp voice, for a little while. He didn't want to admit he was scared too. It was one whopper of a mess. But it wasn't all Sunny's fault. He was just as much to blame. He'd also taken Faraday's bait: hook, line, and sinker. The fella was slippery as an eel. He wished he knew what to do. Wished he had someone to ask. A man. Being too dependent on Sunny wasn't such a good idea. Sunny was smart, all right, but she was still a woman, and there were just some things you needed to discuss with a man. Just then, as though in answer to his wish, Tracy saw a man crossing the muddy street and coming straight toward him. He looked familiar somehow. Why, it was the wagon train scout, Webb Chandler. The man glanced his way, and Tracy saw that he recognized him. Tracy smiled shyly, and the man stopped. A slow grin creased his tanned face.

"Did your wagon and supplies show up yet?" he asked.

Tracy shook his head. "Nope. I guess he's long gone. We sure got took."

"It happens. They should post signs for greenhorns: 'Look out for con men, hold on to your money purse.' Too bad, young fella. But you can probably hitch on to some work—"

"My sister, Sunny, says—," began Tracy.

"*Sunny?*" Webb Chandler repeated, eyebrows lifted. "Your sister's name is *Sunny?*"

Tracy's mouth twitched at Chandler's incredulous reaction. "Yes. . .," he answered hesitantly.

Webb laughed. "Sorry, but she don't strike me as being exactly the *sunny* type. More like a prickly pear."

Tracy fought an urge to join in the man's chuckles. *Serves Sunny right that she gives folks that impression,* he thought. *She is too durn bossy. Like a burr under a saddle a lot of the time. 'Nuff to make a man downright ornery, with her pickin'*

33

and naggin' at him... But on the other hand, I owe her a lot. Shouldn't join in any joshin' about her behind her back—even if it is in good fun.

Tracy tried to change the subject instead. "Well, I wuz thinkin' about applyin' for one of them Pony Express rider jobs." He thrust out his chin in an attempt to look self-confident and at the same time tried to gauge what this hardened westerner might say, whether he would encourage or discourage the idea.

"Well, it's a possibility. That is, if you're—" Webb's glance swept over the lanky young man, then he said, half joking and half serious, "It'll make a man of you in a hurry if it don't kill you first!"

Sunny woke with an uneasy feeling. She sat up feeling groggy and disoriented. The room was in shadows. How long had she been asleep? She swung her legs over the side of the bed and padded in her stocking feet to the window and looked out. It was getting dark. Where was Tracy? She hoped he hadn't got into some kind of trouble. She had seen some rough-looking characters out there in those streets. How long had he been gone? Deciding she'd better go out looking for him, Sunny hurriedly thrust her feet into her shoes and was just struggling to get them fastened with her buttonhook, when a tapping came at the door.

"It's Tracy, Sis," came her brother's voice.

With relief Sunny went over, unlocked the door, and flung it open. Glad as she was to see him back safe and sound, her voice was cross when she demanded, "Where have you been? I've been worried sick."

"No need." Tracy came into the room.

"If I'd known what was ahead of us, I'd never have come," she said grimly. "I should never have left our home, left Meadowdale. It was wrong of me. I'm sorry, Tracy."

34

"It's all right, Sunny. Anyway, things are going to work out. You'll see."

Sunny looked at her brother. Tracy's eyes were shining and there was something different about him, a cockiness that she wasn't used to seeing in him. She felt a funny sensation, a premonition that he was about to tell her something she didn't want to hear.

"Listen, Sunny, and don't say nothin' till you hear me out. I've got a job and we can stay here until we have enough money to get us to California."

"What do you mean, you've got a job?"

"Just what I said. I got me a job, so you don't have to worry—"

"Worry? Of course I have to worry. What kind of a job? Where? What do you mean?"

"Now, promise not to get all het up?"

"I won't promise anything of the kind. Not until you tell me what this is all about."

"Well, after I left here, I run into Webb Chandler. You know, the scout with the wagon train—"

"Oh, *him*! That impossible man—"

"Ah, Sunny, you got him all wrong. He's a fine fella. It was him that told me to go apply for the job I got."

Sunny looked at her brother aghast. "And what kind of a job would someone like Webb Chandler suggest?" She felt her stomach tighten in apprehension.

Tracy proceeded cautiously, speaking slowly. "In the first place, it pays a whole lot more than working as a ranch hand or in the livery stable in town. He told me to go to the Express office, that they were hiring"—he halted, still a little hesitant—"riders to carry the mail."

"Oh, no!" Sunny struck her forehead in horror. She remembered very well the wording of the advertisement they'd seen for Pony Express riders. "You *didn't*! You didn't *ever*! *Did* you?"

35

Tracy nodded. "Yep."

"Well, I won't hear of it! I won't let you."

"I already signed up. Just gotta be sworn in. It's a done deal, Sunny."

Sunny's anger flared. How dare that Webb Chandler take it upon himself to encourage her little brother to apply for such a dangerous job! Furiously she grabbed her jacket, jammed her bonnet on her head, and tied the ribbons under her chin so tight they pinched her skin.

"Well, we'll see if it's a 'done deal' or not! You're underage and you can't sign on to anything without my permission."

"Ah, Sunny, will you listen? If you'd just come and talk to the man who runs the Express office. His name is Mr. Graham, and I told him my sister would—please, Sunny." He threw his hands up in a helpless gesture. "Have you got any other ideas? What else can we do?"

That question stopped Sunny cold. Tracy was right. What else did they have? The fact was, they only had enough money to last them until the end of the week if they stayed at the hotel. Then what? Sunny's fury diminished. Instead she regarded her brother with reluctant admiration. He had the gumption to go investigate the possibility of a way for them to survive. Faced with the reality of their situation, Sunny made a quick decision. The least she could do was go to the Express office and meet this Mr. Graham. "All right, I'll go with you."

Chapter 5

*I*t was beginning to get dark as they left the hotel. The late-spring afternoon had grown cool and Sunny shivered, as much from nerves as from the chill wind.

As they hurried along the wooden sidewalk there was evidence that the town of Cottonwood was livening up for the evening. Men who had made an early start were already staggering as they pushed through the swinging doors of the saloons that lined both sides of the street. Music blared from the dance halls and taverns. When the doors swung open, Sunny caught glimpses of the garishly lighted interiors and flashily dressed women. Her heart sank. It seemed as if they had somehow stumbled into a kind of Babylon. "Watch it, Sunny," Tracy cautioned, throwing out his arm to keep her from stepping into the street. A wagon with an arched canvas top rumbled past, swaying with the weight of its load. Emigrants on their way to Independence going west. Sunny's heart wrenched. *That's what we should be doing,* she thought. She had dreamed of wide prairies, majestic mountains, and clear, flowing rivers. Instead here they were on their way to talk to a man about Tracy taking some kind of foolhardy job. What had she got her young brother into? Sunny felt weighted with renewed guilt.

37

"The Express office is right over there," Tracy said, taking her arm as they hurried across the street before another large wagon came looming down on them.

Tracy opened the door into a sparsely furnished outer office. Over a wooden counter, the "infamous" poster advertising for riders was conspicuously displayed. Sunny averted her eyes. She didn't want to see those ominous words again. She suppressed a shudder.

Beyond, a door leading to another room stood ajar. Through it she saw a dark-haired, broad-shouldered man sitting at a desk.

Sunny looked at Tracy questioningly. "Well?"

He moved awkwardly forward, then knocked tentatively at the door. "Mr. Graham, sir? I'm back. I've brought my sister with me. She'd like—*we'd* like to talk to you, sir. That is, if it's convenient."

Tracy was blocking Sunny's view of the man to whom he was speaking. Then she heard the sound of a chair being scraped back, footsteps approaching. The door opened wider, and the Express company manager stepped into the doorway, his height filling it.

Tracy haltingly introduced her. "Mr. Rhys Graham, this is my sister, Sunny Lyndall. Mr. Graham runs the Express company, Sis."

"Good evening, Miss Lyndall."

Sunny was taken completely by surprise. She had not expected anyone like this man—well dressed, impeccably groomed. In the three days she had been in town, the only men she had seen were roughly dressed ranchers, cowboys, wagoners, and emigrants. None dressed like this. Mr. Graham wore a smoke gray broadcloth jacket, white linen shirt, a vest of paisley silk across which hung a gold-link watch chain. What on earth was someone like this doing in this rough-hewn border town?

"Please, won't you come into my office, where we can talk?"

His courteous manner—although it coincided with his appearance—put her on guard. She had the feeling she was being coerced in some way, coerced to allow Tracy to do something that everything within her told her was fraught with danger. Maybe she should turn around, leave before she agreed to something she would regret. But Tracy looked so eager, so hopeful, that she hesitated only for a second. Then as Mr. Graham held the door for her she entered his office.

"Please sit down, won't you both?" He moved two chairs forward in front of his desk, then went behind the desk. He and Tracy remained standing until she had sat down. Once seated she had a better look at Rhys Graham. His thick, dark hair swept back from a high forehead. He might have been considered handsome, except for the thin, white scar that ran diagonally across his forehead, cutting into his left eyebrow, giving him a strangely quizzical expression. His face was thin and clean-shaven, which accentuated the high cheekbones and the deep-set eyes that were regarding her now with interest. Their very intensity made her uncomfortable.

"Now then, what can I tell you about our company, which your brother wants to join as one of our riders?" he asked. His voice was low, well modulated. The term "gentlemanly" described him perfectly. But in spite of his genteel manner, was he someone to be trusted? The image of that sly Faraday—if that was his real name—flashed into Sunny's mind. This man might also be taking advantage of their inexperience. Luring her brother into a situation that was not only dangerous but at worse could be fatal. She must not let Mr. Graham's manners disarm her. She must take charge of this interview, she decided, and state her objections, thank him for the chance to discuss the situation, then leave gracefully. She directed what she hoped was a firm gaze upon him.

"Mr. Graham, as both our parents are deceased, I am my brother's legal guardian. I want to know exactly what he is signing up for as a Pony Express rider."

"I am glad you came, Miss Lyndall, and indeed I appreciate your concern. It is very responsible of you. Let me outline for you our operation here. We appreciate our riders, admire their skill, their courage, their loyalty. They are as interested as we are to give the western territories what they long for and need: news from home, what's happening in the country, the world. We carry the top newspapers and periodicals from back east so that they can keep up with what's going on while they do their own brave bit of exploring, developing our great country. The fact that your brother—and I must say, I have never interviewed a finer applicant for this position than he. Tracy has all the qualities we look for in an employee. I have no doubt he will make an outstanding addition to our roster of excellent riders, high-minded young men we have hired in the past and continue to hire for this special kind of work. He will be part of a select group of young men whom history will remember and future generations will read about and be inspired by."

Slowly all Sunny's resolution crumbled. Rhys Graham's explanation was persuasive. His gaze, riveted upon her as he spoke so movingly, convinced her these were the eyes of an honest man.

Graham got up from his desk, walked over to the window, and looked out for a minute or two as if to give Sunny time to consider. Then he turned back, saying, "We require a strict code of behavior from our riders and maintain close observation upon them to see that these regulations are kept by them to the letter." He pulled open a desk drawer and drew out a paper, handing it to Sunny. "I'd like you to read the statement we have each rider sign before they're

40

hired. It will give you some idea of the caliber of young men we want."

Sunny took the paper and read, "While I am in the employ of this Express company I will under no circumstances use profane language; I will drink no intoxicating liquors; I will not quarrel or fight with any other employee of the firm. So help me God."

Her doubts disappeared. Perhaps this *was*, as Tracy had pointed out, the solution to their problem. At least temporarily. Her brother was an excellent horseman. That should be no problem. And it would provide them some cash, keep them from starving. But they still didn't have a place to live. *She* had to find work. She'd find something, somehow. In the meantime Tracy could do what he did best: ride horses.

Sunny raised her eyes from the printed agreement. "This seems a very good requirement for such a job," she said slowly. Then, after another moment's hesitation and a fervent prayer that she was doing the right thing, Sunny asked, "Where do I sign?"

Graham handed her a pen from his desk and placed his finger on the line for her signature. As she wrote her name he smiled reassuringly at Tracy and said, "Now let's get your brother sworn in."

Sunny held the Bible while Tracy took the oath, and in her astonished eyes her little brother seemed to grow two inches.

She'd hardly had time to absorb her mixed emotions, when she became aware of Graham's gaze regarding her speculatively.

"I was just wondering, Miss Lyndall, if you knew of my other proposal? Did your brother mention that at the Express station there is an important opening we've been trying to fill for some time? One that you might be interested in? After talking to your brother and now having met you, I'm certain it is one that you would be capable of filling." He paused, waiting to see if she showed a spark of interest. When Sunny leaned forward, he continued. "It's managing the station, taking in the mail and packages, sorting and packing the pouches for the riders. This job would mean taking care of the ponies, much the same as you must have done with your own horses on your family farm. Then there'd be cooking meals for Tracy's relief and alternate riders, packing lunches for them to take in their saddlebags. It's not a difficult job but a very responsible one. We need the right person." He paused. "I think *you* might be just the right person."

Sunny could hardly contain herself. Was this the answer to their desperate prayers? It seemed almost too good to be true. *O ye of little faith,* she thought contritely.

"Are you interested?"

"Oh, yes!"

"The Express station is located outside of town. The building is not much more than a bunkhouse, but there's a big kitchen, and two smaller rooms can be used for bedrooms. It's not in too good a condition, but it's livable and your brother and you can stay there rent free. It's been empty since—well, since our last manager left. Our riders have been staying at one of the boardinghouses in town. At the widow McDowell's. That's working out, because she likes the company and they like her cooking." Graham chuckled. "So there'd only be you and your brother occupying the place. I like the idea of having the station manager there, where the mail is brought in and stored until the riders go out. The barn's in good shape, with six stable stalls and a corral. So do you think you can handle it?"

A job, a place to live! All coming at once. Sunny nodded. "Oh yes, I'm sure I can."

"Good! Then it's a done deed." Graham clapped his

hands together. He noticed a slight smile touch her lips; there was yet anxiety in her eyes, but he ignored it.

After their departure Rhys Graham swiveled his chair around from his desk so that it faced the window looking out onto the street. He watched the two figures moving away in the quickly gathering dusk of evening: the tall, lanky boy, the slim, straight young woman. Odd, though, that they should appear so suddenly in his life, just at the point when he was on the brink of making a decision. . . .

The Lyndalls, brother and sister. Tracy and Sunniva. He had been startled when he saw her signature on Tracy's Express rider application. Sunniva. He said it over to himself a couple of times. An unusual name. A theatrical one. It was the sort of name an actress used, or one that was given to the heroine of one of those romantic novels his cousin Emeline used to have her nose in all the time. What kind of parents named a girl child Sunniva? Sunny, Tracy called her. Rhys tried that. He thought he liked that better. It suited her. He smiled to himself. Like a day full of sunshine and blue sky, like a meadow blooming with daisies and lupine. Sunny. He said it a couple of times aloud, the syllables rolling over his tongue. Yes, Sunny was just right for her.

Strange that they should come across his path just now. Lately he had been struggling with his dark cloud: the thick, smothering, foglike depression to which he was subject periodically. Was their arrival chance? Fate? Luck? Or divine coincidence?

The sister of the young man he'd just sworn in as one of his riders had had a disturbing effect on him. Something about her was so reminiscent . . . a memory, a faint echo of something intangible . . . something he had put behind him but which still haunted him . . . that sweetness of what he had lost, irrevocably, through his own actions, his own fault . . . guilt that grew heavier with each passing year . . .

43

He'd almost forgotten there were women like her—*ladies* like her, he corrected himself. He had noticed all the refined touches: the gloves, the cameo pin at the fluted collar emerging from her neatly fitted jacket, the bonnet framing her face. A natural, unaffected beauty so different from the over-rouged cheeks and kohl-rimmed eyes of the "girls" at saloons like So Long or Trail's End.

Her candid eyes had jolted something within he'd almost forgotten. Rhys closed his eyes, rubbing long, thin fingers across his suddenly aching head.

No, perhaps it was not the right time. He turned back to his desk, to the clutter of papers awaiting his perusal. The past lay upon him like a heavy cloak over his shoulders. The bottle in the lower left drawer of his desk tempted. He resisted. His hand reached for the drawer, then he slammed it shut. "God help me," he groaned between clenched teeth.

On their way back to the hotel, Tracy could hardly contain himself. Relishing his victory, no doubt, Sunny observed wryly. What galled her most was that his rebellion had been encouraged by the advice of that scout, that insufferable Webb Chandler. What right had he to advise *her* brother over all her misgivings and objections?

She prayed that her impression of Rhys Graham was correct. He seemed sincere. She had found herself being swayed as he waxed eloquent about how worthwhile carrying the mail cross-country to California was, how patriotic the riders. But hadn't she been taken in by the apparent honesty of that despicable Faraday? She had thought *he* was honest and reliable, too! And Rhys Graham seemed a man who kept his inner self hidden, protected.

She would just have to trust that it was as it seemed. The pledge Tracy had taken was almost as solemn as one you'd make in church. When Rhys Graham had asked Sunny to hold the Bible while Tracy placed one hand upon it and repeated the promises, it had actually brought tears to Sunny's eyes.

She looked at her brother now and saw how he was bursting with pride. She recognized Tracy's need to prove himself "the man of the family." Actually, it had all turned out much better than she could have hoped. The unexpected offer of a job for her! At least now she could look after Tracy properly. With both of them earning good wages and with no rent to pay, it might not take them long to squirrel away enough money to set out for California again.

They reached the hotel and were just entering the lobby when Chandler came sauntering out from the Gentlemen's Bar and Card Room. The sight of him filled Sunny with resentment. He walked with such self-confident assurance. She turned her head, prepared to ignore him. However, before Sunny could stop him, Tracy brandished his employment certificate and greeted the scout with a wide grin. "I got the job. I'm an Express rider."

"So you signed up, boy! Congratulations," Webb said heartily. Then, his eyes glinting wickedly, he added, "That took a lot of pluck. Seeing as how you had so much opposition."

Sunny gave him a withering glance.

"I hope you are satisfied, Mr. Chandler. Are you in the habit of advising boys to take life-threatening risks?"

"No, ma'am, but I always like to urge a young fellow to stand on his own two feet or sit in his own saddle, as the case may be."

Sunny had not expected such a sharp-edged rebuttal. Webb Chandler seemed to be purposely needling her. She tried to think of something cutting to say in response, but nothing came to mind. Frustrated, Sunny disdainfully drew aside her skirt and attempted to pass. But he was blocking the way. "If you will *excuse* me, Mr. Chandler—," she said coldly.

45

Webb's face twitched with amusement. "Allow me," he said, and stepping to one side, he bowed, battered hat in hand.

Without looking back Sunny, head high, swept past him and crossed the lobby to the stairs, inwardly seething. It irritated her especially that Chandler did not seem to feel the least snubbed. Almost as if he hadn't noticed it. Probably too thick-skinned. To her annoyance his voice followed her. "Not all ladies feel about the Express riders like your sister does. Let me tell you, you're in for some new experiences," he told Tracy, who had lagged behind.

Infuriated, Sunny swung around. Why on earth was he filling Tracy's head with a lot of nonsense! Why didn't he mind his own business?

At that very moment Webb caught her furious glance. A mischievous grin crossed his face. He slapped Tracy on the back and raised his voice. "Well, good luck, fella. Not that you won't need it!" Then he placed his hat back on his head and went out the hotel door, still chuckling.

Chapter 6

The next morning, Sunny and Tracy rented a wagon and set out for the Express station to see their future living quarters. Tracy was to start his training immediately, taking two trips with a regular rider to learn the route. Meanwhile Sunny would move into the Express station and make it into a "home"—an undertaking that, at her first sight of the place, seemed nearly impossible. She tried to hide her dismay after they unlocked the splintery wooden door and stepped inside, but she was horrified at the condition of the place. It would have discouraged the most optimistic.

From the porch, they entered into a large room divided by a wooden partition. Before the wall of one side there was a high counter on which there was a scale for weighing parcels, packages, and bulk mail. Behind the counter were shelves of various sizes, cubbyholes, and a large, square safe. On the other side of the divider was what might be called an all-purpose room. Down a narrow hall were two rooms that Sunny assumed were the ones to be used for their bedrooms.

The dirt floor sent up little clouds of dust as they walked around. The furnishings were few: a table scarred and stained, a few chairs with missing rungs and broken seats, a stove thick with accumulated grease and food spills. In the two small adjoining rooms, one contained four wooden bunks, the other a rusted iron bed with a lumpy straw mattress covered with dirty, striped ticking.

The place smelled musty, of old dirt, burnt food, a stove that didn't draw, and mildew. Beggars can't be choosers, Sunny reminded herself. Not that they were quite beggars. They were employees. They were going to earn their keep here.

Bleakly Sunny recalled the spotless home they had left. Their "house-proud" stepmother's motto had been "Cleanliness is next to godliness," and she demanded that Sunny see to it that the house was immaculate. Sunny was no stranger to applying "elbow grease" and scrub brush. Knowing that Tracy was anxiously watching her reaction, Sunny tried to overcome the urge to throw up her hands in disgust and leave. She couldn't. There was no turning back.

Tracy had not voiced any second thoughts about *his* decision. In fact, he was almost annoyingly cheerful. Sunny could do no less.

With Tracy's help she could at least get rid of the top layer of dirt and get new mattresses. Their trunks were still at the train station, where they'd left them to be loaded onto their wagon for the trip west. In them Sunny had packed quilts, sheets, blankets, pots, pans, kitchen utensils, and other household items that she'd planned to use on their journey and later in their California home. These could now be put to immediate use in the Express station. No sense thinking of what might have been, she told herself grimly. Crying over spilled milk would be a waste of time. She had more immediate—if not *better*—things to do.

"Well, we've got our work cut out for us here," she declared. "We'll have to stay one more night at the hotel; although I think they're overcharging us terribly, we can't stay here until we get this place cleaned. Come on." She whirled around, motioning her brother to come with her. "We'll find a general store and get some cleaning supplies and at least make a start."

Back in town they again had to fight the heavy traffic of the huge "prairie schooners" lumbering through on their way to Independence. They had to pull over to the side briefly to let one of the big wagons get by. Sunny had to keep herself from saying anything to Tracy about her bitter disappointment. He was so buoyed up by his prospective new career as a Pony Express rider, he did not seem at all downcast that they might be stuck in this backwater town for who knew how long?

Tracy went to pick up their trunks at the station while she was at Ardley's General Store purchasing cleaning supplies and some groceries.

The minute she walked through the door, it seemed to Sunny, all conversation halted and heads turned to look at her curiously. The glances varied, from the veiled ones of curious women shoppers to the boldly appraising ones from the group of men gathered around the potbellied stove. Naturally, a stranger in such a small community was bound to attract attention, she told herself, trying not to feel self-conscious as she went over to the counter. A plump, rosy-cheeked woman in a blue checkered apron, her pewter-colored hair drawn from a middle part to a plait around her head, stood behind it and watched her approach warily.

"Good morning," Sunny said pleasantly, bringing out her list. She needed everything from laundry soap and carbolic disinfectant to baking soda.

Verna Ardley eyed her new customer keenly. Verna prided herself on being a good judge of character. Long experience dealing with the public had given her the ability, and she had rarely been proved wrong, even in a first impression. This young woman presented an interesting challenge. She was about twenty years of age, Verna guessed. Nicely dressed, although too nicely for these parts, where most women were too busy with children and chores to pay much attention to their appearance. A bit on the skinny side, but held herself well. Not so pretty as to spark any jealousy on the part of the womenfolk, married or single, but pleasant-looking enough. Verna always noticed eyes. Like the Scripture said, they were the windows of the soul. This girl's eyes looked directly at a body, with not a speck of cunning or dishonesty, and there was a sweetness to the mouth, even though she was holding it now in a tight line.

Of course, her manner was a little uncertain, yet there was a spunky, independent air about her. That was something Verna recognized and admired in other women, because both were qualities she liked to believe she herself possessed. Still, Verna always maintained a wait-and-see attitude with any newcomer before offering more than service. "Yes, miss, can I help you?"

"Thank you, I hope so. . . ."

For a minute Verna thought she heard a note of appeal in the soft voice. She got a hint of insight that this young woman was not as confident as she appeared and that she needed help, more than simply filling her order—all kinds of help. Maybe even more than Verna could give.

Sunny began to read off her list, and Mrs. Ardley went to fetch each item as it was called until they were all stacked up in a pile on the counter. She then began to add up a column of figures, pausing every once in a while to tap her pencil against her teeth. Finally she announced, "That comes to five dollars and twenty-nine cents."

At the sum Sunny experienced a momentary pang of panic. It had come to more than she expected. Perhaps she could do without some of the items. With a show of calm

50

Sunny opened her pouch purse to check its contents. Then she made a quick calculation of her remaining cash, hoping she had enough to pay for it all. How embarrassing it would be to ask for some of it to be put back on the shelves. Especially with everybody in the store an audience to her transaction. As she was quickly adding up her money Mrs. Ardley cleared her throat.

"By the way, miss, you're Sunniva Lyndall, ain't you?"

Startled, Sunny nodded.

"You and your brother are the new employees of the Express station out on Hayfork Road?"

Again Sunny nodded.

"Well, I should've mentioned right off that Mr. Graham left instructions that any items purchased for the Express station were to be put on his account."

"Oh!" A wave of surprised gratitude swept over Sunny. "You're sure?"

"That's exactly what he told my husband, miss."

"Well then," Sunny hesitated, "I suppose—since we *are* employees of the Express station—" Then she reached out and separated the baking soda, the sack of flour, the sugar, the eggs, and the tin of molasses from the cleaning supplies and moved them to one side. "Since these items are for our personal use, I'll pay for them myself."

Sunny was too relieved to notice Verna's admiring glance. With Sunny's statement that she would pay separately for the groceries, Verna's estimation of the newcomer had risen.

"So your brother's going to be a rider?" asked Verna as she began bagging Sunny's groceries.

"Yes," Sunny answered.

Some of her anxiety must have crept into her voice, because immediately the other woman said, "Well, if he can ride a horse, he'll do just fine. Mr. Graham takes a personal interest in his riders, I'll say that. Most of them got no families, and he's like a father to them. If one gets hurt

51

or sick, he sees that Doc Hasting takes care of them. Your brother's lucky. Not all the Express companies are that good to their employees." Verna put the cleaning supplies into a box. "There. Now these I'll just ring up on Mr. Graham's account."

It occurred to Sunny that the storekeeper was probably a fund of information about everyone in town and might possibly be able to satisfy her curiosity about Rhys Graham. Hoping to elicit some information about her new employer, she murmured, "That was most generous of Mr. Graham."

"Oh, he's a capital fella, that's for sure. Folks wanted him to run for mayor at one time, but he declined. For all his fine manners and gentlemanly ways, he can handle himself all right. I've seen him take care of some unruly drunks, as well as a couple of gents who had in mind to rob the Express office. He don't tote a gun, but he's someone to be reckoned with. Don't anyone mess with Rhys Graham but once, I'll tell you."

"My brother will come and pick up all these things in a while, Mrs. Ardley, if that's all right. He's gone to the railroad station to get our trunks and other belongings we left there. I'm going to meet him now, then we'll stop back by after that."

"Sure thing. I'll just put them behind the counter here till you all come," Mrs. Ardley assured her.

It had proved providential that Mr.Graham had arranged to pay for the needed cleaning supplies, since their cash was so low. However, it made Sunny feel slightly uncomfortable. Maybe she should stop by the Express office and make sure that this *was* completely satisfactory.

However, just as she stepped outside, she saw Rhys Graham crossing the street, coming directly to the store.

"Why, Miss Lyndall. Good morning." He took off his hat and smiled at her. His greeting was so warm and friendly that Sunny felt suddenly awkward.

"Good morning, Mr. Graham. Tracy and I are moving some things to the station today, getting it cleaned. I just had to confirm—I mean, I was told by Mrs. Ardley that any supplies I bought—"

"Yes, of course, everything is to be placed on my account. Business expenses, naturally. I hope you got everything you needed? I must apologize for the state of neglect at the Express station. It's only been used as a temporary bunkhouse up to now. There's never been a woman—it wasn't meant to be a proper dwelling place."

"Oh, it's fine! I mean, it will be. We're very grateful, Mr. Graham. You have been extraordinarily kind. I hope I didn't sound foolish. But I just wanted to make sure. I suppose that since we were so outrageously swindled, I've become suspicious of people offering to do something for us—I mean, it's hard for me to accept the fact that anyone is honest or sincerely wants to help. Or that somehow I won't be taken advantage of—"

Graham's eyes seemed to darken. "I can understand that you might feel that way. But don't let that one bad experience sour you on everyone you meet here, Miss Lyndall." A slight smile softened his expression. "Don't judge too harshly, Miss Lyndall. People are capable of many different kinds of behavior. Most react with fear to something they don't understand or haven't experienced. But I think you'll find—especially out here—that most are both generous and willing to help a stranger."

Somehow his words seemed a reprimand, and again Sunny felt awkward. She felt that she had said too much. Had she somehow offended him? Should she make further explanation? However, Rhys Graham had already replaced his hat and started moving on.

"Well, thank you—I do appreciate all you've done," she stammered.

"Not at all, Miss Lyndall. It is a pleasure to see you again.

53

Have no concern about the bill at the general store. Whatever else you need is to be put on my account. I arranged it."

Feeling flustered and unsettled by this less-than-satisfactory encounter, Sunny walked in the direction of the railroad station. Tracy would have retrieved the belongings they'd left there on the ill-fated day they'd been persuaded to get off the train and wait for Mr. Faraday. Just thinking about that rascal made Sunny's blood boil. Thinking of him also made her recall Mr. Graham's gentle reproach. He had taken her to task subtly for her "tarring everyone with the same stick."

Reaching the railroad station, she found Tracy in a discussion with the freight clerk. It seemed their trunks and other possessions could not be found. Tracy did not have any kind of identification, and the storage room was piled high with an assortment of miscellaneous boxes, barrels, and packages. Quickly Sunny dug into her purse, found the baggage checks they had been given, and the search began in earnest.

The storage room was airless, hot, and dusty. Almost suffocating from the heat and dust, Sunny went out onto the platform to get some air, leaving the clerk and Tracy to continue the search. If, on top of everything else, their luggage had been lost or mistakenly put on a train and shipped out, it would be the last straw! Everything she had in the world had been stuffed into her trunk. There was also the box of cherished keepsakes that had belonged to their mother, to say nothing of Sunny's hatbox containing her best bonnets.

The hoot of a shrill whistle announced a train's arrival. It came chugging down the track, then shrieked to a stop with a loud hissing noise. Abstractedly Sunny watched passengers get off and the station manager hurry out to consult with the conductor. She saw the clerk who had been helping Tracy run down to the end of the train to oversee the loading of some crates. Then the whistle hooted a warning, and the train began slowly moving again. This town was only a proverbial "whistle-stop." Sunny remembered how they had been rushed down the aisle and urged from the train by Faraday. Unknown to them, the real reason was to get them off before they changed their minds, and for him to get away—with *their* money! Seeing the train—on which they should have stayed—begin to pull out brought back all Sunny's anger.

Caught up in that past experience, she watched as the train slid slowly by the platform. Suddenly her mouth opened in a gasp. At first she could not believe her eyes. No! It couldn't be! But it *was*! Faraday! Looking out one of the sooty windows. Then he saw her. Their eyes met in horrified recognition. He ducked his head. Totally losing control, Sunny picked up her skirts and began running alongside the train, waving her arms and shouting at the top of her voice. The wind caught her bonnet, tearing it off. On she ran, screaming, "You! You villain!" But the train was gaining speed. All she could see was the top of the biscuit brown bowler on the crouching Faraday.

"Stop! Stop the train!" Sunny yelled, shaking her fist. But the train rolled on. Gathering momentum, it sped along until it rounded the curve of the tracks and became a tiny speck and finally disappeared.

Breathless from running, standing alone at the end of the platform, her bonnet dangling around her neck by its strings, Sunny wept tears of frustration and fury. Slowly she turned and dejectedly retraced her steps back to the station house, where a small group of people were staring at her. Among them were her brother, the baggage clerk, and the station manager. Tracy looked both bewildered and embarrassed. She realized that *again* she had made a spectacle of herself in his eyes. Well, of course, he didn't know whom she'd seen.

With as much dignity as she could muster, Sunny straightened her bonnet and, in as calm a voice as she could manage, asked the station manager, "Where was that train headed?"

"Kansas City, connections in St. Louis, then New York City," he rattled off.

It might as well be Timbuktu, Sunny thought, sighing dismally.

She answered the question in Tracy's eyes with a curt "Tell you later," then asked, "Did you find our trunks?"

"Yep, got 'em in the wagon. 'Fraid your hatbox got mighty badly crushed, Sunny. It was under some wooden crates, and—"

She shook her head and shrugged. "It doesn't matter," she said dully. Nothing mattered except that now she knew there was no hope of bringing that scoundrel to justice, getting back their money, or for that matter getting to California anytime soon.

Chapter 7

*T*his place was a disgrace. Hardly fit for human habitation! Sunny wrinkled her nose in disgust as she surveyed the Express station. Nothing but hard work would change things. And it was up to her to do it. Tracy had gone on his training run with one of the Express riders and would be away two days.

Swaddled in a muslin "Mother Hubbard" coverall apron, Sunny shoved her hair back under a bandanna handkerchief and dug in. Wielding a broom, she vigorously attacked the accumulated dirt, swooping and brushing out old cobwebs where dried spiders nested. Dust flew everywhere. Sneezing constantly, she swiped at her nose with the back of one hand. Tiny beads of perspiration rolled down her face; tendrils of hair escaped from under the bandanna, which by now was plastered against her damp forehead. Every so often she stopped and, leaning on the broom, marked her progress. After she got all this debris out, the floor would have to be scrubbed. Once the walls were clean, she could whitewash them. The windows still badly needed cleaning. She had done a superficial job on them to let some light in so she could see better, but they would have to be done more thoroughly.

It was hot, dirty work. Nostalgically she thought of the cool, shady porch of their Ohio farmhouse under the trees back home. Why had she ever thought it a good idea to leave? If she had only known she would end up penniless, a pauper. . .

No, she wouldn't allow herself to think like that. Back there she would still have been under her stepmother's relatives, who would have been checking on her every movement, watching every misstep, criticizing, waiting for her to make a mistake. At least here she was free. Awful as it had been, this was making her own way. She'd learned from her mistakes. This was the way to earn independence. She had to believe it would all work out in the end.

Sunny would never forget the blow of her father's marriage when she was fourteen. She had been so close to him before he brought his second wife home. Matilda Spencer, a milliner with her own thriving business, was not given either to children or domesticity. With her had come a hired girl and a new order in the Lyndall household. Sunny wondered if her father ever realized his mistake. If he had, he never showed it; he just became quieter, more withdrawn, distancing himself both from his new wife and his children. Martin Lyndall died when Sunny was nineteen, and her stepmother spent most of her time thereafter in town or with her own relatives, leaving Sunny in charge of the farm and Tracy.

That was why Sunny felt so protective, so concerned for him. Wasn't it understandable, no matter what Webb Chandler thought? Thinking of Chandler, Sunny felt a thrust of resentment. What business did he have encouraging Tracy to take the rider job?

Sunny drew a long breath. One good thing about hard work: it kept her from worrying too much about Tracy. She filled the bucket and got out the scrub brush and a cake of yellow soap. Down on her knees, she started sloshing the

58

soapy water onto the floor. Her breath came fast as she pushed the brush back and forth on the boards. Soon the grain began to come through. She sat back on her heels for a minute, resting, admiring the results of her labor. Leaving the floor to dry, Sunny went outside. Hands on hips, she scowled at the scroungy exterior. Whitewash was the only answer for the rough, scaly, splintery wood. When she finished cleaning the inside, she'd tackle the outside of the building.

First things first, she thought and went back inside. She had to get rid of this scummy, dirty water, get fresh water from the well, and do a final wash of the floor. Already her back ached. Her wrist pulled as she carried the heavy bucket outside to empty it, so she had to set it down momentarily. Panting from the exertion, she did not hear approaching hoofbeats. She was unaware that she was no longer alone, until she heard a rich, full laugh.

Startled, she jerked around. There, of all people, was Lucas Flynt's scout, Webb Chandler, seated on horseback, grinning at her!

"Afternoon, ma'am," he said, tipping his hat.

This unexpected appearance upset her unreasonably. Seeing him again reminded her of how condescendingly he had treated her at their first meeting and how he had baited her about Tracy. He represented all her own frustration.

She glared at him. He was smiling as though she should welcome him! What conceit! She didn't like the fellow. Never had. Not one bit. Seemed arrogant, full of himself. Who did he think he was, anyway? Dropping by uninvited. Probably had come to gloat and *laugh* at her situation. He also had the air of a man who somehow thought himself a gift to ladies. She would never have admitted it, but she was annoyed that he had found her looking like this. She brushed her hair off her damp forehead with the back of one hand and demanded, "What are *you* doing here?"

"Just riding by...then I saw you and thought I'd stop, pass the time of day, ma'am."

"Well, now that you've *passed* it, why don't you just ride on by?" she asked, mimicking his Texas drawl.

Ignoring her sarcasm, Webb dismounted. "You look like you could use some help—if you don't mind me sayin' so."

"I *do* mind, and I don't need any advice, thank you. I repeat, Mr. Chandler, why don't you just go on about your business, *whatever that is,* and leave me to my work."

He made no move to leave. Instead he leaned against his saddle and remarked lazily, "You sure are always ready to pick a fight, Miss Lyndall. Fact is, I know your brother is on his route, and I just thought I might—"

She interrupted. "This Express station has nothing to do with you, Mr. Chandler. What we do here or where my brother happens to be is none of your—"

Webb did not let her finish but went on talking in his casual manner. "Well now, this place is pretty far from town...kinda isolated. And it's a well-known fact that sometimes there's money kept out here waiting for pickup or delivery. That might tempt some ornery folks to come out and make...trouble. I was just making it my *business"*—here he emphasized his words—"to check and see if everything out here was...all right."

"Well, now that you've seen it is, you can be on your way." She deliberately turned her back and started to lift the bucket of dirty, soapy water.

Webb moved quickly, intercepting her and grabbing the handle. "Here, let me," he said. An immediate tug-of-war ensued.

"Let go," she said between clenched teeth.

"Don't be a stubborn little fool. It's heavy. I'll empty it for you."

As they struggled the dirty water sloshed back and forth, spilling water on both of them. Sunny felt it soak through

60

her clothes, onto her feet. The harder she pulled, the more water splashed on her. Angrily she gave a savage jerk of the handle and suddenly, swearing, Webb let go. As he did she lost her balance, staggered backwards, and fell, dumping the contents of the bucket on top of her. Drenched and enraged, she sputtered in helpless fury while Webb doubled up with his eyes shut and laughed uncontrollably.

She could have killed him! He was insufferable. As he continued to laugh she scrambled to her feet, tripping over the wet hem of her dress, and rushed toward him, fists doubled, ready to pound him.

"Beast!" she screamed. "You're no gentleman. You're the worst, crudest, most despicable ... ," she ranted helplessly, running out of enough names to call him. Webb made a grab for her flaying arms, his grip like steel, holding her off.

"Now, now, little lady. There's no cause to take on like this. If you'd allowed me to do what I wanted—that is, do a heavy job for you—this wouldn't have happened." He paused a minute while she continued to try to wrest herself from his grasp. "Just take it easy. I don't want to hurt you. I'll let you go if you'll just calm down—"

Seeing an advantage in doing that, Sunny went slack. Webb's hands loosened. She stepped back, then before he could move, she swung around and grabbed up the half-empty bucket, and with all her strength she slung the remains of the dirty, soapy water at him.

Instead of being angry, he started laughing again. He casually brushed the front of his fringed leather shirt where the water had splashed upon it, and gave her a small salute.

"Now I think we're even, miss. So I'll take your earlier suggestion and be on my way." With another tip of his hat brim, Webb swung himself up onto his horse, picked up the reins, and turned his horse's head.

It was only then that, to her absolute horror, Sunny saw Rhys Graham on his gleaming roan horse, standing at the gate to the Express yard. How long had he been there? How much had he witnessed? She thought she might die of humiliation.

Rhys dismounted and walked toward her. He was as immaculately groomed as ever, although more casually dressed in a beige linen riding coat, his boots polished. He removed his hat and acknowledged Webb with a nod.

If Rhys noticed Sunny's sodden skirt, her generally disheveled appearance, he gave no hint of that nor made any comment. She might have been perfectly groomed, dressed for a tea party. Right then and there, Sunny *knew* Rhys Graham was *the* perfect gentleman. Not like some she could mention . . . She threw Webb a poison look.

"Good day, Miss Lyndall," Rhys said. "Sorry to drop by unannounced. But I've been concerned about how you're settlin' in out here. I knew the place was in bad shape. We took it over in a hurry, and the boys used it as a bunkhouse without too much fixing." He included Webb in an ironic smile. "Cowboys are used to sleeping on the ground with only a bedroll and don't expect very much in creature comforts when they become riders. But a lady's different. . .and I've wondered if we shouldn't make some other arrangements for you."

Sunny made an ineffectual swipe at her hair with both hands and smoothed her skirt, knowing neither action helped much. "Oh, I'm fine, truly, Mr. Graham. And we've done quite a lot to improve things. Do come in and see." Pointedly ignoring Webb, Sunny moved to the front door and opened it so that Rhys could walk in and look the place over.

To her annoyance Webb dismounted and followed them inside. Even her daggerlike glance did not intimidate him.

Rhys walked into the middle of the room, looking slowly around without making a comment. However, Webb let out a slow whistle. "Lady, you've done some magic. It isn't the same place."

Sunny followed his glance with a feeling of satisfaction. She had thoroughly cleaned, brushing the ceiling and walls with a stiff broom, sweeping and scrubbing the floor until the wood grain of the planks was now plainly visible. The strong smell of lye soap had replaced the odor of accumulated dirt. Clean windows allowed sunlight in through the once-grimy panes. Sunny had to keep her mouth prim to keep from smiling at Webb's obvious surprise and approval. But even a compliment from *him* was some reward for all her hard work.

"Yes indeed, Miss Lyndall, you've done wonders in a very short time," Rhys nodded. "If there's anything you need in the way of additional furniture, equipment, cooking utensils, or whatever, do feel free to order from Ardley's and, of course, put it on the Express company account."

"Thank you," Sunny murmured, feeling both grateful and a little discomfited to have Webb overhear Mr. Graham's offer. She felt sure that this kind of generosity wasn't usually extended to *employees*. She hoped he would not get the wrong idea. An awkward few minutes followed; both men remained standing there, glancing around as if still examining the interior. Sunny wasn't sure whether or not she should offer them some refreshment. But that might appear to be turning a business visit into a social occasion. Before she could decide, Rhys spoke.

"Well, I'll be on my way now. You too, Webb? If you're going back to town, why not ride along with me? I have a few things I'd like to discuss with you."

Whatever had been Webb's original intention, there was not anything else he could do but accept Rhys' suggestion, and they left together.

Watching them ride out the gate, Sunny thought how different the two men were. Rhys Graham seemed oddly out of place in this frontier town, while Webb Chandler

63

somehow belonged with the hills, the sagebrush, and the spectacular skies.

Webb and Rhys parted company at the fork in the road, and Rhys rode back into town alone. This morning's visit out to the Express station had again opened a window of memory in his mind. One he had kept closed for a long time, one he had thought locked. The Lyndall girl had first pried it open when she had walked into his office the day before.

Both her vulnerability and her strength had attracted and interested him. He admired the way she had tried to hide the fear and the panic he had seen in her eyes and the way she had eventually accepted the inevitable and signed the papers of permission for her brother to become a rider.

Rhys winced. He always had a twinge of conscience when he signed up one of these kids. That's what most of them were—as young as some of the drummer boys who'd run away from home to join up during the war. Foolhardy youngsters bent on adventure—never mind the risk—who learned too soon what war was really like: not a glory road but hell. . . .

Rhys shuddered, thrusting the horror back. He couldn't waste time worrying about boys whose families didn't seem to. Of course, most of them had no families—as the want ad said, "Orphans preferred." He was in business, wasn't he? The mail was important. Someone had to take it— through storms, sleet, and narrow mountain passes, over ledges and canyons, and trails sometimes blocked with rock slides and snow. He tried to see that they were well rewarded—those that survived.

Rhys shook his head as if to clear it. He was in town now and reined his horse in front of his office, dismounted, and hitched the horse to the railing. He went inside and into his private room, then slumped down on the oak swivel chair behind the massive desk. Staring out the window onto the main street, he let his mind wander.

In Rhys' memory was lodged a place where he some-times allowed himself to visit, not often but once in a while, where there was a rambling clapboard house with dark green shutters and a wide porch overlooking a well-kept garden. Beyond that was an orchard, always—in this mental picture—blooming, with pale pink apple blossoms perfuming the soft air. A breeze was forever causing the leaves on the tree-shaded lawn to move gently. It was a world far distant from the looming blue ribbon of hills that rimmed this dusty little town.

Somewhere in this picture was the shadowy figure of a young woman, slim as a willow wand, with a cloud of sun-glossed hair. The features were indistinct, but Rhys imag-ined there would be softly curved cheeks, a delicately formed mouth tipped up at the corners in a gentle smile, and intelligence and wit in her thickly lashed eyes—not unlike Sunny Lyndall's hazel ones . . . .

With an effort Rhys pushed the thought of Sunniva Lyn-dall from his mind. She had awakened memories best not recalled, had stirred a longing to revisit that place he had relinquished and dared not enter again.

Chapter 8

*S*unny woke up with a start, shivering from a bad dream. She hadn't had one of those in a long time. Not since that first night Tracy had taken the mail run alone, after having only twice accompanied another rider. She had hardly slept at all that night; her imagination had run wild, picturing all sorts of horrors happening to her brother on his first trip. Rising before dawn, she apprehensively waited for his return.

To her utter amazement, instead of coming in haggard, exhausted, and discouraged by the hazards of his new job, Tracy had returned jubilant. She had listened in disbelief as he enthusiastically described the excitement of the job, regaling her with stories told by other riders. Finally, reluctantly succumbing to her suggestion that he get some sleep, he had flopped on his bunk bed and slept for the next ten hours.

Now it had only been three weeks since they began running the Express station, yet sometimes it felt as if they'd been here forever. Although Sunny was proud of how well, how responsibly, Tracy was doing his job, she saw him changing before her eyes, becoming self-confident and even cocky as he became a seasoned rider. Maybe it was selfish, but she missed that special place she had always had with Tracy. Daily he was becoming more of a man.

Sunny had to face an unexpected reality. Tracy actually *liked* the job. He had taken to being a rider like the proverbial duck to water. What if he liked it *too* much? That thought haunted her. What if, when the time came and they had saved enough money to finance it, Tracy didn't want to go to California?

That possibility nagged at her as she lay there. He didn't talk about California anymore. Not that they talked much about anything. He was too tired when he came in from his route, and on the days he was off, other chores kept him busy. It troubled her a great deal, but she decided not to say anything to her brother. For the time being she would have to put up with Tracy's boyish pride in taking on a challenging job and proving he could do it. Being a Pony Express rider was the peak experience of his life so far. Gradually the glow would dim. Eventually he would burn out with the long, hard rides, the rough terrain, the winds of winter, the ravages of the trail. She had to believe that. Otherwise she might have to resign herself to staying in this town for the rest of her life. It seemed almost symbolic. Just as Cottonwood was on the border of Independence, the "jumping-off place," remaining here would be like remaining on the brink of adventure, independence, freedom—all that going west had signified to her. No! Sunny threw back the covers and jumped out of bed. Nothing was going to make her give up that dream.

Fighting the mingled emotions of depression and hopelessness, Sunny got to work. It hadn't taken her long to learn how to manage the Express station. She was smart and quick, and she soon caught on to sorting and marking the mail and writing receipts for the payroll pouches and banknotes packed into the riders' saddlebags each day. Doing her job well gave her much satisfaction. However, the more organized and better at it she became, the more time she had to think. The more time she had to think, the more she fretted over their situation.

Today all morning long she felt restless. She got the indoor chores out of the way, quickly deciding that the more vigorous work of taking care of the ponies would take her mind off her problems and keep her from dwelling so much on her own discontent. She had started wearing a pair of Tracy's worn jeans, which she had cut off at the knees, under her skirt when working in the corral or barn. It made bending, stooping, mucking out the stalls, and pitching hay easier. She pulled them on now and tucked the hem of her dress into sturdy boots. Then she went outside.

When Tracy and the other riders were out on their routes, the Express ponies were her responsibility. The fact that her father had taught Sunny to care for her own horse when Sunny was much younger stood her in good stead in this job. But currying and brushing these "critters" was trickier by far than tending to her gentle mare back home. The ponies had a wild streak, were stubborn and resistant to being handled. It took patience—not one of Sunny's strongest traits—and a lot of concentration.

She was doing just that sort of concentrating, keeping a firm hold on a pony's haunches to brush his hind legs, when he suddenly pricked up his ears and whinnied. "Easy, Bramble," she said. Turning around to see what had spooked him, she was chagrined to see Webb Chandler. Leaning his folded arms on the top rail of the corral and placing one booted foot on the lower one, he grinned at her.

"Howdy, Miss Lyndall."

Sunny gave him a cool look. "What are you doing still around? I thought Flynt's wagon train had taken off a couple of weeks ago." She frowned; the idea that she and Tracy *should* have been on it, on their way to California, still rankled.

"Decided not to go this trip. Too much infightin' and wranglin' between the Iowans and the Tenesseans who'd joined up to travel west together. Couldn't see nuthin' but trouble with all that brewin' before they even got started."

"What do you want *here*?" she demanded ungraciously.

"Good golly, Miss Lyndall." He gave a long, low whistle. "I declare, I never met a lady who was always so cross and mad at the world, frowning and working." He shook his head.

"There's a lot of work to be done, and my disposition is my own business, Mr. Chandler," she snapped. "Not that you help it by your constant coming around and bothering me." She went back to brushing the pony's shanks.

A few seconds of silence followed. She felt self-conscious working with him staring at her. Why didn't he leave? But he kept standing there, making no move to go.

"Your brother out on his route?"

She didn't bother to answer. If the man had any sense, he'd *know* this was the riders' work she was doing. She started brushing the pony's haunches.

"How does he like the job by now?" Webb asked.

"What business is that of yours, whether he likes it or not?"

"Well now, mebbe I feel a mite responsible. As you pointed out, I did encourage him some."

All Sunny's smoldering resentment resurfaced. She spun around, hands on hips, and confronted him. "Don't you have something better to do? Other folks have work to do, even if *you* don't!"

He gave her a scrutinizing look. "Don't like to see little brother grow up, do you? Mebbe this is the time to cut the apron strings, let him go."

His words stung like a wasp's bite. Sunny felt her cheeks burn. "Who asked you for advice?"

"I'm jest sayin' that doing a man's job seems to prove he don't need no mother-henning. Only mentioned it 'cause womenfolk don't understand how it is with a young fella trying his durndest to prove himself—"

Suddenly she'd had enough of Webb Chandler. She wasn't going to take any more of his nonsense. She'd tell him off once and for all and make sure he understood. Who did he think he was, coming out here uninvited, handing out advice? "Listen, Webb Chandler, and listen good. I don't like repeating myself. I don't need your advice or your help. Why don't you just go about doing whatever it was you were doing before you came out here?" She grabbed Bramble's bridle, pushed open the corral gate, and started toward the barn.

Webb followed. He stood at the door while she took the pitchfork and shifted some hay into the feeding box. "Sorry. No offense meant."

She didn't turn around or acknowledge his awkward apology, just went on pitching. When she finished, Webb was gone. Still, what he'd said about Tracy had hit a sore spot, and she couldn't forget it.

For some reason, for the next few days Sunny felt lonelier than ever. She felt almost *homesick*. She hadn't realized she would miss some of the things she had grown bored with back home. School friends she had grown up with, gone with to choir practice, ice-cream socials, quilting bees, and taffy pulls. Here there was nothing, no one. No one her age, not one woman in town, had given her more than a curious glance or a cool nod.

Tracy was no company at all. Gone four out of seven days a week, sleeping half the time he was home. The rest of the time, he was busy doing his chores, sharing the barn work and the care of the ponies with the other riders.

One morning Sunny was feeling especially lonesome and sorry for herself when she went to Ardley's General Store to do her shopping. Coming inside, she noticed a box in the corner. In it was the cat she had sometimes seen sunning

70

herself in one of the store windows. Now the cat had kittens. One tiny black face raised itself over the edge of the box and seemed to stare at Sunny with great blue eyes. There had always been cats at home. Oddly enough, their old long-haired gray "Pommy," whom they'd had since he was a kitten, died only a few weeks before they left. Cats were cozy; cats were good company. Sunny suddenly wished she had one. Just its presence in the Express station building would provide another living thing on those long, dark nights when Tracy was gone.

As Clem Ardley stacked her supplies on the counter and bagged them for her Sunny asked tentatively, "Have you found homes for all the kittens?"

With twinkling eyes, he shot her a speculative glance. "You interested in having a cat?"

"Well yes, if—"

"Far as I'm concerned, you can have 'em all, the whole kit and caboodle!" He laughed heartily at his own joke.

"Just one would be fine. Are you sure?"

"Take any one you want."

"I think I'd like the little black one."

Mr. Ardley came around from behind the counter, scooped up the fuzzy black kitty and handed it to Sunny. It was all squeaks, shrieks, and sharp little claws. Sunny juggled it, then stuck it under her jacket, close to her bosom, and refastened the buttons. It quieted at once. Sunny and Mr. Ardley exchanged a smile, then he carried her bundles out to the Express company wagon for her. She kept the kitten snuggled against her inside the jacket as she climbed in, picked up the reins, turned the horse around, and started home.

As soon as she reached the Express station Sunny, still cradling the kitty, jumped out of the wagon and hurried inside. There was a fire in the stove, and she put down the scrap of black fur in front on the hearth where the heat

71

had made it warm. She filled a saucer with milk, which he quickly began to lap up. She found an old, soft, torn shirt that belonged to Tracy but was too tattered to mend and bundled it up into a little nest. When the kitten had finished the milk, she picked him up gently and settled him in his makeshift bed. From that day on the kitten was a joy. Watching him skitter, jump, and play provided entertainment and amusement. Whenever Sunny sat down, he hopped into her lap, twirled around a couple of times, then curled up and went to sleep. He followed her around the house, always at her heels, so much so that she often almost stepped on him or tripped over him. It seemed natural to give him the name Shadow.

Chapter 9

A few weeks later spring seemed to burst into full bloom. The days were so lovely that more and more Sunny was drawn outside. It was too nice for the chores usually done inside. One May morning she carried her metal washtub outdoors. Placing it on wooden sawhorses, she started doing her laundry. Soapsuds were flying and she was scrubbing vigorously on her tin washboard when a familiar voice greeted her.

"Good mornin', Miss Lyndall. Hard at it as usual, eh?"

Sunny inwardly groaned. Not that pesky Webb Chandler *again*? Couldn't the man take a hint?

"Seems like every time I ride by, there you are workin' your head off. Don't you ever take a day of rest? Matter of fact," he drawled with a hint of laughter in his voice, "don't think I've ever seen you lately but with a broom or a horse."

She straightened up, flicked the suds on her hands back into the tub, and glared at him. "What do you want this time?"

"Well, Miss Lyndall, I've been thinkin'. You and me— well, we got off on the wrong foot somehow. I'd like to make amends—"

"Not necessary," she replied curtly.

"Well yes, ma'am, it is. My Aunt Pem, who raised me, always taught me that if you've offended someone—even *unintentionally*—you should try to make things right." With that Webb whipped a bunch of bright yellow daffodils out from behind his back and held them out to her.

Sunny was taken aback by the unexpected gesture. Suddenly she felt a little guilty about the rude way she had treated Webb Chandler. Tracy often accused her of being too quick-tempered, ready to fly off the handle, as well as being "too durned bossy." She knew she had blamed Webb unfairly for their not being allowed to go on Flynt's wagon train. Mostly she had resented his comments about Tracy. Maybe because she suspected he was right.

She wiped her soapy hands on her apron and accepted the bouquet a trifle sheepishly. "Thank you. They're very pretty."

"They're out of Verna Ardley's garden," he told her. At her raised eyebrows he hastened to say, "Oh, she told me to go ahead and pick as many as I liked! She has dozens of 'em. Said they shouldn't go to waste."

Sunny suppressed a smile. Obviously Webb Chandler wasn't an experienced flower giver.

"The Ardleys—well, they're like a second family to me," he explained. "Anyway, the real reason I come out here this morning is—" He paused. "Seeing tomorrow's the Sabbath and they say even the Lord took one day a week off, I thought you might like to ride into the hills where it's cool and have a picnic."

"With *you*?"

"Yes! Why *not* me?" He looked affronted.

Probably never been turned down by a girl before, Sunny guessed. A mischievous idea popped into her head. Taking a moment as if to consider the invitation, Sunny said, "Well . . ."—she dragged the word out—"to answer your question, Mr. Chandler, I most certainly *do* take a day off. I plan to do so tomorrow. And since you pointed out

74

tomorrow *is* Sunday, I will be attending church. If you also plan to go . . .?" she let the supposition dangle.

Church? Webb gulped, nearly letting out a yelp of surprise. *Church?* He hadn't been inside one since he'd run away from his Aunt Pem when he was fourteen. One of the reasons being that she'd insisted on dragging him to church three times a week, twice on Sunday. Not that he didn't believe in the Almighty. He did. On more than one occasion he'd had to call upon him for help, and he'd usually come through. Or given him the idea of how to get out of whatever mess he'd got himself into. But church . . . Somehow that didn't suit his style.

Seeing Webb's reaction, Sunny knew she had hit the mark. At the same moment, she realized she had been, as Proverbs 6:2 said, "ensnared by the words of your mouth." Until just then she had not had the slightest intention of going to church. She had disliked the thought of going to a strange church where she knew no one. Just as her stepmother had always warned her, her wicked tongue had got her into trouble. Now she had no choice but to do what she had told Webb she was going to do.

Webb recovered himself quickly. He had not missed the swift change of expression on Sunny's face. He suspected she had spoken on the spur of the moment. Two could play at that game, he decided. He nodded solemnly. "What a high-minded suggestion, Miss Lyndall. My Aunt Pem would be so pleased that you have reminded me of something I have lately been so lax about: church attendance."

Sunny glanced at him sharply. His tone was sanctimonious in the extreme, and she suspected he was up to something. While she was trying to decide what Webb continued, his drawl pronounced. "Of course, being on the trail as much as I am, Sunday services are a kind of happenstance event, depending on whose wagon train you're with. One time it's the Baptists, the next it might be the Methodists. But then it's

75

all God's Word, as I'm sure you'd agree. Well then, I'll be on my way. And looking forward very much to seeing you tomorrow."

With that Webb swung into his saddle and, smiling to himself, turned his horse around and went through the gate.

Well, we'll just see about that, Mr. Chandler! Sunny said to herself as he rode off.

The next morning broke hot at seven. Getting up and looking out the window at the brilliant sunshine, Sunny regretted her impulsive declaration to Webb Chandler the day before. She dreaded the thought of getting into proper Sunday attire, bonnet, and gloves and driving into town in the heat. *Serves me right!* she thought. She hadn't worn anything but a denim skirt and muslin blouse for weeks. Bemoaning the state of her hands, which were reddened and roughened by all her recent hard work, she slipped a pair of crocheted lace gloves into her handbag to replace the leather driving gloves when she got into town. Finally she put on a blue Irish linen dress and her straw bonnet with daisies, which she had hoped to wear for the first time in sunny California. Satisfied with her image reflected in the wavy little mirror over the kitchen sink, she hitched up the horse and wagon and set off for church.

She was some time finding the town's one little church, which was almost hidden behind the row of stores, taverns, dance halls, and saloons on the main street. Its bell was already tolling as she hurried up the steps. She found a seat in the back pew and sat down. Feeling a little flustered and warm, she wondered why she had made the effort. To impress Webb Chandler? She should be ashamed of herself. Sitting in the small, airless wooden building, Sunny did not feel the least bit spiritual. Why had she even bothered to come? After a few heads had turned for that first curious stare when she entered, no one had deigned to speak or even so much as nod to her. She might as well

GRACE BALLOCH
MEMORIAL LIBRARY
625 North Fifth Street
Spearfish SD 57783-2311

have been invisible. She felt increasingly uncomfortable, miserable. At *that* thought, the small voice of her conscience nudged, *So you come to church to be seen?* Almost visibly shrinking, she tried protesting, *But my intentions were good.* But *were* they, *really?* Next she was struck by the old question: what was paved with good intentions?

After three hymns were sung, Sunny started to sit down, when a fourth was begun. Hastily she reopened her hymnal and flipped through the pages to find the right one and join in a rousing "We Shall Gather at the River." When it was concluded, she waited to be sure the singing was over and the rest of the congregation was seating itself before she took her seat.

"I'm atakin' my text from Matthew twenty-four, beginning at verse eleven," a voice bellowed so loudly that Sunny jumped. Startled, she glanced at the man behind the pulpit. His stature was such that his head of wiry gray hair was just visible above the lectern. With that loud voice, he could have won a hog-calling contest back home. His delivery was dramatic; he rolled his r's and trilled his syllables as he pronounced words like *tribulation.* He accompanied this by waving his Bible aloft with one hand so that its pages fluttered while he pounded his other hand in a fist upon the edge of the pulpit.

Sunny was so fascinated watching him that unfortunately some of the content of the sermon was lost to her. Despite all those scriptural warnings and threats, Reverend Billings beamed beatifically on his flock as he closed his message. Then he moved down the middle aisle, placing himself at the door to shake hands with members of the congregation as they left the church.

No one seemed unduly upset by the dire predictions enumerated in the morning's sermon. All looked cheerful as they shook their pastor's hand and went out into the sunshine. Over and over she heard the comments, "That's

77

12974

preachin'. Amen," "Mighty fine service, Pastor," and "Good sermon, Reverend."

Feeling at a loss as to what to say to him, Sunny waited until he was deep in conversation with an elderly couple, then she slipped past him and down the steps.

Small groups of people stood chatting in clusters in the churchyard. Webb Chandler was nowhere in sight, she saw with both satisfaction and a tiny nagging regret. So he hadn't shown up after all. Not that she was surprised.

She started walking to where she had hitched the horse and wagon, when she heard a familiar male voice greeting her.

"Good morning, Miss Lyndall."

Sunny turned to see Rhys Graham across the street from the church. She stopped and replied, "Good morning, Mr. Graham." As he approached she noticed he was as impeccably turned out as usual.

"Lovely spring morning, isn't it?" he asked, taking off his hat.

"Indeed," she agreed, noting his pearl stickpin in the silk cravat, and the pleated shirt.

From the top of the church steps, Webb saw Sunny talking with Rhys Graham. She was smiling up at him. And Graham looked as if he were enjoying it.

Could anything be going on there? Nah, probably not. Rhys was years older than Sunny. Had always kept to himself. Webb had never heard a hint or rumor of him being involved with any woman. But then, Sunny Lyndall was different.

Webb was even baffled by his own feelings about her. She was a puzzlement to him, and a challenge. His taste in women usually ran to another type entirely. Redheads often, with curvaceous figures, or exotic brunettes, Spanish-looking. She was slender, almost too slender. Didn't look like any of the ladies pictured in some of the gazettes he'd seen. Not really beautiful either. Her nose was too short, her cheekbones too high, her mouth too wide. But in spite of its width, it was a mouth he'd sure like to kiss. He found her mighty attractive.

Webb guessed he'd better wait till they finished talking before he approached her. He wondered impatiently what they were talking about.

Graham smiled down at Sunny. "Attending church, I see."

"Well, yes. My first time here." She was about to make some reference to the rousing sermon, when *his* comment showed he had some acquaintance with the fiery preacher.

"Did you get a good scare or an exhortation?" Rhys asked dryly, a look of amusement in his deep-set eyes.

"A little of both, I think." She smiled. "Although to be truthful, I'm ashamed to say I was so fascinated by his theatrics that I missed most of his message."

"You couldn't know this, of course, but Reverend Billings has quite a testimony. He was a carnival barker before he got the call, you see. Old habits are hard to break. Even after you're saved."

"I take it you didn't hear him this morning?"

Rhys shook his head. "I rarely attend Reverend Billings' services."

"Then you've missed quite a performance."

Suddenly all the humor Sunny imagined she had seen in Rhys' face disappeared.

"Actually, I should have said I don't attend church regularly. I didn't mean to poke fun at Reverend Billings. He is a completely sincere and totally dedicated man of God." He paused, then said, "After all, it doesn't matter *how* as long as the gospel is being preached, does it?"

With that statement Rhys Graham tipped his hat, said, "Good day, Miss Lyndall," and walked away without another word.

Sunny was bewildered by Graham's abrupt change of

manner. Maybe it had been in poor taste to mention the way Reverend Billings conducted his service. But Graham had brought up the subject. Sunny shrugged. It seemed to her that Reverend Billings was not the only person in this town with an unusual history. She had thought from the first that there was something strange and mysterious about Rhys Graham himself. She was standing there looking after his departing figure when she saw Webb Chandler coming toward her, a wide grin on his face.

"Miss Lyndall, wait." He came up to her, and as she started toward the wagon he fell into step beside her. "I saw you in church, and afterwards I was trying to get over to speak with you, but the reverend pulled me aside—" He laughed, straightening his jacket lapels. "I *should* say yanked me by the coat. I've been trying to get away ever since."

"Spotted you as a sinner, no doubt!" Sunny said flippantly.

Webb's grin widened. "Well, he was trying to talk me into getting baptized. Big doings down at the river this afternoon." He laughed. "I finally convinced him I'd been baptized when I was ten and it took."

"Not so anyone could notice," Sunny said archly.

Webb made a show of wincing. "You've got a mean streak, Miss Lyndall." Then he went on. "It kinda spoiled my plans to take you on a picnic at the river this afternoon. I mean the place will be packed." His look of disappointment quickly changed to one of possibility. "Of course, there are other places we could picnic. I know some dandy ones."

"I am just sure you do." They had reached the wagon, and Sunny opened her handbag to exchange her lace gloves for the leather ones. "But it's of no importance to me anyway. I never agreed to go anywhere with you, Mr. Chandler."

His face registered disappointment. "But I thought we'd buried the hatchet! I thought—"

"You thought wrong, Mr. Chandler," she replied sweetly,

taking perverse pleasure in deflating his assumption that she had accepted the invitation.

Suddenly Webb's eager smile disappeared. His eyes narrowed speculatively.

"Well, maybe it wasn't such a good idea anyway. Maybe it wouldn't have been much fun no matter where we went or what we did." He paused and Sunny suddenly felt exposed by the way he was looking at her—*through* her. Then he said slowly, "You know, Miss Lyndall, when I first met you, I was surprised you weren't married. I thought sure it wasn't for lack of chances. But now I think I've got it figured out. It's your tongue. You use it like a weapon, and no man could take that for long." He turned and without a backward glance sauntered away.

His words cut her like the stinging flick of a riding whip. She climbed into the wagon and sat there for a minute, the reins slack in her hands. She wanted to be angry, but the urge to cry was stronger.

She bit her lip. How dare he talk to her like that? And why should she care what Webb Chandler thought? Why had it hurt so much? She answered her own question: because the *truth* always hurts.

81

Chapter 10

The short-lived spring turned into summer. And hot. Sunny missed the long, cool spring of her native Ohio Valley. Here it seemed that spring had come and gone like the snap of a finger.

Even if it had, Sunny was suffering from "spring fever" or some kind of similar ailment. She found herself depressed. Just woke up that way. She couldn't figure out why or find a remedy for it. From the time she dragged herself out of bed, dressed, awakened her brother, cooked breakfast, and packed his saddlebags to send him off on his route, it was an effort. The minute Tracy left, all the dismal thoughts she held at bay fell on her like a sack of potatoes. She could hardly find the energy to do her chores.

It seemed to have started after that Sunday she'd attended church. It wasn't the service, she knew that; going to church was supposed to uplift and inspire you, not pull you down. It might have been the odd conversation with Rhys Graham afterward or the abrasive encounter with Webb Chandler. Whichever it was, she hadn't seen either man since.

She'd half expected Webb to show up, like the proverbial "bad penny," in spite of his telling her off when she turned him down on his picnic invitation. But he hadn't been around. And Graham had sent another rider out to pick up the weekly receipts instead of doing it himself and staying as he usually did for a few minutes' pleasant visit.

Suddenly her aloneness and isolation hit Sunny. She had never felt quite this lonely in her entire life. Better get busy doing something, she told herself firmly. That way she wouldn't have so much time to think, to feel sorry for herself.

She got started on tasks she'd been avoiding, so that she wouldn't be able to dwell on how miserable she felt. Still, her mind was whirling with uncomfortable thoughts.

The confrontation with Webb Chandler preyed on her mind. Why did the fact that he hadn't been around bother her? Hadn't she purposefully discouraged him? To be truthful, she'd been rude. She'd overdone it. He'd had every right to say the things he had to her that Sunday. Now that she'd had time to reconsider, she would have apologized. Not that she'd had a chance. Almost every day, she'd thought he might appear nonchalantly, the old assured grin on his face, his eyes filled with merriment. She almost *missed* him.

And Mr. Graham. She hoped she hadn't offended *him* in some way. After all, she and Tracy were dependent on him for their jobs. She'd gone over and over their conversation but hadn't been able to figure out what she might have said wrong. Sunny frowned and rubbed harder.

I can't stand this place! Can't stand the loneliness. I wish I'd never left Lyman Corners—She stopped short. What was she thinking about? Hadn't she been dying to get away from there? Hadn't she felt trapped in that small-town community? Hadn't she longed for change and adventure?

I'm as bad as the Israelites longing for the leeks and onions of Egypt, she accused herself. So what was she *really* missing? If she only had someone to talk to! Another woman, a *friend!*

By twelve o'clock she was worn out. She still had a long,

lonely afternoon to fill. She washed up, took off her grimy apron, put on a clean one, then plopped down at the kitchen table, chin in hand, and stared out the window, sighing impatiently, "If only something would *happen*—"

The words were hardly out of her mouth when she saw a small buckboard turn into the gate. A woman was driving. Sunny jumped up and rushed to the kitchen window to see who it was. As the woman got down from the wagon and started up to the porch Sunny recognized her. Verna Ardley.

It was Verna, but not the everyday Verna behind the counter at the store. This Verna had on a ruffled sunbonnet and a crisp, flowered calico dress, and she was carrying a basket covered with a checkered cloth.

Sunny was immediately aware of her own appearance. Her first visitor *would* have to be the wife of the storekeeper! Sunny had been here just long enough to know that Ardley's General Store was the hub of the town, the center where all information was passed back and forth, discussed, chewed over, repeated dozens of times. She gave a quick look around. At least the place was clean, as neat and tidy as she could make it. There was no time. She'd have to answer the peremptory knock sounding at the door.

"Why, Mrs. Ardley. What a nice surprise," Sunny smilingly understated. "I'm afraid I'm not fit for company."

Verna held up one hand to stop her apology. "Can't stay to visit. Jest came to ask you and your brother to come for dinner after services Sunday."

"Why, how kind of you. Well yes, I'd love to. I mean, *we'd* love to. He's off on his mail run, but I'm sure he'll be pleased. Thank you very much."

Verna shook her head. "It's nuthin' fancy. I'd have asked you sooner but knew as how you was gettin' settled and all. Well, we'll expect you around one. Come right on over after church." She thrust the basket forward. "I thought you could use some of my strawberry jelly and apricot jam.

Know you haven't had time to put in a garden or do any canning yet."

"Why, thank you, Mrs. Ardley."

"If you'll jest take the jars out and set them down, I'll be taking my basket on home."

"Yes, of course," Sunny said. "Won't you come in?"

"You've done right smart fixin' up this place," Mrs. Ardley commented approvingly as she followed Sunny inside. She stood looking around while Sunny emptied the basket of a half dozen glass jars of glistening fruit preserves. "When I heard a young woman was goin' to be livin' here—well, I said to Clem that place ain't fit for anyone to live in, let alone a *lady* from back east. But then Webb told us—"

At the scout's name Sunny stiffened. She felt herself blush at the idea that Webb Chandler might have been talking about her, giving his opinion to those fellows gathered around the potbellied stove at the general store. It was almost too much to bear. However, Mrs. Ardley seemed to think nothing of the fact that other people's business was discussed openly.

"Yes indeed, you've made it right homey, seeing as what you must've started from." Mrs. Ardley was beaming. She gave Sunny a nod. "And you such a slip of a gal! Who'd have thought it?"

Handing the basket back to her, Sunny walked with her caller out onto the porch. Mrs. Ardley went down the steps, saying over her shoulder, "Well then, we'll see you on Sunday."

"Yes, and thank you again for the invitation."

Sunny watched from the porch as Mrs. Ardley got back into the little wagon, picked up the reins, and trotted out through the gate.

Sunny went back inside feeling more cheerful. What a nice gesture of friendship. And from Mrs. Ardley, of all people. Sunny had never thought the woman to be very

85

warm or friendly when she had gone into the store. It was Mrs. Ardley's husband who joshed with the customers, greeted everyone with a smile and friendly hello. Well, you couldn't always judge right off, Sunny had at least learned that much. She was reminded of the jovial Faraday, with a rush of anger. She would never have guessed him a crook!

When Tracy returned from his ride, Sunny relayed the Ardleys' dinner invitation to him. He gave an exaggerated cheer. "Hey, that's good news! A real, honest-ta-gosh, home-cooked dinner!"

"What do you mean by *that* remark?" Sunny demanded, placing one hand on her hip as she turned around from the stove, where she was frying steak and potatoes.

"No offense, Sis. But our meals *have* been pretty much . . . well, the same old stuff—"

She reached for a dishtowel and flung it at him.

Tracy put up both hands and ducked.

"Better watch those complaints, brother, or you'll find yourself cooking your own supper," she warned, but she was smiling. To herself she had to admit that their menu had consisted pretty regularly of fried steaks, thick flapjacks, gravy, and one disastrous, dried peach cobbler. But that was because she'd been so busy trying to get this place clean and because she wasn't used to baking in this poor clunk of a stove.

Tracy was right, though: it would be nice to sit down at a table and be served somebody else's cooking for a change. Sunny found she was looking forward to next Sunday.

This was the first time for Tracy to attend church, since he was either out on his route or sleeping Sunday mornings. Anxious that they make a good impression, Sunny washed and ironed a white shirt for him and insisted he wear a dark blue string tie. She put a new lace collar on her best dress and pinned it with her mother's cameo brooch.

86

With her daisy-trimmed straw bonnet in place, she was finally satisfied with how both she and Tracy looked.

Because of all their unusual fussing with appearance, they were a little late arriving at church. At the door, one of the ushers stepped forward, shook Tracy's hand, then smilingly showed them to a pew. This friendliness that had not been extended to her on her first visit to church puzzled Sunny. Slowly it dawned on her that everyone in town knew the Express riders. They were recognized and admired for their work in carrying the mail. This was something she had not realized before. It *was* a dangerous job, and people appreciated their willingness to take it on. Glancing sideways at her brother, Sunny felt a warm glow of pride. Much as she had resisted his decision, she saw now that his work was important.

Spontaneously the proverb "A man's gift makes room for him" came into Sunny's mind. Tracy's gift certainly was horsemanship, a kind of reckless courage, and indifference to physical hardship. As a Pony Express rider, all those qualitites were fully utilized. Yes, Tracy had established himself in the community. Yet she had not found her place here.

Coincidentally, it seemed to Sunny, the sermon was taken from James 1:17: "Every good and perfect gift is from above, coming down from the Father." Reverend Billings took this theme further with many scriptural references in rapid sequence, too many for Sunny to keep track of. She did remember the one from 1 Corinthians 7:7, "Each one has his own gift from God," and that it was necessary for each "to stir up the gift of God that is in you." Sunny wasn't sure if she had a gift. If she did, she wasn't sure what it was.

At the conclusion of the service, the Ardleys came up to them right away outside and began introducing them right and left to others exiting the church building. As they walked to their separate wagons Mr. Ardley gave Tracy directions out to their house, and they parted company.

Sunny urged Tracy to drive slowly. "You're not racing to keep your schedule," she reminded him, "and we ought to give Mrs. Ardley time to get home and at least take off her bonnet before we pile in on her. Why don't we take some side roads and look around a little?"

The hotel where they had stayed those first anxiety-filled nights was located at the lower end of Main Street, which was lined with saloons and dance halls. That had been Sunny's first impression of the town. Since then she had been too busy making the Express building livable to explore farther than between it and Ardley's General Store. Now as Tracy drove leisurely along they saw that there were tree-lined streets with pleasant frame houses and neatly fenced flowering gardens. Sunny was chastened. Now she was seeing a whole other side of the town she had decided to dislike. People with families lived here, went to church; their children attended school. These people led lives not too unlike the people back home. More and more Sunny was finding out that first impressions can be very wrong.

"Think we've dillydallied long enough?" Tracy asked. "I'm sure getting hungry." He glanced at her slyly. "That wasn't much of a breakfast you gave me."

"*You!*" she exclaimed indignantly, pursing her lips to keep from smiling. "All right, you can turn around right here. Do you remember Mr. Ardley's directions?"

"Yes, big sister," Tracy droned with exaggerated patience.

"Sorry!" Sunny replied with just as exaggerated meekness. "Just thought I might refresh your memory in case—"

Tracy laughed and they went the rest of the way with their old, easy good-humored camaraderie.

The Ardleys' two-story frame house was set in a grove of aspen trees. It was painted lemon yellow and had dark green shutters. As they drove up front Sunny saw two men sitting on rush-back rockers on the shady porch. They got to their feet as Tracy helped her down from the wagon. To her astonishment she saw that the man standing beside Clem Ardley was Rhys Graham. Sunny was taken aback. Mrs. Ardley had not mentioned she was having other guests. Before she could feel flustered, remembering the odd encounter with him, she returned his courteous greeting along with Clem Ardley's warm welcome.

"Howdy, Miss Lyndall, and you too, young fellow."

Just then Verna appeared at the front door. "Hello there. Come inside, won't you, Miss Lyndall?" she invited. "We'll let the menfolk stay on the porch till everything's ready."

Stepping inside, Sunny looked around appreciatively. The Ardleys' front room had none of the stiffness of most city parlors. Instead it was comfortably cozy. Flowered cretonne curtains at the windows, hand-hooked rugs on the polished floor, comfortable, old-fashioned furniture piled with lots of embroidered pillows that Sunny was sure were also Mrs. Ardley's handiwork. It was a room where a man could be at his ease after a hard day and yet showed the caring touch of a home-loving woman.

"Take off your bonnet, won't you?" Mrs. Ardley suggested. "Then we'll go out to the kitchen. I like company while I finish up the last-minute things. I've just got to mash my potatoes, so come along and we'll have a good jaw while I do."

The pin-neat kitchen was large, bright with sunlight. Copper utensils hanging on pegs glistened. Cabinets were painted a glossy yellow, and there was a big rocker near the shiny black stove.

Mrs. Ardley closed the door to the hall quietly and took Sunny's arm and whispered, "I know you wasn't expecting there'd be more'n just us, a chance to get acquainted. But my Clem, well, he's alyus askin' people out. Most of the time without a 'by your leave.' Not that I mind a bit. I cook

89

more than for two anyhow. So—" She looked anxious. "I hope you don't mind?"

"Of course not, Mrs. Ardley."

"Oh, call me Verna, please!"

"Well then, Verna, not at all."

"Good!" Verna went to the stove, lifted a deep two-handled pan off and took it over to the soapstone sink. She put a colander into the sink, then poured the water out, letting the boiled potatoes tumble into it. She turned them into a big bowl and moved to the square table in the middle of the kitchen and began to vigorously pound them as she went on talking. "I'm surprised Webb didn't come."

At the mention of the scout's name, Sunny started.

"Webb's like family, we don't pay him much mind. He drops in all the time. When he's in town, that is. Mostly at mealtimes." Verna went on, chuckling softly. "But now Mr. Graham—well, it seemed a shame not to include him. He come up to me after church and spoke so pleasant and all, it just popped into my head and out of my mouth to invite him. He being a bachelor and alone and all."

Sunny did not respond to that.

"Funny about Webb not showin' up. He knew you two was comin'. Clem said he overheard Tracy tellin' him at the store yesterday."

Secretly Sunny wondered if *that* might be the reason Webb hadn't shown up. Maybe he didn't want to see *her!* Her cheeks got warm at the probability. Why else would Webb pass it up?

"Mr. Graham thinks the world of your brother. He told Clem he'd never had a fella take to being a rider so easy." Verna turned and gave Sunny a knowing look. "He had some nice words to say about how well you was managing the station, too."

Sunny smiled and said nothing. Of course Rhys Graham would do and say the gentlemanly thing. Webb

Chandler was another kettle of fish. If he didn't want to see her, he'd make that plain. At least she could give him credit for being honest.

Even if it meant missing a delicious meal, Sunny thought ironically as they sat down to dinner. Verna was a marvelous cook. The dinner table practically groaned with platters of fried chicken, a pot of savory baked beans, applesauce, cornbread, buttered turnips, and two kinds of pie—rhubarb and plum.

The conversation was conducted mainly between Clem Ardley and Rhys Graham, with Verna occasionally urging second helpings on everyone. As it turned out, Clem was a great reader, newspapers mainly. He and Graham had much to discuss: national current events, local politics, the settling of the western territories, as well as the progress of plans to build a transcontinental railway across the plains.

"When that happens, of course, that will be the end of the Pony Express," Rhys said. "Cars on steel rails can travel faster and carry more mail." He looked at Tracy reassuringly. "Of course, that won't be for quite a while. Your job's safe for some time."

Safe? Sunny thought. She realized Rhys was using the word in another context, because by no stretch of the imagination could a Pony Express rider's job be called safe. It was risky, hazardous, dangerous. So far Tracy had been lucky. There'd been no accidents, not even a loose stirrup or a pony tripping and falling. The weather remained good. He hadn't been caught in a sudden storm or a flash flood. Nor had he been attacked by Indians. None of the other horrors Sunny imagined when Tracy was gone, the nightmares from which she awoke shuddering with fear some nights, had happened. She just hoped that soon they could accumulate enough money to make new plans to go to California.

"Don't you agree, Miss Lyndall?"

The question jerked her back to the dinner table. She had to beg their pardon and ask for it to please be repeated.

Soon after dinner Mr. Graham took his leave, and since Tracy had to start early the next morning on his route, he and Sunny also said their good-byes, with thanks for such a pleasant day. Verna insisted they take an extra pie she'd baked, then walked with them out to the wagon.

"Now don't be a stranger, you hear?" Verna said to Sunny. "I only work at the store four mornings a week. The rest of the time I'm right here at home. So don't get lonely over there at the Express station when your brother's on his route. I love having company."

Driving back to the Express station, Sunny felt warmed by the older woman's genuineness. It was almost as if her prayer for a friendship had been answered.

Still, there was the small, niggling question of why Webb Chandler had turned down his usual dinner. Was it *really* because he knew *she* had been invited? Did he find her *that* unpleasant to be around? Truthfully, she knew she had been.

Chapter 11

*D*ays passed, then weeks, and the hot, dry summer set in. Sunny was still plagued with the empty restlessness she'd felt in the spring. Their "grubstake" for California was growing slowly. Would they ever have enough? Or would she be forever stuck on the brink of the exciting life she had envisioned for them? Tracy seemed to have found being a rider the most natural thing in the world, as if he had been doing it all his life. He never even talked about California anymore.

One sweltering June day when Sunny rode into town for supplies, she saw a banner of red, white, and blue bunting draped across Main Street, with a sign in foot-high letters:
INDEPENDENCE DAY BARBECUE—EVERYONE,
COME ONE COME ALL
FOURTH OF JULY, TOWN PARK

It was probably intended to whip up enthusiasm in folks to celebrate the nation's birthday. But it did just the opposite for Sunny. A wave of nostalgia for her hometown's annual Independence Day celebration rushed up within her. The firemen's band playing stirring marches from the stand by the lake, families gathering with picnic baskets, happily getting ready to watch the fireworks scheduled to start at dark. Afterward there would be music for dancing in the open-air pavilion. Sunny could almost see how it had been the first year she'd been allowed to go to that part of the celebration—the fireflies dancing in the azalea bushes that surrounded the pavilion, a full moon shimmering on the surface of the lake. Remembering it now, everything seemed better than it really was. Even Billy Taylor—her escort, who had seemed dreadfully dull at the time—was imbued with looks and charm.

Well, she certainly had no plans to attend. It would be just another working day at the Express station, packing the mail pouches for the riders. Tracy was probably scheduled to ride that night as well.

However, Sunny hadn't counted on Verna's insistence. "Of course you're going to come! Nobody misses the Fourth of July here! Even the Express station is closed. The riders don't ride. Of course you and Tracy will be there."

But when the day of the barbecue came, she still lacked much enthusiasm about going. All the previous week she had avoided looking at the July fourth date on the calendar. It was a melancholy reminder that if things had not worked out so disastrously for them, she and Tracy would have been at the halfway point on the trail to California.

Webb tethered his horse to the fence, then with a nonchalant air, thumbs in belt, sauntered unconcernedly to the edge of the crowd. The air was thick with the tantalizing smells coming from the barbecue pit, where a huge steer was roasting on the spit. Nearby underneath the trees, a group of men was gathered. Women in brightly colored dresses were fluttering around the long table that had been set up a little way from the pit. They were chattering and carrying on like a flock of birds as they set out bowls and dishes and large pitchers of lemonade and ice tea. His eyes searched the crowd for a glimpse of Sunny among them, but he didn't see her.

Reckon she wasn't here? Disappointment flooded over

94

him. Suddenly he spotted her, and his heart tripped a mite. She had on a blue dress and was wearing a wide-brimmed straw hat. Relief and excitement spread all through him. He started to go over, then saw she was talking to Rhys Graham. Webb decided to wait awhile.

A couple of men standing in a huddle under one of the shade trees hailed him. Knowing he would immediately become the butt of some rough joshing if he looked too eager to join a lady, he walked over to them. Besides, hadn't he learned his lesson about Sunny Lyndall? Her tongue was like a razor, always at the ready, its blade sharpened to cut deep into a man's very heart—if he let it.

Seeming in no hurry, he traded trail stories for a while but kept occasionally glancing in Sunny's direction. When he noticed Rhys leaving for the refreshment table, Webb saw his chance. With a great display of casualness, Webb left the group of men and sauntered over to Sunny.

Close up she looked even prettier than at a distance, the brim of her hat dipped over the fringe of curls framing her face. It wouldn't do to let her know what a picture she made. She'd most likely turn a compliment into an insult. The way her chin was tilted, she already had her guard up. She had seen him approaching.

Webb took off his hat, smoothed back his hair, and said, "Hello, Miss Lyndall."

She nodded coolly.

"I see you took my advice," he drawled.

"And what advice was that, Mr. Chandler?"

"You know that old saw about all work and no play, don't you? Getting out, mixing with folks, enjoying yourself, being sociable."

Was he deliberately trying to provoke her? It had been weeks since she'd seen him—actually since that day at church when he had told her off so rudely. But she had already decided that if she saw him at the barbecue, she

95

would be civil and polite. So she simply replied, "It's a very nice picnic."

"Yep, folks always told me it was. Most years I've missed it, been on the trail, celebrating Independence Day in the middle of the prairie. Watchin' out for hostile Indians isn't exactly my idea of a picnic."

When Sunny made no response, Webb glanced around and then remarked casually, "I see you're lettin' your brother off his lead for a change?"

Turning to look in the direction Webb had jerked his head, Sunny saw Tracy talking to a very pretty girl. She was tossing her curls saucily and flirting outrageously with him. Tracy, who was usually shy and became beet red and tongue-tied if a girl even glanced his way, seemed to be enjoying it thoroughly.

When Tracy had told her he was going to pick up a friend and wanted to take the wagon, Sunny assumed he was going to meet one of the other riders, so she accepted when Verna offered to come by and give her a ride into town with them. So that's why he'd wanted to use the wagon!

Peeved that Webb had pointed out what she hadn't known, Sunny struggled to conceal her dismay. But her shock must have been apparent to Webb, who was watching her. "Gotta cut the apron strings, or sooner or later he'll bust loose anyway, tearing the apron as he goes," he commented quietly.

At his words all her good resolutions not to rise to his bait vanished. "Don't you have anything better to do with your time but give *unsolicited* advice?"

"Just trying to be helpful—"

"Well, *don't*!"

"Yes, ma'am." He shrugged. Doggone if he hadn't gone and put his foot in it again!

Just then Rhys returned. As he handed Sunny her cup of strawberry lemonade he nodded to Webb and said, "Good turnout today. Best one yet, I'd say. Planning to stay for the barbecue?"

"Don't look like that's goin' to happen anytime soon."

"After the speeches usually. There are dignitaries from back east here today. So I guess it won't be served till after dark, most likely."

"Not much in the mood for political speechifying. Most of it don't ring true, somehow." A slight edge was in Webb's voice. "Don't many seem to remember us after they get back to Washington."

"Guess we have to give them the benefit of the doubt."

Sunny, cheeks burning, sipped her lemonade. She could feel Webb's wary glance, but she wouldn't look at him. Instead she studied the contents of her cup, allowing herself a darting look to where her brother still hovered over the girl.

Tracy *had* changed since he'd become a rider. He was growing up. That remark of Webb's she'd overheard the day Tracy signed up came back into her mind now: *Not all ladies feel about the Express riders like your sister does. You're in for some new experiences.* It had annoyed her at the time, but now she knew it was true, and that smarted even worse. Riders were sort of celebrities in Cottonwood. They were admired for their derring-do, and they all thrived on the adulation. Especially from the young girls.

She came back to the present when she heard Webb say, "Well, I'll be moving along.".

Rhys asked, "You're not staying for the watermelon-eating contest or the barbecue then?"

Webb just shook his head. "Kinda lost the mood," he said, then he tipped his hat. "Good day to you both."

Rhys watched Webb amble back to the group of men still laughing and talking under the trees. "Splendid chap, Webb. Never met a more honest, good-hearted fellow," he remarked. "A *real* Christian. Not like the 'whited sepulchres' who call themselves Christians."

Still smarting from Webb's outspokenness, Sunny was surprised at Graham's comment. It certainly wasn't *her* impression of the man! She felt the twinge of possibility. She had often been too quick to make judgments about people. Could she be wrong about Webb Chandler?

The rest of the afternoon Sunny was too distracted to thoroughly enjoy it. She found herself constantly seeking out her brother and the evident object of his new interest. By early evening she felt as fizzled out as some of the Roman candles that hadn't worked.

After the fireworks display, she sought out Tracy, saying she was tired and would like to leave. Rhys, who was standing nearby, immediately offered to drive her back to the Express station.

"Oh, I don't want to take you away!"

"I wouldn't stay for the square dance anyhow. And I can see Tracy wants to. Please, Miss Lyndall, it would be my pleasure."

Tracy seemed relieved, and there really was nothing else Sunny could do but accept his offer. On the way Sunny was quiet, while inwardly her emotions were churning. Why hadn't Tracy just told her he wanted to spend the day and evening with this girl? He had introduced her as Betty Brownlee. Why had he never mentioned her before? Where had he met her? How long had this been going on? Sunny felt hurt, left out, betrayed in some way. She and her brother had always been so close, but now . . .

Rhys glanced over at her and said, "You're so quiet. Is anything wrong?"

"No," she assured him.

But when they reached the station, Rhys asked again. "You're sure nothing's wrong?"

"No, really."

"You're probably tired."

"Actually, I'm wide awake. Besides, I'll wait up for Tracy."

"You might have a long wait. The last I saw him, he was promenading with that pretty girl, Betty. He'll probably see her home." Sounding amused, he added, "The long way 'round."

"Yes, I suppose that's true." Sunny sounded unsure.

"It's sometimes hard to see people close to us changing." There was a slight pause, then Rhys said seriously, "Younger brothers more than most, I would imagine. I think you have to realize that Tracy is doing a man's job, Miss Lyndall, and doing it well. He's feeling sure of himself, wants to be independent, be his own man. I'm sure that's hard to accept. You've probably heard the saying 'The tighter you hold the reins, the more a horse bucks'?" When she did not respond, Rhys said, "I'm sorry, I spoke out of turn, didn't I? I shouldn't have said that."

"You needn't apologize, Mr. Graham."

"I think I should. Please forgive me?"

"Of course," she murmured.

They came to a stop in front of the Express station. Rhys got out of his buggy, came around, helped Sunny down, and they walked onto the porch. At the doorway, they stood almost shoulder to shoulder—for Sunny was tall for a girl—while she unlocked the door. Then as she turned to say good night and thank him for the ride home, Rhys said, "There's something I'd like to say, if I may. You and your brother have come to mean a great deal to me. I'd like to think we've become friends. Friends out here use each other's first names. Could you—would you—call me Rhys?"

"Oh, I don't know. You are, after all, our employer. It would hardly be proper. . ." Sunny felt awkward, not having expected such a request. She hesitated. "Let me think about it—"

"Well then, perhaps at least in private? I guess what

99

I'm really asking is—I'd like very much to call *you* Sunny." A moment passed, then he said, "Never mind. I won't press you."

Rhys started down the steps, then halted, saying over his shoulder, "Be sure to lock and bolt the door until your brother comes home. Some of those cowboys were celebrating pretty hard, and you don't want some of them seeing your light and wandering in off the road, thinking they've made it home." He went down the rest of the steps. Without turning around, he said, "Good night, Miss Lyndall."

Sunny was thoughtful after she closed the door. It had been an eventful evening on several counts. She had so much to think about. Tracy. Strange that such different men as Rhys Graham and Webb Chandler had given her the same advice about her brother.

Let him grow up, let him be himself. She knew she was afraid to let go, afraid he would wander too far away, go too far, like a colt she was trying to train.

She knew they were both right and that the advice had been given with the best intentions. Why did she accept one's counsel and resent the other's?

She felt uncomfortable about the incident that had taken place at the door. Rhys' request that they call each other by first names troubled her. That and worrying about Tracy kept Sunny wakeful most of the night.

Back in town Rhys Graham was also sleepless. His feelings for Sunny Lyndall had almost taken over his good sense. Standing in the doorway, he had wanted to kiss her. From the first he had behaved out of character where she was concerned. Acting on impulse—something he rarely did—he had offered her the management of the Express station, not even being sure she would accept it. Her courage, strength, resourcefulness, and determination had won his respect. And more. Rhys knew that gradually his feelings had changed, grown deeper. However, knowing where those feelings might lead, he knew he must check them. He did not have the right, not with his background, not with his past . . .

Chapter 12

Sunny woke feeling cross. She yanked the covers. Her blanket and quilt had got twisted with all her turning and tossing throughout the restless night. She didn't remember when she had finally fallen asleep. But she did know that gray light was creeping in the windows when she heard Tracy come in at dawn.

Foolish boy! Staying out till who knows what time, when he had to go out on his route this morning. She just hoped that in his desperate race to prove himself a man, he wasn't thinking of falling in love! But what could she do about it? Gloomily she recalled the advice given her by both Webb and Rhys. Everything seemed to have been taken out of her hands. Sunny sighed, got out of bed, and went to wake up Tracy.

Half dead from lack of sleep, he stumbled out of the bunk room, gulped down a mug of coffee she had brewed. He shook his head sullenly when she urged a bowl of oatmeal and some toasted cornbread. There was no conversation between them. Just as well, Sunny thought, or she might have gone into a tirade about his staying out so late. Finally he shouldered the mail pouches and with a gruff good-bye went out to saddle his pony and leave.

Sunny ranted mentally at that stupid Betty Brownlee. Tracy had probably lingered on her family's porch half the night, trying to work up enough courage to kiss her before saying good night, instead of sensibly coming back to the station and getting a good night's sleep.

Cut the apron strings. Quit mother-henning. Let the boy grow up. These comments echoed hollowly in her mind as she stood at the window, watching him disappear in the morning mist.

It was easy enough for Webb Chandler and even Rhys Graham to give her advice about letting Tracy go; they didn't understand how close she felt to her brother. She remembered the day he was born! The little scrap of a baby bundled in a blanket. "This is your little brother, Sunny. He's going to be *your* special charge from now on," their mother had whispered to her.

No matter how tall or how big or how independent he got, that's how she'd always think of Tracy. She couldn't help it. He was the baby she'd diapered and bathed, the little boy whose neck she'd scrubbed, whose hair she'd washed and cut for so many years. How *could* she not care what he did, what he thought, what happened to him? Their lives were linked—past, present, and future.

Sunny tried to keep busy all that day. She didn't want to think about Tracy. She didn't want to think about Rhys Graham. She certainly didn't want to think about Webb Chandler.

Late the following evening she heard the whinnying of the ponies, and the sound of hoofbeats for which she had been anxiously listening the last few hours. She rushed to the window. Just as she reached it and was peering out, a dirty, disheveled Tracy stumbled into the room. Wearily he staggered over to the bench by the table and flung himself down. He folded his arms on top of the table, and his head sagged onto them. He was too tired to even speak.

"Hard trip?" she asked anxiously.

A muffled groan was her answer.

She hurried to boil water, dragging in the tin tub from the shed and filling it in front of the stove. She unwrapped a new cake of soap and placed it, along with a large sponge, on the bench alongside the tub. Then she turned to her brother. "Tracy, your bathwater's ready. Come get in 'fore it cools off."

Tracy stood, still looking sleepy.

"Here, take off your clothes. They're filthy."

Tracy stared at her.

"Give them to me. They'll have to be soaked before they're washed."

He just stood there.

"Hurry up," Sunny urged impatiently. "Your water's getting cold."

Tracy scowled. "You can git 'em later."

Quickly she turned her back, saying over her shoulder as she left the room, "Well, just drop them on the floor beside the tub. I'll get them when I empty the bathwater."

To her chagrin she again recalled Webb Chandler's words, which had been reinforced by Rhys Graham's sage remarks. Both men had seen what she had been blind to: her brother was growing up. She couldn't treat him like a child any longer. She would have to think of him as— what? An equal partner?

Sunny realized she had come to a crossroads in her relationship with Tracy. She would not be able to make arbitrary decisions as she had in the past. Together they would make the journey that lay ahead, or else their lives would take different directions.

Goodness, there was such a lot to think about! Once life had seemed so simple. Sunny's goal had been clear. To get to California. Then everything would fall in place for them. Had she ever been *that* naive?

Chapter 13

*W*ith so many things on her mind, Sunny longed for someone to discuss her new problems with—someone older, wiser. This struck her as ironic. Hadn't she always resented other people's advice?

Almost as an answer to her need, after church on the Sunday following the Fourth of July barbecue, Verna invited her to come for a visit.

"Tuesday's my day off from the store," she told Sunny. "We can have a nice visit to ourselves with no menfolk around." Verna's eyes twinkled.

Sunny accepted gladly. Maybe she could tactfully bring the subject around to Rhys Graham's interest in her. It was a situation Sunny was finding increasingly hard to handle. One she had not anticipated and one that she felt she certainly had not encouraged. Maybe Verna could give her some sage advice.

That afternoon, after tidying up and finishing her chores, Sunny rode over to Verna's. She tethered the pony under a shady tree on the cool side of the house. As she came up on the porch Verna looked out the kitchen window and called, "Hot enough for you?" then came to the door and held it open for her. "Come on in out of that heat."

Stepping inside, Sunny untied her bonnet strings, drew off her straw hat, and fanned herself with it, saying, "Whew, there's not a breeze stirring out there."

"I made lemonade," Verna told her. "I put it in the springhouse. I'll just go get it, then I'll pour you a nice, cool glass. I'm doin' my berries, making jam, so I'll have to keep at it while we have our chat."

A few minutes later Sunny was seated in the rocking chair, sipping the tangy chilled drink while Verna busied herself at the stove. After a bit Verna looked over, surveyed her guest with sharp eyes, then commented, "You look kinda peaked. Anything wrong? Not got the summer complaint, have you? If you do, I've got jest the thing for it—"

"No, no, Verna. It isn't that. It's . . . well, I think I have a problem."

"If you *think* you've got one, you most likely have. Anything I can do? Help with?"

"I don't know." Sunny sighed. "It's about . . . well, Mr. Graham."

Verna didn't look surprised. "Uh-huh."

"You see, I thought he had always been most generous to us, very kind. It actually was a godsend when he offered me the job of managing the Express station. But now—" Sunny hesitated, debating how much she should tell Verna about the incident on her doorstep after the barbecue. "Well, he seems to have changed. I don't know if it's something I've done or said."

Verna looked amazed. "Don't you see how the land lies, gal?"

Sunny shook her head.

"You'd have to be blind as a bat not to see it!" Verna declared, her hands on her hips. She turned back to the stove and gave the boiling berries a few quick stirs before facing Sunny again. "You should have heard how he jumped at the chance to have dinner with us that first Sun-

106

day you and your brother came." She pursed her mouth and looked over her spectacles at Sunny.

Sunny didn't say anything, just gazed back at Verna. After a while she said, "I wish you hadn't told me. Now I'll feel uncomfortable around him."

"Well, like I said, you'd have to be a bat not to have seen it," was Verna's tart response.

"But it's impossible." Sunny jumped out of the chair, almost spilling her lemonade. She shook her head vigorously. "It's out of the question. Soon Tracy and I will be going on to California, and—" She took a few steps back and forth across the kitchen, paused, then turned back to Verna and said, "Please, don't say anything to anyone else. Especially not to Tracy. We talked of nothing else but California for nearly a year before we came here. I don't want anything to spoil Tracy's dream."

Verna's glance was skeptical. "No dreams of your own, Sunny? No heart's longing for a home, a husband, children?" She pulled a long face and asked, "Are you your brother's keeper?"

Sunny shook her finger playfully. "Don't misquote Scripture, Verna."

Verna went back to stirring, and Sunny picked up her bonnet, put it on, and looped the ribbons into a bow. "Besides, going to California was *my* idea first." She started for the door, then turned back. "I know you have my best interests at heart, Verna, but—"

Verna half turned from the stove, waggling the wooden stirring spoon at Sunny like a teacher's pointer. "Needn't concern yourself about *that*. Just don't come crying to me when it's too late. When you've missed your chance."

Sunny smiled. She realized her friend's tart rejoinder was not an intentional reprimand. She suspected that Verna was beginning to think of her as the daughter she'd never had, wanting the best for her. Rhys Graham, in Verna's opinion, *was* the best any mother could imagine in a suitor.

Outside Sunny untied Bramble and got into the wagon and headed to the Express station. Verna's statement had stunned her. Rhys Graham *in love* with her? Why hadn't she been aware of it or suspected it? She'd never guessed. She had been too self-absorbed maybe, too preoccupied with her new life, her new responsibilities. When she thought of him at all, it was as their employer, actually their benefactor. That's why his impulsive behavior the night he brought her home from the barbecue had been such a surprise.

No dreams of your own, Sunny? No heart's longing for a home, a husband, children? Verna's question brought up something Sunny hadn't thought about much recently. Up until now *her* dreams were Tracy's. The dream of going to California *together,* homesteading, living a new, adventurous life.

Of course, like any girl growing up, she'd had secret dreams of a someday romance. But not lately. And not about Rhys Graham.

He might possess some of the qualities—good looks, status in the community, manners—that might *once* have seemed ideal in the man of her dreams. But her dreams had changed. Out here in Missouri, certainly in California, a woman looked for different qualities in a man. Suddenly Sunny asked herself: When had her romantic dreams changed? What had changed them? Or more importantly, *who*?

Chapter 14

*S*unny was outside hanging out a week's laundry. Even this early in the day it was hot. The sun beat on her back as she pinned up Tracy's heavy, coarse, cotton work shirts and his soaking wet jeans. It was hot, tiring work. Finished, she went back inside and poured herself a glass of the sun tea she had made earlier, and sat down at the kitchen table to drink it.

Tracy had left at dawn on his route. Two long days alone stretched before her. It was too hot to work in the garden or to ride into town or over to Verna's. But Verna would be at the store today anyway, Sunny remembered, sighing.

As often happened when she had time on her hands, unwelcome thoughts came. Was California a far-off dream? One that might never come true? Would she be stranded here forever? If only she and Tracy had gone with the wagon train, they would have been reaching the Sierra Mountains by now. Sunny's thoughts were like ripples from pebbles tossed into a lake: one circle led to the next and the next. Finally she brought herself up short. It was pointless to dwell on this. It only made her unhappy. She should get busy, stop thinking.

So Sunny began straightening out cabinets, rearranging

kitchen shelves. Thus occupied, the hours passed quickly. Suddenly she realized that the sun had moved and her clothes must be dry. She went back outside to bring them in.

It was past noon and the sun was high, glaring. Squinting into it, she unpinned the clothes, piling them into the willow clothes basket as she moved down the line.

Something—some movement—alerted her, and she turned just as two men on horseback rode in through the gate. From that distance she couldn't recognize them. She wasn't expecting anyone. She watched them slow their horses to a walk as they passed the corral, giving the sleek Express ponies the once-over. They halted, leaning forward, pointing, nodding their heads as if discussing the animals fenced there. Who were they? What did they want? They didn't look at all familiar. From her vantage point, shadowed by the side of the building, Sunny observed them with a vague feeling of uneasiness. What were they doing here? They looked as if they might have been riding a long time. Their horses were shaggy, had matted manes, and moved as if weary.

The men didn't see Sunny at first. As they moved slowly toward the Express station building they were talking to each other in low voices. What were they discussing? Sunny stepped out into the sunlight, holding her willow basket in front of her like a shield. The men seemed startled at her sudden appearance.

One of the men nodded to her, muttering something to his companion, who then stared at her. They both reined their horses only a few feet from where Sunny stood. She took a step back. The bigger of the two pushed his sweat-stained hat back from his forehead, pulled the red bandanna from around his neck, mopped his darkly stubbled face. Then he spoke to Sunny. "Afternoon, ma'am. We been travelin' a mighty long way. We'd be obliged iffen we could bother you for some water for ourselves and our horses."

110

She did not want to sound too friendly, as though welcoming neighbors. Cautiously Sunny replied, "There's the well and a trough. Help yourself."

"That's right kind of you, ma'am." He gave what passed for a smile, although there was no real pleasantness in it. He jerked his head to the other man. "You see to it, Jake." They dismounted and he tossed his reins to Jake, who took both horses by their reins and led them over to the trough. The man who had spoken got out a small pouch of tobacco, slowly rolled himself a cigarette. With his thumbnail he flicked the end of a match into flame, lit it. As a swirl of smoke spiraled up in front of his face he squinted, his eyes staring at Sunny. Then he asked casually, "This your spread, ma'am?"

"This is the Express station."

"Your husband run it?"

Something in the man's voice sent a sliver of fear down her spine. Instinctively she knew she must not show it. Nor let them know she was here by herself. For a minute she hesitated. "No, my brother and I do."

His scraggly eyebrows lifted. "Do tell? You look mighty young to be in charge of an Express station."

She didn't answer. Her fingers tightened on the handles of her basket. She wished they would get their water and go. She didn't want to put the basket down or go inside, leaving these suspicious-looking strangers out here.

She saw him look toward the building and the barn. Checking for any sign of someone else around? Under most circumstances if a man were on the premises, by now he would have appeared to check out who had come.

The stranger probably guessed she was alone. Sweat gathered into her palms. The man looked back at her, his narrowed gaze intimidating. Sunny looked away, over to the trough, where the horses drank thirstily. They must have been ridden a long way. Hard and fast, from the look of them. Were these men running from something? The law?

She felt a fluttering in her stomach like a covey of quail coming out of the brush. An inner warning came: *Don't act afraid. Act confident.* Inwardly she was teetering on the brink of panic. The urge to run into the building and bolt the door was strong. She took a few steps in that direction. As she did the man's voice stopped her.

"We're a sight hungry, ma'am. Could use some grub. If you could spare some, we'd be mighty grateful."

Let these two in the house? In sight of the safe, the mail shelves? While she was here alone? She wasn't about to do that. But the man's eyes were boring into her, allowing her no escape.

The other man was returning, leading the horses up to the hitching post in front of building. The man who had been doing all the talking shifted his body slightly, and his free hand smoothed the gun holster on his hip, remaining there provocatively.

Her heart banged and she could hardly breathe. Should she offer to fix them some food? She felt confused, dizzy with fright and indecision. As she hesitated the other man walked over to stand beside his partner. They both stood there at the bottom of the porch steps, blocking her way into the building. She had to either think quickly of something to say or allow them to come in with her.

Before she could think of anything, the man spoke again. "Well, ma'am. We come a long way. Sure are hungry. So's our horses. Reckon you've got a good supply of feed for all them ponies you got. Jake'll jest take a look down at that barn yonder. Mebbe you and me kin go inside and rustle up some food?"

Go inside alone with *him*? Sunny's breath was coming so fast it almost choked her.

The men exchanged a look, then both looked back

boldly at her. The taller man's mouth twisted into a humorless smile. The other one gave a harsh laugh, more of a snort.

If only Tracy were here! Should she lie and say her brother would be back any minute? The threatening gleam in the men's eyes convinced her that they'd see through any such ploy. What could she do? Pray! *Oh my God, an ever present help in times of danger, protect me.* The clothes basket was getting heavy; its handles were cutting into her hands. Impulsively she acted. With all her strength she threw the basket toward them, hitting them hard on their knees, momentarily unsteadying them. She made a dash for the steps, running into the building, slamming the door behind her, and shoving the wooden bolt into place. She fell against it, breathing hard. Next she ran to the window and saw that they were both stumbling about, cussing and snarling. Realizing that because of the heat she had opened all the windows, she rushed through the house, banging them down. From the front window she saw that the big man had drawn his gun and was sneaking around the side of the house. *Oh, dear God!* She clutched her hands to her breast and shuddered. She was alone here, helpless against two men. *Please, help.* They could break down the door. Now that they were angered, there was no telling what they would do! She sagged against the wall, closed her eyes, and prayed.

Never before in her life had a prayer been answered so swiftly. Almost at once she heard the sound of other horse hooves. She opened her eyes, rushed to the window, and looked out. Of all people, Webb Chandler was cantering up to the building. Sunny went weak with thankfulness. The two men had whirled around at Webb's approach. On a horse he looked taller than he actually was. Sunny noticed with some astonishment that his expression was stern, fiercely belligerent. He must have taken in the situation at once. He brought his horse to a skidding halt and the animal

113

reared. Then he spun around, facing the two strangers, his hand resting on the rifle in its holder behind him.

Her ear pressed to the door, Sunny heard Webb demand, "You fellas here on Express company business?"

Jake shifted uncomfortably, glanced at his partner. The other man seemed to take Webb's measure before answering, "Nah, jest stopped to give our horses a little rest and water."

Webb's hand stroked his rifle. "Looks like that's been done, so I suggest you all git movin'."

"Come on, Tanner," Jake urged as he swung himself up into his saddle, holding out the other man's reins toward him.

Tanner took his time walking over to his horse, still watching Webb. He grabbed the reins and mounted, then gave Webb a malevolent look before swiveling his horse around. Both men rode out the gate, stirring up clouds of dust in their wake.

Sunny flung open the door and rushed out onto the porch. "Oh, thank God you came when you did, Webb!" she exclaimed breathlessly. "I've never been so glad to see anyone in my life!"

"Well, that's a nice change from the way I'm usually greeted out here," he grinned. He got off his horse and began picking up the assorted clothing scattered all about, now soiled with dirty hoofprints where the intruders' horses had trampled them in the dust. Holding one item up with a quizzical expression, Webb remarked, "I think you're going to have to do another wash, Miss Lyndall." He chuckled as he gathered the laundry into the empty willow basket.

"Oh, never mind about that!" Sunny retorted impatiently. "How in the world did you happen to come out here just now? I don't know what I'd have done. I was so scared—" Her voice broke. In spite of her attempt to appear brave and unshaken by the incident, to her dismay Sunny suddenly

114

felt limp, sick, and faint. Her knees went weak, and she grabbed hold of the porch post. Clinging to it, she pressed her face against the wood, and tears began to fill her eyes. Shaking with sobs, she was unable to stop crying.

The next thing she knew, Webb was beside her. Strong hands on her shoulders gently pulled her close, holding her firmly. She heard the murmur of his voice soothing, as if to a hurt child, "It's all over now." She felt the roughness of his jacket, the buttons pressing into her cheeks as she leaned against him.

"They didn't *do* anything to you, did they?" Webb asked fiercely.

Choking back sobs, she shook her head. "But who knows what would have happened if you hadn't come."

Something in her longed to remain held in this reassuring embrace. But the independent woman she was trying to be would not allow her. She pulled away and stepped back. Unable to completely stem the tears, she burst out, "Those awful men! This awful place. I wish we'd never come here. I wish I could just up and leave and never see this whole terrible place again." She knew she was making a fool of herself, and in front of Webb Chandler, of all people!

"Aw now, come on. You just had a bad scare, that's all."

She shook her head. "No, I mean it. I can't handle it. I give up."

"Not *you*! Never. You're strong, like a willow. . . .You might bend, but you won't break," Webb assured her. He dug a clean, folded red bandanna handkerchief out of his pocket and handed it to her.

"Well, maybe not. But if it weren't for Tracy, I wouldn't stay." She took the handkerchief.

Webb studied Sunny while she dabbed at her eyes. Even now, with the end of her small nose reddened, her wet eyelashes stuck in little points over the wide hazel eyes, she was doggone pretty. But there was more to her than just that. This little lady had something else he hadn't encountered often. Something he admired. Watching her get ahold of herself, Webb drawled, "By the way, just how did that basketful of clothes get strewed all over the place?"

"I threw it at them!"

"You *what*?" Webb began to laugh.

Sunny smiled somewhat sheepishly through her tears. "I threw it at them so I could make a run for it into the house."

Webb began to roar with laughter. "My oh my, Miss Lyndall, I gotta hand it to you. You're one lady with a lot of spunk! I'll say that for you."

For a minute Sunny basked in his admiring glance. "It didn't help much," she shrugged. "Only made them mad, I'm afraid. That man pulled a gun, you know."

Webb's face got serious. "You know, you ought to learn how to handle a shotgun."

She looked at him in alarm. "Oh, no!"

"You might never need it or have to shoot it, 'cept maybe as a warning. But it's a good thing to know. It's the knowing *how* that's important, should somethin' ever come up you had to."

With surprise she realized Webb was too much of a gentleman to say, "For instance, like today, if *I* hadn't shown up." She also realized she had not thanked him, shown him how truly grateful she was.

"I'll take it on myself to bring one out, show you how to clean and care for it, how to load, and how to shoot."

"Thank you," she said humbly. Then, "The least I can do is offer you something to drink. I have some sun tea made. Will you have some?"

The old teasing grin was back. "Why, I'd be pleased to do just that."

She brought their glasses out onto the porch. They sipped it in silence. Sunny was still recovering from the frightening incident, and Webb seemed completely comfortable not forcing conversation. Before he went, he made it a point to check the barn and suggested she leave the ponies in the corral overnight so she would be sure to be alerted if any intruders came on the property.

"Tracy will be home tomorrow," Sunny told him.

Webb nodded, then promised, "I'll be out first thing to teach you to shoot."

Feeling suddenly shy, Sunny said, "Thank you very much. For everything."

"Don't mention it." He smiled, adding with a grin, "My pleasure."

After Webb left, Sunny couldn't remember much of what they had talked about while they had their tea. She *did* remember the surge of relief at seeing him ride in the Express station gate. The gratitude for the way he had sent those characters packing. Her cheeks grew warm as she remembered how comforting it had felt to be in the protective circle of his arms, so close she could hear his heart against hers.

That night it was a long time before Sunny could sleep. Every creak, every cricket, every faint snort or whinny from the corral, brought her to quivering wakefulness. Webb was right. Having a gun and knowing how to use it would give her some security when she was here alone.

Thoughts of Webb also kept her awake.

She had seen a whole new side of Webb Chandler this day. Strength and tenderness. She recalled Rhys Graham's comment about him: *A real Christian?* What other traits might he have that she had never given him credit for? He had certainly seemed a knight in shining armor riding to her rescue today. An unlikely image to have of the scout.

True to his word, bright and early the next day Webb showed up. Sunny came out on the porch to greet him

"Ready for a shooting lesson?" he asked her as he dismounted.

"I'm not sure. I've always been afraid of guns."

"I'm going to teach you to use one so that other people'll be afraid of *you*. Knowing how takes the fear away. Like I said, you may never have to use it. But *knowing how* is the thing. A woman pointing the barrel of one of *these*"—he unbuckled a double-barreled twenty-gauge shotgun from behind his saddle and held it up—"at you, and seeing she knows how to pull the trigger, will scare any sane fella right out of his boots."

"I'm still not sure," she said doubtfully.

"You'll catch on quick. I guarantee you'll be glad you did."

"Would you like some coffee?" Sunny asked tentatively, hoping to delay the lesson a little longer.

"Sure. Thanks."

Sunny went into the kitchen and poured two mugs of the coffee she had freshly brewed. When she came out, Webb was sitting on the porch steps. She handed him his mug, and as their fingers brushed she felt a little quiver go through her. For a second their gaze met, then Sunny looked away quickly. She sat, thinking it was funny how since yesterday everything about Webb seemed different. Nicer, gentler, sweeter even. Of course, that was nonsense. Her imagination. She was just so grateful he'd come when he had—which reminded her of something she'd wondered about. "By the way, how did you happen to come along out here just when you did yesterday?"

Webb took a long sip of his coffee before answering. There was mischief in his eyes when he did. "Oh, just riding by to pass the time of day," he teased, jogging her memory of the first time he'd done just that and they'd had their disastrous tug-of-war.

She blushed but just said, "Well, I'm awfully glad you did."

Webb finished his coffee and put down his cup, then held out his hand and pulled Sunny to her feet.

"Come on, time for your lesson."

Webb was a patient teacher. He demonstrated to Sunny how to unlock the catch of the shotgun, open the chamber, slip two shells in, cock it, rest it securely against her shoulder, aim, and squeeze the trigger.

With infinite patience he went through the procedure several times, making sure she understood how to load the gun safely. Then he placed a half dozen empty tin cans along the top rail of the fence, behind the barn so as not to frighten the ponies in the front corral.

"Those will be your targets. Let's see how many you can knock off." He showed her how to place her feet, take a position, and focus where she wanted to shoot.

As Webb came and stood behind her he gently helped her prop the gun against her shoulder. At first Sunny was too much aware of him to concentrate. Aware of the sun-smell of his skin, the scent of his leather vest, his muscular shoulder pressing against her back, his fingers on the nape of her neck as he gently moved her head to the right angle to aim . . . Then Webb's steady voice matter-of-factly coaching her quieted the flurry of her emotional response to his nearness. She began listening carefully to his instructions, and before long all her attention was on learning how to use this powerful weapon.

After several times going through the routine of shooting, reloading, and shooting, Sunny's aim improved and a number of her shots sent tin cans rattling off the fence. This brought a low whistle from Webb. Sunny felt inordinately pleased by his "Well done!"

"I told you you'd catch on quick. You'll be a crack shot in no time flat, Miss Lyndall." He gave her a nod of approval. "We better quit for now. Your arm and shoulder'll probably be kinda sore. But the idea is to practice. Keep

119

practicin' and the better you get. Just line up the cans over and over till you can puncture them one after the other, knock 'em all off."

He took the gun from her, unloaded it, and swung it around, shouldering it. "For a first time, you did real good, Miss Lyndall."

Webb was regarding her with unabashed approval. And something more. She sensed it, saw it in his eyes, felt something so strong flowing between them it made her almost dizzy.

I must be getting light-headed from the sun! Quickly Sunny reminded herself of Verna's telling her that Webb had a "way with women." With a chuckle, Verna had told Sunny that many of the local girls had their caps set for him, to say nothing of some of the dance hall "ladies." "He's the kind that grannies want to mother and younger women would like to march down the aisle with, but Webb—well, he's like a wild horse who likes running free on the range and don't want to be tamed. He gets skittish when anyone gets marriage in their eyes. Some men are born bachelors. And I reckon Webb's one of them."

Well, *she* certainly didn't have her cap set for him! And going down the aisle with anyone was a long way off in her future. Certainly not until she got to California. Certainly not with a "rolling stone" like Webb Chandler. With an effort, Sunny dragged her gaze from the blue eyes looking into hers so intently and turned away. She started walking back up toward the building, and Webb fell into step beside her. When they got back to where Webb had hitched his horse, he said, "I suggest you practice every day for a while till you feel at ease with handlin' the gun. You'll do fine. I can see you're a fast learner, Miss Lyndall."

"Thank you for coming—and for teaching me and all."

Webb set his wide-brimmed hat on his head, tightened

the leather strap under his chin, then tugged the brim. "No thanks necessary." He mounted. "So long, Miss Lyndall," he said, turning his horse and riding off.

Following Webb's suggestion, Sunny had a daily practice session. She made a target outside, away from the barn and corral. In two weeks time she felt confident that come any emergency, she could handle herself and the gun. As he had also predicted, "knowing how" had given her a sense of security she did not have before. She had not liked the way she felt after that awful day with those two men. Until she really knew how to use the shotgun, she was jumpy, looking over her shoulder, thinking she saw things. When Tracy was gone and none of the other riders were around, she had to work up courage to go out to the barn, lead the ponies into the corral. All things she had learned to do well and had taken pride in doing. One of the things she had been especially proud of was how she had adapted to life alone at the station. After that one frightening episode, her hard-won independence had been shaken. Now she felt it had been restored. Thanks to Webb.

When Tracy came home the day of her shooting lesson, she'd explained what happened and why she planned to start target practicing every day. He thought it was a good idea, although he seemed worried about her being alone, in case something else happened. While Sunny was regaining her confidence as the days passed, he kept suggesting they should mention the incident to Rhys Graham.

Sunny eventually dissuaded him. "I'm getting real good, Tracy. Webb says just the sight of one of these is enough to run off most anyone who'd come out here with any ideas."

"Well, if Webb says so . . ."

That seemed to satisfy her brother, who admired Webb greatly. Sunny had never understood why—until now.

Nor did she mention the incident to Verna. She didn't

want word to get back to Rhys Graham. He might decide they needed a man to run the station. To lose her job at this point, and the money it brought in, the nest egg they were building up for when they could leave for California, would be a disaster.

Chapter 15

A scorching August led into a September in which the dregs of summer lingered. Everything was dusty, dry. Grass turned brown, sunflowers wilted along fences, the midday sun beat down relentlessly. Sunny felt as listless as the weather as she entered Ardley's General Store one day. She found Verna putting up a poster announcing the upcoming harvest ball.

Sunny glanced at it indifferently, then remarked to Verna, "I've come for some material."

Verna beamed. "Goin' to make yourself a new dress for the dance, I wager?" She finished hammering the last nail to the sign, then hurried to the counter, behind which were bolts of cloth on the shelves. "I've just got in some lovely yardage that'll make up real fine."

Sunny shook her head. "It's curtain material I want, Verna. Calico. Besides, I'm not going to the dance."

Verna looked shocked. "Not going? What do you mean, not going? Of course you will. You *can't* miss it! It's the biggest social event of the year."

"Somehow it doesn't seem much like fall or weather for dancing, Verna—," Sunny began but was immediately cut off by Verna.

"That's just it! It'll get everybody out of the doldrums! It's a great time," Verna said positively. "You'll enjoy it, trust me."

"Oh, I don't know . . ." Sunny sounded reluctant.

"Nonsense! You've been working hard all these weeks, looking after that brother of yours, besides minding the station. You deserve a little fun. Everybody'll be there."

Then Sunny plaintively asked the eternal feminine question, "But what on earth would I wear? I haven't been to a party or a dance in—months." Actually, it seemed like forever. Her workday life at the Express station precluded any sort of dress-up clothes. Mostly she wore a clean shirtwaist and cotton skirt—and sometimes, of course, Tracy's old jeans underneath, which not even Verna knew about.

"Didn't you bring a party dress along in your trunk?" Verna demanded, raising a quizzical eyebrow. "Didn't think they danced in California, eh?"

Sunny had to laugh at her friend's satirical question. "I had other things on my mind when I thought about California."

"Well, be that as it may, you've got to have something pretty to wear to the harvest dance. It's the one time in the year all the ladies wear their finest. And I've got some yardage at the store I want you to see. Matter of fact, had you in mind when it came in."

She would not take no for an answer.

Verna Ardley had taken a great interest in Sunny. Since her first wariness, she had come to admire the young woman. Her lack of whining and complaining over a situation that might have caused others of her kind to go into mild hysterics and take the next train home had won Verna's staunch support. "That gal has gumption," Verna had told her husband. "She needs a hand up, a listening ear and a strong shoulder to lean on if need be." Clem nodded and wisely didn't put in his two cents worth. His private opinion—"The Lyndall gal is pretty as a picture and twice as smart"—he'd expressed to Rhys Graham and Webb Chandler and some others, all of whom seemed to share it.

"Now, here it is, Sunny," Verna said, bringing out a bolt of cloth from under the shelf and placing it on the counter for Sunny to see. Verna lowered her voice confidentially. "I've not shown it to anyone else. But it'd be just right for you. Your colors and all. Wouldn't it make up into the sweetest dancing dress?"

Sunny shook her head regretfully. Their budget and the amount she was trying to save each week didn't allow for extras.

"No thanks, Verna. I've decided I'm not going."

"Land sakes! What are you talking about?" Verna asked incredulously. "Nobody misses the harvest dance!" Then her face softened as she realized what the problem might be. "This is specially priced, 'cause I knew there wouldn't be much call for it. There'd just be about enough for someone the size of you. Just look at how pretty it is," she coaxed.

"Oh, Verna, don't tempt me . . . ," Sunny pleaded. But it was too late, as Verna held out a length for her examination. It was periwinkle blue lawn printed overall with tiny clusters of daisies and buttercups tied with trailing ribbons of deeper blue. Sunny weakened. Lightly her fingers traced the delicate pattern.

Watching her, Verna knew she had made a sale. "See, it can be trimmed with this," she suggested, laying a roll of Swiss eyelet ruffle beside the material.

"I really shouldn't," Sunny sighed. "But—"

"Now, no buts. You're going and that's the end of it. I'll put it on next month's account," beamed Verna, quickly measuring out several yards, adding the trim and lace, placing both on top of the curtain calico, wrapping it all together in brown paper, and tying it with a string. Verna turned to one of the shelves behind her and brought out a wheel of ribbon. "What color ribbon for your hair?" she asked, pulling her fabric scissors out of her apron pocket.

Sunny laughed helplessly. "Violet, I guess."

"There you are. And you'll thank me when it's done." Verna smiled.

In spite of some guilty pangs, Sunny left the store with the wrapped parcel of dress material, trim, and lace. She found she was even looking forward to making herself a new dress and attending the harvest dance.

Back at the Express station she dragged the battered, leather humpbacked trunk from the corner and opened it. Lifting off the shallow top tray, she searched the contents for some of the things she had almost forgotten she had brought with her. Tucked into tissue paper at the bottom were dancing shoes, lace mitts, and a fan. Perfect accessories for the dress she planned. It might really be fun, and it would certainly be a break from her monotonous routine.

With Verna's help the dress was cut out, sewn, and ready for her to wear to the harvest dance. Sunny was thrilled with the result. It had tiny pink and blue flowers scattered all over a lavender background, a frill of lace at the neckline and at the elbow-length puffed sleeves.

The dance was being held at the town hall. Tracy would be back in time to take her. For once Tracy didn't seem to object to the prospect of wearing a white ruffled shirt and a string tie.

Life had been so humdrum, so hard, these past months that the closer the time came to the night of the dance, the more excited Sunny got. *You'd think it was a ball at the governor's mansion,* she chided herself, but that didn't stem her excitement.

That afternoon she washed her hair in the water from the rain barrel first, then boiled water for the tub. Sunny bathed, lathering lavishly with the special scented soap she had experimented making. All they had at Ardley's General Store were the big blocks of harsh, yellow soap. This, of course, was sufficient to clean off the dust, grime, and grit of the trail for Tracy when he got home, but it was very hard on delicate skin. Sunny had saved all the grease she could manage, melting the accumulated fat from bacon rinds, tallow, and drippings. Then she poured it into the lye water leached from woodstove ashes simmered in a huge kettle for hours. Into this she stirred a mixture of crushed clover and some dried lilac petals from a bouquet Verna had cut for her from a bush in her yard. The result had not been perfect. But at least she had been able to mold several small cakes for her own personal use.

By the time Tracy got home, had his bath, and dressed, Sunny was ready and waiting. Tracy didn't so much as mumble one complaint when Sunny insisted on trimming his hair. She was so preoccupied with her own appearance, she never discerned the reason for his unusual compliance. That is, until they arrived at the dance and he made a bee-line to the side of Betty Brownlee.

Deserted on the threshold of the dance floor, her foot spontaneously tapping to the sound of fiddle music, Sunny glanced around, not admitting to herself for whom she was looking. When she saw him, her heart gave an astonishing little flutter. He looked all slicked down, hair dark and smooth, crisp white shirt, flowing tie, boots polished to a high gloss. Seeing her, he smiled and made a move as if to cross the room to her. At the very same moment Sunny heard a voice beside her say, "Good evening, Miss Lyndall," and there was Rhys Graham. "May I have the pleasure of the first dance?"

Reacting spontaneously, she accepted the invitation. The minute she did, she wished she'd waited for Webb, but it was too late. Rhys was holding out his arm to lead her onto the dance floor, which had been freshly sanded and waxed for dancing. As she reached for the loop on the side of her skirt to lift it she caught a glimpse of Webb's disappointed expression before he turned away.

Rhys held her rather stiffly as they circled the floor, saying, "You'll have to forgive my awkwardness, Miss Lyndall. I've not had much opportunity for this sort of thing. I was brought up by a Quaker grandmother, and dancing was considered—" He smiled ironically. "Well, it wasn't included in the rest of my education."

For all of his deprecating, Rhys was a smooth dancer. Sunny was also somewhat out of practice, she discovered, but they managed to complete the set reasonably in step. Again Sunny wondered about this man. Little by little Rhys dropped hints about himself, like mentioning a Quaker background. Still, he seemed to cloak himself in shadows, only at rare moments revealing bits and pieces of what made up his personality. He still seemed out of place here in this "gateway to the West" town, remaining an enigma.

Sunny soon found out it was the custom here for everybody to get a chance to dance. There were no wallflowers. All it took was a tap on a dancer's shoulder and an "if you please," and away that dancer went with another partner. Sunny circled the floor with two or three before the music stopped and Rhys was at her side again, suggesting they get some cooling punch. He took Sunny to one of the chairs at the side of the room, then excused himself to get the drinks. Left alone, Sunny looked around interestedly at the roomful of people. It was quite a mix. As Verna had forewarned her, *everyone* came to the harvest dance. She recognized some of the ladies she'd seen at church, along with the schoolmarm, Miss Eddy, who Verna had introduced her to one day at the store. All ages were represented. She saw the church organist, a lady nearing seventy if a day, young women holding babies that they bounced in their laps in time with the tunes, middle-aged "grannies" who gossiped on the sidelines and watched the dancers, and children of all ages dancing together. Evidently no one was excluded. With amazed disbelief, Sunny spotted some extravagantly gowned and "painted" ladies, obviously girls from the dance halls. They would've been hard to miss. Their brightly colored dresses were in sharp contrast to the "best" calicos and cottons of the other women in attendance. However, tonight they were a little less flamboyantly attired and less rouged than they probably were when "at work." But they did not act the least ill at ease, hobnobbing this once with the more conservative citizens. Neither were they being snubbed or ostracized.

Sunny was just wondering where Webb had disappeared to when suddenly he was standing right in front of her. He smiled down at her, his teeth very white against his sunbronzed skin. "Howdy, Miss Lyndall. If you don't look a picture tonight."

"And so do you!" she retorted. "I hardly recognized you!" He *did* look handsome as could be.

"Would you like to dance?" he asked.

Remembering how she felt before in his arms, Sunny wondered if she should risk being that close again. She flicked open her fan, fluttering it to cool her suddenly-flushing face.

"I'm surprised, Mr. Chandler. I didn't know dancing was among your many accomplishments."

"Oh yes, ma'am. Some do say I'm quite a *terpsichorean*." Webb drawled the word elaborately, looking pleased at being able to roll it out so grandly.

"Oh, my! Is it catching?" Sunny asked in mock horror.

He laughed and held out both hands. "Try me and I'll prove it."

The band was playing what sounded like a waltz, and Webb whirled her into its rhythm with a sure, strong lead. Over his shoulder she saw Rhys return to where he had left her. Holding two punch cups in either hand, he stood glancing around until he saw them. His puzzled look turned into one of disappointment. Sunny felt guilty. That soon vanished when Webb drew her closer, whispering, "You smell like lilacs." For a moment she shut her eyes, a sensation of delight sweeping through her. It was such an unexpected, romantic thing for him to say. Flattered but a little flustered, she felt the need to regain their old adversarial rapport.

"My apologies for doubting your word, Mr. Chandler. You're every bit as graceful on a dance floor as on a horse."

"What kind of compliment is that?"

"The only kind I know to give. Just an honest opinion."

"That's one thing I can sure say about you, Miss Lyndall: you're nothing if not flat-out honest about your opinions." His eyes were laughing as he looked at her. "An unusual thing in a woman!" he added mischievously. "Most lead you on till you think you've made some headway, then *wham—*"

"You sound very experienced in the ways of women, Mr. Chandler."

Just then the music came to an end as Milton Beemis, in charge of the dance, climbed onto the band platform, held up both hands, and announced, "Comin' up next is the Cinderella."

"Ah, doggone it, they always do that!" Webb said.

"What on earth is it?" Sunny asked.

"You'll see."

Milton Beemis' voice rang out. "Ladies, take off your left shoe and, holding it in your hand, start moving in a big circle to the music. Gents, form a circle outside the ladies. When the music stops, ladies, toss your shoe into the middle and make way for the gents to scramble in for a shoe. Gents, when you grab a lady's shoe, it's up to you to find the lady it belongs to—and *she's* your partner for the next set."

Webb relinquished her as the circles began to form. "What kind of shoe are you wearing?" he asked. She didn't have a chance to reply, because Webb was jostled out of the way by a large, burly cowboy and pushed as others crowded in, and they were separated.

Amid much laughter, little shrieks, and exclamations, the ladies began untying, unbuckling, unbuttoning, the shoe from their left foot. Hobbling a little on her one stocking-clad foot, Sunny joined the circle of ladies. The music began again and everyone started moving. The band entered into the fun by slowing down as if they were going to stop and then picking up the melody again, and the circling continued. When it finally came to an abrupt stop, there was a wild tossing of shoes. A mad scramble followed as the men dashed through the ladies' circle, searching for the shoe whose lady they wanted to dance with next.

Holding her breath, Sunny stood waiting excitedly to see who her partner would be. She was taken completely by surprise when a red-faced, broad-shouldered fellow with muttonchop whiskers, holding her small kid slipper in the palm of his beefy hand, turned up. He introduced himself as Harper Nelson, a cowboy at the Bigelow ranch. Before he swung her practically off her feet as the music started for the next set, Sunny saw Webb still standing in the middle of the circle. In his hand was a red satin slipper, its curved French heel studded with rhinestones.

Sunny lost track of him after that. The dance became a free-for-all. It seemed all a man had to do was tap another man on the shoulder to exchange dance partners. Sunny did not lack partners. She was whisked from one to the other. She danced with a hefty rancher who pumped her arm so energetically as they two-stepped around the floor that some of her hairpins fell out. Grateful for an excuse to catch her breath, she excused herself to repair the damage. She went to find the "refreshing" room set aside for the ladies.

As she left the dance floor Sunny saw Webb dancing with

the girl she'd heard someone call Juanita. She was an exotic-looking dance hall girl with dark hair swirled into a loose knot, curls tumbled randomly down on white shoulders. She wore ruffled black lace on a crimson gown with a flounced skirt short enough to reveal slender ankles. Curiously Sunny glanced at her feet. She was wearing red satin shoes with heels that sparkled. With a jolt she realized Webb was *still* dancing with the girl whose slipper he'd found. Most people had changed partners a dozen times since the ladies' shoe toss. To Sunny's discomfort, they looked as though they were enjoying each other's company enormously. Sunny's mouth tightened. All her easy acceptance of the dance hall ladies being made welcome at the community dance disappeared. With a sharp jab something else replaced it: jealousy.

She hurried outside, around the back of the building. The path leading to the refreshing room skirted the long wooden porch that circled the dance hall. Couples taking the air between dances strolled there, and small clusters of people chatted in low voices, their figures indistinguishable in the darkness unless they were touched by the glow of the lighted windows.

The ladies' room was empty at the moment, and Sunny was glad. She needed time to collect herself. She felt upset. Impatiently she took out the rest of her hairpins and began to rearrange her hair. The mirror was chipped and mottled and so her image was somewhat distorted, yet it revealed her petulant expression. That irritated her more. What did it matter to her who Webb danced with? Why should she care anyway? Reluctantly she answered her own question. Something had happened tonight while they were dancing. All her old animosity toward him had faded. She had felt pleasurably lighthearted, light-footed, light-headed . . .

Ever since the day he rescued her, something had changed between them. She was too honest not to admit she was strongly attracted. It was more than just gratitude toward him for teaching her to shoot. She recognized the feeling. She had felt it twice before in her life. Once, when she was fourteen and in love with her piano teacher. The other time, with the young assistant minister that had come one summer to help Reverend Dorsey, their regular minister, who had fallen from a ladder while cleaning the bell tower of the church, breaking his arm and several ribs. Sunny had spent hours gathering flowers to take over to the church, making all kinds of excuses to go by there. She had suddenly become a regular attender at the Wednesday night prayer meetings. After he returned in September to the seminary in Louisville where he was a student, Sunny had pined all winter. She had written letters she never mailed, written poetry she tore up, daydreamed constantly about being a parson's wife.

Had she unconsciously been drifting into the same kind of thoughts about Webb Chandler? She must be out of her mind. A man—a man's man—a wagon train scout! A man with no roots, reckless, irresponsible. To feel the same way about someone like him as she had about a teacher and a preacher? Impossible!

The trouble was, her feeling toward Webb was stronger. Lately she had felt a kind of underlying purpose in all that had happened. Could it have been more than coincidence for she and Tracy to be stranded in this town on the edge of Independence? Could they have been delayed here for a reason somehow, so that . . .? So that they could meet certain people, fall in love? Was there *really* a kind of destiny that overruled people's plans?

There was, *if* you believed all those silly romantic books. Which of course she didn't. Sunny slammed down her brush, shoved it into her reticule. She wanted to get back to the dance. It was getting late. There was still time to dance with Webb again, to see . . . She gave a final pat to her hair and hurried out.

133

Outside a delightfully cool breeze was blowing. Sunny stopped for a minute to breathe deeply of it before going back into the warm dance hall. As she stood there she heard a woman's low, soft laugh. Something made her turn her head. There against one of the supporting porch posts she saw two figures, male and female, silhouetted against the light from the windows. The woman's head was thrown back, tossing a mass of curls as her full-throated, seductive laughter came again. The man, one arm stretched over her head, leaned toward her. He was speaking in a low, teasing voice Sunny recognized, even though she could not make out the words. It was that Texas drawl she had teased Webb unmercifully about. It was Webb, and the girl must be the enchanting Juanita.

Sunny's cheeks grew hot. It was shaming. Her heart felt bruised, hurting painfully. She didn't want to feel this way—not for someone like Webb Chandler. She clenched her hands. She didn't want to go back in to the dance, but she couldn't stand out here. She shivered. The cool wind had begun to make her feel cold. On the verge of tears, she hated the idea of walking back into the lighted room filled with music, the sound of dancing feet, the laughing voices and gaiety. But she had to. She could never let him know what she'd seen or how it made her feel. Straightening her shoulders, she took a deep breath and went back inside.

Intermission over, the band struck up again. This time a familiar melody she particularly loved. She had just successfully got her emotions under control when she saw Webb strolling toward her, and she panicked. Suddenly she couldn't move but stood there at the edge of the dance floor as if her feet were frozen.

"I've been lookin' for you," he smiled, holding out his hand to her. "My dance, little lady?"

Something cold hardened Sunny's longing to move into his arms and dance with him again. "I'm afraid not,

134

Mr. Chandler," she said icily. "I've already promised the next set. But I'm sure you can find another partner without any trouble."

Webb's eyes narrowed. He looked bewildered, almost stunned. Sunny took perverse satisfaction in the hope that she might have hurt him a little. At least punctured his ego. Over his shoulder she saw Rhys coming across the hall. She smiled and waved with her unfurled fan. Webb turned to see to whom she was directing this flirtatious gesture, and when he saw Rhys, he gave Sunny a long, knowing look, then stalked away. Rhys hurried to her side.

Sunny couldn't remember much of the rest of the evening. She talked, laughed, and danced, but it was all forced. She kept seeing that silhouette against the windows, the sound of low voices, the intimate position of the two figures. Why had she allowed herself to be caught up by the slow-talking charm of that Texan—that "lady-killer," as Clem Ardley jokingly called him?

The night she had looked forward to so happily was ending for her on a sour note. She wanted to go, to escape. Impulsively she said, "Oh, Mr. Graham, could I ask you to take me home? I have a slight headache, and I'm afraid Tracy isn't yet ready to leave."

"Of course. It would be my pleasure."

Immediately Sunny wished she hadn't given in to the impulse. Rhys seemed almost delighted at the opportunity. After what Verna had told her, she had purposely avoided doing anything to invite Rhys' personal attention. Now he might think she was making an occasion to be alone with him. Irrationally she blamed Webb. If she hadn't been so upset about seeing him with Juanita . . . But it was done now. She would just have to be completely impersonal, talk about Express business on the way home.

When she came back from getting her shawl, Rhys was waiting for her. She couldn't resist the urge to take a last look to see if Webb was dancing. But he was nowhere in sight. Probably out on the verandah again with Juanita! Sunny was glad that in the darkness her burning cheeks could not be seen.

On the ride out from town, Sunny tried to still her churning emotions, to carry on some kind of conversation. She didn't succeed in doing either very well. Anything that came to mind to say seemed too banal or artificial, so she decided to remain quiet. He too was silent until they reached the Express station, then he asked casually, "Did you enjoy yourself tonight?"

When she didn't answer at once, Rhys glanced over at her. "Did something happen to make you unhappy? I thought I saw an expression on your face that—" He hesitated. "Don't answer if you don't want to."

Astonished, Sunny said, "You're very observant."

"Not always. Not unless ... well, I noticed, that's all." When she didn't offer any explanation, he got down, came around, and helped her out of the buggy. A pale moon shed a milky light over everything, softening the harsh outlines of the building.

Sunny felt again the rise of humiliated anger. She was still smarting from seeing Webb flirting with someone else. Well, she'd just have to get over it. He wasn't worth her giving him another thought! Her foolish feelings were probably brought on by the frustration of being trapped here and lonely ...

With a start she realized Rhys was talking to her, and she had to ask him to repeat himself.

"I just said it was a lovely night, the moon and all—you weren't listening, were you? It's been a long evening, and you're probably tired. I noticed you didn't miss a dance."

"Yes, it *was* quite an evening."

They walked slowly over to the building. When they reached the porch, Sunny put out her hand to thank him.

Instead he captured it in both of his, holding it. "You know, I searched for *your* shoe! I blamed myself for not checking what kind you were wearing. I didn't get a chance to dance enough with you."

Sunny tried to withdraw her hand, but he held it fast.

"I've grown very fond of you, you know," Rhys went on. "You *and* your brother. He's growing into a fine young man. Dependable, serious. You should be proud of him."

"Oh, I am," Sunny replied, wondering where all this was leading.

"He's intelligent too. Not just a rider. I think I could train him to be a very good station manager, to take on more responsibility if and when he tires of riding."

"But you know we're going to California."

"I thought maybe you'd changed your plans." Rhys' voice was hopeful. "I know Tracy is quite interested in one of the local girls, Brownlee's daughter. He has a huge spread, lots of cattle. He'd probably welcome a son-in-law with Tracy's qualities."

Sunny tugged gently at her hand. "Tracy's still very young, Mr. Graham—"

"*Rhys*, please."

"I don't think he has settling down or marriage on his mind."

"You sure about that?"

She drew in her breath. "Well, he hasn't said anything to me."

"Maybe I spoke out of turn," Rhys said. "It's just that your and your brother's plans are important to me. *You* are important to me, Sunny."

Sunny felt a little dart of alarm. Rhys had called her Sunny! The use of a first name of someone of the opposite sex, except to a close relative, assumed intimacy. Between a young woman and man it meant an affectionate relationship. Rhys had spoken it so naturally, Sunny realized

137

he must think of her in these terms. Now it had inadvertently slipped out. He didn't even seem to realize what he'd done, because he went on speaking. "Have you any idea of how much you have come to mean to me?"

His hands tightened on hers, his voice grew intense. He leaned toward her, and for a minute she thought he was going to kiss her. She stepped back, and reluctantly he let go of her hands.

"I'm sorry. I've offended you, haven't I? I spoke too frankly. I think I've frightened you. I didn't mean . . ."

"No, no, of course not," Sunny said breathlessly. But she drew away, opening her purse, fumbling for her keys. "Thank you for bringing me home."

He seemed chastened. "It was my pleasure. And if—" He started to say something more, then stopped.

"I'll say good night now," she said, opening the door.

"Good night," Rhys said. Then softly, "Sweet dreams, Sunny."

Sunny went inside. She leaned against the closed door, listening to the sound of Rhys' buggy wheels gradually fading as he went out through the gate.

What an evening it had been! It was all too bewildering. Sunny slipped off her dancing shoes and folded her shawl. She sighed deeply. Tracy had better get home soon. Not keep her waiting up.

She was suddenly weary. She wanted to go to bed, go to sleep. She didn't want to worry about what Rhys Graham had hinted or what was happening to all her plans—most of all she wanted to stop thinking about Webb Chandler.

Chapter 16

The day after the harvest dance, Sunny set to work cleaning the stove. *Just like Cinderella after the prince's ball. Back to ashes and cinders,* she thought grimly, remembering the ladies' shoe toss. At least her mind was taken up with the grubby job rather than her humiliation at seeing Webb Chandler with the dark-eyed Juanita. Sunny brushed harder, faster. Why should she care? Still, the memory caused resentment to tighten inside her. Whatever amused him so that he threw back his head and laughed set Sunny's teeth on edge. The whole intimacy of the scene bothered her most.

Only a half hour before, he had danced with *her,* had whispered, his lips against her hair—then he was out in the moonlight with Juanita! Sunny gritted her teeth and shoveled out the ashes with a vengeance. She wished she'd let him know she had seen them, shown him how tacky she thought they were being. However, if she had done *that*, he might have assumed she *cared* . . . Oh, figs and apples! What possible difference could it make? None whatsoever!

Then why did she feel so betrayed? Before last night

hadn't she discouraged Webb? Why now should she feel rejected? Why this grating sensation of jealousy?

The truth was that ever since that terrible day when he had come to her rescue, something unspoken but very real, something she couldn't explain away, had happened between them. Even that day she realized her feelings about Webb had changed.

She had been excited when she went to the dance, expecting to see him, anticipating his reaction when he saw her in her new dress, hoping—well, Sunny wasn't sure just what she'd been hoping. For a brief time it seemed as if everything would turn out happily, just as she had imagined. Until . . .

No use going over all that again. Sunny got up from her knees, emptied the ashes into a bucket to take outside. She was not going to waste another minute thinking about the incident. It was stupid and childish and she was going to forget it.

At one time she might have fretted about such things. But not anymore. She had changed, grown up! Everything that had happened had changed her. She had plenty of better things to think of. Decisively Sunny went out to her garden to pull weeds.

She weeded two rows, priding herself on how strong she had become. Her slender body had toughened; there were muscles in her slim arms and wrists now. Working with the ponies had increased other skills as well. She felt she could handle them better, that she had more patience. She was capable of so much more than she had ever thought possible. Coping with the Express company business, keeping up with daily chores, unexpected tasks. She could do lots of things as well as Tracy—hammer a nail, shoot a rifle . . . *That* thought naturally made her think of who had taught her. She quickly thrust it away. She'd given Mr. Chandler enough of her thoughts today!

As if thought could produce reality, she heard the sound of hoofbeats. She turned around just as the very subject of her inner turmoil cantered through the gate. In sudden confusion she went back to yanking the stubborn weeds out of her carrot patch.

"Mornin', Miss Lyndall," he greeted her cheerfully. Her mouth straightened into a hard line. *Just as if nothing had happened!* she thought indignantly. She was torn between two urges: one to ignore him, the other to confront him about Juanita. Neither was a good idea, she decided.

She leaned back on her heels and lifted her curls off her neck, securing them with her bandanna handkerchief. Why was it he always came when she looked her worst? And why should that bother her? Putting up one hand to shield her eyes from the sun's glare, she watched him saunter over. It galled her to find pleasure in his trim, muscular frame, his oddly graceful stride, as he walked toward her with his usual confidence.

"Had a good time last night, did you?" he asked casually. "You got away so quick, I didn't get a chance to say—"

"*You* seemed to be enjoying yourself," Sunny retorted crossly, then she could have bitten her tongue. She shouldn't let him know she noticed. Without intending to, she blurted out, "Having too good a time to even notice when we left."

"Oh, I saw you leave, all right. You and Rhys." There was insinuation in his tone of voice.

Sunny's eyes widened. "Well, you could've said good night."

"I was just trying to tell you I didn't have the chance to say *good-bye*. That's what I come out for today. To say good-bye."

"Good-bye?" Her surprise was genuine.

"Yep. Signed on with a wagon train leaving day after tomorrow."

His announcement hit her like a stone landing on her

141

chest. She dropped her trowel, straightened up, and looked at him in surprise before managing to say, "Isn't this awfully sudden?"

"I would've told you last night. But like I say, I didn't have the chance."

"You through with scouting?" she asked, surprised.

"Nah! Jest wanted a change. As a matter of fact, I've been hankering for a change of sorts. And this was too good to turn down. Pays good. Actually, it's as escort to a group of English *gentlemen*." He emphasized the word with a trace of sarcasm. "They're on a hunting expedition. Want to actually *see* the buffalo they've read about. They need an escort to Fort Laramie."

"Huh!" Sunny swallowed this added bit of information, then said, "I thought you hated the way men were hunting buffalo! I believe the word you used was *slaughtering*."

He shrugged. "They're paying me a heck of a lot of money."

"Oh? Well then, I suppose *that* would be enough to make *you* change your principles," Sunny snapped.

He gave her an odd look that made her wish she hadn't said it.

"Money's not the reason. Besides, I never said I *approved* of it. They just need someone who knows the territory, buffalo country. You see, they're a new breed of hunter. They've got a lot of newfangled *photographic* equipment. Want to take pictures more than to shoot. Seems like back in England people are interested in slide shows of the American wilderness. One of them plans to write a book to go along with the pictures."

Sunny felt chastened. As usual she had spoken too quickly, had jumped to conclusions. She started to get to her feet, and Webb stretched out a hand to help her, then quickly plunged his hands in his pockets instead.

"Anyway, the main reason I rode out before I left was to

142

see—" He broke off, glancing around. "Haven't had any unwelcome visitors, have you?"

Sunny was ashamed. Had she been wrong about him? *Again?* Maybe he really cared about her, was concerned about her safety. She shook her head.

"Well anyway, I was jest thinkin' it might be a good idea for you to have a dog out here. With your brother gone so much and all." Webb looked around, not meeting her eyes directly, and said almost indifferently, "So I wondered if you might want to keep my dog, Dandy, for me while I'm gone. He's a great watchdog. 'Course, his bark is a whole lot worse than his bite. He's a real good companion. I got him when he was a pup, but I can't take him along on my scouting trips. I've sometimes left him with the Ardleys, but their dog's just had pups, and Verna has her hands full. There's other places I could leave him, I reckon—" He paused. "He gets lonesome. Figured you might get a tad lonely, too. Reckon you two could keep each other company?"

Taken aback by the offer, Sunny stared at him for a moment. This man was always putting her off balance. Blowing hot and cold with her. Showing interest one time, indifference the next.

"He's a real nice dog—gets lonely when he's left, that's all."

At Webb's affectionate tone of voice, something softened within her. Her impulse was, of course, to keep the dog. She loved animals. Then just as quickly Sunny remembered the scene she had inadvertently witnessed the night before. If she agreed too quickly, he might get the idea—

"Well . . .," she dragged it out as though she were considering it. Then perversely she decided to put it on the basis that *she* was doing *him* a favor, not the other way around. "Why, I suppose—if you can't find someone else to keep him for you, I'd be glad to."

A knowing smile briefly touched Webb's mouth. His eyes

seemed to say, "I'm on to you," but all he said was, "Good. I'll bring him out later on so's you two can get acquainted."

With that he turned and strolled back to where he'd hitched his horse. He mounted and without looking back rode out the gate.

Sunny stood motionless, looking after him with a mingling of regret and wishful thinking. He hadn't mentioned last night, as if *their* three dances had never happened!

Sunny felt confused, unsettled, unhappy. She felt as if she were caught in another tug-of-war. Her heart was pulled one way, then another. She was attracted to Webb yet suspicious of that attraction. He was so hard to figure out. She recalled something Rhys Graham had once said about him: *Webb likes to put on a tough front. He's like a chestnut—hard on the outside, soft and mellow inside. Keeps his good deeds to himself. But he's done plenty of 'em that I know of personally. He really cares about people.*

He certainly seemed to care about her and her safety, Sunny conceded. The question was, how much? And dare she allow herself to care about him?

Later that afternoon Webb arrived with his dog, a brown and white spaniel-cross. When Sunny saw Webb ride through the open gate, the dog was running alongside him. Sunny came out on the porch to meet them. Webb walked over, stopping at the bottom of the steps. He squatted down, sitting on his heels, stroking the dog's head, saying in a low voice, "This here's Dandy. And this is Miss Lyndall, fella. You're to watch out for her, protect this place, y'hear?" He looked up at Sunny. "Maybe you should come down, put out your hand, let him get your scent. Let him get the idea that you're takin' my place for now."

Sunny came down the steps, tucked her skirts around her, sat down, and held out one hand to the dog's muzzle. Velvety brown eyes turned questioningly to Webb. "It's all right, fella," Webb said soothingly, fondling the silky ears.

The dog made small whining sounds of pleasure. "He'll do all right here. He's got a mighty good bark. He'll keep you safe, won't you, boy?"

Sunny hadn't meant to say it, but she'd been puzzling over it all day, so it just popped out. "What's the real reason you're going off like this—taking this job with the hunters?"

Webb looked up at her again. His expression held mockery and something else indefinable. Under his steady gaze, she felt her cheeks flush. "There's reason enough," was all he said, and she was silenced. Then Webb stood up. "Well, I think you two'll do fine. I'll be takin' off."

The dog moved, too, running to the side of the horse, quivering in anticipation that they were starting the familiar race back to town or wherever his master led. But Webb whistled him back to his side.

"No, fella. You're to stay here. Stay." The command was firm. For a split second the dog seemed to hesitate, then he came, whimpering low in his throat. "Take your place." Webb gestured with a downward movement of his hand. The dog did as he was told. Webb glanced at Sunny. "He knows. He minds well. Just speak quietly, firm."

"When will you be back?"

"Can't say for sure. Maybe a month, maybe more. Maybe I might even stay out west, if I've a mind to. Might even give up scouting after all, settle down!" He smiled wickedly. "If I don't come back, Dandy's yours. If you don't want him, I have someone else who does." He took off his hat and made her a sweeping bow. "You were my first choice, Miss Lyndall, being you're so *sweet-tempered* and all. Thought Dandy'd have a right good home till I get back." He walked over to his horse and mounted. He tipped his hat, swung his horse around, smiled, and said, "So long." To Sunny there seemed an awful finality in his words. As she stood watching him until he disappeared in the clouds of dust raised by his horse's hooves old feelings of being forsaken, of losing something important to her, washed over her.

Just then Dandy threw his head back and gave a mournful howl. It was as if the dog knew Webb's leaving might be for good. An instant empathy for the animal prompted Sunny. She leaned down to pat his head comfortingly. But Dandy moved away from her and with a sigh flopped down in the corner of the porch, putting his nose onto his paws.

That night, emotions Sunny thought she had long ago put behind her surfaced. She discovered that the old wounds of losing her father when he married Matilda had never really healed. To her utter surprise they were some-how now mixed with Webb Chandler's leaving. Seeing him ride off had brought an instant sadness, a soreness to her heart, a loneliness to her spirit. Almost the same way she had felt seeing her father ride off from the church, newly married. She had promised herself then that she was never going to love someone so much again. Her father's remar-riage had broken Sunny's heart, because it excluded her, changed her life. Even at that tender age, she'd decided that loving someone gave them the power to hurt, and she would never let it happen to her again. Being vulnerable was a weakness. Sunny had determined to be strong. That night she wept, not knowing exactly why or what it had to do with Webb Chandler.

Chapter 17

*S*unny missed Webb. More than she cared to admit. Missed those impromptu visits, those teasing remarks, the provocative look in his eyes. Dandy missed him, too.

Webb's dog proved both a comfort and a challenge to Sunny. Master and dog were a strange pair, she often thought. Why Webb had brought the dog here Sunny could never quite decide. Although obedient, Dandy maintained an aloofness, seeming only to suffer her attentions.

It puzzled and hurt Sunny a little that the dog kept his distance. Eventually he allowed her to pat him or talk to him when she fed him or placed a pan of cool water by his dish. But for the most part Dandy kept up a wall that no amount of coaxing or petting overcame. Dandy daily took his place on the station porch, facing the gate as if waiting hopefully for his *real* master's return.

At first Shadow showed his indignation at the arrival of a new animal into the household by scurrying on top of the table, the hutch, or the rocker, arching his back and hissing. Soon, however, a truce was reached between the kitten and the visiting dog. In fact, one day Sunny found her black cat curled up back-to-back with Dandy, both asleep in a patch of sunshine.

147

A week after Webb's departure, Rhys came out to the Express station. At the sound of Dandy's barking, Sunny went out onto the porch just in time to see Rhys leaning over and patting Dandy, whose tail was wagging. Rhys looked up at Sunny and remarked, "Nice dog, isn't he? Belongs to Webb Chandler, right?"

Feeling as though she should explain, Sunny said, "Yes. We're keeping him for Webb while he's away." She purposely said *we* to give the impression it was Tracy's friendship with Webb that had resulted in Dandy's stay.

"Good idea," Rhys nodded. "*I* should have thought of giving you a dog of your own. For protection when you're here by yourself, as well as for company. We'll have to see about that when Webb comes home and wants Dandy back." He came toward the porch steps. "So is everything going all right out here? You need anything?"

"No, thank you. We're fine. I don't have last week's receipts yet, but it won't take long, if you want to wait. Or I can have them for you tomorrow."

"Whichever is best. I might as well wait."

"Come in then, and I'll get them together."

"How's Tracy?" Rhys asked as he followed her into the front of the building, where the office was.

"Fine, I guess." She gave a rueful smile. "I hardly see him, though. When he's in town, he's either sleeping or doing chores or with his rider friends."

Sunny went behind the divider and unlocked the safe. Rhys, on the other side, leaned his elbow on the counter and asked, "Does it bother you that your brother is finding other interests? Friends of his own?"

"Oh, maybe a little. It's not his fault, and it's only natural. I suppose it's just that I've always kinda looked after him, especially after both our parents died. I have to keep reminding myself he's growing up. He's not my little brother anymore."

A smile touched Rhys' mouth, but his eyes weren't smiling. "It happens like that sometimes," he said. "Overnight, boys become men. It happens often in the West. Life moves faster out here. Too fast sometimes. Differences that should be settled by discussion and debate are taken care of by guns." Sunny saw something flicker in Rhys' eye, glint there for a single second, then vanish. What was it? Anger? Bitterness? She could not guess. "I've seen it happen too often," he continued. "Small disagreements escalate into violence. Out here, without the constraints of a more settled kind of life, family reputation, church, the law—all the influences that keep society civilized—are sometimes forgotten. Men seem to elevate recklessness more than honor, hatred more than tolerance or compassion. Hatred is demonic. It turns men into brutal beasts. It robs them of their humanity."

Rhys' face suddenly underwent a change as if he were remembering something vividly. Then just as quickly he said, "How did we get on this subject? Forgive me. The only reason I mentioned it was I thought maybe it might help you understand about circumstances causing people to change. Like your brother is doing with his new responsibilities. It has nothing to do with you, his feelings for you. He's growing up, that's all. Don't take it personally."

"You're right, of course," Sunny agreed, wondering why it was so much easier to accept Rhys' comments about Tracy than Webb's. "And I am glad Tracy is happy, is making friends."

"This isn't a bad place to put down roots, you know. It's a good community, good people. Not growing too fast like a cattle town, nor does it draw riffraff like a gold strike would. Not even too close to Independence, for that matter. It'll develop at its own speed. Be a fine place to settle down, raise a family."

Suddenly conscious that their conversation might

become too personal and remembering Verna's warning, she quickly changed the subject. "Well, this is everything. All the receipts, dated received." She stacked them and slid them across the counter.

"Thanks. You're doing a fine job, Sunny. I appreciate it," Rhys said, opening a leather packet and putting the receipts inside. But he made no move to leave.

Sunny felt awkward. She was uncertain of how to treat this visit, as business or social. Usually when Rhys came on business, he maintained a very formal manner. Especially since the harvest dance and what happened after, she could no longer treat him as simply an employer. She would have to be blind as a bat, as Verna put it, to not see Rhys had more than a passing interest in her. How to handle it?

Trying to seem natural, Sunny came out from behind the office enclosure and moved toward the kitchen. At the stove, she lifted the still half-full coffeepot questioningly.

"Yes, thanks," Rhys nodded and walked over to accept the cup she handed him. Dandy had trotted after them into the building and remained by Rhys, his tail wagging hopefully. When Rhys sat down, Dandy went over to him and rested his head against Rhys' knee. For a minute Rhys silently caressed the dog's head, then he looked over at Sunny and picked up the thread of conversation he had been pursuing. "For myself, the longer I was here, the more I felt like staying. I suppose there comes a time in a man's life when he wants to settle down, put down roots, establish a home—wouldn't you agree?"

"I really couldn't say. Tracy and I have talked of nothing else but going to California for over a year—since our stepmother died. Coming here was to be the start of the great adventure of our lives."

"I understand. But you don't think maybe Tracy has changed his mind? Especially since he's been courting rancher Brownlee's daughter? I heard he's been talking about buying some land *here*—"

Jolted, Sunny turned wide-eyed to Rhys.

"I didn't know that! I mean, I knew he often rode out to the Brownlee ranch on his days off, but about buying land, no—" The conviction in her tone faded. "At least, he hasn't said anything like that to *me*."

"I'm sorry if I've spoken out of turn, Sunny. I like your brother very much. He's smart, bright, got a good head on his shoulders. He's becoming a man capable of a lot more than riding the Pony Express. He's got a future, and it may be here." He paused. "Any chance *you* would change *your* mind? Or be willing to?"

Sunny bit her lip, shook her head.

"I've not even thought about it. We—or at least I—have always thought . . ." She lifted her chin a little. "As far as I'm concerned, nothing's changed. We plan to move to California as soon as possible."

What Rhys said about Tracy's plans shook her badly. How could Tracy go behind her back, talking about things he never discussed with her? She felt left out, betrayed. After all she had done for him! For Tracy not to have shared something so important was a hard pill to swallow. She struggled not to show her hurt. To cover up her emotional reaction, she scooped up Shadow from the pillow on the rocking chair, cradling him in her arms.

She wished Rhys would leave, give her a chance to sort out her thoughts. But he kept sitting there, regarding her thoughtfully. Then he said, "About California—I guess it has a lure for everyone. I had in mind to keep going on to the coast myself. But now somehow I feel different. I'm not running away anymore. I think I've found what I want, what would make me happy."

Sunny felt a vague uneasiness. She had the feeling they were heading into dangerous territory.

He seemed to notice her discomfort. "I'm afraid I might have said something to upset you. If I have, please forgive me. I value our friendship too much to ever do anything that might offend you."

"I know that."

"You must know what a high regard and respect I have for you. I will never bring up any subject that might cause you distress under any circumstances, unless—unless you give me reason to believe that it would be acceptable to you."

The more he said, the more uncomfortable Sunny became. She wanted to bring this conversation to an end.

Taking the hint, Rhys got up, placed his empty coffee mug on the table, picked up his hat, and moved toward the door. Sunny followed him out onto the porch, still holding Shadow in her arms as if for a shield.

At the edge of the porch, Rhys gazed into the distance, and Sunny again was struck by the nobility of his profile, the almost classically Greek structure of his high-bridged nose, his strong chin. He pointed toward the rim of blue hills beyond the gate, saying, "Someday I'd like to take you up into the hills not far from here. I want you to see a remarkable view. It's where I plan to build my house."

Without thinking, Sunny asked, "To live in by yourself?"

Immediately she was sorry. Her question posed an answer she might not want to hear. Even though the brim of his hat shaded his eyes, Sunny felt their thoughtful speculation as he turned to look at her. Then he said slowly, "I hope not. I sincerely hope not, Sunny."

Watching him ride out, Sunny had the feeling that their relationship had crossed some line and that nothing would ever be quite the same between them again.

Back in town at the Express office, Rhys had questions of his own to confront. Had he said too much? Gone too far? Had he dared to hope again? Was it possible to recapture all he had abandoned? To find in this woman the tenderness, the passion, the beauty, of a life he had lost? The constant loneliness had its source—a source he had to keep hidden, but it could not be denied. He had forsaken his right to the sweetest part of life, had kept its possibility locked away at a distance.

Did he have the right? *That* was the final question. If she knew—

Rhys moved his hand to the lower left drawer of the desk, then drew it back as if it contained a poisonous snake. No! Never that again. The only chance for true happiness was honesty. A picture of Sunny's eyes came into his vision—their candor, their innocence, their trust.

Forming a fist, Rhys banged it on the desk. Until he knew, until he asked Sunny outright, he could not decide what to do. He had to risk her rejection before he could seek her understanding.

During the next two days, Sunny could think of little else except what Rhys had said about Tracy. She did not risk bringing the subject into the open. But her inner resentment grew day by day, building a barrier of unspoken tension that had never existed before between brother and sister.

Maybe it was mostly rumor; after all, Rhys had only hearsay evidence. Yet rumors always seemed to have a germ of truth. Certainly Tracy hotfooted out to the Brownlee ranch every time he could. So what if it was all true? What if he *had* fallen in love with Betty Brownlee? What if he *did* want to settle down here and become a rancher? What then was *she* to do? There was no way as a single woman Sunny could go to California by herself. Lucas Flynt had made that clear enough before.

Thoughts of California—of the snowcapped mountains, the golden poppies, the oranges as big as melons, the constant sunshine—were what had kept her going all these dreary months. Were they all doomed to be just idle day-dreams, unfulfilled fantasies?

Simultaneously Rhys Graham's feelings for her began to have some unexpected impact. The fact that he had originally planned to go to California himself came into her mind at odd moments. Several times he had mentioned that in a few years, after the transcontinental railroad was completed, the trains would carry the mail, and then the Pony Express would be obsolete, his business gone. Would he *then* be content to build a house on a hillside here? Alone? Or might he again consider going west?

She still hadn't dared ask Tracy about his possible change of heart or his intentions. She knew she was avoiding learning something that just might break her own heart.

Fall was in the air. Although the days remained sunny and warm, the afternoon sun departed sooner and the evenings became cool. Sunny felt a strange melancholy that had nothing to do with the change of seasons. Or at least she didn't think it did. Yet a pervasive feeling of sadness hovered.

One particular evening Sunny was alone and fighting this creeping self-pity. Tracy had gone out. After coming in from his route and grabbing a few hours' sleep, he'd washed up and changed clothes. Then, mumbling some excuse to Sunny about going into town, he'd saddled one of the ponies and left. Sunny was sure whatever errand he might drum up in town, he was headed out to the Brownlee ranch to visit Betty.

Resolutely determined to be cheerful, Sunny lighted the fire and got out her mending basket. She had just started darning one of Tracy's socks when there was a knock at the door. Dandy's head rose, a rumble of a growl deep in his throat. He got to his feet with hackles quivering and approached the door, where he braced his back legs and stiffened, awaiting a word from Sunny in case it was necessary to attack an intruder.

She placed a hand on the dog's head and called, "Who is it?"

"Rhys, Sunny." She immediately threw back the bolt, opened the door, and he stepped inside. It had been almost two weeks since she had last seen him.

"I hope I'm not disturbing you, Sunny. I haven't the excuse that I was just riding by and decided to stop. I've come for a special reason."

"Of course." Her heart gave a queer little thump. She remembered some of the things he had *not* said, and at the same time she recalled the things Verna *had* said. "Come in."

He declined the cup of coffee she offered and pulled up a chair on the opposite side of the stove. He sat forward, leaning his arms on his knees, his hands clenched.

"Sunny, I'm sure you've sensed that I've grown to care for you a great deal. More than care—" He halted. "Do you know what I'm trying to say?"

Sunny shook her head, her heart uneasy. "That would be presuming—no, but I have a feeling it might be better left unsaid."

"If you don't want me to, of course, I won't."

Not knowing what to say, Sunny said nothing, and Rhys continued.

"I don't think I've done a very good job of keeping my feelings for you secret, Sunny. I've stayed away, trying to think things through. I understood that you did not wish me to go further the other afternoon. Why I was not sure. Perhaps duty to your brother? Reluctance to give up your original plans? And I respected your wishes. However, since then I've come to the conclusion that to withhold speaking frankly of my intentions is not forthright. I should do so and let *you* have a chance to consider my proposal. May I?"

Knowing she could not deny him that privilege, Sunny said, "Of course."

"Since you have no older male relative, at least none that I know of, and Tracy is not legal age, I must ask you directly. Would you do me the great honor of marrying me?"

Sunny chose her words carefully. "I'm flattered Rhys, but really—"

"Wait!" He held up one hand to keep her from interrupting. "As I mentioned the other day, when I started west some years ago, I planned to go on to California. But when I got to Independence—well, several unexpected things happened to delay me. Not unlike you and your brother. Although my experiences weren't as devastating as yours. Still, they were of the kind to make me stop, rethink my plans. Challenges, opportunities. The Express company seemed a stroke of good luck at the time I bought it. The thought of California began to fade somewhat. I grew to like it here, the town, the people—but what I wanted to tell you is this: if you would do me the great honor of marrying me, I would certainly consider the possibility of heading west again."

When Rhys left, a light rain was falling. They had talked for over an hour. He got back in his buggy and, sighing heavily, picked up the reins and headed back toward town. He felt inordinately let down. The fragile hope he'd had earlier was replaced by the old despair. At one time this disappointment might have led him to seek solace in drink. At least he felt no temptation to do that now.

What had he expected? Sunny had not rejected him out of hand. Neither had she seemed completely surprised by his proposal. Maybe he should have pressed for an answer once he'd fully explained his intentions. He hadn't dared to risk that. It was so recently that he'd allowed himself to imagine what it might be like to love and have someone love him in return.

At least she had not turned him down or refused to consider it. He had been quick to tell her to take all the time she needed, that he was willing to wait. He had lived long enough to know that nothing worthwhile in life comes easily. As he entered town Rhys felt a stirring of new hope rise in his heart. He felt more than ever that Sunny Lyndall had come into his life for a purpose. Was that purpose to give him a second chance? Hadn't he paid his penalty? Served his term? Suffered regret, remorse, repentance?

Night after night he had awakened from a nightmare— reliving the act that had brought him to this place, this moment in time. . . . The terrible loneliness, the scalding shame, would sweep over him. Then he knew he could not bury the past. His mind, his conscience, his soul, would not allow him that release.

Now for the first time he felt some assurance. The possibility that he could at last put it all behind him. After all the guilt and self-doubt, the wasted years, he saw a chance for a new beginning. His only fear was that Sunny would not be able to accept what he had not yet told her: the truth about himself and his past.

After Rhys left, Sunny could not settle down. Dandy seemed restless, too. Rhys' visit had probably been unsettling for him as well. Rhys' male scent had reminded the dog of his missing master. He prowled around, pacing back and forth on the porch, making small whining sounds in his throat. Taking pity on him, Sunny sat down on the top step and caressed his head. The dog's eyes revealed his loneliness, his bewilderment, and Sunny responded, saying, "You miss Webb, don't you, fella? Well, I do, too."

Her feelings about Webb were perplexing. She remembered how much she had disliked him at first, but since then . . . He had reached out to her in many surprising ways. She couldn't figure him out. He certainly wasn't someone you could count on. Here today, gone tomorrow. Even his showing up that awful day when those men had come had been by happenstance. Hadn't it? She was never sure. Still, a girl would be crazy to fall in love with anyone as undependable as Webb Chandler. Fall in love? What made her even *think* of that?

Sunny spent a sleepless night. In the morning she still couldn't get answers for any of the questions that had kept her awake. The simplest chore seemed almost too much to concentrate on, and soon she gave up trying. Her mind was in turmoil. Webb Chandler's absence and Rhys Graham's proposal were all she could think of.

Sunny had come to think of Rhys Graham as a benefactor. He had thrown her a lifeline when she was drowning, given her a job and then a place to live. But marriage! She had never thought that. She remembered how she had dismissed Verna's comments as nonsense. Now it made sense. Little things came back to her, small kindnesses, thoughtful gestures, that all added up to something more than friendship. But *marriage*?

Suddenly the Express station felt confining. She needed to get out. She needed someone to talk to, someone to confide in, someone she could trust to help her sift through her mixed-up feelings, find the truth. Verna. *Of course* Verna.

Sunny checked the bread she had rising on the table, tucked the cloth back over it. She fed the ponies and turned all of them but Bramble out in the corral. Then, snatching up her sunbonnet, she hitched him to the wagon and drove to the Ardley home.

Verna was putting up pickles and looked surprised when Sunny knocked at the kitchen door, then walked in.

"Hope I'm not barging in at a bad time?" Sunny asked

158

rather sheepishly. Looking around the kitchen, she realized at once that Verna was busy as usual.

"Not so I couldn't stand some company," was the tart reply. "I'm puttin' up my bread and butter pickles, but I'm most ways through."

"Can I do anything to help?" Sunny asked vaguely.

Watching Sunny aimlessly circle the room a couple of times, Verna concluded, *Something's up*. But she decided to wait until Sunny was ready to tell her the real reason she'd come.

"I got to go on here with what I'm doing. I'm jest now mixing the brine. I got more cucumbers in my garden this year than I know what to do with, and I'll have plenty to give away. Why don't you light somewhere while I finish up?"

Sunny nodded but remained where she stood, twisting her bonnet strings nervously.

Verna gave her a sharp look. *Something is sure enough wrong with the girl*. Making another try, she pointed to the rocker. "Pull up that chair and you can watch me. Mebbe you'd like to have this recipe for yourself."

Sunny did as Verna suggested but was too distracted to pay much attention as Verna resumed working, talking all the while.

"This recipe's been handed down in my family for goodness knows how long. Won prizes at county fairs many a time," Verna said as her hands moved deftly, measuring out the chopped onions, chunks of bell peppers, half a cup of salt, five cups of vinegar, five cups of sugar, teaspoons of clove, turmeric, mustard and celery seed, combining them in a bowl, then putting the mixture in a large pan and setting it on the stove to boil. "Now all's left to do is pour it into the packed jars," Verna said with satisfaction. But when she turned around and looked at Sunny, she realized Sunny would never be able to duplicate the pickle recipe.

What on earth was troubling the girl? "How would you like some fresh, sweet cider to have while we visit?"

Sunny glanced at Verna as one coming out of a trance, as if she had not even heard Verna's question, then announced solemnly, "Verna, you were right. About Rhys Graham."

Verna didn't need further explanation. She nodded. "Didn't I tell you he was plumb loco about you?"

"He's asked me to marry him."

Verna pursed her lips, then asked, "And what did you say? Did you accept?"

"Not yet. I told him that—well, that I'd have to think about it."

"Hmmm."

Sunny flashed her a look. "What does that 'hmmm' mean, Verna?"

Verna raised her eyebrows slightly. "Just hmmm." She gave her head a shake. "I'm thinkin' how many gals hereabouts would swoon clear away at such a proposal, give their eyeteeth for such a chance. Fine-looking man with a thriving business, no question of his being able to provide for a wife—"

"I *know* that he's considered a good catch." Sunny looked thoughtful. "But is that enough? There's love—isn't there?"

"You must be wanderin' around with your head in the clouds." Verna looked scandalized. "Most women out here don't have that luxury, child. A strong, healthy man, sober, God fearin', a good provider—that's what most are looking for, hoping for, and can't find."

Abruptly and disconcertingly that ended the conversation. But Sunny found it wasn't the end of Verna's uncanny discernment. A few days later Verna came out to the Express station. After plunking down a batch of raisin bread and two baskets of freshly picked blackberries on the kitchen table, she said, "These are the last of the season.

160

Better find some use for them right away iffen you don't plan to make jelly. They don't keep very good; they soften." Then she folded her arms, pierced Sunny with her direct gaze, and demanded, "It's Webb, isn't it?"

Startled, Sunny blinked and immediately denied it. "No, of course not."

"You sure?"

"What makes you think such a thing?"

"Oh, I dunno. Just something about the way you two look at each other when you think no one else is. The way you spar all the time, spittin' and scratchin' like two cats in a gunnysack." Verna sniffed with mock impatience.

"Webb Chandler! I declare, Verna, where in the world you got such an idea I'll never know."

Verna pressed her mouth into a straight line. For a full minute she was silent, then she said, "Well, I guess I do give you credit for better sense than that. Don't get me wrong. I love Webb like he was my own son. My *prodigal* one. And if I had a daughter, I'd tell her to keep away from him. Not that he don't have his good qualities. He's honest as the day's long, loyal to his friends, braver than he's got any right to be, but"—and here Verna paused significantly—"you know what they say, 'A rolling stone gathers no moss.'"

Sunny absorbed this but then said slowly, "However, Verna, he did hint that he was about through. Tired of taking people to California and then turning around and coming right back. Sounded like he might be getting ready to stay here and settle down—or move out west and homestead."

Verna threw up her hands. "If that just don't sound like something a fella like Webb *would* say. I doubt it seriously. He's been scouting ever since I've known him, and—"

"People can change, though, don't you think?"

Verna speared her with a skeptical look. "Can a leopard change his spots? Not very likely. Not in my experience. Folks stay pretty much the same. *Unless*—" She paused.

"Unless somethin' nobody could account for happens to 'em."

After Verna left, Sunny mulled over her pithy comments. She had to admit the older woman was wiser than anyone she had ever known. Maybe she should pay attention to what she said. Could Verna be right?

Nothing happens by chance. She'd heard that somewhere. *"Man proposes, God disposes."* Did God have anything to do with their being here in Missouri instead of California? Was she meant to meet Rhys Graham? Or was it Webb Chandler?

Chapter 18

*R*hys' proposal weighed heavily on Sunny. She was torn between feeling flattered and burdened by it. He had said, "You might learn to love me. I would do everything I could to make you happy." Sunny knew this was true. A man of Rhys' honor and integrity would be true to his word. But she had never thought of him romantically, and the idea of marriage without mutual love her conscience would not even consider. There was no one she could really confide in. Verna's advice was practical but born of the frontier way of thinking. In Verna's mind Rhys Graham was a godsend, meeting all the requirements of protection and provision a woman needed. Sunny would be a fool to turn him down. Sunny knew she could never make Verna understand the deeper need inside her that such a marriage would not fulfill.

In a way, she felt guilty not telling Tracy, but her brother had his own secrets. Until she knew what was going on with him, she did not want to say anything that might influence him one way or the other.

Rhys came out to the Express station more frequently, and never empty-handed, even if it was simply a bouquet of flowers. Sunny could not help being touched by his desire to please her, his carrying on an old-fashioned courtship. She already admired and respected him and now was more aware of his nobility of character, his sense of honor. He kept his promise never to mention his proposal of marriage again. Although she could not give him the answer he longed for, the appeal she saw in his eyes moved her. Intuitively she knew he had been deeply hurt by something—or someone. A terrible loss of some kind? Yet there was no bitterness in his expression, more a forlorn weariness and loneliness. Whatever it was, Sunny wished she could help or heal in some way. It wasn't as simple as "learning to love." Searching her heart for the right answer, Sunny knew that before she could be free to try to do that, she would have to do something else: forget Webb Chandler.

The longer he was gone, the more she had to admit she missed him, regretted some of her past actions. Her anger at the scene she had inadvertently witnessed at the harvest dance really seemed childish and foolish now. Wasn't it possible that the same easygoing charm that she herself found attractive about him would be irresistible to other women—even one as experienced as Juanita? Maybe she had overreacted, imagined something that didn't exist, that had been just a playful, flirtatious moment.

On the other hand, was she making excuses for him? She did not want to believe there was anything more going on between Webb and the dance hall girl. Was it so important because she wanted to believe Webb genuinely cared about *her*? Hadn't he been concerned enough for her safety to teach her to shoot, to bring his own dog for her protection? He *had* to have some special feeling to do all that. *She* had felt something real between them. It had not been her imagination!

As long as that was there, how could she consider Rhys Graham's proposal seriously?

But as Verna, who loved him like a son, pointed out,

what kind of husband would a man like Webb make? She had called him a rolling stone.

The argument went on in Sunny's mind endlessly, day after day. What was she looking for anyhow? In her girlhood dreams, she had imagined that one day she would meet a man who would match her own adventurous spirit. That is, once she got to California!

Now that she had a taste of what rough frontier life demanded, Sunny realized her dream had changed. Now she wanted not only someone to share her dream but a man who would recognize her independence, her ability, her strength, treat her as an equal partner. Or was that an impossible dream?

Weeks passed and Rhys remained outwardly patient. When he came on Express station business, he maintained a businesslike manner. Only the tenderness in his eyes betrayed the fact that he regarded her as more than an employee.

Although Sunny was sure Verna had not violated her confidence, somehow the word seemed to have got around on the notorious "small-town grapevine." Every time she went into town, she saw it in people's faces: the curious looks she got at the general store, the watchful eyes, the sly smiles, the knowing glances, on the street or in church when people greeted her. Rhys Graham was well thought of by everyone; therefore there was a natural interest in anything that concerned him.

Sunny did not know what to do to stem the tide of gossip. She was helpless to put an end to all the speculation. She knew people would talk no matter how small the grain of truth. In the meantime the tension building between Tracy and her reached a crisis.

With October weather arriving, each morning was colder and colder. Sometimes Tracy now had to wear a sheepskin-lined coat, leather chaps, and a wool scarf when he went out on his route. He talked of running into snow in the narrow passes, of winds whistling down the mountain canyons, of the pony's breath coming in icy puffs as he braved it along the frozen trails. This one particular morning Sunny awakened thinking mournfully about Christmas back home. Maybe it was the weather, which was bleak, overcast with heavy, gray clouds. As she went about the dark kitchen banging the stove door, getting a fire started, clattering the coffeepot when she set it on to boil, she grew increasingly wretched.

When Tracy came out, he seemed to be in just the opposite kind of mood. Sunny threw him a wary glance. Why was he looking so happy? Didn't he miss the same things she missed? No, probably not. Too cow-eyed over Miss Betty Brownlee, she thought irritably, plunking down his plate of flapjacks in front of him.

"What're you in a pucker about, Sis?" he asked as he poured molasses over the stack.

"I'm not in a pucker!" she retorted indignantly.

"Sure actin' mighty ornery," he said placidly, taking a large forkful.

"I am not."

"Well, could have fooled me."

"Don't talk with your mouth full!"

Tracy started to laugh.

Sunny turned her back and began pouring more batter into the pan. She knew Tracy was right. But somehow she couldn't get over feeling put upon, unhappy. She didn't respond and nothing more was said. She could hear him scrape his plate, then slide back in his chair. He came over, bringing his plate to the sink, then refilled his mug with coffee.

"Sorry if I made you mad, Sis."

She turned around. "I'm sorry, too, Tracy. I don't know what's got into me lately—"

166

"Maybe this will help," he said and dug in his jacket pocket and brought out a small leather pouch and set it on the table. It made a clinking sound. "Mr. Graham gave us fellas a bonus for takin' extra rides when Fergus broke his arm last month. I want you to use it and buy yourself somethin' pretty at the store. I know how hard you've been workin', Sunny. And I know ladies need to have some fancy doodads to make them happy."

"And where did you learn that piece of feminine wisdom? From Betty Brownlee?" Sunny's voice was edged with sarcasm. Tracy blushed a deep pink, and instantly she was sorry. She hurried to make amends. "I'm sorry," she said, but it was too late. Tracy was really angry.

"Doggone it, Sunny—"

"I didn't mean it—"

"Yes, you did. You can't stand for anyone else to be happy when you're miserable, can you?"

His words hit her hard. That's how it probably seemed to Tracy. Lately when he'd been coming or going to see Betty, Sunny had never failed to make some caustic comment. She was ashamed.

"Oh, Tracy, I really *am* sorry." She picked up the little money bag, opened it, and gasped when she saw what was inside. "Why, these are gold pieces, Tracy. My goodness! That was generous of Mr. Graham."

"He said we deserved it," Tracy said sullenly.

"He's right, of course. You *do* deserve it. And I don't deserve having such a kind brother! Forgive me, Tracy. But I can't spend it on myself. This will go a long way to fattening our nest egg!" She was excited. "Why, with this we could buy most of the equipment we'll need to go west by next spring."

Tracy turned away from her.

"What's the matter?" she asked, puzzled.

"That's not what it's meant for. I wanted you to use it for something nice, for yourself."

A cold certainty gripped Sunny. The unbidden thought came. *He's going to tell me he's changed his mind about going to California.* She clutched the little leather pouch in tight hands, waiting.

Tracy's voice was muffled. "You still set on going, then?"

"Yes, of course. Aren't you?" she demanded. "*Are* you?"

Slowly Tracy turned around. "Dunno. I kinda like it here."

"*Here?*"

"It's a nice town, nice folks . . ."

"You're certainly not thinking of—"

"Well, Mr. Brownlee's offered me a job on his ranch if I ever quit riding. 'Course, I'm not about to do *that*—least-ways, not yet!"

Sunny swallowed. "You're not—you *can't* be thinkin' of getting married, are you, Tracy?"

"Well, we've talked about it, me and Betty—"

Something in Sunny exploded. "Are you out of your mind? You're not old enough to get married, for heaven's sake! And you can't get married without my permission. You're not even legally of age!"

Tracy's hands balled into fists. His face flushed and angry, he confronted her. "Doggone it, Sunny, you alyus gotta control everything, everybody, don't you? You gotta run the show. Mebbe I ain't old enough 'cording to the law. But I'm sure old enough to know my own mind. What I want to do and what I don't. I'm doin' a man's job right now. You've got no idea what it's like to ride the mail route—no notion what I face out there each time I go out. Mr. Graham knows, and he thinks I'm old enough. So does Mr. Brownlee. If you weren't so set in your own ways, you'd see I've grown up. I'm not the little brother you can boss around anymore."

168

With that Tracy grabbed his hat and jacket off the peg by the door and slammed out.

Sunny sank down on one of the kitchen chairs. She felt as if she'd been beaten by Tracy's words. Was that how he really saw her? Was that how she really was?

Salty tears ran unchecked down her cheeks, and Sunny began to sob bitterly.

What would Christmas be like here in this desolate place? Sunny stared out the window, watching rain send rivulets steadily down the pane. A tide of nostalgia for past holidays washed over her.

Christmas was snow, sleigh bells ringing in the frosty air, sledding down the snow-covered slopes on starry nights, bonfires blazing, hot cranberry punch and spiced apple cider, carols and church chimes, tiny candles sparkling on gilt-and-tinsel-trimmed cedar trees.

How could she celebrate Christmas here?

She had to do something to make up to Tracy, to let him know how sorry she was to have quarreled. She would make him his favorite cake, walnut with brown sugar icing. That meant an extra trip to Ardley's General Store to get all the ingredients, but it would be worth it.

Quickly Sunny got her cape and bonnet, her grocery basket, then hitched up the Express wagon and rode into town, imagining her brother's grin when he saw his special dessert. As simple a gesture as it was, it might be just the thing to break the ice between them.

As luck would have it, she met Rhys as she was coming out, her arms full of packages.

"Here, let me," he said and started taking the bags.

"That's not necessary. My wagon is right over there. I'm going right home."

"Well, at least let me carry this across the street for you," he said.

She hesitated a split second, then relinquished her bundle.

As Rhys took the packages he said, "Actually, I was thinking about you just now. Not that you aren't often in my thoughts these days." He smiled at her fondly. "As a matter of fact, I intended to drive out this afternoon to see you. If that's all right with you. May I?"

Sunny hesitated. She could hardly refuse without seeming ungracious. Besides, Rhys *was* her employer. He had a legitimate reason to check things at the station. "Of course."

He helped her into her wagon. "I'll follow you," he said and crossed the road to get into his own buggy.

On the way out to the Express station, Sunny felt nervous. Perhaps Rhys had decided he'd waited long enough for an answer to his proposal. In spite of his pledge not to pressure her, Sunny felt her position was becoming increasingly uncomfortable. If they only had enough money to plan seriously to leave on one of the wagon trains this spring, it would be so much easier to explain her refusal. Tracy hadn't actually given her a firm answer when she confronted him about still wanting to go to California. Until she knew that, how could she plan her own future?

Rhys was right behind her when she turned into the station gate. He was out of his buggy and at the side of her wagon before she had braked. When Rhys took her hands to help her down, he exclaimed, "Your hands are like ice! I didn't realize it was so cold. Let's go inside. I'll make a fire. I guess winter's really on its way."

Sunny unlocked the door and they went inside.

"Keep your cape on until I get this going," Rhys said and knelt to open the stove and ram some crumpled newspaper into it, along with some sticks of kindling. Soon the room glowed with soft light and warmth. Rhys got to his feet and came over to where she stood and helped her off with her cape. He moved away from her as if afraid it would be too difficult to remain so near and not touch her.

As the silence stretched Sunny felt the need to break the invisible tension. "Did you want to check the ledgers? The account books?"

He dismissed the suggestion, saying slowly, "No.... In fact, I've come for a personal reason." He paused and, frowning, said, "I'm afraid I may have put you into an awkward position. Perhaps I have taken too much for granted. My feelings for you are so . . . so deep that I've expected you to respond in a different way, a way you have not—perhaps cannot. There is, after all, a difference between love and friendship."

"Rhys, I value your friendship. I admire you very much. You have been more than generous to me and Tracy. We are so grateful—"

"I don't want your gratitude, Sunny." He made an impatient gesture. "Nor do I want your friendship. I want your love."

His expression of expectation and hope twisted Sunny's heart. She *did* admire him so much. He had all the qualities most women looked for and wanted in a husband and seldom found all in one man, but—

As if reading her mind, he said, "But you don't love me. That's it, isn't it, Sunny?"

"Rhys, I—"

"Is there any possibility, given time, you *could*?" he persisted. There was such longing in his eyes that Sunny hesitated.

"I don't know, Rhys. It's just that I never thought of you that way . . . before . . . until . . ."

Hope lit his eyes. "Do you mean you are *now*? Oh, Sunny, if I thought there was a chance . . . I'll wait. However long it takes, however much time you need."

"I can't promise anything, Rhys, I—"

"Of course not. I understand that."

He glanced at the stove, where the fire was now snapping

171

and burning brightly. "That should keep you warm through the rest of the day." Then, picking up his hat, he started toward the door. Sunny followed him. His hand on the latch, he turned and said, "I won't bother you with this again, Sunny. Let me know if and when you want to see me." He lingered a moment longer as if he would say more, then decided not to and left.

Sunny turned back into the room. The only sound in the room was the thrum and crackle as the fire burned, snapping once in a while. After a while she got out a bowl and sat down at the kitchen table and began shelling the walnuts she'd bought.

Uncertainty filled her with troubling thoughts and doubts. Why couldn't she love a man such as Rhys Graham, who had everything to offer her: steadfastness, security, devotion?

If only . . . Her thoughts drifted. If only what? What did she really want? Whose love would satisfy that empty place in her heart?

Chapter 19

*D*ecember brought none of the snow Sunny longed for to give her a sense of Christmas. Back home in Ohio there had always been white Christmases, skating on the pond near their farm, sledding on the hillside back of the barn. This December was gray, heavy with clouds, and brought a cold, raw wind. It had also brought Webb Chandler back.

Or at least that's what she'd *heard*! Sunny lifted the heated flatiron off the stove and angrily plunked it down on the trivet on the end of her ironing board. She was as angry as she could ever remember being. Most of all, she was angry with herself for *being* so angry.

It was so silly. It had all started when Tracy said he ran into Webb Chandler at Ardley's General Store that morning. Her brother had mentioned it offhandedly as she packed his saddlebag lunch before he left on his mail route. Webb was back in town.

She'd been too surprised at the news to find out more. Besides, she hadn't wanted Tracy to see how eager for details she was. So Tracy rode off and Sunny was left with all sorts of unanswered questions. How long had Webb been back? Days? Weeks? No matter. It was odd he hadn't come out to the Express station, at least to check on Dandy!

She glanced at the sleeping dog curled up contentedly in front of the stove, Shadow beside him, and thought indignantly, *How about that? Your master not even bothering to see if we're alive or dead? You'd think that is the least he could do.*

Of course, that wasn't the only thing bothering Sunny. She and Tracy had not regained their easy, comfortable relationship since their quarrel. She felt that her brother was being secretive, keeping his real feelings and true thoughts from her. She couldn't blame him. After all, when he had tried to express them, she had lost her temper. And at the idea he was even *considering* marriage, she'd flown at him in a rage! Even that he was courting that little piece of fluff, Betty Brownlee, was bad enough! Imagining her as a sister-in-law was too much to contemplate. What about all their dreams, hopes, and plans? Had Tracy totally forgotten those?

Sunny banged the iron down over the starched sleeve of Tracy's shirt. The hot iron made a hissing sound as she slid it back and forth. He was wearing these more now that he spent his evenings at the Brownlee ranch. Guess *she* wouldn't stand over an ironing board doing his shirts as his sister did!

Sunny took another of Tracy's shirts from the basket of damp laundry, unrolled it, and shook it out. Carrying on a furious mental conversation, she smoothed it onto the board, reached for the flatiron, and set it down. It stuck! The iron made a sizzling sound as it hit the cloth. The smell of scorch rose into her nostrils. Quickly she removed the iron, but it was too late. There was already a V-shaped burn on the back of the collar. Slamming the iron down, she snatched the shirt off the board and went over to the kitchen pump, where she held the mark under the sloshing water, then rubbed the cloth vigorously. This was about the

174

last straw of a day that had got off to a bad start. Absurdly, tears spurted into her eyes. *Sometimes it all seems too much,* she sniffled as she scrubbed at the stubborn burn. It was futile. Giving up, she flung the shirt onto the floor in frustration.

"Hello there, little lady."

At the sound of the familiar teasing voice, Sunny looked up, startled. Webb! She had been too preoccupied to notice Dandy's ears pricking up or the skittering of his paws on the wooden floor as he made a dash for the door. Neither had she heard a knock or the door open. But there he was, leaning against the door frame, hands in his pockets, regarding her as if he'd just "happened by to pass the time of day"—three months later.

Seeing him like this, so unexpectedly and with no warning, Sunny's heart gave a leap. In the flash of a second, she realized how much she had missed him, how empty the weeks had seemed since he left. At the same time, she felt caught unawares. As a result, she was flustered.

While Dandy made half-strangled sounds of recognition and bounded across the room, barking madly, Sunny tried to get her breath and gather her scattered thoughts. She made some ineffectual swipes at her hair and smoothed her apron, telling herself she must look dreadful. As for Webb, she quickly observed, he looked better than ever. Taller, leaner, and handsomer than she remembered. Weeks out on the plains had deepened his tan, making his eyes blue as prairie skies. It was all she could do to hide her pleasurable shock at his appearance.

Dandy was dancing around Webb in a paroxysm of joy, leaping up frantically. Webb went down on one knee and embraced him, looking over the dog's head at Sunny.

"What are you doing here?" was all she could manage to say.

"Aren't you supposed to say somethin' like, 'You're a sight for sore eyes'?" he laughed. He got to his feet and started toward her, with Dandy prancing at his side. "Or better still, 'Welcome back'?" His gaze met hers, and at its impact she flushed.

Quickly she transferred her attention to Dandy.

"I suppose you came for your dog." Her voice sounded sharper than she intended. She felt a little stab of jealousy at seeing how happy Dandy was to have his master back. She tried not to show it. After all, he *was* Webb's dog. However, during the past few weeks, Dandy had seemed to become *her* dog. At least Sunny felt he had, but the dog now seemed to have immediately reverted to his true allegiance. Watching them reminded Sunny poignantly of how alone she was. Self-pity suddenly overcame good sense. Betraying tears sprang up in her eyes, and to hide her irrational hurt she turned quickly away from the scene of affectionate reunion. She replaced her flatiron on the stove. Behind her the room was very still.

Without looking at Webb again, Sunny turned around and smoothed out another shirt to iron. For a moment the only sound was the iron moving against the fabric. Then Webb spoke slowly.

"That isn't all I came for."

"I can't imagine what else you would come for," Sunny said petulantly, knowing she must sound ridiculous but being unable to help it.

"Can't you?" he asked, then drawled, "And I thought you were bright as well as pretty."

She went on ironing, not daring to look up at him, wondering what he was going to say next.

"Well then, if you can't, I reckon the rumors I've been hearing around town are true," he said.

She stiffened but still didn't look up. "What kind of rumors?" She thought he might have heard something about Tracy and Betty Brownlee and that her brother was thinking of buying land. That alarmed her. If Webb, being

GRACE BALLOCH
MEMORIAL LIBRARY
625 North Fifth Street
Spearfish SD 57783-2311

just back in town, had heard it, it could be true. But that wasn't it.

"About you and Rhys Graham."

Sunny nearly dropped her iron. Oh, my! Her cheeks flamed and she felt as if the breath had been knocked out of her. She hadn't expected *that*. Webb was regarding her with unusual intensity, as if he really wanted to get an answer. She swallowed and tossed her head and retorted, "You listen to small-town gossip?"

"As they say, 'Where there's smoke, there's fire.'"

"Why do you always have to use something out of the farmers' almanac to say what you mean?"

"They're as good as anything and mostly true." Webb shrugged. "Anyway, it looks like I hit the nail on the head."

Sunny started to say, "What business is it of yours?" But instead she burst out, "Why did you go away? Really?" She was thinking that if he hadn't gone, Rhys might have noticed the attraction between *them* (after all, Verna had) and never proposed, and she wouldn't have been in this awkward situation. If Webb had ever given her so much as a hint that he was interested in her—well, *romantically*—maybe things would be different. How she wasn't sure, just *different*. Now she just felt angry, confused.

"Why? You mean the real reason. If I'd told you then, you wouldn't have believed it. Now there's no use to tell you."

"What do you mean?"

"It's too late, from what I hear. A smart gambler knows when to fold."

Sunny knew little about gambling but recognized the term Webb was using. It meant when things look hopeless, you don't keep playing; you cut your losses and pull out of the game.

What did he mean? That he felt he had no chance against someone like Rhys? That Rhys held all the winning cards? That's what it sounded like.

177

12974

The flatiron steamed on the stove burner. Sunny grabbed a pot holder and picked it up, slid it back onto the ironing board. Pretending to concentrate on the shirtsleeves she was pressing, she did not look up. She could not bring herself to meet Webb's questioning look. Conscious that Webb was moving toward the door, her hand tightened on the handle of the iron. She wanted to stop him, ask him to stay, tell him it wasn't too late, she hadn't promised Rhys anything. She tried to think of something to keep him from leaving. Anything! Then she heard the sound of Dandy's anxious whine. He was afraid he'd be left behind again.

Webb spoke softly to the dog. "Well, I guess there's no use us hanging around here any longer, old fella. Looks like we've worn out our welcome."

She panicked. How to stop him? How to keep him from leaving? The first thing that wildly came to mind was, of course, the wrong thing.

"I guess I get no thanks for keeping your dog all these weeks. Not that I expected any." Even to her own ears, her words sounded waspish. She knew they were perverse and wrongheaded and utterly untrue. It was *she* who should have thanked *Webb* for bringing Dandy to her!

"Thanks." There was undisguised sarcasm in Webb's voice. To Dandy he said, "Come on, fella."

Oh, why hadn't she bitten her tongue before saying that? Sunny kept on ironing. Then the door closed with a final click.

What a fool she was! Why did she behave that way? All the time Webb had been gone, she had thought about him. In fact, she had not been able to stop thinking about him. She had relived encounters, conversations, especially that pivotal night at the harvest dance. She had rehearsed what she would say, if she had a chance, to undo some of the misunderstandings, the tiffs they'd had. Then today she had ruined any possibility—

But why had her knees weakened, her pulse raced, when he walked in? The truth was, Verna was right: she was in love with him!

Why then had she not asked him to stay? Sadly, Sunny knew the answer. She was afraid. Afraid that if she let him know, he would break her heart. Better that he thought she was engaged to Rhys Graham. Safer.

Sunny put down the iron and ran to the window just in time to see Webb climb into a small buckboard, Dandy leap up on the seat beside him. Miserably she watched Webb ride away, too proud to call him back.

To her dismay, just as he reached the gate, Rhys Graham's small, shiny buggy rounded the bend. They passed each other at the entrance. Sunny's heart sank. Now Webb would be sure those rumors were true.

Chapter 20

$\mathcal{T}$hat evening a kind of hopelessness set in on Sunny's usually determined optimism.

Even the fact that her walnut cake had turned out perfectly, the brown sugar icing spread in luscious swirls and peaks, didn't make her feel any better. Somehow Tracy hadn't seemed to enjoy it as much as he used to. She supposed it was too much to expect a mere cake to heal the growing gulf between them.

Was she really as bossy, self-centered, and stubborn as he had called her? If she was, why would someone like Rhys Graham want to marry her? Or why, as Verna believed, had Webb Chandler been attracted to her? Well, there was no use even thinking about Webb anymore. She had finished any hope of his returning under any circumstances.

Webb's showing up as he did had upset her. Rhys' unexpected visit had also been upsetting. He was going to St. Louis on business, he told her, and would be gone about a week. Rhys lingered awhile as if trying to find reason to stay longer. It was as if he wanted to say something personal or hoped she had something to say to him. Sunny kept very busy, moving about, straightening the ledger books, tidying the mail. She could tell Rhys wanted to kiss her good-bye, but she knew that would only encourage his hopes. Finally Rhys accepted her unspoken no with his usual graciousness, yet she could see the deep disappointment in his eyes as he bid her farewell.

After Rhys left and she was alone again, Sunny was plagued with indecision about everything. Just a few months ago her vision had been so clear, California her goal—right there beyond the horizon, like a distant dawn awaiting her coming. If Tracy had now lost interest in going, had found another direction he wanted to travel to find happiness, what then for her?

Of all the words Tracy had hurled at her in anger, what had hurt most was that he'd accused her of not wanting anyone else to be happy. She *did* want her brother to be happy. His welfare had always been her primary concern. All his life she had cared for and looked out for him, dreamed for him—but maybe now he had his own dreams, and they didn't include her.

Sunny had always prided herself on being honest. Now she had to be scrupulously honest, face the facts of her situation. *I'm at a crossroads, that's all,* she thought. *I've just got to figure out which one to take.*

No amount of soul-searching, however, calmed Sunny's unquiet spirit that evening. She felt restless and worried. She thought about what Verna had said when she told her about Rhys' proposal: *Whenever I don't know which way to go, I rely on the Good Book. That's my map.*

Sunny felt conscience stricken. Lately she hadn't been faithful about reading her Bible. Her prayers had usually been haphazard and fleeting. She hadn't even attended church regularly. She was always so busy. With Tracy often gone over the weekends, she didn't feel she could leave the station unattended. Payrolls, money orders, cash enclosed in personal letters, valuables in small packages, were kept in the safe. The ponies always had to be taken care of, fed, curried.

Not that any of this was an excuse to neglect private daily devotions. Convicted, Sunny got down her Bible from the shelf. Ashamed at the dust collected on it, she wiped it carefully, opened it, turned over the pages randomly. What should she read? Where would she find *her* map?

The Lord is always faithful, she remembered Verna saying. *I've never asked him for help in vain.*

Sunny tried not to worry that her negligence might cause the Lord not to be disposed to answer her, help her. She would trust Verna's faith. Wisdom is what she needed. Proverbs, she decided. But somehow she turned to Jeremiah instead. Her fingers slid down the thin pages, her eyes searching. Then she saw a verse that seemed to spring up from the print. Jeremiah 6:16: "Stand at the crossroads and look; ask for the ancient paths, ask where the good way is, and walk in it."

The word "crossroads" struck her. Coincidence or guidance? Sunny wasn't familiar enough with the interpretation to be sure. But she did remember one verse of Scripture she'd learned in childhood: "Ask and ye shall receive, seek and ye shall find, knock and it shall be opened unto you." That's all she could do—ask to be shown *her* path.

A dreary succession of days followed, then a week went by. At the end of it Rhys came out to the Express station. He seemed quieter than usual and did not bring up the subject of his proposal, for which Sunny was grateful. With Tracy's plans still not disclosed and her own future uncertain, she did not feel ready to discuss it. They handled the Express matters that needed to be attended to, and then Rhys said his business in St. Louis had not been satisfactorily completed and he would have to make another trip before the first of the year.

"Since I may not be here for Christmas, I brought you

an early present." He handed her a package. When she opened it, Sunny drew out a light, fringed, paisley shawl.

"Oh, Rhys, it's beautiful! But I haven't a present for *you!*"

"I didn't expect one. You know the only thing I want from you, Sunny." He smiled but his eyes looked sad. "I really wanted to give you something else—an engagement ring. I even looked at some at a jewelry store, but then I was afraid it would be presumptuous." He looked at Sunny almost shyly. "I suppose that's too much to ask or even hope for?"

"Oh, Rhys, I wish I could say what you want me to say, but—"

He held up his hand to halt her. "No, Sunny. I didn't mean to press you. I said I was willing to wait, and I am."

After he left, Sunny thought, *I don't deserve him. I wish I could love him the way he wants me to, but I just can't. I don't know if I ever can . . .*

Christmas came and went and Sunny hardly noticed. She gave Tracy the wool scarf she had knitted, then he went to spend the day with the Brownlees at their ranch. She'd been invited, too, but had declined, saying she had a scratchy throat and felt she might be coming down with a cold. She had also turned down Verna's invitation to spend Christmas with them. Verna was expecting her two sisters and their families. Much as she appreciated both invitations, Sunny wasn't up to pretending holiday cheer she just couldn't seem to muster. She had spent the day feeling sorry for herself and actually ended up nursing a fever. *Serves me right for fibbing!* she admonished herself.

The week after Christmas it rained sporadically, not helping Sunny's already low spirit. No matter the weather, Tracy had taken his route, and Sunny was left on her own. She assumed Rhys was still in St. Louis. At least, he hadn't been out to the Express station. Maybe his business trip had taken longer than he had planned.

Sunny had continued her renewed habit of Bible reading and prayer. Surely God would recognize her good intentions and give her some insight about what she should do. She memorized the passage from Jeremiah as though it were some direction that she should put to the test.

What was the "good way"? Did "ancient paths" mean the trail worn by thousands of emigrants going to California? Did that mean she and Tracy should go on with their original plan? Should she be trying to talk Tracy out of an ill-advised marriage to Betty Brownlee? The more she thought, the more confused Sunny became. Maybe she wasn't doing it right. Maybe she should talk to Verna about her method of prayer.

One evening she was alone, busy knitting some heavy wool stockings for Tracy. The weather had turned so severe, he needed several layers of warmth for his feet, as his leather boots were no real protection from the bitter cold.

Her thoughts were as tangled as the ball of yarn that had fallen out of her sewing basket and become Shadow's plaything. She still hadn't settled anything in her mind about what to do. The only accompaniment to her mental debate was the soft pattering of an icy rain on the roof, the click of her knitting needles, and the occasional snap of the fire in the stove. Then suddenly the quiet was broken by the sound of buggy wheels outside. She straightened up in alarm. Who could that be on this cold, rainy night? Instinctively her eyes moved to the shotgun Webb had given her, which was on the rack he'd nailed in place for her near the front door. She got up, heart hammering, and moved slowly across the room toward the door. Before she reached it, there was a loud, steady knock, and a familiar voice called, "Don't be frightened, Sunny. It's me, Rhys."

Surprised and relieved, Sunny hurried to slide the bolt back and open the door. At the same time, she felt some apprehension. Rhys had promised not to pressure her for an answer. What had brought him out here tonight?

She opened the door and Rhys stepped inside. His caped slicker was dripping, and she took it as he shrugged it off, then she hung it on one of the pegs.

"I had to see you, Sunny." He held up a hand. "I did not come to pressure you. In fact, over the past few weeks I've kept my distance. But now I've come, because—well, it's important. To us both. I just realized I couldn't put it off any longer."

Puzzled, Sunny said, "Why, of course, Rhys, come in," and ushered him into the kitchen. Motioning him to one of the chairs, she sat down on the rocker she had drawn up to the stove.

"This is probably an intrusion, Sunny. But I've thought of nothing else for days, and I knew I'd have no rest until I talked to you—told you." Rhys leaned forward, clasping his hands in front of him so tightly that the knuckles whitened.

What on earth could it be? Rhys' face was haggard, and there were deep circles under his eyes, evident signs of stress.

"I would give anything if what I've come to tell you had never happened. Anything if I didn't feel you must know. But since I have asked you to marry me, there can't be any secrets between us. It would be wrong." A shudder shook him. Clearing his throat, he said, "Sunny, I want you to know that when I proposed, it was because I'd met some-one with whom I wanted to spend my life. Someone I love, respect, and admire with all my heart. And it is because I do that the conviction grew that I must lay my soul bare. It would've been unfair to expect you to make as serious a decision as marriage without knowing everything there is to know about me. The dark side. Things in my past."

A sudden chill went through Sunny. What terrible thing was Rhys about to confide?

"I've never told this to a single soul before. I thought I had put it behind me. I thought I could forget it." Watching his face intently, Sunny thought she saw him almost wince. "But before I tell you, I release you from any feeling of obligation to me whatsoever. Any necessity of giving me an answer is hereby dismissed. I am putting away the hopes I had, because I now realize those hopes were unfounded. Do you understand?"

Speechless, Sunny nodded.

"This will come as a bad shock to you. Or maybe you have suspected there was something I was holding back? You seem to have an uncanny way of seeing through people. But this I do not think you'd have ever guessed—" Rhys paused, obviously struggling with what he had come to say. "Sunny, I've killed a man. I'm a murderer."

Sunny's hand involuntarily flew to her mouth, stifling a gasp, and she felt the blood drain from her face. One look at his anguished expression, however, brought a swift reaction. She reached her hand out to him. "Oh, Rhys, there must have been reason—outlaws, robbers at the Express station ..."

He shook his head. "No, it didn't happen out here. It was back east—as a matter of fact, in Philadelphia." He gave a harsh, derogatory laugh. "The City of Brotherly Love. I can tell you there wasn't much of *that* a few years ago. But first I should tell you a little about my background. My parents died when I was a small boy. I was sent to live with my grandmother"—a faraway look came into Rhys' eyes, for a moment dulling their intensity—"a saintly Quaker lady, and my Uncle Jason. I was reared in a home where conflict was always avoided, where any kind of violence was abhorred—that's what makes this all so incredible."

Rhys sighed, clenched and unclenched his hands, and went on. "Growing up I didn't realize it fully, but both of my relatives and their immediate circle of friends were

186

deeply committed abolitionists. Against slavery as an institution, and the degradation it meant to the individual, both owner and slave. What I didn't know until I was twenty was that my uncle was very involved in the Underground Railroad, the secret group helping slaves to get out of the South and escape to safety, usually in Canada. I found out about it quite by accident. Coming home from college unexpectedly one night, I found they had three runaway slaves in the house. I was shaken. I knew the danger this put us all in. Uncle Jason did not want to tell me much. He felt the less I knew, the better. He was afraid that it would get me into trouble. He wanted me to finish my education. He wanted me to return to school, try to forget what I'd seen. Of course I couldn't forget. Nor did I want to. I was deeply affected by his bravery and the risk he was taking to help these oppressed people to freedom. I was young, idealistic, and now newly awakened to the abomination of slavery, fired up with what I felt it was doing to our country. The bitterness, the divisiveness, growing between the different regions of the country, eroding the unity of the nation."

Rhys paused and took a long breath before continuing. "I did return to college. But I began to attend meetings at which famous antislavery leaders were speaking. I believed ardently in what they were saying. It was confirmation of the Quaker teachings that I had been exposed to by my grandmother, the intrinsic value of each soul. Well, to make a very long story short, one night I was caught in a riot following an abolitionist meeting. Hired toughs broke into the building and mayhem ensued. They were using clubs, swinging them wildly, hitting everyone in sight. People panicked. I can't tell you what it was like. A man standing next to me was beaten to the floor. He was bleeding profusely, and as I knelt to help him I was hit on the back and shoulders several times. Then the police arrived and started arresting everyone they could put their hands on."

Rhys heaved a deep sigh. "I was grabbed, my arm twisted behind me, and dragged off, shoved into a vehicle, and taken to jail. We were booked for inciting a riot. We, the victims, not the perpetrators. We were thrown into a cell with drunks and worse—" He shuddered again at the memory. "No medieval dungeon could have been worse. It was beyond description. Filthy, cold, no place to lie down or even sit, twenty or more men crowded in a space meant for four."

He halted, shook his head. "I didn't know what to do. I knew they would distort the truth when we were hauled into court for trial. Right then I knew I had to find a way to escape. All I could think of was how to get out. We were there for three days and nights. No air, no sanitation. I cannot tell you the horror of it. The fourth night, we were marched out to the yard, and I saw my chance. There was only one guard on duty. Most of us were too weak from lack of food and air; some were sick. Anyway, I still had the strength and the desperate determination to act. I watched and waited, fell behind the others, then slipped up behind the guard and grabbed him by the throat. He struggled but I was stronger. I heard him choke, gasp for breath, but I pressed harder, and finally he went limp and slumped to the ground. I didn't stop to see if he was still living. I stepped over him and left him. I wasted no time. I vaulted over the brick wall and ran for my life."

Sunny went cold, felt herself tremble.

Rhys' voice roughened as he continued. "For days I hid in the woods, running at night, sick with fear. Hunger had weakened me. I didn't think I'd make it. I began to not care if I did. All I was afraid of was they'd recapture me and I'd have to go back to that hellhole and stand trial for something I didn't do, maybe spend the rest of my life in jail—"

His voice broke. He shook his head as if to rid it of the scene. "I can't tell you the desperate thoughts that went through my head. If I was going to die, I wanted to die a free man. I knew all the feelings, the emotions, of the escaping slaves my uncle had tried to help."

"What happened?"

"I knew I couldn't go home, contact my family, because they would then be implicated, and maybe their own actions would come to light. I couldn't risk that. If they were arrested, taken to prison themselves—well, I couldn't bring that upon those who loved me and whom I loved."

Rhys' voice again broke a little, but he managed to go on. "I traveled by night, finally made it to a farm, where I hid in a barn. I stole eggs from the henhouse and ate them raw, but at least it gave me some strength."

Rhys stood up, paced a few times back and forth before continuing. "It was quite an odyssey. A miracle, you might say. I got help. Providentially—I don't know any other way to say it—the farmers themselves were Quakers, and when I explained, they were sympathetic. They gave me food, a change of clothing. Still, I didn't want to get them in trouble, so I left, traveling blindly, still not knowing what to do. Soon I knew my absence at school would be noted; perhaps they would notify my uncle. I didn't know which way to turn. A few miles farther along I saw a "Wanted" poster ... and knew I was now a fugitive. I started traveling farther, to the West. I thought I could lose myself, change my identity. I knew if I went back, somehow it would be known that I killed that guard, and I'd be hung. I was sick, sick of everything. Worst of all, I knew I couldn't go home."

Rhys turned to face Sunny, his face etched in agony. "I had murdered a man. I could never get that off my conscience. It haunted me day and night. I dreamed about him—that faceless man I'd grabbed from behind, choked, *killed*. He began to have a face! I thought about him all the time. Was he married? Did he have a wife, children? Perhaps by now people who loved him were grieving for him—his widow, orphans, aging parents! I nearly drove myself insane. I kept moving farther and farther west."

Rhys sat down again, buried his face in his hands. His shoulders shook under the fine wool coat. Sunny put out her hand in a spontaneous gesture of comfort, then drew it back. It didn't seem the right thing to do. Somehow she understood that her letting him pour out his soul was what he needed now.

When Rhys began to speak again, his voice was husky. "Some men might be able to forget—probably most, excusing the act because of the extraordinary circumstances. They'd call it self-preservation, tell themselves it was acceptable. But I couldn't. For me it was different." His voice broke. "I never thought I'd kill someone! Never thought I *could*. Not even in self-defense. I was supposed to be a different kind of man." He raised his head and looked at her for a long moment. "You see, Sunny, when this happened I was attending seminary, studying to become a minister."

Sunny drew in her breath. Yet this explained so much about him that had puzzled her. His aloofness, his dignity, his familiarity with the Scriptures even. Rhys went on. "For me the memory of what I'd done became a living hell." He raked his fingers through his thick hair. "I thought I could run. If I got far enough away ..." Rhys shook his head. "But I couldn't stop mentally looking over my shoulder, expecting someone to recognize me, arrest me."

Sunny said nothing. She could think of nothing to say or do but listen to this strange tale of violence and trauma. The room was silent for a few minutes, then Rhys began to speak again, his voice calmer, steadier.

"Anyway, my original plan was to go farther west, to California. It seemed the farthest, safest place I could go. I thought it would be the ideal place for me to make a new start with a clean slate. I figured nobody out there would care where a person came from, what his past had been." His smile was ironic. "But when I got to Independence, the 'jumping-off place' for emigrants going west, I saw all sorts of opportunities no one else was taking advantage of in the rush to go to the goldfields and all that California promised. I saw these just waiting for someone with some intelligence, some vision, to develop. Like the Express business. Here. So I decided to settle here. People accepted me for what I appeared to be. I thought maybe I could make a life here, with no reminders of the past."

There was a pause and then, with another ironic smile, Rhys continued more slowly. "I had to learn that you can never lose yourself completely. Not that anyone ever *did* come to get me. I was damned by my own conscience. And when a man has that, he needs no other kind of fear." He sighed. "I tried to blot that out by drinking too much. That didn't work. Nothing worked. Until—" He looked at Sunny for a long time. "Until you, Sunny."

"Me?"

"Yes. You with your youth, honesty, ideals, dreams. You brought back to me all I'd left behind when I ran away. Any chance of the life I'd always planned I'd have someday, a life of purpose and meaning, shared with a woman of virtue, beauty, and character." He hesitated and then, with his voice shaking a little, he told her, "I was foolish enough to think I had paid my dues in some way." Rhys shook his head. "But now I know I can't. I was wrong to ask you to marry me, Sunny. Wrong to ask you to share a life that was dark with secrets. More than that, to share the shame of punishment that may still be in store for me if I go back east and face whatever justice my act deserves, make some kind of restitution, perhaps even go to prison."

Involuntarily Sunny gasped. Was it possible they could still convict a man for something that happened so long ago? But *murder*. She shuddered. Didn't that mean hanging? She prayed that would not be Rhys' fate.

191

Rhys sighed deeply and stood up. "I must go. I didn't come to beg your pity or your absolution or for you to tell me it doesn't matter. I have to figure it all out for myself. The thing that *did* matter was to tell you the truth."

"I know that," Sunny said with quick compassion.

Rhys took her hand. "Thank you, Sunny, for listening. I hope I haven't burdened you too much with what should be mine alone to bear?"

"Oh no, Rhys, please don't think that."

He kept holding her hand as though he could not relinquish it.

"Oh, Sunny, I wish to God it could have been different. I wish I could have come to you with an unsullied past, could have honestly offered you my heart with no shadows of regret. It would have been easier if you never knew. But I couldn't do that. I care too much about you." He sighed again. "Your coming into my life is a bittersweet blessing. I cannot tell you what it has meant to know you, fall in love with you. Now to have to give you up . . ."

Sunny sensed Rhys' struggle to keep a check on his emotions. She recognized it because she herself was struggling with the impulse to tell him she would stand by him, wait until he settled whatever unfinished business he had left back east. But she couldn't. She didn't love him. Not like that. Not enough. All she could be was a compassionate friend, when he wanted so much more.

"Sunny, no matter what, loving you has been the one perfect thing that's happened to me in the last six or seven years. I thank you for that." His fingers tightened around her hand, then he raised it to his lips, kissed it. She saw in his eyes the battle he was waging against passionate desire restrained by honor. He pressed her hand with both of his to his breast. She could feel his heart pounding. Finally, with an effort he said, "I really must leave."

Sunny walked to the door with him. When he opened it,

a cold wind rushed in, chilling her. She stepped back. Rhys looked at her again. This time she saw infinite tenderness in his eyes, infinite sorrow.

"Good night, Sunny. Bless you."

Sunny closed the door, stood there until the sound of Rhys' buggy wheels faded away, then she returned to the kitchen. She was shivering. Hugging her arms, she got close to the warmth of the glowing fire.

It had been an amazing evening. In the space of a few hours, so much had changed.

She wondered what Rhys would do. Go back east? Give himself up to the authorities? If he did, what would happen to the Express station, to Tracy and the other riders, to *her*?

It seemed ironic that in different ways, she had now lost the two men who had become part of her life here. Webb because he thought she was engaged to Rhys, Rhys because of his past and his conscience.

Chapter 21

*T*wo weeks into the new year, it continued to rain off and on. Skies hung gray and heavy with clouds threatening more. Rivers were swollen; there was talk of possible floods.

One morning Sunny woke to the sound of rain pelting the window like pebbles flung by a furious hand. Groaning, she huddled into her quilt, dreading getting up. Finally she pulled herself up and out of bed, fighting the urge to dive back under the warm covers and go back to sleep. As she dressed the steady rain increased. What a morning for Tracy to have to set out on his route!

In the dim kitchen, she lit the oil lamp and set it on the drain board so she could see to make coffee. Shadow came stretching out, curling around her ankles until Sunny put down a saucer of milk for him. As she did she felt something clutch her heart. She missed Dandy, who had always greeted her with a wag of his tail, then waited patiently at the front door to be let out. She missed the dog. She missed his master too.

Determinedly Sunny thrust away the thought of Webb. What good did it do to look back in regret? He was probably not giving a thought to *her*!

She sliced bread, cheese, and ham to fix a lunch for Tracy to pack in his saddlebags. When the coffee was ready, she poured a mug, then took it in to Tracy. She bent over his bunk and shook him gently awake. A few minutes later he came into the kitchen, fully dressed but still groggy, and filled his mug again. He threw a yellow rain slicker over one of the chairs, walked over, peered out the window, and remarked, "Comin' down cats and dogs, ain't it?"

Tracy, who like everyone else had been aware of Rhys' interest in his sister, had been pleased when Sunny first told him of the proposal. When Sunny, without betraying Rhys' secret, told him that it was off by mutual agreement, he was disappointed. Since their relationship had remained stiff since their quarrel, Sunny and Tracy did not discuss it further.

Sunny had not dared bring up again the subject of going to California. She tried to think how she might revive Tracy's interest in going west. Could she persuade him to seek his fortune in California, as so many others were doing, *then* return to marry the girl he left behind?

Frying his sausage and eggs for breakfast, she wondered if this might be a good time to bring it up. Might give him time to think about it as he sloughed through the rain, wind, and mire on his route. Make him pine for sunny California. She placed his plate on the table and poured him another cup of coffee.

"You're gettin' to be some cook, Sunny," Tracy said, looking up at her with a grin.

The smile caught Sunny off guard. It was their mother's smile, the mother Tracy didn't remember. Yet there it was in his half-boy, half-man face. His thick, curly hair needed cutting, but Sunny checked her impulse to touch it tenderly. It was silky still, a child's head of hair. The gap between his two front teeth still gave him a little-boy look. Sunny felt a melting tenderness for her brother. Hadn't she

195

practically raised him single-handedly? She felt the old protective urge. A new determination to not lose their dream of finding that distant rainbow, the two of them together, gripped Sunny. She would not let him be swayed by a temporary infatuation, not let him do something so foolish as rush into an ill-advised marriage. Impulsively she launched into the subject.

But it was the wrong moment. The words, "Tracy, I hope you haven't made any foolish promises to Betty Brownlee—" were hardly spoken when she realized she'd put the proverbial foot in her mouth. She should have talked about California first, not mentioned Betty.

Tracy gave her a furious look. His jaw jutted, his expression hard, his eyes cold, he shoved back his chair, stood up, flung his napkin down on the table beside his unfinished breakfast.

"I ain't going to discuss Betty with you, Sis. You don't like her. Without even gettin' to know her. Without even tryin' to. And this ain't a good time to talk about going to California. You don't seem to realize everything's changed." He strode over to the coatrack, grabbed his jacket, and shrugged into it. "Just because things have turned sour for you don't mean I've got to go along with your ideas, Sunny. I've quit tagging along after you like some little puppy. From now on, *I* decide what I want or don't want to do. Now I gotta go." Grabbing his hat and mail pouch, Tracy stormed out, letting the door slam after him.

For a minute she stood looking after him in shock. His shouted words and the banging of the door reverberated in her ears. At first she felt a reactive rush of anger. What had got into Tracy? Couldn't she even talk to him anymore, express an opinion, make a suggestion? Full of indignation at the way he had treated her, she snatched her shawl from the peg beside the door and stepped out onto the porch. The wind knifed through her, and she pulled the woolen shawl closer as she stomped down the steps and through the puddled yard to the barn.

Her brother was tightening a pony's girth and strapping on the saddlebags when she entered. "Tracy—," she began.

"No, don't start in on me, Sunny. I said all I mean to say on the subject. This ain't no time to discuss goin' to California. Right now I got to get on my route. The mail's got to get through—and it's gonna be a hard ride this day."

Sunny realized he was right. She couldn't have picked a worse time. Sunny said, "All right, but we will have to sometime."

"I said leave it alone, Sunny!" Tracy mumbled. He adjusted the bridle on the pony and backed him out of the stall. Sunny had to step back as he walked the pony to the open barn door.

Unwilling to let him go like this, with all this anger between them, she called, "Wait! Wait, please wait." But if he heard her, Tracy gave no sign. He swung himself up onto the pony's back, gave it a quick prod with his spurs, and without a backward look galloped out toward the station gate. He was soon lost from sight in a gray veil of rain.

She knew her brother was very angry. And it frightened her. It was her fault again. The ancient adage "Fools rush in where angels fear to tread" rebuked her. Just as her stepmother had predicted years ago: *Your tongue is your worst enemy.* Hadn't Webb Chandler said almost the very same thing to her? Truth, no matter what the source, was hard to take. This break with Tracy, further eroding the closeness they'd once had, was almost too much.

Sunny returned to the house feeling burdened and disconsolate. The sense of loss was heavy. All the things that mattered to her were slipping away. Perhaps even her dream of going to California, which had sustained her so long. Was she to lose everything? Even her brother's love?

The weather did not help. Fresh bursts of rain continued

197

during the long, lonely day. Late in the afternoon the storm broke with an unleashed fury. Wind slashed at the windows, sending the rain pounding against the panes. The wild sound of the storm made Sunny shudder; it was as if even nature bore a grudge against her. The walls of the Express station building seemed to close in upon her, while outside the storm raged. She tried to read and distract herself, but all she could think of was her brother on his dangerous trip in this terrible night.

Finally she went to bed, but sleep eluded her. She shivered as she lay there and listened to the wind howling, rattling the windows, and hissing down the chimney.

Dear God, please protect Tracy. Keep him safe, Lord, and guard him as he rides. Her prayer was repetitive, while her thoughts zigzagged from Tracy to her own dilemma. What was she to do now that Tracy no longer wanted to go west?

That same evening, Webb Chandler left Rhys Graham's office in a muddled state of mind. This was something he'd not counted on. Maybe he'd thought he could find out something just by casual conversation, a little prodding. But he sure hadn't expected the information he'd got.

Rhys Graham was selling out, going back east. Leaving Missouri. No real explanation other than he wanted to move on, do something else with his life.

Webb had been too shocked to be tactful. Jolted by the surprise of Graham's statement, Webb had stammered, "But I thought—I mean, I heard you were probably going to get married, settle down—" He flushed, realizing he was repeating gossip.

A rueful smile lifted the corner of Rhys' mouth slightly. He shook his head. "No, I'm afraid that's not so. There's no truth to whatever you've heard, Webb."

Webb also realized Rhys Graham was too much of a gentleman to discuss a lady, so the next question that sprang to his mind couldn't be asked. The fact that Rhys was pulling up stakes, giving up a lucrative business, and leaving Missouri could only mean one thing. Either he had asked Sunny and been turned down or there had never been anything to the rumors.

It gave a man pause, that's for sure. Had he got things figured all wrong? Maybe he should go out and talk to Verna and Clem. They were like the folks he'd never had—they always treated him as if he belonged to them. Maybe Verna would straighten him out on Sunny Lyndall. Webb shook his head. Women! They sure were a mysterious breed. He couldn't understand them. Used to be he could take 'em or leave 'em. Mostly he'd got along pretty well with the ones he was interested in. Not that he'd ever done any serious courting. But this was different. Webb leaned against the post of the boardwalk and surveyed the scene. Rain coming down in sheets. Main Street a river of mud. Should he ride out and face Sunny tonight, just come right out and say what was on his mind, in his heart?

A picture of her floated into his mind. Webb remembered the first time he had seen her, his first impression of her. The small, determined chin, the wide, lovely eyes that held fear she was trying too hard to hide, the soft, pretty mouth, its lower lip trembling a little—still, even then he had recognized grit, courage, spirit. Something he admired greatly in a man, a horse, *or* a woman. Something he hadn't seen a lot of in any of these. But Sunny had it. He remembered thinking at the time that she was feisty, though, like an unbroken colt.

Of course, he felt and thought much differently about her now. He saw so much more in her than that first male admiration of a pretty woman. He saw a strength more than beauty, a character honed by hardship, a stubbornness refined to a determination to endure.

She still looked fragile somehow, as if in spite of everything she needed taking care of. The question was, would she let anyone, would she let *him*? He knew he would have to choose his words carefully. Not tread on her new independence, her confidence gained by what she had done. Yet he wanted to let her know how much he cared, how much he wanted her.

Still, it might not be a good idea to ride out there tonight. Might frighten her if he came out like that in the middle of a storm. Might take her by surprise, get her dander up, like other times he'd come unannounced.

No, he'd wait until tomorrow. Think of some reason to ride out. What he didn't know. He'd think of something. Doggone it. Why did the idea seem so—well, so uncomfortable? All she could do was turn him down, say no.

Webb moved on to the small house he had rented since his return. He walked past the hotel, from which he could hear the sounds of the tinny piano. He imagined the smoky scene inside, the loud voices, the clink of glasses, and the smell of tobacco. That didn't interest him anymore somehow. Not that it ever did much. He'd just gone there out of loneliness mostly. He thought of the kitchen at the Express station. Sunny had sure fixed it up bright and cozy, with the walls whitewashed and the little flowered curtains. Something in Webb pictured what it might be like to have a home of his own, to be sitting with his feet up on the stove's fender, looking over at Sunny, the lamplight sending little sparks of light through her hair and onto the sweet curve of her cheek as she worked on some sewing, maybe mending some socks—*his* socks!

Man! If *that* wasn't wishful thinking. More than likely the truer picture would be Sunny riding beside him or galloping on ahead, looking back over her shoulder, laughing at him, daring him to catch her. The possibility of losing what he'd never had made Webb feel as though a steel band were tightening around his chest.

Chapter 22

*U*nable to sleep, Sunny got up toward dawn and peered out into the darkness. The rain had become a steady downpour whipped by a ferocious wind. She shuddered. Soon she would have to brave the gale to go out to the barn and feed the ponies. Drawing her shawl close around her shivering shoulders, she went out to the kitchen, stoked the fire, put the kettle on the stove. Where was Tracy out in all this? Had he reached the next station safely?

Prayer for her brother came as naturally as measuring coffee into the pot. *Lord, please be with him as he rides, protect him*—The words of the psalmist, memorized in childhood, sprang spontaneously into her mind: *O God, our refuge and our strength, a very present help in trouble*—

Trouble, danger, peril of all kinds, were a rider's constant companions on the trail. Although Tracy had been lucky so far, other riders had had accidents. Sunny felt a sharp twinge of fear but quickly thrust it away. *It's just me*, she told herself. *My own uncertainties, anxieties*—

She poured herself a steaming cup of coffee, held it in both hands to warm them, and brought it to her mouth. If only they hadn't quarreled before Tracy left. If anything happened to him ... Sunny felt a hollow sensation. A premonition? She gave herself a mental shake. That was simply superstitious. She was feeling guilty, that was all. She'd make it up to him when he got back, tell him she was sorry.

Trying to escape from these dark thoughts, she got on with her chores. But a strange restlessness kept her uneasy. For some reason she kept going to the window, looking out into the gray, misted landscape. Once in a while she glanced at the clock. Tracy should be safe at the other station by now, she thought. Probably sound asleep. Not worrying about her or their quarrel. Her strange apprehensions were all just her overwrought imagination.

Then, on one of these seemingly pointless trips to the window, she saw a figure stumbling through the Express yard gate. As she watched he staggered forward, grabbed one of the corral posts, clung to it. For a moment she could not move. Then she recognized the yellow poncho. The man was one of the Express riders! Her next thought was, *Tracy?* With a horrified gasp Sunny whirled from the window and bolted out of the building. Outside she ran, slipping and sliding on rain-slick mud, toward the man slumped against the rails of the corral. Reaching him, she saw her worst fear realized. It *was* Tracy. His face was blood-streaked and swollen, one eye nearly closed. He had kept himself from falling completely only by holding with one hand to one of the rails; his other arm hung uselessly at his side.

"Tracy! My God, what happened?"

One eyelid opened with effort. A glint of recognition flickered briefly. "Ambushed. Attacked. . . . Looked like Injuns," he mumbled hoarsely.

On her knees in the mud beside him, Sunny placed her arm around his shoulders to help him stand. He let out an agonized groan. "No! Don't touch me. . . . I think some ribs are broke—my arm's been shot, too. Tried to fight 'em off, but there were three of them. . . . They beat me up pretty bad, and—"

"Never mind that now. You can tell me later. First we've got to get you inside. Here, hold on to me—I'll try to be careful."

Sunny was weeping, her tears mixing with the rain that fell steadily and soaked her hair and dress. "It's a wonder you weren't killed."

"I played dead, or they would have finished me off," moaned Tracy. "I managed to lie on top of one of the mailbags. They got off with everything else."

"Where's the pony?"

"Spooked—run off. They were shootin' and hollerin'. It's a wonder it was only my arm they hit."

Sunny used all her strength pushing and pulling Tracy to his feet amid his heart-wrenching moans, telling him, "Hold on to the corral railing as long as you can, then lean on me, and I think we can make it up to the porch."

Tracy's breathing was shallow. Sunny knew he was close to the end of his endurance. How far must he have come from his attack? His clothes were sodden. He might have been unconscious, lying out in the rain for hours. Through her anguish at her brother's condition, Sunny prayed. *Dear God, help us, please. Give me the strength to get him inside. Please, please.*

Afterward Sunny wasn't sure how they managed to drag themselves up the steps and into the building. Her tears streamed helplessly as she got him onto the bed in her room, which was the closest. The leather mailbag Tracy had concealed and then stashed in the large inner pocket of his rain slicker dropped to the floor, and she kicked it out of the way while she attended to her brother. His hat, with its dripping brim, had fallen off as Tracy collapsed, a dead weight, onto the bed. She removed his soaked boots, then covered him with a blanket.

Looking down at him, Sunny stifled a sob. Gently she brushed back the thick hair that was plastered to his forehead

203

by the rain and blood. His face was ashen. Both eyes were nearly shut, and she realized he was slipping into unconsciousness. He was probably in shock from loss of blood and the stabbing pain of his arm and broken ribs.

What to do? Should she leave him? Ride into town, get the doctor? Sunny stood by the bedside, looking down at her wounded brother in a confusion of indecision. The slightest move caused him agony. She could see his arm was in pretty bad shape. She would have no idea how deep the gash on his head was until she washed away the dirt and blood. It probably needed to be stitched. *Oh, dear Lord, what shall I do?*

The old adage "First things first" activated her. Disregarding her own wet clothes, Sunny hurried into the kitchen and put water on to boil. She filled a basin with hot water and carried it back into the bedroom. Tracy was moving his head from side to side on the pillow, mumbling incoherently. Sunny put her hand against his cheek, and it was burning: he had a fever.

"I'm here, Tracy. I'm going to take care of you," she murmured soothingly. As gently as possible, she lifted his arm, biting her lip as Tracy let out a groan. With her sewing scissors, she cut through the leather jacket and flannel shirt. It took some doing, but she finally was able to examine the wound. It seemed the bullet had torn the flesh but not lodged in or shattered the bone. However, the wound bled profusely. She staunched the blood temporarily with the wadded material from his shirt. Then she ran to get some of the cotton batting Verna had given her to use as underpadding for the quilt top she had started. This she folded, and with strips she tore off one of her clean petticoats, she wrapped and tied it securely for a bandage on the jagged wound. Tracy might need stitches later, but for now this would keep him from losing too much blood.

That done, Sunny looked at his forehead. Her hand

trembled as she took a folded cloth, dipped it in the water, and began to remove the crusted blood from his forehead. Tracy flinched and she withdrew it quickly. Fresh blood began to trickle out of the cut. His eyes opened and they were glazed. For a second they focused, and then he recognized her.

"Sunny, you gotta saddle up one of the ponies. I gotta get back on the trail, carry the mail through. Fred Miller's waiting for me—" He tried to struggle into a sitting position, but the pain was too severe, and he fell back against the pillows with a spontaneous cry.

Sunny knew he meant that the rider at the next station depended on receiving the mail from this one so he could carry it on to the next. But she knew what Tracy in his delirium didn't. He was in no possible condition to ride now—or anytime in the near future. She also knew she had to keep Tracy calm, or he would do something more to injure himself. A sudden move would put him in danger of one of the broken ribs piercing his lungs. Then there would be no hope. At all costs, she had to keep him still.

The only medicines they had on hand were bicarbonate of soda, iodine, eucalyptus oil, and a tiny bottle of tincture of opium, which the doctor in Cartersville had once given Tracy when he went there with a toothache. She wasn't sure whether it had cured his toothache, but it *had* put him sound asleep for a number of hours. Maybe that was what she should give him.

She went to get it, measured several drops into a small tumbler of water, then took it in to Tracy. Raising his head gently, she pressed the glass between his lips, forcing the liquid into his mouth. He sputtered, coughed, then swallowed at least part of the dosage.

Exhausted from all the effort, Sunny started out of the room. She wanted to get out of her wet clothes, which clung to her chillingly. As she was about to leave Tracy mumbled something. She went back over to the bed. Seeing him so battered, bruised, filled her with tenderness. This was her little brother, but he was a man—a brave one who had courageously battled the band of ruthless Indians and outwitted them. At least he had salvaged part of the mail he'd sworn to protect. He had lived up to his responsibility.

As she leaned over him Tracy licked his dry, parched lips, lifted his head and tried to say something. Sunny knelt down beside the bed, bending close to hear what he was saying.

"The mail . . . gotta get through—"

She eased him back onto the pillow. "Hush, hush. Don't worry." A wild thought entered her mind. "It's taken care of." Even as she spoke the words Sunny knew what she had to do.

In the months she had worked at the Express station, Sunny had learned and understood the importance of the mail getting through on time. Payrolls, telegrams, mail, medicines that people were waiting for, cash, even jewelry—a wedding ring for an anxious bride and a nervous bridegroom, as well as less sentimental things. Everyone relied on the intrepid riders to come through the rain, sleet, or snow. . . . Tracy, a true Pony Express rider, had risked his very life to protect the mail.

Everything combined to argue Sunny out of the idea that had come and burrowed into her mind: the weather outside worsened with every passing minute, and she worried about leaving Tracy alone and unattended. Still, the idea lodged ruthlessly in her brain. Why not? It was only ten miles. Ten *hard* miles, in a terrible downpour, she reminded herself. But hadn't she ridden six miles each way to school every day for years, with Tracy behind her on the saddle when he got old enough to go? Hadn't their father always declared she could ride as well as any boy? Her stepmother had wailed over the fact that she rode astride. And until Matilda put a stop to it, she'd ridden bareback whenever

206

she had a chance. Hadn't she taken care of the ponies all these months? They knew her; she could handle any of them, especially Jericho.

It seemed the right thing to do, the *only* thing. If she rode into town and told Rhys that he would have to find a relief rider, time would be lost. Riding over to the Ardleys to ask Verna to come would waste precious moments.

Sunny changed the cloth on Tracy's burning brow. Wringing out a new one in cool water and placing it on his fevered forehead, she heard herself saying, "It's all right, Tracy. Someone's taking it. It'll get there."

Leaving him, she quickly unbuttoned her dress, stepped out of it, unfastened her petticoats, and let them drop to the floor. She grabbed a pair of Tracy's jeans that had been hanging on the drying rack near the stove and pulled them on. Next she put on a flannel shirt and dragged on her boots.

Just to be certain he would sleep until she returned, Sunny measured out a few more drops of the opium tincture, mixed it with water, and returned to the bedroom. She tilted Tracy's head up a little, forced open his mouth enough to get the rest down. That surely would keep him asleep for a couple of hours. She hated leaving him, but she had to get started before the rain turned to sleet.

If only there were someone she could depend on. If only someone would come to help. But there was no one. She only had herself to rely on. And God. She would have to trust that she was doing the right thing and that God would take care of Tracy and her. If, after she delivered the mail to the next station, she turned around and came right back, she still would not get back before noon tomorrow. She would have to trust God to protect them both.

Hastily she twisted her hair up into a knot, then jammed a woolen stocking cap over her head and ears and put Tracy's suede slouch hat on over it, drawing the leather thongs tight under her chin. Then she went to the bedroom door to take a last look at her brother. His breathing came heavily but regularly. *He'll be all right. Please, God.* No matter her anxiety, she couldn't linger. To make up for the lost time, she had to leave now.

She picked up the mailbag and went back to the kitchen just as there was a loud, insistent banging on the front door. A tremor of fear passed through her. Had those savages followed Tracy back to the station, bent on getting more loot? She hesitated there a minute while the banging continued. She realized she hadn't bolted the door. She glanced over to where the shotgun hung on the wall. Did she have a chance to get to it before they broke in? There wasn't time. The door, caught by the strong wind, swung open and banged against the wall. There on the threshold stood Webb Chandler.

Relief exploded through Sunny. "Oh, thank God, Webb! You're an answer to prayer!"

At this unexpected greeting he look stunned. A smile tugged at his mouth, and he started to say something comical in response, when his startled gaze took in her altered appearance. "Why in the world are you git up like *that*? You look like a dadgum *boy!*"

"I don't have time to explain," she said. "Tracy's been hurt on his route."

"What do you mean, hurt? How?"

"He was attacked by Indians. He fought them off, saved a mailbag—but a bullet got him in the arm, I'm afraid. Anyway, Webb, will you ride over and get Verna? Then get Doctor Hayes?"

"Well sure, but—" Webb frowned. His puzzled gaze swept over her again. Sunny looked slim as a young boy in the well-worn jeans, and the old, gray felt hat that was pulled down over her ears concealed the sunshine gold hair. "What the blazes are you doing in that getup?"

Sunny was sure that he would object to her plan, but she had no time to argue. The situation was too desperate.

"I'm going to take Tracy's route, get the mail through."

"You out of your mind? You can't do that!"

"No?" She turned away and drew on leather gloves, saying, "Just watch me!"

"You little fool! You can't. That's no job for a woman."

In a few quick strides Webb crossed the room. He grabbed her arm, swinging her around. His grip was so tight it hurt, and she reacted. Her other hand swept up and smacked his face. As her fingers felt the sting of the slap Sunny gasped. She had never struck anyone in her life before. Instantly she felt sick and ashamed. Immediately something snapped. The built-up tension of the past twenty-four hours—the quarrel with Tracy, her remorse, followed by the shock of his return—suddenly broke loose like a cracked damn. She burst into tears.

For a single second Webb's grip on her arms tightened, then his hands loosened and he drew her into his arms, holding her securely. He cradled her gently, rocking her a little against him. For a moment she sobbed, then pulled away and looked up at him.

"I've got to do it, Webb. The other riders are waiting—it's what Tracy would want. You *know* I can ride."

"That's not it. It's too dangerous. Those Indians, they may still be out there somewhere. No, Sunny. *I'll* go."

She shook her head, stepping back out of his arms. "You can't. You aren't an Express company employee. I am."

"I won't let you go." His mouth tightened. "Besides, Graham would have me strung up if I did."

The mention of Rhys brought a flush into Sunny's pale face.

"I'm going with you and that's it," Webb said stubbornly.

"All right. But first couldn't you get Verna? Tell her what's happened, see if she'll stay here with Tracy? I've

209

given him a heavy dose of laudanum. He'll sleep for hours."

"Right. Clem can go for the doctor. OK. I'll make it as fast as I can." He gave her a little shake, his eyes riveted on hers. "Promise me you won't leave until I get back?"

"Yes, I promise," Sunny nodded, then as Webb turned to leave she said, "Webb, I'm sorry about slapping you."

He gave her a small salute. "I understand."

After Webb left, Sunny went back to the bedroom to check on Tracy. He hadn't moved an inch. He was breathing evenly. She drew the covers higher over his chest and shoulders. "Dear God, watch over him, please," she whispered. "And thank you for bringing Webb."

She hurried back to the kitchen, put on Tracy's heavy jacket, and went out to the barn to saddle Jericho. It had stopped raining momentarily, but the sky was still dark with clouds.

Sunny led the pony out of his stall, slipped the bridle and bit on him, threw the folded blanket over him. She was tightening his girth, securing the saddle, when she heard the sound of hooves. A minute later Webb entered the barn. "Verna's on her way in her buggy. Clem'll ride into town for Doc Hayes," he told her. "Can I ride one of the other ponies? I rode my own horse pretty hard; he's probably not good for the long trail to the next station."

Quickly Sunny got Plato out of his stall, and together they got him saddled and ready to ride. After buckling the mailbag under her saddle, Sunny swung up onto her pony's back. Webb led both ponies out of the barn and shoved the doors closed. Webb and Sunny were both silent with tension.

"All set?" Webb asked. "Then good luck and God bless!" he said between clenched teeth.

"You too," she said and gave her pony a slap on the flanks, a kick in the ribs with her boot, then she and Webb galloped forward.

210

They had not gone far when they ran into heavy rain. Sunny dug her spurs in and hunched over the pony's neck. Wind and rain stung her eyes. The trail was rougher than she had figured. Once or twice Jericho seemed to stumble and slide on the muddy ground. Maybe Webb was right. Maybe what she was doing was foolhardy. Maybe it would have been wiser to go into town, get one of the regular riders. But all that would have taken too much time. Tracy was sworn to the duty of making his schedules—no matter what. She would try not to let her brother down.

They rode for miles over the rugged terrain, Sunny in front, Webb following closely. The sound of his pony's hoofbeats back there made her feel safer somehow. But ahead loomed darkness and uncertainty.

The trail seemed to go on forever, and Sunny was beginning to search anxiously for signs of the station. Suddenly she heard Webb shout behind her. She tugged on her reins to slow Jericho down as he came riding alongside her.

"You ride on ahead, Sunny. I'm going to double back. I saw something suspicious I want to check out."

Before she could ask what it was, Webb whirled his pony around and soon was lost in the rain that now came down in sheets, obscuring her view. Her heart pumped wildly. Had he seen the marauding Indians who attacked Tracy? Maybe they should have alerted the sheriff about the mail robbery. Then he could have rounded up deputies to form a posse to go after them. She hadn't thought of that. Now Webb was putting himself in danger. Not for the Express company but for *her*. She'd misjudged him, all right. Even tonight. There had been something in the set of his jaw, in his eyes, even after she slapped him, that her heart instinctively recognized. When this night was over, she'd have a lot to make up for to that man. But after what she'd done, would Webb Chandler forgive her? She couldn't think

211

about all this now. All that was important was making these next miles ahead.

As she rode through the lonely night Sunny knew fear in all its starkness. She was so scared that she could hear her blood pounding in her ears. Hostile Indians might be lurking anywhere along the trail. Everyone knew the Pony Express mail route. They could be waiting around the next bend. Her lungs pushed the breath up and out through her mouth as she leaned over the pony's neck. Riding astride on a saddle contoured for a man was difficult; she'd always preferred riding bareback. The reins cut into her palms even through the worn leather gloves.

The wind whipped her hair into her eyes, and the rain plastered it to her forehead. Was there no end to this? Every breath she took burned her lungs, and her face felt raw from the sting of the wind. She had not ridden this long or this far in years. Every muscle ached. Her wrists were growing weak, and she had to grit her teeth to keep some strength in her hands. Her fingers cramped as she clung to the reins, urging the tiring pony onward.

Where was Webb? Had anything happened to him? Had the Indians lain in wait for the next rider, planning to attack again? She strained to hear the comforting sound of Plato's hooves behind her. She longed to feel the assurance that Webb was back on the trail again. But all she heard was the whistle of the wind in her ears. She prayed, "Oh, God, an ever present help—" The words were carried away in the wind.

Finally she saw a faint light far ahead. Peering through the darkness and the rain, she saw the outline of a building. Jericho, exhausted now from being ridden so hard, tripped and almost stumbled. She jerked his head up with a sharp pull of the reins. She knew that must be the Express station. She halted the pony and slid off, grabbing the reins in one half-frozen hand. She staggered forward, dragging the pony with her. The wind-driven rain almost blinded her. Then she saw a lantern swinging in front of her. With extreme effort she took a few more slogging steps. The wind was behind her now, pushing her, thrusting her forward.

"Hello!" a voice called.

"Hello!" she shouted back with her remaining strength. "I'm here! Rider with the mail!"

Chapter 23

*S*unny opened heavy-lidded eyes and for a moment did not know where she was. The room into which she awakened was dark. A narrow wedge of light shone through a ragged canvas cloth, a makeshift curtain pulled over a window high in the wall opposite where she was lying. She lay there for a second, dull with sleep and confusion. Then she remembered. She had made it! Barely able to walk, she had staggered into the Cartersville Express station, where the rider was ready, his pony saddled to take the mail on to the next station.

She had been almost too tired to do more than take a few scalding sips from the mug of bitter coffee someone thrust at her. Then Sunny took the blanket he handed her and went into the riders' sleeping quarters. A jerk of the station manager's thumb indicated the way. Without bothering to remove her hat or boots, she wrapped the blanket around herself and slumped onto the lower bunk. Her last thought before falling into a dense slumber was the desperate hope that Webb was all right.

That was also her thought as she lay awake now. All the events of last night rushed into her consciousness. Webb. Tracy. Feeling uncomfortable from having slept in clothes and rain-stiffened leather boots, Sunny began to raise herself up on her elbows, when she heard two men's voices coming from the other room.

"Nah, our rider got off—a little late, but with this kind of weather all along the Missouri border, they know down the line we might be slower than usual getting through."

"That was some attack, but they weren't Indians after all. They was rigged up like Indians—headbands, feathers—to give that idea. Three no-good outlaws. All of 'em got a price on their heads. Lookin' for gold they'd heard was in the mail."

"Is the kid they ambushed all right?"

"He'll be out of commission for a spell. But nuthin' too serious."

"Could have been killed, that's for sure."

"Could've been worse, and that's a fact."

"The mail got through, though."

"Durned brave youngster that did it."

"Very brave."

"Not many young fellas would do that—storm and all."

Slowly Sunny swung her legs over the edge of the bunk. Holding on to the splintery post of the bunk bed, she pulled herself into a standing position. Every muscle cried out in protest. Her whole body was sore. Taking careful steps, she moved to the door, hoping she could better hear what else was being said in the other room. The squeaking floorboards made her miss the next part of the conversation. What she *did* hear was an astonished exclamation.

"A *girl*? You say that was a *girl* come in here last night?"

"A very brave young woman," a new voice said. Sunny was startled. That was *Rhys'* voice! "It's her brother who was hurt. She rode for him. That's the main reason I drove over here this morning. To take her back to our station."

Sunny drew a long breath, then held it. So Rhys had driven over to get her himself? Where was Webb? And what had happened? Curiosity banished any thought of her appearance. Sunny pushed back the flimsy canvas curtain that separated the riders' sleeping quarters from the office. At her entrance all three men turned to look at her. Two of the faces wore expressions of amazement, as though the men did not quite believe what they saw. Only Rhys' face was unreadable. What was it she saw there? Before she could say anything, he crossed the room.

Speaking in a low voice so the others might not hear, he said, "Sunny, you shouldn't have—it was much too dangerous, too much of a risk. You should have sent for me. I'd have found another rider." Then he spoke more loudly. "You and your brother are both a credit to the Express company. We shall certainly see that you are rewarded for your bravery."

"And Webb?" Sunny asked through dry lips. "Webb Chandler? Is he all right?"

"Another brave one. When he had seen you safely to almost within sight of this station, he went back to check something strange he'd noticed a little off the trail. He came upon the three men who attacked Tracy. They were camped in a makeshift shelter, out of the storm. They'd built a fire, and Webb had seen its glimmer and suspected it might lead to something. He got off his horse and crept up on them. They were huddled together, passing a bottle around. They all were half drunk. It looked as if they might have been planning to wait for the next rider—who knows what they were up to?"

"Was Webb—I mean, he wasn't hurt or anything?"

"He's fine." At her anxious question, something curious flickered in Rhys' eyes. "He says in their condition he didn't have too much trouble getting their firearms, then trussin' them up and bringing all three back to jail. Webb found headbands and feathers at the camp—they'd tried to pass themselves off as Indians. The sheriff said they've all got warrants out on them. They're in custody now. So all's

216

well that ends well." He smiled slightly. "Now, I'm sure you want to get home, see your brother, and—"

Suddenly Sunny was conscious of her straggly, uncombed hair, the fact that she was still dressed in Tracy's jeans and shirt. Standing beside Rhys, who was, as usual, impeccably groomed and immaculate, made her feel even worse. But there was nothing she could do about it. After bidding the two still-astounded Express station employees an awkward good-bye, she left with Rhys.

Outside Rhys helped Sunny up into the seat beside him in the buggy. She felt self-conscious with no skirts to spread over her knees and felt ridiculous as she folded her hands demurely in her jean-clad lap. Before Rhys picked up the reins and urged his horse to start, he glanced over at her and said softly, "Thank God you weren't hurt, Sunny. When I think what could have happened, what those rene-gades might have done if they had caught up with you . . . I don't know what I would have done—" He didn't finish his thought. He gave the horse a flick with the reins, and they moved forward.

The first person Sunny saw when she walked into the Express station was Verna Ardley. She might not have looked like an angel to anyone else, but to Sunny she certainly did. Good smells were wafting through the place from whatever Verna was cooking. Tracy, pale but on his feet, his arm in a sling, was grinning from ear to ear.

Sunny felt tears gather in her eyes at the sight of her brother, but when she rushed toward him, he backed away, holding up his one good arm.

"Whoa! No hugs! I gotta couple of cracked ribs!"

That brought laughter and more tears, and even Verna joined in, wiping her eyes on her apron. She soon took charge. "I've got water on boiling so's you kin have a nice, hot bath and git out of them clothes," she told Sunny.

"Not that I *need* it!" Sunny laughed, only too glad to obey.

Using his good arm, Tracy helped Verna drag the tin bathtub into Sunny's bedroom. Then he carried in a bucket of hot water to fill it. Verna followed with a kettle of boiling water to add to it for the right temperature. "There now," she said with satisfaction. "Go to it. We'll have supper on the table when you finish."

Never had a warm bath and soap been so welcome or felt so good. Resting her head on the edge of the tub, Sunny closed her eyes. The sensation of comfort and safety was mingled with the feeling of accomplishment, of having overcome fear, flouted danger, pushed herself beyond expectation. Perhaps for the first time she *really* understood Tracy's pride in being a Pony Express rider.

Dressed in fresh clothes and feeling herself again except for some lingering stiffness and soreness, Sunny went back out into the kitchen. Clem Ardley had arrived, and he added his hearty congratulations to the others Sunny had received, declaring, "It was the durndest thing for a little slip of a girl to do I'd ever heard tell of."

While she basked in his admiration Sunny noticed with a small twinge that Rhys was gone. In all the confusion he must have slipped out. Hadn't anyone thought to ask him to stay for supper? She didn't have long to dwell on the omission, because Verna, turning from the stove, announced, "Come on, sit down, folks, or else everything'll get cold."

They all gathered at the table, and Verna said a heartfelt grace. "Heavenly Father, we do thank you tonight for the safe return of loved ones, for your gracious protection, and for your bountiful provision of this food which we are about to partake." She said her "amen" like a question, and everyone echoed it enthusiastically.

While they consumed a savory stew and cornbread, followed by sweet potato pie and apple cake, Sunny picked up all the missing pieces of the harrowing story of her brother's attack. Then she told a rapt audience of her own part of the episode. She was sure all the details of the Lyndalls' adventure would be repeated and discussed around the potbellied stove at the store for weeks to come. When the Ardleys finally left, Sunny was barely able to keep her eyes open and hardly remembered climbing into her own clean, sheeted bed.

The following morning Sunny woke up early. She lay there relishing the fact that she was safe and sound, then she wondered about Webb. Why hadn't he ridden out to see her? To find out how she had weathered her wild ride? There had been something so caring, so protective, in the way he had treated her the other night—even after she'd slapped him! It was as if he'd really understood. There had been no condescension in his attitude. He had accepted her decision to ride and given her due respect, acknowledging that she was capable of doing it. That meant more than he'd ever know. She also remembered how she felt when he held her, how she was tempted to remain there, secure, sheltered, and then how knowing he was riding with her had given her courage.

After what they had gone through together, she would have thought that he—but then, she had never been able to figure out Webb Chandler. What he thought or how he felt. Would Webb Chandler always be an unanswered question in her heart? Sunny dared not explore her feelings for him too closely. She feared having her heart broken. It was better not to think of what might have been. Better to burn her bridges behind her when she and Tracy left here. *If* she and Tracy went on to California, she amended. She still wasn't sure about her brother's plans.

Even though it was early, she couldn't go back to sleep. She looked in on Tracy, who was still sleeping like a baby, then tiptoed past his room. Grinding coffee in the kitchen, she still couldn't seem to stop thinking about Webb. Then suddenly she heard the clatter of hooves outside. Hope leaped up in her heart, and she rushed to open the door. When she saw it was not Webb but Rhys Graham, she quickly hid her disappointment. He came up the steps, smiled, and handed her a bouquet of early tulips and jonquils.

"For a very special lady," he said. "May I come in? I have something important to say to you and your brother."

"Tracy's still asleep."

"In that case, don't disturb him, please. Anyway, I have some things I'd like to discuss privately with you."

"Come in then. I've just made fresh coffee," she invited.

"I can't stay long," he said, following her through the office into the kitchen. "First I want to extend the Express company's gratitude to both of you for your loyal, brave actions in protecting the mail and, at great risk, carrying it through to the next station." He placed a small leather bag on the table. "That is only a small token in comparison to the fact that you both put your lives on the line. If anything had happened to you—to *either* of you—I would have never forgiven myself." He paused. "Of course, I have enough to forgive myself for as it is—as *you* already know."

With a slight shake of her head and a dismissing gesture, Sunny indicated that he need say no more. She poured him a mug of coffee. But Rhys made no movement to take it. Instead he went on seriously.

"Since we talked, since I told you about ... everything, I've made a decision, the *only* decision I could make. I've at last come to the conclusion that although nothing will erase what I did, my only salvation will be to make something out of all this pain. I can't give that man back his life, but I *can* do something with the rest of mine. Something better, more worthwhile, than making money and trying to forget the past." He drew a long breath. "So I've decided to go back east, back to the seminary, finish my training, then spend what life I have left doing whatever the Lord purposes, wherever he sends me. I don't mean to sound pretentious—" He broke off as if embarrassed.

"It doesn't sound pretentious, Rhys. It sounds humble—and very sincere."

He looked at her fondly. "Thank you, Sunny. You always seem to know the right thing to say."

She had the grace to blush. "Oh no, not always! In fact, I know other people who would take quite the opposite view of that," she said lightly.

Rhys smiled, too. "Well anyway, besides bringing you the reward money, I've come to say good-bye. I've sold the Express station, and I'm taking the noon train. There was no use to delay once I'd made up my mind."

All at once Sunny felt a lump rise in her throat. She felt an unexpected sorrow, a regret that she had not been able to love this man—at least, not enough. She realized that Rhys Graham had come to mean a great deal to her and that she would never forget him.

They stood for a moment looking at each other. Then, as with immense effort, Rhys moved toward the door. Sunny went with him. There his eyes moved over her, almost as if he were memorizing her face, and he said, "I want you to know how much knowing you has meant to me, Sunny. You were, without knowing, God's instrument in my life." He opened the door and stepped out onto the porch, then turned and spoke quietly, unable to keep the sadness out of his voice. "I wish you all good things in whatever lies ahead for you and your brother."

This was, they both knew, farewell. They would probably never see each other again.

That night, Sunny and Tracy sat up talking long into the night. Drinking mug after mug of coffee, they shared the way brother and sister had never done before.

When they had counted the award money, the amount stunned them both. It felt like finding the pot of gold at the end of the proverbial rainbow. It doubled the money Sunny had put in their nest egg.

Tracy's eyes regarded Sunny with new respect. "I still can't get over your doing what you did, Sunny. If it hadn't been for you—well, none of this would be happenin'." He lowered his head and, looking embarrassed, said, "And I want you to know I'm really sorry about—you know—giving you a hard time. I can't go back to riding for quite a spell, Doc Hayes says, and besides, I've been thinkin' a lot about what you said. I really ain't ready to take on a wife and family. I mean Betty's a nice girl and all, but—well, I been thinkin', and I think we should go on with our plans. Go to California."

"Really, Tracy? That's what you *really* want to do?"

"Yep, I sure do, Sunny." He grinned. "Cross my heart and hope to die."

"Well, with the reward money, we'll certainly have enough for everything ...," she said slowly. "If that's what you want to do."

"I heard Lucas Flynt is getting a wagon train come spring," Tracy said.

"Lucas Flynt?" Sunny exclaimed, horrified. The image of the red-mustached, poker-playing, cigar-smoking, hard-as-nails wagon master who had heartlessly turned down her pleas to allow them to work their way to California came back into Sunny's mind. "After what he did to us?"

"Ah, Sunny, let bygones be bygones, right? Besides, *this* time we ain't greenhorns, Sis!" He laughed boisterously, slapping his knee at his joke.

"No, we're certainly not that," she agreed grimly. What she didn't say was that the mention of the name Lucas Flynt also brought up the name of his scout. She *had* to stop thinking about Webb Chandler. He was as much out of her life as Rhys Graham was now.

The important thing was that the reward bonus would

enable them to buy the wagon, mules, and equipment necessary for their westward journey. But why didn't her enthusiasm match her brother's excitement? It had all been *her* idea from the very first, hadn't it?

Again. They were on their way again. Going to California to find—what? For a moment Sunny's eagerness drained away completely. The whole plan struck a hollow note. Something was missing. Her joyous anticipation, the adventure of it, the challenge, all seemed somehow pointless. How could she have lost what kept her going all these dismal months?

It was probably just that she was tired. Worn out from the unusual physical exertion of the last few days, the fear and tension she'd been under. She was exhausted emotionally. Surely now everything would fall into place. They were free to pick up their dreams and follow them again. To look forward to the overland journey, to homesteading. This had only been a detour on the way to the new life that awaited them in California.

However, Tracy was so fired up after their conversation, he didn't seem to notice *her* lack of enthusiasm. He started shopping for the best bargains in the equipment they would need. Even with his arm still in a sling, he managed to ride around getting things lined up. When he learned that Lucas Flynt's wagon train was getting filled up, he made reservations for them to ensure they would be among the ones heading out from Independence the second week in April.

Sunny was still managing the station, sorting and packing the mailbags and taking care of the ponies, while two other riders were alternating taking Tracy's route.

In the meantime she had been doing some packing for their trip. From what Rhys had told her, it would only be a matter of months until all the Pony Express stations would be closing. The nearly completed transcontinental railroad would take over the transportation of mail across the country. Soon the gallant riders, and the little stations dotted all through the western territories, would be forgotten. But Sunny knew she would never forget her own experience nor the people she had met, the friends she had made. She knew that when it came time to leave, she would of course miss Verna and Clem. Rhys had already left. The person she knew she would find it hardest to forget was Webb. She didn't even know if she'd get a chance to say good-bye to him.

Sunny felt a stab of resentment but mostly frustration. If he really cared, if he was at all interested, if what she thought she had glimpsed in his eyes had any truth—then why hadn't he come to see her? Surely he couldn't still believe that gossip about her and Rhys. Not when Rhys had sold out and left town.

There was no use worrying about it. She should know better than to expect Webb to behave in any normal way. A man with his own code—unpredictable, undependable, irresponsible. A "rolling stone," Verna had called him. And yet not easy to forget.

"I'm just not going to think about him anymore," she told herself resolutely. She had other things on her mind to do. More important things. Making lists, for one thing. She tried to remember all the necessities that the scoundrel Faraday had told her they had to have to complete their equipment and supplies for the journey west. Ironically Sunny recalled how meticulously she had written everything down, with the estimated cost beside each item, and then so naively counted out to him the money with which to purchase it all for them. Even though they had been swindled and had never seen a penny of the amount she had given him to pay for it all, Sunny still knew the list almost by heart. Now she went over her notes in order to better advise Tracy when they shopped for the best equipment. Naturally she had planned to go with Tracy to make the final decisions. That's why she was surprised and more than a little miffed when he came in one day, his eyes lighted with excitement, and told her, "Sis, I've got us a rip-roarin' deal. Mr. Ardley told me to go out to the rendezvous place, that he'd heard tell of a fully equipped wagon for sale, all outfitted and ready to go. Seems like the man who bought it was fixin' to go west with the wagon train. Well, at the last minute his plans changed—his wife decided she wouldn't go or some such fracas—and he wants to get at least some of his money out of it."

Sunny blinked. It seemed too good to be true. "And you went out to see it?"

"I sure did. And it's just like Clem said. It's a good, sturdy wagon, already has boxes and shelves built inside, plenty of storage space—"

"Mules to go with it?"

"No, he'd already sold the livestock he was taking. Anyways, the fella who showed it to me said it's better to take oxen. Oxen's the most durable for the long trip. Don't require much care, are strong, easily driven. We'd need at least four to spell them pulling the wagon in case one got lame or they got sore necks. But they're cheaper than mules and we can sell them for four times as much when we get to California." Tracy halted only long enough to catch his breath, then rattled on. "And we should have a milk cow but Clem said he'd sell us one of his and—"

"Wait a minute, Tracy, wait! Are you *sure* this is all as it's supposed to be? I mean we're not being taken again?"

Tracy assumed a pained expression. "Come on, Sunny! Don't you think I remembered we was hornswoggled once? I've smartened up some since then. Besides—" He started to say something else, then stopped. "Get your bonnet and shawl and come see for yourself. Seein's believin'."

Reluctant to admit she resented her younger brother having taken on so much on his own without consulting

225

her, Sunny hid her feelings and kept herself from saying more. Instead she did as he suggested. A few minutes later they were in their small wagon, riding out to Oakmont, the gathering place for the wagons forming the Flynt train.

On the way out there, Sunny took herself firmly in hand. If they were going to make this long, hazardous journey together, she would have to remember that Tracy was no longer a boy. In the past several months, her brother had come a long way from being the boy with whom she had left Ohio. He had become a young man, having proved himself capable of handling responsibility, exercising good judgment, and showing courage.

When they pulled to a stop at the edge of the circle of wagons, Tracy jumped out and ran around, ready to help her. Sunny straightened her bonnet, adjusted her shawl, then put out her hand and got down, asking, "So where do we go? Where is the wagon you want me to see?"

"Over there." Tracy pointed.

Just as she turned around to look in that direction, she saw Webb Chandler sauntering toward them.

"Miss Lyndall," he said as casually as though it had been only yesterday they had seen each other. As though they had not ridden through a stormy night, risking danger and ambush. As though he had never held her so close in his arms that she had heard his heart beating as wildly as her own . . .

Sunny just watched him coming, unable to move or respond to his greeting.

"Mornin', Webb," Tracy hailed him and stuck out his hand to grasp the other man's in a friendly shake.

Like two men on equal terms, Sunny thought. Although she was impressed with her brother's display of new maturity, seeing Webb was disconcerting. She was determined not to reveal the hurt she felt that he had obviously been avoiding her since the night of her wild ride. Acting cool as the proverbial cucumber, he was. As if nothing had passed between them! Well, two could play at this game, Sunny decided.

"You've come to look at my wagon?" Webb spoke to Tracy, but his eyes moved to Sunny.

"*Your* wagon?" surprise made Sunny blurt out. She turned an accusing glance on her brother. "You didn't tell me *that!*"

Tracy looked just as surprised. "I didn't know. How come, Webb?"

"Well, I kinda felt sorry for the poor fella—," he drawled. Then, as if he didn't want to be presumed softhearted, Webb quickly amended the statement. "He would have been taken by grafters, he was so desperate. The main thing is, it's a good rig, one of the best I've seen. Besides, I've been thinking for a while now of mebbe"—he paused, pushed the brim of his hat back off his forehead with his thumb—"staying out west this time. Homesteadin'." He glanced at Sunny, then went on. "I could let you have it for half of what I paid for it. Then when we get to California, we could sell it and split whatever we got for it. Sound fair?"

Tracy looked at Sunny. When she didn't say anything, he answered. "Sounds fair to me."

Sending Tracy an insinuating glance, Sunny found her voice and said primly, "*Before* we make any commitment, I'd like to see the wagon."

Webb looked amused. "Sure enough, Miss Lyndall. Let's take a look."

The wagon was everything Tracy had said. Sturdily built, its twelve-foot-by-four-foot frame covered by yards of oiled canvas stretched over arched supports, its wheels rimmed with iron. Webb held out his hand to assist Sunny's climb into the wagon by means of pull-down steps at the back. There was a split-second hesitation before she placed her hand in his. Something within her both wanted and

227

dreaded the contact. But not to do so would have seemed rude. His fingers grasped hers firmly. She stepped up and inside the wagon, the vehicle that—if they purchased it—would be their home for months to come.

The interior was as well ordered and constructed as the exterior was. Wooden storage bins had been built on either side, pockets for extra storage had been sewn on the inside between the wooden hoops holding the canvas ceiling, space had been provided for a small cookstove, cooking pots, and utensils, and shelves had been made for supplies.

"Well, what do you say, Sunny?" Tracy asked eagerly. "Isn't this a jim-dandy outfit?"

There was no question of that. Again, coming into such a fine wagon, already outfitted and supplied, seemed like some kind of miracle. Was it happenstance? Or was there more to it than that? One of those old adages she'd accused Webb of employing now flashed into her own mind: "Don't look a gift horse in the mouth." Not that it was exactly a gift. But it was certainly a good price for such a windfall. And they still had to buy oxen.

"You'll want time to discuss this together and decide," Webb said after they were all standing outside the wagon. "I've got some things to tend to. Let me know if you want it." With that he walked back into the circle of wagons, leaving brother and sister alone.

"How does Webb figure in all this?" Sunny asked Tracy.

"He's Flynt's scout on this trip. I guess he was in on the whole thing when the man who had signed up to go west come to Flynt and told him about his wife getting sick or whatever the reason was that he'd decided not to go. Guess Webb wanted to help out."

Sunny's reaction to the fact that Webb would be the scout on this trip was mixed. Would it be a daily struggle not to show her changed feelings toward him? Or would they all be too busy to let personal feelings interfere? She had the suspicion that being around Webb now would be like a hurting splinter in the soft regions of her heart. But the outfit for sale was too good a deal to pass up. She couldn't let Webb Chandler's effect on her keep them from the best bargain they would ever find on an outfit to go west. She would just have to deal with it. She was going to California and that was it! Nothing was going to stop her this time.

When a triumphant Tracy came back after closing the deal with Webb, Sunny asked, "Did you sign something?"

"Nope. Just a handshake."

"Was that wise? I mean—"

Tracy shot his sister a withering glance. "We trust each other, Sunny." He picked up the reins and turned the wagon around, headed back to town. "Webb's as sterling as silver. I heard Mr. Graham say so. That oughta be enough for *you*."

That silenced Sunny. It wasn't the deal of buying the wagon. It was the months ahead that worried her. Maybe she could trust Webb in a business transaction. It was with her heart she was unsure.

Determined to put her own feelings aside, Sunny smiled at her brother and gaily repeated the words on the signs she'd seen proudly posted on some of the wagons. "Then it's 'Ho for California!'"

A few days later Tracy went with Mr. Brownlee to select the oxen they would hitch to their wagon. Sunny was alone at the Express station, doing her final packing. As she gave the living quarters a final sweeping look, searching for additional things to take with them, her gaze rested on Webb's shotgun. She'd forgotten she had it, that it belonged to him. How could she get it back to him?

As if beckoned by her thoughts, to her amazement Webb rode through the gates of the Express yard less than an hour later.

Flustered and trying not to show it, Sunny opened the door to his knock. He tipped his hat brim. "Mornin', Miss Lyndall. Wondered if I could have a few minutes of your time."

Why the sudden formality? Sunny thought as she stepped back so he could enter. "Why, sure. Come in. Matter of fact, I was just thinking about you . . ."

"You *were?*" He looked wary.

"About your shotgun, actually," Sunny said hastily. "How I'd get it back to you."

"Has Tracy got one for the trip? Every wagon should have a rifle or a shotgun—in case of Indians. Not that I'm looking for that to happen. Flynt's pretty savvy with Indians, knows how to deal with them. S'long as I've been scouting for him, he never run into any trouble with Indians. So if your brother hasn't got one yet, you might as well keep that one."

"Well, if you're sure . . ." Sunny sounded hesitant.

"I'm sure." Webb stood looking around, twisting the hat he'd removed upon entering. He shifted from one foot to the other uneasily, brushed back an unruly strand of hair from his forehead before saying, "It weren't 'bout the shotgun I come." He cleared his throat. "Well, what I come for was to say—to be truthful, I had something else in mind when I bought that wagon off the fella I told you about."

"Oh, you don't want to sell it to us after all?"

"No. I *do*. I mean it was *you* I had in mind when I bought it."

"*Me?*" she repeated softly, conscious of—as she often was in Webb's presence—her heart beating very fast and hard.

"Yes, ma'am. You."

Suddenly the room seemed very quiet. Webb was looking at her steadily. Sunny's knees began to tremble. She moved behind one of the kitchen chairs, steadied herself by holding on to the back.

"I don't know exactly how to put this," Webb began

slowly. "For quite a while I've had in mind making this my last trip to California. I've had a hankerin' to settle down, put down some roots, homestead. Guess that comes from seeing some of the men who come west on the trains I've been scout on prosper once they get there, make a good life for themselves and their families. I'm about done crossing the prairie and the mountains, then turning right around and coming back." He paused and looked directly at Sunny and said in a softer tone, "The trip's a lot harder than folks tell you or want to believe. But then at the end there's California. And it's just as pretty as they say it is, even better maybe. It's a great place to build a home, raise a family—"

Sunny heard Webb's words but wasn't sure she quite understood where they were leading. Stiltedly she echoed his words. "Build a home, raise a family? Homestead? *That's* what you plan to do?"

"That's sure what I'd *like* to do." Webb paused. "But a man can't do that alone." He put his hat on the kitchen table and took a few steps toward her. Sunny did not move. Gently prying her fingers from their grip on the chair, he moved the chair out of the way. Now they stood only a breath apart, looking into each other's eyes. Sunny saw in his what she had longed all her life to see in a man's eyes. He reached for her hands, and the minute he touched her, she felt a strong current pass between them. She had felt the same thing the very first time they met. Or something like it. Then she had thought it was antagonism. This was even stronger. She quivered as if electricity were coursing through her entire body. She felt both weak and excited, frightened yet happy.

Webb dropped her hands and took her face between both his hands, looking at her as if searching for something. His question was asked and an answer given without a word being spoken. With a little sigh Sunny closed her eyes as Webb leaned forward to kiss her. It was a kiss both had long dreamed of, and now they experienced it in all its tenderness and promise. He gathered her to him, holding her against his heart, and whispered, "I love you, Sunny."

The strength of his sheltering arms was familiar and comforting, and she whispered back, "I love you, Webb," knowing it was true.

Sunny almost laughed. For joy. How could she have been so blind? Had she not known it before this? Had she not seen that Webb Chandler was the kind of man she had always secretly wanted?

All the misunderstandings, the misgivings, of their prickly past relationship faded away in this newfound certainty.

This was a man she could trust, knowing that he loved her in spite of what she seemed to be. Here was a man with whom she would never have to pretend. With whom she was free to be who she really was. He knew her weaknesses, admired her strengths, shared her faults of being opinionated and quick-tempered and her good qualities of loyalty and honesty.

Perhaps this is what it had all been for, the swindling, the delay, the time of waiting "in the desert." It had all been for a purpose. She had grown, matured. The girl she had been when they arrived had changed. That girl was almost a stranger to the woman she had become. Sunny rejoiced in the thought that what the Scripture said was true: "Everything works together for good." *Maybe even the things we think we don't want, things that are hard and difficult, that seem to thwart our desires, in the end prove to be the best. Maybe this is what I came west for, what I've been hoping to find all this time.*

"So when we get to California, will you consider marrying me?" Webb sounded anxious.

"Oh yes, Webb, I will." Her voice rang with happy conviction. Webb kissed her again, caught her up in his arms,

GRACE BALLOCH
MEMORIAL LIBRARY
625 North Fifth Street
Spearfish SD 57783-2311

and swung her around, singing out, "Then it's 'Ho for California!'"

Sunny had planned to conquer the trail to California on her own. Now she knew that if she accepted Webb's proposal, she would never look back, there would be no regrets. Loving Webb and agreeing to be his wife would be the beginning of the greatest adventure of all. It might take a long time for two such stubborn people to really get to know, understand, and accept each other. But it was a long way to California, and they still would have the journey of a lifetime before them to learn all the lessons love teaches.

12974

ORDINARY PEOPLE SHARING THE EXTRAORDINARY LOVE OF GOD

A needy child enjoys our Mont Lawn Camp

ISN'T IT reassuring to know that good books are still being published in America? That's the whole idea behind Family Bookshelf ... "Since 1948, The Book Club You Can Trust."

We're proud of this distinction, because it clearly defines the kind of literature we offer — from books that emphasize the importance of family values to self-help, fascinating biographies and exciting fiction. All are written by today's foremost authors. *All of the editions we print are exclusive and not available from any other book club.*

Family Bookshelf is also part of a circle of compassionate ministries which have been reaching out to the poor and needy for more than a century. Our ministries are supported by "ordinary people sharing the extraordinary love of God" — living proof that people can make a real and lasting difference in the lives of others.

Our Christian Herald ministries started in 1878 with a mission to help alcoholic men repair their shattered lives. Today, our care also extends to homeless women and even children. At our new Women's Center in New York City, mothers once caught up in the misery of drugs are regaining their dignity and self-respect through professionally-administered recovery programs.

Our ministries are also a mainstay in the lives of deprived youngsters. Every year, urban children are brought to our Mont Lawn Summer Camp in the serene Poconos of Pennsylvania. Here, far away from the city's vicious streets, they can hike, fish, swim, and enjoy the bountiful beauty of God's great outdoors. It's gratifying to see the smiles on the faces of these small children, and to watch them grow in this nourishing environment. While at the Camp, many discover Christ and feel His love for the first time. And when Camp is over,

most leave with a new and enduring sense of family values.

But our youth ministry doesn't end at Camp. All year long "our kids" and their families receive assistance through a number of programs, including Bible study, holiday meals, tutoring in reading and writing, teen activities and college scholarships.

So you see, Family Bookshelf is much more than just a book club. It's also a ministry of Christian Herald. With a worthy mission to provide the kinds of wholesome books — fiction and non-fiction — which will help develop strong family values and morality. *The proceeds from the book you are holding in your hand – and every book you purchase from Family Bookshelf –help us to fulfill our vital mission.* And we thank you for your support.

If you wish to help even more, you may send a tax-deductible donation, in any amount. Simply make your check or money order payable to The Christian Herald Family Bookshelf. We sincerely appreciate your kindness.

OUR CHAPEL AT FAMILY BOOKSHELF

PLEASE JOIN US IN PRAYER ...

On every Monday morning, Family Bookshelf employees and our ministries staff join together in prayer for the needy. If you have a prayer request for yourself or a loved one, simply write to us or call us at (914) 769-9000.

FULLY ACCREDITED MEMBER OF THE EVANGELICAL COUNCIL FOR FINANCIAL ACCOUNTABILITY
FAMILY BOOKSHELF, 40 OVERLOOK DRIVE, CHAPPAQUA, NY 10514

MR 5 '98

NE 3 '98

4 '99

'99